IN MEMORIAM

For Meme,
whose love, faith, and optimism endure. I miss you, always.
Wherever your spirit is, I am there also.

TO CAROL SHETLER

Thank you for your encouragement and insight.
You were with me through every iteration of the manuscript,
scene change, and plot twist. You asked the tough questions
to move the work forward. I could not have finished this
project without you in my corner.

CHAPTER 1

Melee Tragnor ran through the corridors of the detention center on the grounds of Plant 13. The technician was desperate to escape from the Fordham, modified humans who used psychic sensors to track human emotions.

Every employee at the plant was currently lining up for interrogation. They were as sheep to the slaughter, blindly marching toward the torment of correction. Melee longed to bring them out of their sedate consciousness for her fellow citizens did not understand the linked nature of pleasure and pain. They were numb to how happiness could spring forth from sorrow, and how strength rose from the so-called burdens of a heavy heart laden with disappointment.

Beta Union claimed to rid its population of negative emotions by replacing oppressive and obsolete feelings with a hollow utopia devoid of personal attachments and self-centered desire. If citizens were free from such a smokescreen, they could face the evil of Beta Union's constitution, a code despising everything but joy, which robbed its citizens of the capacity to experience all their feelings. Melee believed these were essential for balanced emotional health. Without such experiences, how could her people call themselves whole?

There was very little time to contemplate the answer to the question. The Fordham, led by a senior sentinel named Prell, were relentless in their pursuit and as they closed in on Melee's position, the realization of that dream became more unlikely.

Her legs felt like gelatin, wobbly and ready to slide from underneath her hips. No matter how tired Melee was from the arduous chase, she could not stop to rest.

Melee remembered the last time she encountered Prell and his guards just before she slipped from their grasp. His tight jaw reflected a determination to extract the truth surrounding the fire raging within Plant 13.

Prell paused at an intersection, continuing to tune his senses to Melee's vibrations. She was close, the scent of her fear distinct. Two more Fordham crept behind him with rail pistols in hand. A single beam of red pulsed down the center of their faces, indicating the presence of antagonistic feelings.

"This way," Prell said, pointing to the right. "She is trapped and there is no escape."

His assessment of the situation was correct. Melee had reached a dead end, a locked gate for which she had no code key. She frantically pushed buttons on the gate's keypad, hoping for a miracle exit. There was none. She turned around, pressed her back to the door, and listened to the sound of the sentinel's clicking heels encroaching on her position. There was but one recourse left.

"I won't go!" Melee shouted to Prell and his band. "I don't need to atone. There is nothing wrong with me!"

"As it stands, you are guilty of expressing hostile vibrations," he responded. "Your present state of agitation testifies to that fact."

"What I am is real and what you enforce is a lie," she breathed, her chest heaving at the thought of what was to come.

"Arrest her," Prell motioned to a female guard standing beside him. "She is to be taken for treatment."

The woman came forward, gripping Melee's arm, but the technician had no intention of surrendering. Instead, Melee fought her captor, seizing the sentinel's weapon and knocking her to the floor.

Prell aimed his pistol at Melee. "Think on your decision," he said. "You need not die, but we will oblige you if deemed necessary."

"I'm dead already, just like everyone in this vapid world."

Before Prell and his cohorts could react, Melee placed the weapon against her forehead and squeezed the trigger mechanism. A burst of energy erupted from the weapon, turning her head into sanguine pulp, and depositing a mess of flesh and bone on the wall.

Prell wiped a palm along the resulting stain, smearing the spatter. He raised his fingers to his nose, rubbing them together in a macabre gesture. The sentinel's eyes then gleamed white, choking the color from his irises.

"Technician Tragnor was obviously very ill and beyond redemption," he said with a mechanical grin to his comrades. "This cure was best for her. She will not contaminate others."

Crawford Lear exhaled slowly as he stared out of a window toward Unity City's skyline. His arms were crossed and his face blank. The sunset beyond the translucent State Building heralded the coming of the night with its burnt orange glow. Beta Union's capital was indeed magnificent and in Crawford's mind, no other city in the habitat came close to its beauty.

The metropolis featured towers and hubs combining metal, crystal and natural stone. Prefabrication and plastics were used sparingly in the striking buildings. Most boasted floor to ceiling windows that let in maximum natural light.

Other structures, laced with suspended apparatuses, almost defied gravity. For the most part, much of the architecture was firmly rooted in the earth. Everywhere you looked, there was something pleasant to see. Plaza fountains flowed generously with water and elegant blooms dispensed lush fragrances into the air. Public screens, in quadrangles and other open spaces, provided daily news and various programs such as sporting events, plays, and musical performances.

The streets were a bustle of noise as light trains traveled swiftly on shimmering tracks and citizens clothed in shades of the spectrum moved about with fervent energy. Everyone wore attire specific to their occupation: green for harvesters, yellow for vendors, and gray for the technicians. Fitted blue uniforms, in the hues of cobalt and cerulean, graced the bodies of Aero and Aqua employees. Crimson signaled scientific and medical vocations. Robes of aubergine cloaked senators while esteemed engineers, like Crawford, donned chocolate brown.

Last, there were the Fordham in their sleek white uniforms. Most wore accompanying capes, the better to conceal the deadly weapons they carried. Crawford often wondered why none of them were outfitted with stun rods. It seemed to him that if the habitat's main credo was built on anti-violence and the abolishment of all negativity, then the Fordham should not carry such weapons. In the wrong hands, the very nature of the instruments made them detrimental to a peaceful society.

Crawford turned away from the sight, his thoughts shifting to the next morning when at the age of thirty-four he would officially become the youngest Grand Architect of Beta Union. It would be a daunting task, managing the entire infrastructure of the habitat, and supervising the many engineers and constructs who would be under his charge. In this, he felt no apprehension. What he felt was sheer excitement.

The responsibility was a challenge Crawford accepted with great personal pride even though pride was fast waning in Beta Union. Pride was once a source of individual satisfaction, a sense of a job well done. Now, it was a perversion, lumped in with the other professed negative vices, believed to have no value to the human spirit. Joy, gratitude, serenity, amusement, and loyalty to perpetual elation were the sole hallmarks of Beta Union's doctrine. These precepts were created by its founders roughly a century ago and upheld at all costs.

Hence, the Fordham, Crawford inwardly reminded himself.

Crawford was familiar with the early measures taken to create Beta Union's utopia. The first step took place when political radicals seceded from the Birth Born Coalition who ruled the founders' home planet of Enoch, a world riddled with persistent contradictions on every ideology imaginable. On Enoch, there were too many religions, too much discrimination, too little resources for the aging and impoverished, too much violence, and an unhealthy imbalance of power.

The Birth Born Coalition's concepts provoked wars against families, an extreme gap between the privileged and working classes, and forced allegiance to an absolute religious rule. While radical secessionists agreed with the Coalition's beliefs on the majority of the seven deadly sins and their respective contribution to demoralization, they surprisingly defended lust and sloth as a human right, which if all else were corrected, people could enjoy to their heart's content as no one would need to be burdened by a depressive life on Enoch.

To the radicals, lust was a natural biological trait. Love and marriage were selfish acts leading to jealousy and violence. In fact, love in all its forms, whether familial, monetary, religious, or romantic, was deadly. This declaration caused the Birth Born

Coalition to banish the radicals from Enoch and exile them to the stars. It was widely believed that the radicals would die in search of a world.

That belief proved false as the radicals found a place to suit their "immorality." Their forced migration led them to a planet they chose to christen as Tal. In their new environment, repression of humanity's darker half, and the reordering of consciousness allowed them to pursue an alternate hierarchy of needs. To create a fresh history, the founders and their successors concealed Enoch's history from citizens, choosing instead to offer a safe environment with widespread financial security, and isolation from foreign influence and fanaticism.

The founders introduced what appeared to be an egalitarian regime favoring all races, sexual orientations, genders, and abilities. Yet, though Beta Union was far away from the scattered conflicts of Enoch, some things remained unchanged. Its clandestine history was privy to those at the highest levels of government but not ordinary citizens.

They'll change soon enough, Crawford pondered.

He continued watching the activity in the street while ruminating in silence. Crawford was alone with his thoughts but not alone in the room. A woman, dressed in red, sat a few paces behind him in an oversized gray leather chair. She held a square sheet of translucent material in her lap. It was no thicker than ordinary paper but pulsated with information. A glowing white orb sat beside her on an end table.

"Do you see something interesting?" she asked, tucking her dark brown hair behind an ear.

Crawford turned around, relaxing his six-foot frame against the window glass. "Not particularly," he said, unfolding his arms. "It's a typical evening. Business as usual."

"What would someone born and raised in Delphia know about a typical evening in Unity City?"

"It's not as if I've never been here before," Crawford responded, taking a seat opposite the woman. "Betera used to bring me here when I was a boy. She said Unity City's residents were the epitome of proper decorum and everything Beta Union expects from its citizens."

"Does that mean you think residents in other provinces aren't good examples of how people should behave?"

"No. Every province is the same for me."

"As they should be," the woman said softly. "Delphia once enjoyed an elevated status above all other provinces until a time came when its reputation was sullied."

"I'd prefer not to discuss that this time if you don't mind."

"It is only important that you never forget what you learned," the woman said. "No province can stand above another. Exultation is for everyone. It is something we must share, never to keep to ourselves."

"I suppose," Crawford murmured, pushing his hair away from his eyes. The motion exposed silver strands blended throughout his dark locks.

The woman looked at the sheet in her lap again. "Your record is perfect. You have never come to therapy. Is there something you feel you need to purge now?" she asked, focusing on Crawford's youthful face and verdant eyes.

"Not really. Everything is as it should be."

The orb changed color, flickering from white to yellow. The woman tapped something on the sheet. "You are experiencing some mild stress."

"It's not telling you something more explicit?" he asked, poking fun at the sphere.

"No, the Fordham are far more accurate, but I doubt you will ever have to be in their orbit. You strike me as very compliant," she said.

Crawford let out a huff and rose from his seat to return to the window. "I'm certainly not stupid enough to ever require the Fordham's particular remedies."

"In the time we have remaining, you may express any feelings of concern on the subject."

The orb's color shifted back to solid white. Crawford was suppressing his feelings, returning to an even-keeled state of normalcy. "That's not necessary," he said. "I grew up in the groups. I know why they were made the way they are."

"They are beneficial. We don't have to tag as often."

"Have you ever tagged anyone?"

"Once," she said, her voice low, almost a whisper.

"Did you feel sorry for them?"

"No. They were in error. Violations can't be tolerated if we are to remain a healthy and prosperous society."

Crawford's gaze swept to view the street once more. "Aren't dark emotions necessary to mature and learn about one's self?"

"Negative emotions hinder our well-being. They hurt us, they hurt others, and have no value anymore," she said. "Complete health is achieved by sustaining bliss at all times."

Crawford backed away from the window and crossed the floor towards the exit. He put a hand on the door, pausing to turn back to the woman.

"The past doesn't do anyone any good, but are you sure we did the right thing by getting rid of that baby with its bathwater?"

The woman said nothing to the question he posed. She stared blankly at Crawford as he made his exit. Crawford's pocket began to buzz as soon as he left the office. He pulled a triangular device from the compartment, recognizing a call from Delphia waiting on the other end. He squeezed the apparatus, causing a small projection to emanate from its base. A woman sentinel began speaking from the display.

"Your presence is required at Plant 13, grand architect."

"Is it an emergency? My role isn't official until morning."

"There is a fire at the plant," she said in a monotone voice. "You are needed at once."

"Tell the duty officer I'm on my way," Crawford said, closing the communication.

Why put off till tomorrow what you can destroy today?

CHAPTER 2

Crawford stood examining the burnt façade of Plant 13. Smoke and ash drifted like a thousand snowflakes in the veil of night. Though automatic suppressors had extinguished most of the blaze, the charred atmosphere stung Crawford's nostrils.

The dead and wounded were everywhere. Those among the living were scared, choking in agony against an invisible threat. Crawford heard wheezing, sounds of life seeping from shrinking corpses whose bodies bled queer-colored fluid. The vision was consistent with those he experienced as a child. Every instance brought the same reaction, an itching beneath the skin of his left forearm, which was often raw from him clawing at the flesh.

Crawford bit his lip, hard enough to draw blood. The self-mutilation distracted him from the haunting images. The architect continued his survey and observed two deceased forms laid out perpendicular to each other. Crawford thought it an odd way to lay out the bodies, but Fordham had strange idiosyncrasies when it came to how they cleared deceased residents.

He had watched them many times, as they removed expired citizens from homes or wherever life ended. Fordham handled dead people like most discarded objects. They were efficient, performing tasks without emotional attachment. This fact, reinforced by six Fordham sentinels lying motionless in a haphazard array, further emphasized their lack of interest in death's once sacred ritual.

Crawford shook his head, dismissing his musings while unleashing Thalo, his jackal sidekick, to survey the scene. The canine bounded up to the bodies, sniffing for clues.

The Fordham lying on the ground were in a state of helplessness, evidenced by the white tone of the emotive markers splitting their faces. Under ordinary circumstances, the sensory markers were neutral gray until activated by intense emotions. If they were dead, the stripe would be black.

Crawford studied the patchy bruising on their smooth skin, freakish purple and green welts, which dotted their complexions. It occurred to him that their injuries might not be an accident or a result of crowd control. No, these markings seemed to be a product of forceful trauma.

From the corner of his eye, Crawford saw a plant technician rushing to meet him. "Tech Xander," Crawford called to the approaching figure.

"Grand Architect Lear," Xander said with hurried breath, "Some first day, huh?"

"There's always a first time for everything, even when it's not official until tomorrow," Crawford joked. "Where's the master officer?"

"We can't find Master Julian."

"I didn't know Julian was posted here."

"He was assigned just yesterday," Xander said in a tone indicating he thought Crawford knew every personnel change.

"When did you lose sight of him?"

11

"He was checking the reactor before the fire started," Xander replied. "Tech Tragnor found his ID inside."

"And where's Tech Tragnor now? Is she with another group of supervisors on the grounds?"

"She's been taken to the detention center. Everyone's being adjusted no matter the readings they're getting."

Crawford nodded silently. As he continued his survey, he spotted the sentinels Prell and Karno approaching with backup. Their bleached uniforms converged, forming a cluster of bulbous clouds, ushering in a shower of relief mingled with rebuke.

"You know the procedures as well as I do," Crawford said, turning from Xander to scan the wafer-thin tablet in his hand, which displayed Engineer Tama's assessment. Crawford ruffled his dark hair. "Forgive me, Xander. I've got to get on with the inspection."

Prell approached Crawford from behind, standing level with the architect. The Fordham's icy gray eyes stared straight-ahead as he spoke. "Grand Architect Lear, is your evaluation ready? Consul Farah has called a meeting of the senate."

Crawford faced the sentinel. "The fire started in a stairwell and spread along a floor. We'll have to bring constructs in for repairs."

"And is the reactor intact?"

"It's sound, no damage. Besides, we aren't dealing with pre-story fission here. That thing would do more harm," Crawford jested, pointing to the electromagnetic rifle slung on Prell's shoulder.

"Are you attempting to be humorous or sarcastic?"

"I was going for humorous, but that's obviously above your paygrade and totally lost on you."

Despite Crawford's sarcasm, Prell's visage remained unchanged as his sensor exuded a happy tone. His voice told another story. "Tread carefully, grand architect. You will provide the senate with the information you have gathered in person," he said. "The remaining staff can report any additional information from their observations directly to Zelda."

"You don't think my visit can wait?"

"The Senate must have all available accounts if they are to assist these people. They need assurance everything is well and there is no cause for alarm."

"Xander said Master Julian is missing," Crawford said. "I'll need to speak to Melee Tragnor."

"That is no longer a possibility."

"I know you've taken her to detention, but she's next in rank, so I need to hear if she has more details."

Prell stared into Crawford's eyes. "She has expired."

"I'm sorry. What did you say?"

"Tech Tragnor refused The Stretch and was subdued by other means after a pursuit."

"You didn't have to terminate her."

"Your response is presumptive," Prell responded. "The Fordham pursued and took actions per approved protocols in place."

"You just said she expired."

"The woman took her own life. It was most unnatural," Prell said, "and the act of a guilty party."

"You can't be sure of her state of mind without an assessment," Crawford said. "I've got dead techs, Fordham injured, and people missing. She may have been our only source as to what happened here."

"Technician Tragnor was evidently involved."

"I don't believe it. You don't know anything about her."

"It does not matter what you believe," Prell said. "Your duty is to find the cause of the fire and report those findings to the senate. That is what you are required to do."

"Trust and believe, I'll do just that," Crawford said, signaling Breen Novak, one of his senior engineers.

Breen sprinted to Crawford's position. "Yes, sir."

"Take charge here. Relay what we have so far to Consul Farah's aides," Crawford said. "Make sure the report reaches Zelda's ears or I'll never hear the end of it."

"I'm on it," Breen said, walking away toward a team of specialists gathered on a slope.

Crawford looked once more at the plant then back to Prell. "Consul Farah and the senate won't like what's happened here, especially with regards to Tech Tragnor."

"The record will show Tech Tragnor was demented, willfully disobedient, and beyond cure," Prell said. "Think about it no further."

Crawford wanted to say something but kept quiet as Prell examined his features, ready to tap into the slightest thread of intense feeling. Despite the sentinel's probing efforts, nothing in Crawford's fixed visage betrayed him.

Consul Farah Aver lounged in the garden of her abode, amidst the trees and flora of its grassy acreage juxtaposed against the city's urban landscape. She was oblivious to the fact that her quiet evening was about to end. Adario and Garnette, both Fordham sentinels, were moments from her door. Both had dashed to her location to deliver news of the fire at Plant 13.

"A shutdown?" Farah asked, pacing the foyer as she took in the news. "Is this on the communications wave?"

"The communications center was discreet," Adario answered. "There has been no contamination among residents."

"What do we know of the situation?"

"Engineer Novak reported a fire and casualties," Garnette said. "Two technicians have expired, and six Fordham are incapacitated at this time."

Farah breathed evenly, before asking, "Are they dead?"

"No, madam. They are merely unresponsive. That is how the engineer phrased it," Adario explained.

"See they are transferred to Dr. Sorenson for a full examination," Farah said. "Who are the techs?"

"That information is unknown at this time," Adario said. "Their cellular damage made recognition difficult."

Farah stopped in front of Adario. His wide grin and amber eyes slightly unnerved her, causing the hairs on her neck to stand at attention.

Garnette's sensors registered the slight change in Farah's mood. "You are experiencing fear, Consul."

"Are you impugning my right to experience it in my home?"

"No, madam. You have the right, though it is unwise not to seek a remedy when needed."

"I will do what is necessary, but never forget my rights," Farah admonished, before continuing the previous conversation thread. "Have you spoken to Crawford Lear?"

"He is onsite, but there is no direct communication from him," Garnette answered. "Constructs are proceeding to the border."

"What vessel is assigned to transport them?"

"The *Zephyr*, under Commander Jaxon," Adario replied.

The doorbell rang; Farah directed Garnette to answer it. Senator Orin Novak rushed in, his bold brown eyes searching the consul's face. "What do you need me to do?" he asked.

"Containment is our number one priority. We must continue to divert attention away from the incident."

"We can open the dispensaries and distribute the appropriate measures of Joi and Solace."

"That would be good for Delphian residents and any citizen who may have heard about the incident," Farah said, turning her attention to Adario. "Tell Karno and Prell to report to the Delphian province. I want them on the ground."

"They are already present, madam," Adario responded. "Prell is questioning the workers as we speak."

"Excellent," Farah exhaled. "Make sure he retrieves the shift schedule. I want to know who was minding the store."

Orin watched the Fordham leave. Once the door closed, he directed Farah to the sitting room and addressed her in a frank tone, "You realize this could be costly?"

"We won't know anything until we receive the grand architect's report."

"Either way, if this gets out, there may not be enough Joi or Solace to keep control."

"I've been thinking about our inventory for quite some time," Farah said. "The efficacy of our methods is not what it used to be, but there are alternatives."

"I do not follow you."

"Culling," she said boldly. "It was effective in the past."

"Farah, that is an extreme solution I would rather avoid."

"I will do everything necessary to protect this habitat."

"And I hope it does not come to that," Orin said. "The last sweep crippled the Delphian province's population."

Farah ignored his observation. "The situation will remain under our control if Prell does his job effectively."

"You should give a State of the Habitat address as soon as possible. I can arrange it through the broadcast center."

"That will do. I also need to see Severn Novak. We will need a full account of our inventory across the habitat."

Farah approached a communication box on an end table. As she passed her hand over it, a light protruded from a wide beam. An image of Zelda, Farah's guard, filtered through. Her black hair, slicked back from her russet features, gave her a militant appearance. Her large golden eyes were flat, unencumbered by emotion.

"Consul Farah."

"Find Severn Novak. Have him report to me at The State Building first thing tomorrow," Farah said. "Also, have the commanders of the *Zenith*, *Halo*, *Horizon*, and *Compass* placed on standby. We will require their services."

"They will be informed immediately, consul."

"Tell the rest of the senators we will assemble at The State in thirty minutes," Farah said before closing the communication.

"It is going to be a long evening," Orin said. "You will want to change."

Farah looked at her dressing gown, its gossamer fabric unsuitable for the events to come. "Wait for me," she said, starting up the stairs.

She paused mid-flight, looking upon the spot where Adario stood moments before. Farah shivered. *He knew I felt fear. There is never a moment when they do not know. Betera saw to that.*

"Farah?" Orin remarked, breaking her trance. "Is something the matter? You look anxious."

"Everything is fine. I will return momentarily," she said, disappearing into the upper level. "Then, we will deal with this."

CHAPTER 3

Severn Novak leaned over an island in the center of his laboratory, staring at his reflection in its glass surface. It was the first day of a new week and his birthday. He drew a hand down his cheeks and cupped his chin. Severn smiled.

His appearance and overall health had not shifted since the birth of his progeny some twenty years before. Severn took note of his modest nose between broad cheeks, an upper lip slightly thinner than the lower. There was nothing miraculous or uncommon about his brow, but he found satisfaction in the soft hazel eyes that complemented his fair hair and even skin tone. Overall, he had a handsome face.

Fifty-four. Not one blemish or deterioration, he mused. *I suppose that does call for a celebration.*

The average citizen, adhering to a faithful routine of social activity and a consistent therapeutic regime against vice, could live well beyond a century. Most of Severn's acquaintances did just that. The result? They were blessed with graceful looks and the vigor of youth unadulterated by amendments to the flesh.

Only the Servers, a group shrouded in anonymity, bore the burden of immortality, living in a silent retreat far in the northern border's harsh climate. Severn knew little of the entities beyond their custodial duties to Beta Union, and he often wondered about their peculiar "donation" to society.

The chemist rested a hand under his chin as the equipment in the lab hummed quietly. He tilted his head slightly to the left to continue examining his features. With his finger, he rubbed the imprint on his temple, a symbol of the Beta Union's ever-present omnipotence.

The network knows and senses every breath we take, he pondered to himself. *Every heartbeat is recorded for perpetuity.*

Severn's thoughts drifted back to his former partner, Agora Zadi, mother to his children, Kemble and Breen. He remembered how much he enjoyed her company and educating their offspring together. A soft voice spoke from behind before he could delve deeper into the memory.

"Dr. Novak? Commander Tragnor signaled he will map in soon. He expects you to be ready."

Severn turned to a petite figure wearing a fitted red dress. Bristol was a vision of arresting beauty. Her alabaster legs were sheathed in thigh-high-boots. Blue eyes sparkled beneath her full lashes and loose blonde waves flowed about her slender shoulders. She always seemed so serene, but the projection of peace she displayed belied the many processes whirling in her Fordham brain.

"Thank you, Bristol," he responded, studying her closely.

Bristol was an excellent lab assistant, keenly interested in their work, and tasked with protecting his studies and demeanor. Everyone knew Betera Eaton's creations detected shifts in temperament with powerful accuracy. Their predecessors were augments, part of a defunct military program trained to monitor crime within the society and keep order among citizens.

Unfortunately, they were overly compassionate and lenient, too human and sentimental to be efficient as police. The Fordham replaced them as a new, more intrusive legion of enforcers. Under Betera Eaton's tutelage, these psychic constabularies became terrifying weapons in a campaign against censored sensations.

With their physiology altered with neural grafts from The Servers, the Fordham's amplified brains collected and dispatched emotive information and processed these signals to create an individual sensory file on every resident in each province. Additional modifications to their emotional centers resulted in dissociation from personal feelings, which eliminated clashes with citizen moods. They behaved mechanically, administering penalty without prejudice; establishing order with an appropriate level of pugnacity.

A cool blue emanated from the stripe on Bristol's sweet face, indicative of Severn's placidity. "Shall I escort Commander Tragnor into the lab?" Bristol asked.

"Yes, please do."

Bristol pivoted away, stopping suddenly to face the chemist. "Happy birthday, Dr. Novak," she said, the corners of her mouth turning upward.

Severn accepted her gesture with a nod, turning his meditations to his daughter Kemble's superior officer, Mallet Tragnor. Mallet was Severn's most recent mate and over two decades his junior. The age difference was hardly uncommon in sexual pairings among matured citizens. Severn's association with Mallet was open and respectful of prohibitions against long-term partnerships.

It always amazed Severn how well the indoctrination against loving relationships worked, though it was hardly the case for him when Mallet entered his life. Severn's association and subsequent coupling with Mallet had quickly transformed him into a criminal, replete with feelings of attachment that Mallet readily and enthusiastically reciprocated.

In the beginning, the two tried convincing themselves their union was only a release of sexual energy, a source of natural ecstasy. That idea proved false. Severn found himself wishing nature had made him a woman. If he were a woman, he might have been chosen to brace with Mallet and rear children with him.

The process of bracing occurred once in a lifetime between ages twenty and forty. When selected, citizens became Pares, cohabitating and instructing their offspring to be exemplary citizens. Pares still enjoyed and were encouraged to frolic with multiple partners.

Through their Pares, the young gleaned crucial knowledge needed to become well-rounded, happy people adherent to the status quo. By age thirteen, the "family" unit dissolved, leaving teenagers to pursue higher education so that they were prepared to enter the workforce and become self-sufficient. All these ruminations mattered little for despite Severn's longings, nature and science, stubborn as they were, resisted altering the long-standing order of procreation.

A pulse of light from a sleek panel broke Severn's concentration. The north door of the lab slid open revealing a tall, dark-haired man whose cropped hair and delightful smile set off attractive features.

"What are you doing?" the man asked, greeting Severn. "You need to step away from that. It's time to get ready to go."

"Why? So, Kemble can surprise me with an outing I don't want?" Severn joked, finding joy in Mallet's sun-kissed face as his gaze trolled over the commander's athletic form.

Symbols on Mallet's sleeves rippled over well-defined arms. The rich hue of his uniform matched his cobalt eyes. To Severn, Mallet was exciting and his strategic intelligence, coupled with his brusque attitude, was refreshing to the chemist. Mallet had an opinion on everything, which he expressed freely. Severn chuckled to himself, wondering how Mallet, with all his histrionics, avoided the unpleasant correction administered by The Stretch.

"Do you think I'm getting old?" Severn asked, looking once more at his reflection.

Mallet laughed aloud, the corners of his eyes crinkling. "Years ago, people would think you did plastics."

"That's disgusting. I'd die rather than have someone cut or inject something into my face."

"Well, they say people were vain back in the day."

"They still are in a way, but I'm fortunate that with my presumably huge ego, I've never faced correction," Severn said, smoothing his cheeks. "I never intend to either."

"I hope not. Your mind is far too beautiful to be ruined."

"And I certainly wouldn't want to be dead."

Mallet was wise to move away from the topic, as it was Severn's least favorite subject. "We should get moving or we'll be late," he said, caressing Severn's shoulder.

"I'll need to stop home and change," Severn replied looking down at his crimson lab coat and matching scrubs.

"I think I can help you with that," Mallet said, starting to the door. "In fact, I'd be delighted to get you out of that gear."

Severn returned Mallet's sentiment with a seductive grin of his own. He arranged a few tubes and shallow dishes in a neat row on the island before heading in Mallet's direction. He stopped suddenly, and lingered for a spell, taking in a view of the lab. His eyes turned toward the ceiling where an emotive receptor glowed.

Like Fordham, the monitors were part of the general environment, taking the shape of pillars, signs, and ornaments, and serving as an extra layer of insurance in mood surveillance.

The devices also supported Server coordination of transportation, mechanics, food and energy supplies, utilities and more.

We'll never be free of this system, will we?

Severn joined Mallet at the door as the lights in the lab went dim and the sound of equipment faded. When the door sealed shut, Bristol's shadowy figure crept across the floor from an alcove, her face producing a single beam of rosy luminescence that pierced the darkness, going unseen by the specter above.

Severn and Mallet walked leisurely through the capital. The month of Olanda was in full swing; a temperate breeze cooled the air. Pink blooms around the perimeter released heavy sedation. Severn's delight lay in the liveliness, enthusiasm, and activity of the metropolis.

The chemist looked up at the wispy clouds, watching the birds soar in small flocks. The sun began its descent toward the horizon, inviting lamps along the avenues to come alive with a soft radiance. Once darkness settled, the beams of three moons would bathe the violet sky with shades of rust and ochre.

As the couple continued along, residents greeted Severn with smiles and nods. This was in keeping with his lineage as a descendant of the initial founders.

"Does it ever annoy you?" Mallet asked.

"Don't be ridiculous. No one gets annoyed," Severn said, smiling at the youthful and pleasant faces in the crowd.

"I suppose not," Mallet replied. "We're all supposed to be equal, but people show you a lot of deference."

"They're smiling in gratitude for everything we have," Severn said returning the pleasantries. "Besides, everyone across the habitat knows my position. I'm largely responsible for their congenial moods."

"I'll agree to disagree. Everything in this place seems hierarchical and hypocritical to me," Mallet said, smiling at passersby. "We're supposed to be above all that nonsense."

"Be careful of that opinion. It's not healthy, especially in public where anyone can hear you and the Fordham are near."

Mallet changed his tune and with it, the conversation. "I was thinking of going over to the west coast."

Severn shook his head. "There are too many beaches if you ask me. Plus, I don't like sand in my toes."

"I'll hear no words against the beaches. The surf is where it's at and you could use the distraction."

"Yes, and terror from six-legged slimy monsters with claws the size of a man's fist."

Mallet chuckled at the comment. "At least they're tasty."

"True," Severn replied. "Are we having them tonight?"

"I didn't plan the menu, so you'll have to wait and see."

Severn's smile grew pensive. "There's only one flaw in your plan. Only harvesters and engineers have clearance to cross the western plains."

Mallet returned his comment with a sigh, putting the adventure aside to focus on Severn instead. The duo's pace was slow as they passed a meditation garden where groups reclined on soft grass surrounded by Fordham. The bursts of colors on the sentinel's faces shifted with the tranquil melodies erupting from hidden speakers. Mallet stared in awe at the symphony of light, its composition devoid of jarring notes.

By his side, Severn watched children bask in playful moods while remaining conscious of his proximity to Mallet. Although they guarded their mutual feelings closely, Severn deliberately increased the distance between them. Neither wished to face the consequences associated with a veiled romance.

"You think this is better than the way things were?" Mallet asked, still surveying the pleasant scene.

"I wouldn't really know. I wasn't here in the time before."

"I don't think enslaving tempers is an improvement on anything. In fact, it's probably a detriment to the psyche."

"You shouldn't be talking about it," Severn whispered.

"That's right. It's not safe for any of us to think otherwise."

"And it's certainly not safe to act on it."

"Are you actually getting upset?"

"No, but I don't want to debate the law," Severn said. "The Fordham are everywhere and they're very sensitive."

"They're always watching, waiting, and ready to pounce," Mallet said, his sarcasm showing.

"Could you please stop with the brazen attitude?" Severn quipped. "You consistently tempt fate."

"Nonsense. I'm the picture of perfect health."

The chemist was not amused. Even with delight filling the quadrangle, there were others in the background, their languid faces and ailing bodies a testament to the penalty of indulgent, persistent, and objectionable behavior.

Severn shivered as they passed two haggard figures on a bench. "Let's pick up the pace," he said with frantic eyes. "I want to get home as soon as possible."

Mallet recognized the change in Severn's disposition. He obliged his request, guiding the chemist through the glass doors of his dormitory and ushering him quickly past the foyer. Emoticons lining the walls flared yellow as the two men entered the lift.

"You need to calm down," Mallet said to Severn whose heart rate eased with each breath.

Severn looked at the tile above, its monitor moving from gold to black. His tension was passing. When the doors flew open, a tall Fordham, sporting a high-collared white coat, faced them. Severn was immediately on edge, recognizing the sentinel as Karno, third in the Fordham chain of authority behind Zelda and Prell, and just as intimidating.

"Good eve, Dr. Novak," Karno said. "Are you all right?"

"Yes. I feel fine, just a bit of nausea."

Though his ebony features remained tranquil, Karno's sensory mark displayed distress. The sentinel's hand hovered near his sidearm. "You appear in need of assistance."

"No, I just need to sit down," Severn said, balancing himself against a wall.

"I'm taking him to his quarters," Mallet said, taking a firm hold of Severn's elbow.

The sentinel's eyes passed over Mallet, sweeping his body from head to toe and back again. "Dr. Novak is a valued citizen. See that he remains so."

Mallet stepped around Karno, guiding Severn down the hall. The sentinel lingered in the hall until both men disappeared. He then walked away, his coat whipping the air with his movements.

Inside the shelter of his apartment, Severn sank into the cushions of his sofa. The pressures and expectations of Beta Union weighed upon him. It was difficult enough being an example for citizen perfection.

When coupled with his responsibilities regarding citizen health, life became almost unbearable. Severn's job as a chemist consisted of overseeing the creation, production, and distribution of drugs inhibiting undesirable emotions. Without them, the utopia of Beta Union might descend into mental anarchy.

Mallet came to rest beside Severn, circling an arm around his waist. "We have to get away from here," he said.

Severn's head popped up from its resting place against Mallet's firm chest. "Where do you intend to go?"

"Anywhere but here."

Mallet's response spoke of a hope Severn frequently dreamed of, but the reality of the proposition remained elusive. So far, this birthday was the most depressing of any. All he could think about was crawling into bed, allowing Mallet's touch to comfort him.

"I suppose I should be grateful we didn't run into Adario or Garnette," Severn breathed. "I don't think we would have fared well with either of them. They both seem to be trigger happy."

"Don't think about it," Mallet said. "We need to get on with the evening. Let's get you up and dressed."

Severn complied, planting a kiss on Mallet's lips. "Are you coming home with me?"

"If you're nice."

Severn bounded to his room, leaving his companion alone. Standing before a mirror in his bedroom, the chemist pictured the evening to come. It would take more than a party to convince him that humanity could persist in a state of perpetual happiness. Without profound change on the part of the senate and the citizens it governed, Severn and Mallet remained chained to their clandestine relationship, forever living under the pretense of dispassion.

CHAPTER 4

The senate's members arrived at the State Building, as Consul Farah ordered, for a briefing on the Delphian incident. Crawford and Prell presently appeared on screen in the senate chamber to offer their accounts of the situation.

The architect looked less than pleased to be taken away from the investigation, but when Farah called, the best thing to do was comply with her wishes.

Farah's hands were laced under her chin and she leaned forward, eagerly anticipated answers to her many questions. "What is the status of the situation?" she asked.

"The fire's out and constructs are to arrive within the hour," Crawford said, abruptly.

"How soon can the workers return to duty?"

"The north section was the only affected area," Crawford answered. "Since there wasn't any damage to the other sections or any crucial systems, they can return to their duties now."

"You are forgetting something, grand architect," Prell said. "The receptors were damaged."

"I didn't forget. I didn't think it was worth mentioning."

Farah perked up at this detail. "What happened to the receptors?"

Crawford looked down, collecting his thoughts. "They might have been vandalized. Slightly."

Orin was next to question him. "You mean deliberately, don't you, grand architect?"

"There were a few…" Crawford paused.

"There was a mob," Prell blurted out. "The technicians acted wildly, madam. Several Fordham were overpowered, and additional forces did not arrive in time to quell the disturbance."

Zelda came forward, bending to Farah's ear. Whatever she whispered into Farah's ear had the consul exhaling sharply. "So, which of you was going to tell me about the injured Fordham?"

Crawford clenched his jaw, hard enough to force his lips into a grimace. "If you're referring to those that were unresponsive, I'll have a physician prepare the analysis, which will arrive—"

"I do not care when it arrives," Farah griped. "You have a duty here and that is to inform us about everything regarding this incident."

Zelda took Farah's arm. As if by magic, she produced a small satchel and handed it to Farah. The consul accepted the pouch, closed her eyes, and inhaled its sweet fragrance.

"Elation is restorative," Zelda whispered.

"Thank you for reminding me," Farah said, returning to the immediate conversation. "Prell, at least tell me that your inquiries are completed."

"The majority of the techs who were questioned cooperated. Others needed additional encouragement," the sentinel answered. "Unfortunately, they seemed to know very little about what transpired here."

Senator Rivan, seated to the left of Farah, leaned forward with his inquiry at the ready. "Doesn't it seem odd that no one saw anything or heard anything?"

"There was one technician who possessed intimate knowledge of the event," Prell replied. "She evaded The Stretch, and therefore, her mind was not explored."

"You let her slip out of the detention center?" Orin asked.

"She chose her solution before we could submit her to the probe," Prell answered. "Another unfortunate occurrence."

Farah looked around the room, gauging the expressions of the members assembled. They were befuddled. "What solution do you speak of, Prell?"

"Technician Tragnor committed an act of suicide, madam," Prell replied. "All evidence points to her as the arsonist."

"That's a lie!" Crawford hissed.

Prell's sensitivity to the remark quickly showed onscreen. "Is it, grand architect?" he questioned. "Or are you being overly sensitive? There are remedies for such behavior."

Farah's eyes narrowed, her brow wrinkling in disapproval. "You would do well to calm yourself, grand architect. I do not wish to see you under the influence of stretching, especially not on your first day of the assignment."

"Calm or not, it's a lie," Crawford said, mimicking Farah's expression. "Melee Tragnor was a competent technician. She and the rest of the staff are under my supervision. Her work ethic is beyond reproach."

"If that were the case, there was no need for her actions," Farah said. "Pleasant and loyal citizens do not harm themselves or anyone else."

"Believe me, consul, she wasn't a rabble-rouser."

Farah passed over Crawford's testimony. "Prell, bind every mind at the plant and residents within a ten-mile radius. Let no information regarding this situation escape across the territory."

"With all due respect, Farah, the injury is done," Crawford said. "Those people have already been exposed to stress and you know as well as I do that binding isn't always successful."

"I did not ask for your opinion," Farah retorted. "Resistance can be dealt with by alternative means."

"You mean culling?" Crawford asked. "That's not exactly a tidy way out, not to mention it's violent to boot."

"Fear and stress destabilize contentment. They bring nothing but depression and illness," Farah responded. "If that means we must sacrifice a few to save many, then so be it."

"Farah, on this occasion, I agree with the grand architect. We cannot be so extreme as to wipe out nearly an entire area," Orin said. "We should be transparent in case the binding process fails and someone talks through unpredicted channels."

"What do you suggest as far as transparency, Senator Novak? Is the consul expected to divulge all the details?" Senator Hyatt asked, arranging the drapery of his robe.

"Consul Farah will address the people at midday. She can assure our mechanisms are sound and we can have a sale of euphoric stimulants to bolster citizen confidence," Orin said. "Grand Architect Lear, you should be there and deliver your full report to me for correlation through the Servers."

"I have to go to the Citadel at dawn, but I'll show up," Crawford said. "Now, if you'll excuse me, I have an investigation to finish." Crawford abruptly closed the channel, leaving the senate members to stare at a blank screen.

After a bit of silence, Farah motioned Zelda to her side. "Tell Severn Novak to bring the full inventory of stimulants within the habitat's factories with him to our morning meeting," she said. "He will coordinate the dispersal of the product to the squares with assistance from the fleet."

"Do you wish to alert the fleet commanders to continue standing by?" Zelda asked.

31

"Yes. This will be all hands on deck," Farah answered. "One more thing, Zelda, bring me the shift schedule Adario retrieved from Plant 13."

"Karno has it, madam."

"Then send him in with it," Farah said, waving Zelda out.

With Zelda gone, Senator Hyatt focused his attention on Farah. "As you know, when last reported, our inventory was lower than expected. A wide-scale sale could significantly deplete what remains."

"I thought Dr. Novak recorded a surplus available among the stock," Orin said.

"That was months ago. Sales have increased more than thirty percent since then," Rivan said. "The longer people use the products, the more they build a tolerance to them."

Farah quieted Rivan with a reassuring glance. "I believe we are safe," she said. "Dr. Novak is meticulous in his counts and he is constantly developing new formulations."

Karno entered, crossing to Farah's side. "You require something, madam?"

"Bring me the names of the laborers at the plant."

"It was given to Zelda to collate."

"She said it was in your hands."

"She is in error, madam," Karno replied.

"I do not care whose responsibility it is. Find it and bring it to me, then see to it the fallen Fordham and civilians are delivered to Dr. Sorenson." Karno smiled, obeying without question.

"This incident in Delphia is troubling," Rivan said to his colleagues. "It has been nearly what? A decade or so since..."

"Everything is under control," Farah said. "You need not worry yourselves."

"We are fortunate to have procedures in place to deal with these issues," Orin responded, dryly. "I shudder to think what would have happened if we were not prepared."

"Indeed, though no one was seriously injured, like Rivan said, the previous Delphian issues come to mind," a woman senator by the name of Castillo noted.

"Those issues were resolved swiftly," Hyatt said.

"That is not entirely true," Castillo said, "and besides, I refer to the incidents in the years after Rand's secession."

"Those were nothing compared to this," Rivan said.

Senator Castillo looked to Rivan. "I hardly call those morbid deaths minor."

"Did we ever discover the cause?" Farah asked.

"There were many theories, but no definitive answer was ever supplied," Hyatt said. "Those cases contributed to the demise of therapy as a remedy."

"I do not think this issue is related."

"Neither do I," Rivan said. "There have been very few disturbances until now."

"But let us not forget, they did happen," Castillo said. "The stain on Delphia cost that province its place as the premier jewel of the habitat."

"The past has no bearing on today's events," Farah said. "Beta Union is secure and Delphia has no need of an honored reputation since its purpose is the same as all the provinces—it serves the entire habitat."

"We will stand by you when you give your address," Hyatt said. "Until then, I believe this meeting is adjourned."

"I concur. We have had enough excitement for one day," Farah said, bidding each of them farewell.

Orin stayed behind to speak with Farah in private. "The grand architect didn't mention any ramifications to the Servers."

"Perhaps there are none."

"There are twelve sensory receptors around the plant. All of them carry significant amounts of energy."

Farah smirked. "Now you are an engineer, Orin?"

"No, but I cannot imagine it is not important."

"I am sure a diagnostic is on his list of things to do when he arrives at the Citadel tomorrow."

"Another thing, Crawford Lear's reaction to Prell's accusation was volatile," Orin said. "Does his behavior not concern you?"

"He knew Melee and obviously trusted her," Farah replied. "His trust may have been misplaced, but it was noble of him to try and salvage her honor."

"Nobility is one thing, but disobedience is another," Orin mused, his dark eyes filled with suspicion. "I would like to accompany him on his next inspection."

Farah's eyes widened at Orin's suggestion. "You know that is impossible," she said. "No one except the grand architect and members of their engineering corps can ever enter the Citadel. I cannot use my office to grant you access."

"Surely now is not the time to proceed carelessly."

"I suggest you be candid in your evaluation of Crawford Lear," Farah replied. "If you are questioning his abilities, you have leave to say so."

"He is new to the position, a human being, and therefore fallible," Orin remarked. "I only suggest he may be trying to cope with a situation beyond his capabilities."

"His engineers and the senate support him."

"No one need know I am present, Farah."

"The answer is no. None of the other senators will agree to it," Farah retorted, "and as I have already said, I cannot circumvent their authority."

"Very well," Orin said, backing down. "I hope you are right, and Crawford Lear proves a worthy choice."

"Good eve, Orin," Farah said, departing for her office.

As she walked back to her sanctuary, Farah reflected on their conversation. She was unwilling to challenge Hyatt and the other senators. That action would border upon favoritism and she could do without that trait.

Without further evidence, the senate and Beta Union's populace would have to rely on Crawford's knowledge and fidelity.

CHAPTER 5

The sails of the *Zenith* rippled in the gentle wind as its keel bobbed in the harbor. Kemble Novak, dressed in a fluid emerald dress, glided along the ship's deck.

The view was breathtaking, and the ship's sleek hull reflected the rhythm of the water's dance. Lanterns along pathways and aboard ship blazed with mellow fire in the night, their radiance complementing Kemble's honey brown skin.

What's keeping him? He's never late.

Kemble could not imagine what delayed her father. He needed this outing more than the other guests did. Her eyes fell to a metallic chain hanging from her belt. At its head was a small woven orb encasing an opal sphere. She lifted it to her nose, and inhaled deeply, the sweet odor releasing tensions in her body.

Kemble's attention returned to the streets, spotting Severn and Mallet approaching the ship. She beckoned them to the plank as Tovah, her brother's pare, appeared at her side. Tovah's pale complexion, raven hair, and seductive dark eyes stood in marked contrast to Kemble's warm features. Kemble found her stunning, if not a bit haughty. Mallet and Severn reached the deck, accepting embraces from both women.

"What took you so long?" Kemble asked.

"I couldn't come dressed in a lab coat," Severn said, "so, we stopped at the dorm and I changed."

Kemble giggled at Severn's relaxed attire. "You look splendid," she said before addressing Mallet. "Good eve to you as well."

"And a good eve to you," Mallet sneered.

Kemble took Severn's arm, guiding him toward the guests. "Look who's finally arrived," she called out.

Breen came forward, clasping his father's forearms. He was taller than Severn, but like his sister, the engineer's short curly brunet mane framed a face much like that of his father. Severn marveled at his children's physical beauty just as he admired their intellect. Their education yielded adept awareness; their training was evident in their mannerisms.

"It must have been difficult, tearing yourself away from work," Breen said.

Severn inspected Breen's uniform. "You're obviously more attached to your duties than me."

"We're going to the Citadel at dawn, so Crawford granted me leave this evening."

"How are you supposed to pursue and enjoy the pleasures of life if you're always working?" Severn asked.

"Crawford needs all the engineers he can get," Mallet said with a wink. "Beta Union couldn't function without them."

"Labor is a boring subject," Tovah injected. "It's a celebration, we should be joyous."

"Quite right," Severn said. "Shall we?"

The absence of prying sensors comforted Severn. He recognized many faces in the party, his brother Orin and several notable scientists among them.

Severn turned to Mallet. "Where's Melee?" he asked. "I thought she'd be here."

"She wanted to be," Mallet answered, swiftly. "She had to take a shift but sends her regards."

Breen shifted, rubbing the back of his nape. He alone was aware of why the technician was absent, and it was obvious Mallet did not know. Mallet had not seen his sister in a long time and his display set Kemble off balance. She expected sarcasm to leap from his lips. It was improper to possess less than friendly thoughts about him and she struggled to keep them at bay.

Kemble never wanted to dislike him, but like swarms of stinging insects, touches of discord jealously buzzed in her mind to antagonize the pilot. The feeling never failed to rise to the surface whenever he was near.

Her psyche felt drained by some invisible menace, its sensitivity intimidating. Kemble's distaste of his person began before Mallet's introduction to her father and the couple's subsequent rapport did not dispel it.

Severn approached an elaborate table setting heaped with delicacies. "This looks lovely."

"Sit here," Kemble said, showing him to a seat at the head. "I'll tell the watch officer to get underway."

Mallet cut an eye at her as he settled into a seat next to Severn. "She'd pilot the ship herself if it weren't a party," he mumbled.

"What'd you say?" Tovah asked.

"Nothing."

Kemble peeked at Mallet's face as she proceeded to the wheelhouse. The remedy she took earlier finally kicked into gear, allowing her to dismiss the twist of his mouth. She suspected Mallet was a deviant.

One day, his expressions will get the better of him, she thought.

Severn saw their subtle exchange. He reached under the table to place a hand on the commander's knee. "I'm fine," Mallet responded.

"Sooner or later, the two of you should get over it," Severn said. "This competition isn't doing either of you any good and it's likely to get you tagged."

"She can't stand the fact I was first at Aqua."

"Kemble was first at Aero and you can't seem to stand it. Let it go before it causes trouble."

Mallet dropped the argument. "I'll need this if I'm going to get through tonight," he said, removing a clear, petite tube from a pocket. He clicked the button on its underside, igniting the turquoise crystals within. He drew on the mouthpiece, exhaling rings into the air. The drug took effect immediately, dilating his pupils, and settling him into a private haze.

"What is that?" Tovah asked.

"It's new," Severn remarked, watching Mallet slip into a relaxed state. "I think it's the best of the bunch."

"I'll take your word for it," Mallet said in a drowsy voice. He offered the tube to Tovah, but she declined.

"I'm good on my own. Natural joy is best."

"Not everyone is as disciplined as you," Severn replied.

"No one complains, and everyone stays cheerful," Mallet groaned, twirling the tube between his fingers, the crystals within charred. "Be happy or be stretched."

"Are you a killjoy?" Tovah asked.

"No. There's no cause to ask me that."

"Good. I'm glad to hear it," she replied. "People like that make everyone miserable. They're worthy of tagging."

"Do we have to talk about this?" Breen asked. "I'm sure we can find a better topic for conversation."

Kemble returned to rest in an empty chair to her father's right. In the background, she heard soft laughter from the group. They were whispering in each other's ears, playing a game.

"Are you enjoying yourself?" she asked Tovah.

"Absolutely."

Mallet raised his head, eyes bright with excitement, a delightful grin spread across his rugged face. "I'm definitely enjoying this."

Kemble watched his movements, delighted by the sight of his pacification. "Your remedy seems to be working," she said to Severn in a hushed tone.

"You'd better eat something before you pass out," Tovah said to Mallet. He ignored her concern, attempting to eavesdrop on Severn and Kemble's conversation.

"I'm still testing it," Severn said. "So far, it provides a worthy successor to Easel and it lasts longer."

"What about the after?" Tovah asked. "Are there any lingering side effects to note?"

Severn was lost in his reflections when she spoke, imagining how many others were in Mallet's condition, drugged, and lost to the full knowledge of their emotions. It took him a few moments to return to reality and answer Tovah. "We haven't seen anything significant yet, but everyone metabolizes medication differently," Severn said. "Weight, physiology, and overall health come into play every time you prescribe something."

The effects of Kemble's alleviation, now dissipating, allowed a wicked idea to creep into her consciousness. "It would serve him right if he wakes up feeling heavy," she said. Heads turned, looking at her with scolding eyes.

"What possesses you tonight?" Severn asked.

"I'm sorry. I don't know why I said that," Kemble replied, shaking her head. "It won't happen again."

Orin slide out from his chair at the far end of the table, standing up, raising his glass, and calling for a toast. "To Severn, my sib," he began. "The years have been good to you. May your life be filled with abundant joy, prosperity, and above all— purity, and loyalty to the Union."

The party attendees echoed Orin's sentiment with glee. Mallet did not rise to join in on the accolades given to Severn. Instead, the commander sat enjoying the warm air, breathing shallowly and peacefully, with his eyes closed against frolicking people surrounding him.

Kemble could not help but peer in his direction. The longer she focused on him, the stronger her disapproval. Her behavior was a source of consternation, bewildering Severn. It was to her credit that she acquiesced. If Fordham were near, they would not hesitate to correct the pilot's insolence.

Severn realized, for the first time, the degree of his daughter's revulsion for Mallet. It was deep-rooted, needing a watchful eye and a firm hand. Nothing terrified him more than the knowledge of what would happen to Kemble should she let her feelings off the leash. He decided to remind his daughter of this fact even if it meant pushing her further into the abyss he wished to wash from his hands.

The festivities ended late with Breen and Tovah the last to leave. When they arrived home, Tovah checked on their children before joining Breen in the living area then plopped down on the couch, making polite conversation.

"That was a beautiful celebration of Severn's life."

"Yeah, it was," Breen said, spreading himself on the cushions, "and a good turnout as well."

Tovah extended an elbow along the back of the sofa before resting her head in her palm. "Mallet was in rare form."

"How's that?"

"He says inappropriate things."

"Everyone falls short from time to time."

"He seems to fall often."

Breen stood up. "You sound like Kemble."

"She knows it as well as me."

"He'll get it under control."

"The sooner the better, he's becoming a real killjoy."

"You're thinking of tagging him, aren't you?"

"Someone should," Tovah answered, "His behavior isn't normal, and it could contaminate someone else."

"Give him a chance to correct it on his own," Breen said, starting for the front door. "I'm sure he'll see the wisdom of it."

"Where are you going?"

"I forgot to get some specs for the grand architect," Breen answered. "He needs them for tomorrow, and I won't be long."

"Curfew starts soon," Tovah reminded the engineer. "Whatever you have to do should wait until morning."

"It can't wait. Crawford answers to the senate," Breen said. "And I answer to him."

Tovah strolled to the stairs and began to remove her dress. "Then you'd better hurry," she said smiling.

"I will," Breen winked.

By 2:00 a.m., the curfew blanketed the city. The streets and squares were devoid of citizens, but Fordham remained on constant patrol. Breen moved cautiously in the stillness doing his best to avoid the dim monitors scattered throughout the grounds. He was thankful the rendezvous point set up by his contact was close.

With his back against a pillar, he stole a look at the pathway leading to a bountiful row of trees laden with soft red needles, a reasonable distance, two meters at most. Running was not his best option, but if ever there was a time for action, it was now.

Breen peeled away from the wall and stepped out into the street, moving quickly behind a dense bush. The lush arbor enveloped him, his hands grasping its foliage. This is madness.

"Where are you?" he whispered. He felt a soft brush caressing his hand, which caused him to spin around and search the void for a presence.

"Be still," came a muted voice from the dark.

Breen tried to focus on the speech but did not recognize it. "Say what you need and then I'm going," he replied.

"Your services are needed," the voice continued. "Obtain the public communication codes for the network and deliver them to us."

"They're classified. What do you want them for?"

"Do not concern yourself with this."

"If I'm going to get them for you, I want to know what you're planning to do with them."

"You know our purpose and you have pledged to assist."

"Do you know how difficult it'll be? Do think the grand architect will just hand them over?"

"We are confident you will succeed."

"You're really not going to tell me anything, are you?"

"All will be revealed soon. Remember, the welfare of all citizens is at stake," the voice spoke in a determined tone. "Restoration cannot wait."

Breen strained his vision to see beyond the trees, but the contact had already slipped away, leaving him fearful of his alliance with a faceless and nameless ally bent on a rebellion.

People are happy. Why destroy what little peace they have?

His wavering thought cooled after remembering the words given to him at the beginning of the proscribed journey. The message spoke about freedom of will, the balance of emotion, and something called love. The latter was a complicated concept for Breen. When asked about his feelings for his father, he did not truly know how to answer.

Severn added to his happiness through the wisdom he imparted, yet Breen often wondered if the warmth he felt went beyond gratitude, straying into forbidden territory. When he first departed home, his desire for Severn's company was strong, but he was against seeking it. Breen eventually came to reconcile the behavior, but now and then, he caught himself wishing for a substantial connection with his parent.

It can't be unnatural.

Breen's thinking drifted to his children, Somiel and Lerner. The actions he was about to carry out would shame them. This bothered him for a moment, but his course was set, and he wanted to discover what new experiences the mysterious emotion would introduce.

The engineer silently made his way back to his dormitory. Just as he was walking up the path, he heard movement behind his position. Breen halted in place, waiting to hear who was on his heels. He suspected a Fordham and like many of his colleagues, he preferred certain sentinels more than others. The engineer took a chance and turned to face this new shadow. Breen's gut reacted when he saw Adario.

The Fordham looked inquisitively at Breen. "Curfew is in effect," Adario said in a stern voice. "What are you doing outside at this hour?"

"I was retrieving a system log from Pump 5," Breen replied as calmly as possible.

Adario's thin lips formed a disturbing smile while his amber gaze remained cold and feral. "You know the policy. Your activities should have been completed before curfew."

"The grand architect needed some vitals," Breen responded, "He's going to the Citadel this morning."

"For such an important errand, you seem to have forgotten the data," Adario said, pointing to the engineer's empty hands.

Breen watched the hues on the sentinel's face edge up the spectrum. "I have a storage disc in my pocket," Breen fibbed, praying to an unseen force that Adario would relent.

But the Fordham was not fooled. "Then you will have no problem producing it for inspection."

The engineer swallowed hard as he reached into the slit of his pants for a disc that was not there. Just as he started to feel a surge of panic rising, Tovah called across the length of space.

"Breen, what took you so long?" Tovah asked, sprinting from the entrance. "Somiel woke up asking for you."

"It took a while to find the log," Breen called over his shoulder without taking his eyes off Adario's sensor band.

"Come inside," Tovah said, catching up to him, and taking his arm. "Somiel wants you to read to her before bed."

Adario reluctantly backed away from the engineer. "Take care that you do not break the rules next time," Adario warned.

Breen's skin crawled even as Adario walked away. "Trust me, there won't be a next time," he breathed.

With a sigh of relief, Breen joined Tovah and together, they walked into the dorm building. Breen was thankful Tovah had saved him from Adario's menacing interrogation and the aftermath of what would have surely been a trip to the detention center. Just like his father, only hours before, Breen had narrowly avoided catastrophe.

CHAPTER 6

The gunship, *Azimuth*, skated swiftly to the northern border under the new morning sky. The vessel served as a guardian of Beta Union's borders, along with its sisters, the *Zephyr* and *Corona*. Its crew underwent extensive training for security clearance processes, allowing them to ferry the grand architect and the engineer corps to secure locations outside civilian boundaries.

The vessel's sapphire sails sparkled in the white sun as the collected warm rays. Men and women busied themselves with the rigging, some aloft, others scampering around the deck. Fordham stood at attention, surveying the actions of the crew while Crawford stood in the wheelhouse looking out of the command center's porthole with Commander Odonna Ragas. His beloved companion, Thalo, lounged on the floor, slumbering.

Crawford rubbed his palms together vigorously. "Shouldn't your pilot be with his navigator?" he asked.

Odonna sniggered, clapping Crawford on the back. "Are you nervous?"

Crawford moved toward the compass at the center of the room. "No, but my hands are cold."

"I've heard you're the coldest man in the western hemisphere, but I can always turn up the heat for you."

It took every ounce of courtesy from Crawford to resist uttering a witty comeback. "That won't be necessary."

"Is it true? Are you as perfect as they say?"

"I'll never tell."

"Come now, Crawford. You're not supposed to any have secrets from anyone."

"I don't. What you see is what you get," he replied, studying the map, "and right now, you're not getting to me."

Odonna stepped in front of him, pausing to regard the slumbering animal at her feet. "Be a good sport. I've heard you get on well with Consul Farah."

Crawford noted how appealing Odonna's lithe body looked in her indigo flight suit. The net of the fabric hugged Odonna's curves, accentuating her pleasing physical attributes. "I don't know what you mean," he grinned.

"I know you've had her, and I can't blame you. She's an exquisite creature."

"Do you have an interest?" Crawford asked, leaning against the pedestal surrounding the globe.

"I'd have been there already if she weren't so busy."

"Maybe you can pry her away from the senate?"

"I doubt it. Running this place seems more important to her than sex."

Crawford laughed. "Well, the truth is, you're not missing anything."

"I don't believe it, considering the number of times you're rumored to have bedded her."

"You're keeping count?"

"It pays to keep abreast of the competition."

"I'm not attached to her if that's what you're thinking."

"That's right, you play by the rules," Odonna said. "I'd love to know who's next on your list."

"I'm sorry?"

"It's not good to go without too long."

"I've never gone without anything," Crawford snickered.

Odonna stepped closer to his side, the swell of her breasts brushing his arm. She blew hot breath in his ear and motioned him forward with eager eyes. There was no pretense in her proposal. Before he could consider her offer, the *Azimuth*'s pilot thrust her head in the entranceway.

"Commander, we're nearing the border," the pilot said.

Odonna reluctantly withdrew from Crawford's side. "Did you alert the patrol to our approach?"

"Belmont and his guards signaled they'll meet us at the LZ," the pilot answered.

"I'll be up in a moment. Maintain course and speed."

Crawford bent to check on Thalo. The jackal lifted his head and planted a wet nose on its master's face. "I should take him out before we land."

"Are you trying to get away from me?"

"You actually want the truth?"

"No holds barred."

"Then, yes. I've no wish to be mauled by you or any other tempting creature," he said, reaching for Thalo's leash, "at least not today."

"Then it's true. Farah does have power over you or maybe it's someone else."

Crawford chuckled at her response. "We've already had that conversation. Let's not rehash it."

Odonna bit her lip. There was nothing more to say. What he possessed was his to give, and he enjoyed dangling it before her, casting the reel then yanking it back before she tasted the bait. As he slipped away, Odonna rushed to the window to see him appear on deck, puzzled by Crawford's rejection. The man she knew would not have passed on such an opportunity. Taking to the steps, she crept on deck, stopping a safe distance behind Crawford, her annoyance alerting Prell and his squad.

Prell came to her side. "Are you feeling well, Commander?"

Odonna met his smoky eyes, their glassy appearance reflecting the lime flow on his facial sensor. She unzipped the neck of her suit and extracted a small square from the shoulder region. "It's a bit of frustration," she said, peeling away a thin film coating the object before pressing it to her skin. "There's no need for concern."

Crawford and his engineers got off the ship at the border's hub, a fair distance from their destination. The team assembled in two hovers to journey across the icy and desolate region. With their equipment secured, communication devices at their throats and thermal units within their attire, they were well prepared for the final leg of the journey.

The Citadel, an extraordinary obsidian structure, lay carved into the mountainside. Its mammoth façade, discovered by the first planetary expedition, was of practical design, and its shadow cast a grim eye on a crystalline courtyard.

It took years to interpret the pictographs scrawled on its walls, yet once deciphered, the Citadel proved an invaluable resource. Passes leading to the building held certain death for those unfamiliar with the maze-like geography. Crawford naturally navigated the route with ease, guiding the engineers who moved as one in their chocolate uniforms that blended into the woodlands.

After a time, Crawford led the corps through the grand entrance, into a lofty but warm marble atrium. "Narlin, you, and Alcott take the Red Wing," he instructed. "Make a thorough assessment of the points."

Narlin acknowledged his orders, waving Alcott and two sentinels to follow him. "This way, folks."

"Tama and Hensley, you're on the Blue. Check the filtration pumps and energy cells," Crawford continued. "The rest of you, come with me."

"Sir, have you spoken with Commander Tragnor about Melee?" Breen asked, following Crawford's lead.

"No, there's not much to tell."

"How did her session go?"

"I'm not sure. When I left, she was still being questioned," Crawford lied.

"I'm sure he'd want to know."

Crawford found Breen's concern for Mallet surprising. His insistence suggested a level of unwholesome compassion beyond the set norm. "I haven't had time to pursue the matter," the architect said. "If you see him and he asks, which he shouldn't, you've nothing to tell him."

"I understand," Breen said in low voice. "I just know I'd want to be apprised of the situation."

"Good thing you do understand," Crawford said, ignoring the rest of Breen's statement. "Now let's concentrate on the task at hand."

Breen motioned the others to pick up the pace. The interior, with its sculptures and other decorative elements lining the halls, was a stark comparison to the exterior. Pyramid-shaped lamps, swinging from the ceiling, beamed with fluorescence, every detail more magnificent than the last.

Three gates protected the Server hive, requiring passcodes unique to every grand architect, locked away in his or her mind.

The only other entity who could access the encryption was the assigned key maker and they dared not violate the sanctity of the hive unless legally ordered by the senate. Any unwarranted intrusion would result in death.

Crawford stepped forward, standing a slight distance from the last gate. A brilliant beam engulfed him in pure white light. Seconds later, a hole appeared in the door, its size formatted to accommodate him. "All of you stay here," he said, moving inward.

Once inside, his presence brought the circular cavity to life. Hundreds of identical modules filling the room sparkled with starlight, illuminating the captive organs serving society in a marvelous installation of bioengineering. A limpid web, channeling powerful energy, sat above the glow, its pulsating energy forming a communications channel between Fordham and The Servers.

Working in tandem with the network device was a supportive foundation behind the austere trophies. Its elaborate array of twisting braids formed spiny pipes connected to pools of bio-substances. This sophisticated setup essentially forced the entities to perform as Beta Union's slaves.

Crawford approached a pentagonal floor pad sitting in front of a sleek podium at the center of the room. With a sweep of his hand, a display with a fluid visage appeared suspended in the air. All functions looked normal, but a 360-degree inspection was mandatory.

"Round," he commanded the pad.

It lifted from the floor, beginning a slow spiral through the height of the space. Crawford inspected each level with meticulous care, but halted midway through his survey, finding fault amid the collective. Clusters of modules on level H were mottled, their color drained and sallow. He turned around the room again, observing muted tones looming in other areas.

Crawford wheeled the mat over for closer inspection while removing a slender wand from his belt. He struck its metallic surface like a match and blew across the tip. Globular fluid seeped from the stick forming a viscous bubble, which he floated gently toward one of the units.

The sphere attached itself and spread in a gluey patch. With a wave of the baton, Crawford probed inside the specimen discovering critically elevated levels of fluid surrounding the intelligence. His brow tightened at the results.

It's dying.

Crawford returned to the floor to call up another display and run a new diagnostic. Just as he assumed, vulnerabilities existed within the modules, yet the conduit binding the sentinels to The Servers continued to absorb and transmit information.

Let's see how long it lasts, he thought while shutting down the presentation to activate the voice unit in his choker.

"Breen, I'm coming out. Have Narlin and the others meet us in the atrium."

CHAPTER 7

The State Building received a steady flow of employees as the daily routines of the morning commenced over Beta Union. Farah, an early riser, arrived at 6:15 a.m.

She took her place behind her desk and began poring over a translucent page, sliding her finger from right to left and back again, reading notes and studying images. Of all the places in the city, this space was her favorite. Here, luxury and power surrounded Farah.

"What is different?" she muttered, looking up from her work to survey the room.

After a brief pause, she recognized the latest additions to the décor. Ebony timber formed curvaceous legs on a smoky quartz table laying opposite from the tinted floor-to-ceiling windows, which overlooked the bay. The chairs accompanying the table were of dark blue stone with ivory-colored arms. The complete set complemented couches of fine hide, and various plants decorating the room. Each piece fit naturally with the office's pallid walls and artwork, alive with bountiful tints.

Orin criticized her taste, calling the paintings explosions of ovaries unsuitable to the environment. In his opinion, they were queer and perpetuated a conceptualized sanctity of motherhood. Farah refused to remove them. They made her happy, as every item in the office, right down to the crystal paperweight bearing her initials, F.I.A. The item was a vain accoutrement, a last reminder of her birth line. The "I" was for Ivanova, her mother's surname.

At the height of her career, Sabina Ivanova was one of Beta Union's brightest economists with twenty years of service at the State Building. Her match with Dorian Aver was a successful one, producing their daughter within the accustomed timeframe and without incident. Farah learned the business of leadership and responsibility from both Sabina and Dorian, but the hardline she took on the law flowed directly from the latter.

Farah struggled to remember Sabina's face. The only memorable thing that came to mind was Sabina's fiery red hair, which her daughter inherited, and the way she always seemed to speak with authority in her musical voice. Farah could not even remember a time when she smiled, as she always looked serious.

Did I get anything from her? she wondered.

Farah put aside her meditations and returned to the charts. Her breakfast, a modest plate of curly red leaves dotted with speckled fruit, went untouched. The senate would convene at ten, its members to arrive no later than 9:30 am. Farah's eyes moved to the surface of her marbled desk where she traced a small inlay to summon Zelda to the room.

"Is Dr. Novak on his way?" Farah asked, concentrating on the forms.

"Bristol is coordinating his arrival."

Farah looked up from her work. Even with the plethora of prescriptive elements Farah ingested, the sight of Zelda elicited incomprehensible chills down her back. Too often, she found her mood challenged by Zelda's stalking specter, yet as one of the most capable guards in her arsenal, she was too efficient to dismiss.

"Inform me when he arrives."

"Yes, madam," Zelda said, touching a link in her ear.

Farah grimaced, envying her apathy. It is easy for them, she thought. They have no inner turbulence.

The consul believed contentment and inner peace through medical means and communal pleasantries worked, yet the practice of purging in residences impeded full compliance. Farah pushed the senate to establish household censoring, but they opposed the strategy, arguing the faithful consistently identified and tagged offenders.

"You may go, Zelda. I need to prepare for this afternoon."

Zelda left Farah to her routine. Farah touched another control on her desk, activating a wall screen. She relaxed in her chair to review footage from a historical archive more than fifty years old. Founder Linus Rand appeared on the screen, his dark hands and curly black hair splotched with blood. A row of robed officials sat before him.

Farah recognized several of the judges, former bastions of society headed by her father Consul Dorian Emmett Aver. Senator Philippa Taylor, a fair-haired woman known for her unwavering stance on morality, sat to the consul's right and next to her was Senator Mitchell Manning, an ardent supporter of Beta Union's longstanding isolationist policy.

"You have heard the charges against you, Linus Rand?" Aver asked.

"Your charges mean nothing," Linus said. His deep brown eyes pierced through the tribunal. "You can't hide behind what we did."

"We eradicated irrelevant ideologies and negative emotions," Aver said. "We brought the people to a new way of life, devoid of the Birth Born sins."

"You gave us ultimate pleasure, but you removed deeper aspects," Linus said as the documentary continued. *"If our past taught us anything, it taught us that love and commitment are sources of strength."*

"Those ideas breed sickness and ill-will," Senator Taylor said. *"They give rise to pride, jealousy, prejudice, and violence."*

"The people of Enoch clung to self-seeking ideas and delusions of superiority," Aver said.

"They waged war against their neighbors."

"As we did here," Linus said. *"We came and conquered, becoming the very people, we despised at home."*

"You had no difficulty doing your duty," Senator Manning said with a huff, *"and for that, you were graced with life beyond the average years."*

"If I'd known the consequences, I would never have done what Austin wanted."

"You were seduced by this new world," Aver said, *"a world that is separate from the life we led on Enoch."*

"We're no better now," Linus said. *"You think you can suppress what's natural forever?"*

"The dark age of humanity is gone. It served its purpose," Aver said. *"Our present ways are superior to the evil within we left behind."*

Orin walked into Farah's chamber. "The meeting is about to start," he said, eyeing the archival footage.

"I will be there in a moment," Farah responded, still watching the screen with rapt attention.

"There was an accident in Delphia. We should start now."

Farah hushed him. A close-up on the screen showed Linus Rand, hanging his head and taking deep breaths. Prompted by Dorian Aver's words, the courtroom doors swung open. Two guards walked beside a stone-faced woman with alabaster skin, sunken cheeks, and red rings clustered around her golden eyes. Her hair, the color of moonlight, lay in loose, messy waves about her shoulders. Linus Rand gave Betera Eaton a look of longing, but her expression remained the same.

"There is Betera," Farah breathed, "Crawford Lear's pare."

"A noble symbol for Beta Union," Orin remarked, as Senator Taylor came into view.

"It was she who deceived you, Linus Rand," Senator Taylor said. "Every facet of your plan passed from her hands to ours."

"Your affection was misplaced," Dorian Aver said.

Linus stared at Betera, searching her face. She continued staring straight ahead, arms at her sides. The guards closed in on Linus, grasping his limbs, dragging him from the chamber.

"One day you'll regret what you've done as I do," he shouted, wrestling against their muscle. "Justice will come, and it will end the way it began."

"A threat?" Senator Manning asked, standing at Aver's side.

"There will be no retribution," Aver said, motioning the guards. "It dies with you."

Senator Manning and his fellows watched as the guards took Linus from the room. "What of Delphia and Betera Eaton?"

"Delphia is to be culled. Betera Eaton will live to serve as our standard," Aver said. "Her allegiance will be a model for all."

Farah smiled when the program concluded. "I would have liked to meet Betera Eaton."

"I am sure you would have enjoyed that."

"Indeed, she was a marvelous and noble contributor to the cause."

"I understand she passed from a rare disease," Orin said.

"Unfortunately, we have not found a cure for every frailty," Farah said, standing to depart. "Dr. Novak will be here soon. I expect good things from our discussion."

Orin stopped Farah before she reached the door. "Why do you watch it?"

"You know why."

"I know why I watch it, but not your reasons."

"My reasons are the same as yours," Farah said. "Duty must be bolstered every now and then."

"If citizens knew what we know," Orin began, "they would never understand it. They might even think it vile."

"Fortunately, they will never know," Farah said. "Their ignorance is bliss. They need not be concerned how it was attained."

"Are we so changed, Farah?"

"We are living proof that our past is in our past," she said, making for the exit. "What happened before has no bearing on today."

"I wonder," Orin whispered following her out. "The thief is meant to be caught and punished. Rand said so himself."

"The dead can punish no one."

"And what about the living?" Orin asked.

"They just keep living," Farah replied, "as you and I must do for the security of everyone. Let that fact assuage your guilt."

CHAPTER 8

Severn lay awake staring at the ceiling; Mallet slept beside him with his face buried in a pillow. At any other time, Severn would be dead to the world, but his thoughts were full of issues that needed sorting. Production plans for the new euphoric Vapital were going slowly and it faced steep competition from its predecessor, the current standard Morfenya, known commercially as Joi.

Joi was a potent medication exuding the highest increases in euphoria, energy, and sexual desire. It continued to surpass the expectations of second-generation remedies, including a third, Solace. The drug's added advantage was a myriad of ingestion methods, the most popular being inhalation through atomizers or pipes. Its only downside was short duration and a propensity for "flaking" or "fogging."

Vapital was without such side effects, promising greater benefits at marginal cost to consumers. The main enticement of the drug was its ability to inundate the mind with congenial and arousing memories.

Severn thought of the work he and Bristol had put into the project. It was nothing for her kind to be up day and night; his body was tired and begged him to rest, but citizen comforts outweighed his own. Just as he was drifting into sleep, the front door chimed.

It's too early for this.

He felt around the foot of the bed for his robe and walked downstairs through the dimness of his quarters, shoving his arms into sleeves. The floor was chilly under his bare feet. When Severn opened the door, Bristol stood smiling pleasantly in candy-red attire.

"Dr. Novak," she said. "Consul Farah wishes to see you immediately."

"Now?" Severn asked, squinting against the bright hallway light.

"Now is the definition of immediate."

Severn huffed. "Come in. I'll get dressed."

Bristol slipped inward, staying close to the entrance, her watchful stare lingering here and there on objects in the room. In tall case, a group of images spread the length of a shelf. Bristol found the collection interesting and waited for Severn to disappear before approaching the pictures. In a neat row were holographs of his descendants at several pleasurable locales. Though much younger, she recognized Breen and Kemble, their expressions jubilant, smiles wide with sparkling teeth.

Though she recognized an irregular sentimental value in Severn's possession of the items, Bristol ignored the offense. She parted her lips, fixed her jaw in the fashion of the faces, and felt her enamel while holding an awkward smile for a minute before allowing it to fade. She then turned slightly toward the staircase hearing voices on the upper floor. Commander Tragnor was awake.

Severn came down the stair dressed in lab attire. "I'm ready," he said with a half-hearted smile.

"Commander Tragnor and the *Meridian* are to be placed on standby."

"I'll let him know," Severn said, heading for the stairs.

"Zelda will communicate with him," Bristol said, barring his retreat. "You will go to your lab and retrieve the full inventory before meeting with Consul Farah."

Severn nodded in agreement and followed Bristol. As the door slid closed behind him, he heard the wave link buzzing inside.

Bristol accompanied Severn to Farah's office where they waited patiently for her arrival. The chemist watched Bristol looking around the room, admiring the fashionable furnishings. Her attention was peculiar to him, as he never saw her in awe of anything outside of their lab work.

She had a delightful enthusiasm for the work they accomplished together. Severn attributed this to her training and national pride. In the stillness of the moment, he tendered a thought. *She must have feelings of her own. Repressed or not, she must feel something.*

"I know that better than anyone," he muttered aloud.

"What did you say?"

Severn shook himself away from his analysis. "It's like a gilded cage, isn't it?"

"That reference is unfamiliar, but these objects do have a certain aesthetic quality."

"At a considerable expense, no doubt."

"What is the relevance of your observation? Is it not simply a matter of taste?"

Severn laughed. "One could say so, or you could call it a borderline extravagance."

"The dissolution of corporate identity makes these items available to every citizen."

"Yes, because greed is no longer good."

"Are you quoting a publication from The Cellar?"

"Yes. I've read and seen many interesting things there."

The Cellar was a modest library of sorts where Severn devoured books devoted to medicine and novels about fanciful happy adventures without romance, political drama or anything construed as immoral. Handbooks, readily available in print and electronic editions, spanned a wide array of subjects from economics to emotional vigilance, diet, and law. Other volumes advised on medication, sexual stimulation, and overall good citizenship.

Abridged chronicles detailing the time before Tal's settlement avoided the history of Enoch, one of the first colonies established by humans after venturing beyond their native solar system. The chronicles told of the original three Talian colonies, but very little regarding its previous inhabitants.

The ancient structures and marvels suggested construction by an advanced civilization long departed. The buildings, combined with new edifices lent a strange, but beautiful sight to the lay of the landscape. Severn never questioned the omissions about the founder's previous homeworld or any of Tal's mysteries.

"Fordham do not go to the Cellar to read," Bristol said.

"Did you know there was a time when the attainment of wealth was a virtue?" Severn asked. "A selfish one."

"Some chose not to reach for it and others, not to share what they had, but I will say this, I'd welcome a bit of competition in the market right now."

"Competition is unhealthy. It creates jealousy and pride."

"It does, but I wouldn't be the only responsible party," Severn said somberly.

"Responsible?"

"It doesn't matter, back to the former," Severn said, glancing at Farah's paintings. "I prefer the minimalist approach."

"Your taste is to be admired, Dr. Novak," Bristol said in a charming tone.

Farah and Orin entered the office, ending Severn and Bristol's conversation. It was a rare occasion for Severn to see his brother, as circumstances usually kept them out of each other's immediate orbit.

"Severn, good to see you," Orin said to his brother.

Severn wanted to hug Orin but contained himself. "I assume the matter is urgent, madam,"

"It is indeed."

"I've brought the inventory you required. Is there anything else I need to do?"

"We need to distribute euphorics to all public squares in advance of my midday address," Farah instructed. "You will coordinate the supply of the fleet. I intend for citizens to enjoy a sale of goods and sample anything new you can muster."

Severn opened the inventory and scrolled to the data. "There is a surplus of Joi, Delight, and Solace. As far as new medications, we may not have enough Vapital yet for every square."

"Do we have a label?"

"Considering its recall capabilities, we settled on Evoke."

"I like it, simple and elegant."

"Who would not want to recall happy times?" Orin asked with a smile.

"Everyone would," Severn replied.

"I agree," Farah said. "You will go to the factory and gather the necessary items and your subordinates will do the same in their regions."

"We should start straightaway, Dr. Novak," Bristol said.

Severn followed his assistant, stopping at a kiosk to dial Unity's largest production facility. A woman answered the call.

"Dr. Novak."

"Isabel," Severn said. "I'm on my way. We have to check stocks."

"Shall I prep now?" she asked.

"Pull half of Joi and Solace and count what we have in Vapital," Severn instructed. "We'll need to deliver to Aero what's available immediately and we only have a few hours."

"I'll start right now."

CHAPTER 9

While Severn started to implement the latest of Farah's latest plans, Mallet wandered the *Meridian*'s deck on the other side of the city. He watched supplies flowing aboard the ship, his crew completing their task with precision. The *Azimuth* lay adjacent to the *Meridian*, having recently returned from escorting engineers to the Citadel. Mallet watched as Odonna strolled the length of her deck, deep in thought.

The ships would soon depart, blanketing the provinces with stimulants and serenity. His comm unit rang several times during his vigil, but he neglected to answer. Serious and more pressing matters preoccupied him. When Zelda woke him, duty was the last thing on his mind.

"Do me a favor," Mallet said as Kemble came to join him after finishing preparations in the wheelhouse. "Go over the routes again with Commander Ragas. I don't want any overlap."

"We've been over them already."

"Go over it again."

Kemble huffed and left him to his own whims. The comms device tucked away in his uniform buzzed again. This time, he moved to answer it, hoping it was Severn. It would be good to see his face. He squeezed the device and to his surprise, Breen appeared in the bubble.

"Commander Tragnor, I have information regarding your sib," Breen said.

"What's Melee done now?" Mallet asked.

Breen paused. Crawford instructed him not to say anything, but his conscience bothered him. "She was taken for questioning after the fire."

"What fire?"

"There was a fire at Plant 13 while Tech Tragnor was on duty."

"Is she still there?"

"I'm not sure. There are a lot of workers here," Breen said, seeing distress in Mallet's features. He reasoned his assumptions were correct. Mallet had a bond with his sister. He continued relaying information. "The GA went in with her. He should have more information."

"Thanks. I'll check with him," Mallet said.

Mallet knew Melee was smart. He was confident she could take care of herself. Mallet turned his thoughts away from the subject. He looked toward the stern seeing Odonna cross over with Kemble. The pilot gave him a nod as she slipped off to the command center, leaving Mallet alone to face Odonna.

"You didn't have to send your pilot to me," Odonna said. "These routes were checked a hundred times."

"Okay, you know the plan then," Mallet said, snatching the pane, to go over the assignments.

"I'm taking this route. The *Halo* and *Compass* are supplying Osler. *Horizon* is at Iona."

"And the *Zephyr*?"

"It's in the plan. They'll rendezvous with the *Horizon*."

"I thought the *Squall* was assigned the territory."

"You said you read the plan, Odonna," Mallet smiled. "It doesn't seem like you paid attention to the details."

Odonna rolled her eyes. Mallet was behaving like his usual self, blunt, in command, and slightly immature. "Prell and his troop are with me," she said, turning on a heel, "and I see Karno has arrived for you, so I'll be on my way."

Mallet was happy to see her go. He started for the wheelhouse issuing orders for departure. "All right, people, let's get underway and engage the field. Anyone who wants to keep their arm had better hang back off the railings."

A flash appeared around the outer edges of the deck, signaling the activation of the ship's force field. From the helm, Mallet watched the men and women outside, thinking back to his first flight with Severn. It was a spontaneous trip on Mallet's part. He coaxed Severn into a journey, thinking it would be a fun voyage, but Severn spent the greater part of it in panic, and the rest ill.

The chemist was not suited to the clouds, preferring travel by sea. Besides, he was more than doubtful about the safety margin and Mallet's detailed lecture did nothing for Severn's anxiety. If he could not touch it, see it, or taste it, he had no faith in it.

"It's a lifting body," Mallet said, explaining the vessel's workings. "There's an energy field surrounding the deck protecting us from the air pressure."

"As far as I'm concerned, birds are the only things that should fly," Severn said, belittling the concept.

"You'd have never made it in a spaceship. It's basically a flying can."

"How are you steering this thing?"

"Uh, it's called a yoke, but it looks like a wheel," Mallet laughed. "There's a rudder too."

Mallet jolted out of the memory as turbulence shook the craft during its rise. Kemble came up to him with an update.

"Ivar estimates three minutes to the first site," she said, relaying the navigation officer's estimate.

"Very well," Mallet replied. "Half ahead."

Though it had just started, he longed for the mission to conclude. The sooner it was over, the sooner he could return home to Severn's arms.

Farah stood before the mirror in her bedroom mentally reciting her afternoon speech while guests in the garden enjoyed ease among the flowers, fountain, and various sensualities of the consul's villa. Zelda moved around the room, laying out several garments for Farah on the bed. Each incorporated rich purple in a unique style. Farah took her time selecting the most attractive, finally choosing a one-shouldered frock with exquisite draping about the bodice.

"This one, I think," she said, holding the dress up to her figure.

"You will look regal in it," Zelda commented, handing the other items to a servant for removal.

"Thank you, Zelda. Have you and Karno straightened out the data on the plant workers?"

"Yes, but Dr. Sorenson must confirm the identity of the two technician casualties."

"If you examined the list and eliminated those who are alive, you should have your answer."

"There were persons on the list scheduled to be on duty but were not present."

"Do not let Dr. Sorenson's report delay your efforts," Farah replied. "I want the list."

"Yes, madam."

Farah turned on the wall monitor as she dressed. The preparations for the speech, carried via live broadcast, generated enthusiasm throughout the viewing area. Orin's marketing plan used special invitations to entice citizen participation. Farah did not remember the exact verbiage. The advertising piece publicized the event as a clearance sale. It was to commence at noon and conclude at three with everyone receiving eleven milliliters of Joi and Solace at a significant discount, plus a sample of Evoke free of charge.

Farah's viewing screen continued displaying images of vibrant activity. She expected nothing less, as cheerful people meant happy sales. Vendors in every province, anticipating the excitement of the crowd, assembled in the squares flanked by stores opening early.

The large area accommodated all types of merchants, all of whom were anxious to begin selling their goods and engage in deals of the day. Stimulant vendors joined those selling clothing, accessories, décor, and delicacies.

"Everything is on schedule," Zelda said, securing a hook closure on Farah's gown. "Has the grand architect returned from the Citadel?"

"He arrives shortly."

Farah stepped away from the mirror to observe her makeup. She loosened several strands of hair around her oval face; the flame-red tresses fell about her shoulders, imparting a youthful, less severe look. Chatter and laughter encroached from below as senate members arrived for the pre-broadcast reception.

"You must join your guests," Zelda said, heading for the door, stopping shortly thereafter to allow Farah to take the lead.

Senator Hyatt greeted Farah at the bottom of the stair. "Consul Farah, you look resplendent."

"Thank you," she replied. "This is a momentous day."

"It is," Hyatt said, taking Farah's arm and ushering her to the garden.

Farah caressed several arms as she passed through the throng. Orin watched her procession in silence, too consumed with the day's festivities to shadow her. He busied himself organizing notes for the speech before the lenses began recording. After kissing her hand, Senator Hyatt handed Farah off to Orin.

"So far, the spectacle is a success," Orin said. "I rarely question your skills. I have some things you should review before you go on air."

"I am either ready or I am not."

"There is no question you are ready," Orin responded. "I merely drafted these points, should you wish to incorporate additional items into your address."

"Thank you, but I intend to stick to my script."

"As you wish."

Crawford Lear appeared in the archway of the garden, his watchful eyes skimming the area, meeting Farah's through the crowd. He proceeded into the arena with a stealthy stride, coolly acknowledging other guests as he made his way toward Farah. Contempt hid behind his smile as he took account of the ample drugs and drink offered.

You'd think it was candy.

Senator Rivan came to Crawford, blocking Farah from view. "It is so good of you to join us, Grand Architect Lear."

"Where else would I be?"

"I assume the situation in Delphia is under control?"

"We're wrapping up restoration efforts," Crawford replied. "Engineers Novak and Narlin have authority over the project."

"Good to know there are those you can count on," Rivan smiled.

A server bearing a tulip-lipped bowl of pastel dust approached the men. "Evoke," he said, offering the drug.

Rivan took up a petite spoon and placed a small amount on the back of his hand. Crawford watched with cloaked aversion as Rivan snorted the substance. The served offered the powder to Crawford.

"No, thank you."

"Come now, you must have many pleasant memories to savor," Rivan said.

"I do, but they're close to the surface already. I carry them with me daily," Crawford demurred.

"Then indulge in them now."

The garden fell silent, all eyes on Crawford, desperate to see him use in a social setting.

Crawford let go of his resistance, took a portion, and sniffed hard. He coughed a bit, clearing the bitter taste from his throat. The drug's effect was immediate, unbalancing his senses.

Crawford glared into the space beyond Farah's form, seeing people and nature rippling like water in a pond. Unsure of his forthcoming reaction, he fought the high in futility, but its influence gripped his reason. Crawford closed his eyes and sank onto a polished bench in a corner.

"There now, enjoy the moment," Rivan said, moving along to enjoy his oblivion.

The sea of bodies surrounding the architect melted away into the reality of his boyish past. A vision of a young woman appeared, her dark hair shining, her skin dewy. He recognized the slim figure sheathed in pale yellow silk and uttered her name as she tenderly stroked his brow. Janessa.

"I love you," Janessa said. "You're my life."

The memory was alive with sensation, every detail complete and unadulterated. The recall occupied his cognizance, lulling him deeper into distraction, changing, illuminating what was and

71

never would be again. Janessa's naked body, underneath his, pressed upward against his forward motion, her husky voice urging his passion.

"Tell me how you feel," she mouthed.

The words were there, but he could not mouth the words. Instead, he basked in the comfort of her form and the tantalizing discoveries of adolescent sexuality.

Farah slinked over, resting next to Crawford, reveling in his experience. Crawford did not detect her company nor those of the guests who gathered around him like lecherous vultures, their lusty appetites intensified by the writhing movement of his body. Farah's hand slid up his thigh, creeping lightly towards his groin. Crawford snapped awake with a gasp, his eyes dilated, his mouth salivating. The watchers dispersed, grinning with satisfaction.

"Thank you for a titillating show," Farah said.

"You'll never witness it again," Crawford said, rising from the bench and smoothing his uniform.

"Community sport is healthy," Farah said, clasping his arm. "Come with me."

Despite the events dredged from his memory, Crawford stepped into place with Farah, composed before the media, internally hating the intrusion into his past. Crawford never intended to revisit his memories of Janessa, but the drug forced the issue. The experience was a costly lesson Crawford vowed to heed.

CHAPTER 10

Severn and Mallet joined Kemble and Tovah within the packed square outside the State Building as citizens huddled and chatted together, awaiting Consul Farah's speech. Fordham encircled the space at every angle, ensuring order.

"This is too much," Mallet said.

Kemble arched her neck. "We're doing our civic duty."

"I'd rather be asleep."

"How is it you only think of yourself?"

"You'd be thinking of yourself if Crawford were here," Mallet teased. "In fact, you'd be ducking in and out of this crowd."

"It's not funny," Kemble said, clenching her teeth.

"Ask yourself why you're resisting," Mallet said, murmuring in her ear. "I'll bet you don't have nice thoughts."

"If I don't, it's because of you."

"Sounds like a personal problem. Don't drag me into it."

"Hush, you two," Tovah said. "It's a good thing you're here. You both need an adjustment." Mallet shifted his feet. "When's this thing supposed to start?"

"Should be any minute now," Severn replied, scoping the area.

"I wonder what Consul Farah will wear," Tovah said.

"Whatever she wears, she'll look so beautiful," replied Kemble.

A tone sounded, followed by the appearance of Farah standing confidently with Orin, Crawford and a slew of dignitaries. Mallet immediately tuned out, but Severn was not so easily distracted.

"Welcome, citizens. Today marks a happy occasion for our mutual bliss. Joi and Solace are available to you today for a fraction of the retail cost. Please accept this gift of Evoke, our newest euphoric, as a token of what we all hold dear," Farah said to the crowd.

Citizens stood mesmerized by Farah's stately presence, absorbing her every word in silence. "Remember the ideals of The Founders. The world we live in belongs to all. Your happiness fuels my happiness," she continued. "Every notion of bringing pain is gone from us. Revel in this. Guard yourselves against negativity, protect one another and give yourselves over to joy, for it is truly restorative."

When Farah finished, citizens rushed to secure their place in line. Mallet, who had tuned out during the broadcast, took a final look around, ready to vacate the premises.

"This is your contribution," he whispered to Severn. "This is your legacy."

Kemble and Tovah proceeded toward the vendors to claim their share of the new drug. "Are you coming?" his daughter asked Severn.

Mallet turned his back on Severn and started away. Severn contemplated following, but a sentinel, lingering a few paces away, was measuring his reaction. Tagging behind Mallet would give further credence to his guilty emotions.

Severn plastered a smile on his face. "I'm coming," he said, falling in line with Kemble and chancing a peek back at the Fordham. It was gone, but for the second time in less than a week, the precarious ledge he trod hovered on the verge of collapse.

At the close of the assembly, Crawford drove to Cleft, a lounge in downtown Unity City. He needed a real drink, anything to squelch the sour feeling of the festivities. He sat in his hover outside the jeweled doorway of the club mulling over his irritation. His head was a jumble of ideas, his thoughts on his rise to grand architect.

Crawford's allegiance to Beta Union, family legacy and brilliance in engineering allowed him to take the reins at thirty-four, six years sooner than the average candidate. Grand Architects generally served twelve years, supervising the engineering corps, technicians, and constructs in the maintenance and expansion of technology and infrastructure.

Attaining the office was no small feat. Besides intelligence and skill, a nomination required a perfect emotional record and an elevated degree of integrity. Candidates for grand architect underwent a less invasive form of probing devoid of the mental torment and torture unique to each delinquent. They were not, however, exempt from its physical effects.

Crawford was the first incumbent from Delphia, his success a surprise considering the province's history where Rand's attack bred fear of instability, saddling Delphia with a regrettable reputation. Citizens of the time did little to suppress the revolt and paid for their passivity.

When the government, in the fashion of the obsolete god, performed numerous executions in the Great Sweep, Crawford's mother turned the paradoxical event to her advantage, betraying Rand to assure her existence and

Crawford's. Betera's actions in favor of Beta Union saved Crawford from peril after the Delphia Museum incident, and at the same time buttressed the destiny laying before him.

You're either going in or you're not, Crawford thought, relaxing in his vehicle. *She could be in there.*

Crawford rarely chased after things or people, but the idea of pursuing Kemble Novak excited him. Unlike other women, she closed herself to his advances, rebuffing him despite his pleasant, dashing, or subtle behavior. Crawford laughed and sank back into the driver's seat, instinctively examining the structure and the patrons entering the club.

If she were wound any tighter, she'd be a knot.

He wondered if Kemble was inside flirting with someone, having a good time. Just as he decided to find her, Crawford saw Dinaria Burns, an old acquaintance. She also knew Kemble. He followed her gait. Dinaria's path led her to the lounge. If the object of his affection was there, he wanted to give Dinaria a chance to warm her up.

Crawford sat tight, mulling over his intentions, as wrong as they were. He reflected on a conversation he had with Betera, his mother. Crawford was six years old. On this day, he sat in the front of a classroom, way past the hour of dismissal. Betera busied herself correcting homework from the last class. Crawford shifted in his seat, unable to concentrate on the assignment she had given him as a reprimand.

When Betera looked up from her work, her golden eyes were soft and warm. He could see she had no interest in punishing him for his lapse in judgment at recess.

"Are you finished carrying on?" she asked.

"Yes," he whispered.

Betera eased herself from behind her desk. "I know you are fond of Mallet Tragnor, but you have to be more careful how you behave in front of the others," she said, smoothing a lock of platinum hair behind her ear. "There's a time for such behavior, but it's not now."

"Why do I have to pretend?" Crawford asked with childhood innocence. "You said it's good to know how I feel."

"It is," Betera answered, "but it can hurt your future. You are special, Crawford. Your destiny is different from others."

"What's destiny?"

"It's what we're meant to do. Fordham children have very different paths. Theirs cannot be yours."

"What's mine?"

"To be as important as you can," Betera said. "To serve as I have served, for the good of our people. One day, after I've taught you everything you need to know, you'll understand."

"What are you going to teach me?"

"I will teach you about justice and how to obtain it."

Crawford's mind returned to the present. He let out a breath and exited the vehicle. The grand architect moved at a calculated pace. Once inside, he took up residence in the back of the room. He spotted Kemble sitting at the bar alone. He figured she was relaxing after the tedious deliveries she and Mallet's crew performed around the habitat.

Crawford leaned against the wall, waiting for an opportune moment to approach. It would not be long.

CHAPTER 11

Kemble fiddled with a glass in front of her, her mind recalling the morning. Mallet, obsessed with cleanliness, ran students up and down the deck, cleaning every centimeter of the ship after the assignment. When he checked their progress, it was usually not with praise for a job well done.

It took several years in the field after Mallet's studies at Aero and the Aqua Academy for the *Meridian* to come under his command. It was a beautiful, swift vessel built in the likeness of a clipper, and capable of sail and flight. A sophisticated barrier field kept its crew protected from the atmosphere while giving Mallet a complete view of the land and air. Its pliable metallic sails used solar energy at sea with engines enabling the crew to make a run between the Aqua hub and the Green Zone in less than two hours.

To see Pleuran technology, Mallet once took the boat to the edge of its border. Kemble was against it, but Mallet's curiosity needed satisfaction. The crew spied a Pleuran submarine patrolling the waters, its menacing shape coming to a shallow depth, threatening to act on the trespass. Mallet smartly changed course to avoid confrontation.

Kemble took a sip of the elixir she ordered and twirled on her stool. The lounge was crowded with citizens enjoying the soft buzz of colored lights in tune with live music. For a moment, she wished she had snagged a chaise, but she knew she would likely fall asleep in its velvet clutches, only to wake at closing. Her eyes never caught sight of Crawford, cloaked by the bodies of the people directly in front of him.

Whirling around like a child once more, she saw Dinaria Burns, striding through the entrance, looking resplendent with her golden hair swept upward, her glittering onyx dress enhancing sculpted shoulders.

"Hi!" Kemble said, waving Dinaria over to the bar. "What are you doing here?"

"I was bored so I figured a night out would provide a lift," Dinaria said, taking a seat. "You look wonderful."

Kemble gestured to her hair. "You like the cut?"

"Looks good. I wish my hair was thick."

"You can fix that," Kemble replied, patting her smooth cropped hair. "You can fix just about anything."

"How's Breen?"

"He's good. Tovah and he are pares now."

"When do you believe you'll be called?"

"It's getting late. I may not be called."

"It's not necessary," Dinaria said. "You just have to keep stepping out with all sorts of subjects."

"What have you heard?"

Dinaria lifted Kemble's glass, tasting its contents. "I know the grand architect is interested."

"So, everyone knows?" Kemble blushed.

"Of course," Dinaria laughed. "Your welfare is everyone's business."

"I'd rather talk about your welfare."

"I'm enjoying a Cellar worker."

"Librarians are too cerebral," Kemble said, rolling her eyes.

"She's not," Dinaria said. "In fact, we're making a third."

"It's been a long time since I've been in one."

"You should revisit it or try for a quad."

Kemble shook her head and faced the bar, poised to order another drink. "We'll see, but it won't involve Crawford Lear."

"It's immoral to deny yourself."

"I don't deny myself anything," Kemble said, "but I'm not obligated to surrender myself either."

"Surrender? Why'd you use that word?"

"Because I feel pressured."

"It's not that serious, he can't make you do anything, but remember you do have an obligation to share yourself."

"I'm reminded all the time."

"Well, well, from your lips to his ears," Dinaria said, looking towards the rear of the lounge. Her eyes fixed on a familiar figure. "Look who's here."

"Not now," Kemble whispered, as Crawford crept forward.

"I think you should put in for an attitude adjustment," Dinaria said, getting up. "Think on it while I go say hello."

Kemble watched Dinaria skip to Crawford's side. He turned away from his conversation with an attractive female, giving her his undivided attention, and perked up when Dinaria mouthed in his ear. He then stroked Dinaria's neck in farewell before working his way through the crowd to Kemble.

"Good eve," he said. "Having a girl's night out?"

"It was a chance meeting," Kemble responded, gripping her glass tightly.

"You don't look pleased," Crawford said, motioning to a man behind the bar. "How's the teaching going?"

"I don't have any students right now."

"Who's teaching navigation?"

"I am, but Aero's semester is over."

Crawford thought the innocuous conversation would put Kemble at ease. He did not wish to frighten her away. Her intelligence charmed him, as did her dove-like eyes, slim waist, and long legs. Something beyond the physical occupied his thoughts, the same forbidden feeling he possessed for Janessa in his early youth.

Kemble felt his penetrating stare. Her cheeks flushed with an overwhelming sensation of strange origin. Crawford took many females to his bed and Kemble believed, if inclined, he would do the same with the male population.

"You know people used to drink just so they could be depressed," Crawford said, lifting his glass, inspecting its contents.

"I need to go," Kemble said, throwing down two etched metallic coins. "I have an early morning."

"You're bailing on me?"

"I'm not in the mood for a discussion on psychology."

Crawford stroked the stubble on his face. "You're hard to reach."

"You mean breach."

"Your words, not mine."

"Good eve, grand architect," Kemble said.

As she stepped outside, the balmy night surrounded her. She approached a tram station across the street, waiting patiently for the train to come into view, partially glad to get away from Crawford.

Why are you resisting him? There's no logic to it.

The tram appeared before she could unravel the source of her ambivalence, and Kemble crossed the threshold, leaving her feelings about Crawford behind.

Back in the club, Crawford shook the ice in his empty glass. Despite the flurry of gaiety surrounding him, the vibrant atmosphere of Cleft felt diminished by Kemble's retreat. He turned back to the bar, his slightly sullen mood interrupted by a commotion on the floor, instigated by a man and woman engaged in a struggle over a young female.

Their argument floated above the blaring music, making their animosity clear. Patrons, drenched in chemical bliss, laughed and pointed at the tussling pair as emotive receptors swelled with violent color. Crawford stood up, approaching the trio, intent on ending the skirmish.

"She's coming with me," a tanned woman in an ivory dress said.

"She belongs to me!" the man screamed.

The woman lunged at the man, but Crawford caught her in his arms, restraining her movement. The youngest of the trio looked on in delight at the commotion.

"I had her before you!"

"Well, I have her now."

"Sir, I think you should leave," Crawford said.

Before the man could sprint off with his prize, Crawford's captive wriggled from his grasp. She clawed at her opponent, tearing a hinged bangle from his wrist as he rushed past the young girl and knocked her to the floor. The offender headed for a TransMap portal at the far edge of the space. Several Fordham, alerted by the sensors, started into the establishment

"Stop!" they commanded, raising rifles.

It was too late. The man punched a panel and disappeared. The elder female, already in custody, kicked at the sentinels, but her assault was no match for their strength. Crawford retrieved the bracelet while helping the fallen girl to her feet. He looked at the jewelry before handing it to a sentinel.

"Are you harmed, grand architect?" she asked, appearing confused and off-balance, her strip blinking intermittently with a milky light.

"I'm fine," Crawford whispered, mesmerized by the curious anomaly. It was the first time he had seen a sensory fluctuation, a momentary break in Fordham functioning.

"Please come with us and fill out a report," the sentinel said.

Crawford nodded in response, falling in line with the troop. There was no trepidation in his mind, just a simple thought. *It's really happening. Nothing they do will stop it.*

CHAPTER 12

Kemble opted to walk most of the distance home. She took a few detours on the way, stopping to view a display in the storefront of a clothing shop. The mannequins in the window wore pleasant smiles. Kemble pondered the garments' shapes and color palette. They were clothed in the latest Beta Union fashions inspired by the rough-hewn landscape west of the city.

Most citizens did not stray beyond the borders of their province, let alone the habitat. Even she, as a pilot, had not ventured so far; therefore, Kemble concluded the designer's inspiration had to be flawed.

Knowledge of the western territory was limited to the engineer corps. These men and women rarely discussed their missions, especially those in proximity to Zara's Pillar. Many rumors surrounded the obelisk. Some said Linus Rand built it to mark the forbidden domain.

Others were convinced the object belonged to the former dwellers of the planet. No matter its true origin, Zara's Pillar did not often come up in polite conversation. It was not considered as beneficial to or bearing a significant role in the present lives of Beta Union citizens. The pillar was a relic of the past, an obscure mystery, best ignored.

The sound of hover traffic diminished as Kemble proceeded across the market square. She stepped into another establishment, intent on refilling the alleviator within the jewelry around her waist. The store was crowded with customers transacting sales. A clerk bounded to Kemble's side.

"May I assist you with something?" he said.

"I need another pearl," Kemble said, unhooking her belt chain.

"Certainly. I'd be happy to help you," he said, guiding her to a case filled with shiny orbs. "Do you want the same formula or something new?"

"The same will do just fine," Kemble said, looking around. Her eyes fell on a display of tubes containing red crystals. "What's that?" she asked, pointing.

"Ah, that's the new formulation of Érotique."

"What's wrong with the old one?"

"Nothing," he said, guiding Kemble to the display. He picked up a tube, holding it out for her inspection. "This one guarantees women multiple pleasures as opposed to one or two."

"And men?"

"It's the same in addition to greater sensitivity and endurance."

"That should make it a bestseller," Kemble muttered. "I'll take it."

The clerk led Kemble back to the counter. He placed her items into a box before bagging them. "That will be thirty-six and eighteen. Flash payment or coin?"

"Um, flash," she said.

The clerk swiveled the register screen. Kemble leaned forward, prompting a scan of her temple insignia and an automatic deduction from her funds.

"Do come again," the clerk said, handing her the items.

Kemble smiled. She turned to leave, but the sound of breaking glass stopped her at the door. Kemble's eyes sought the direction of the noise. She eyed several store associates rushing to a spot in the middle of the store.

"You come near me and I'll cut you," a voice screamed.

"Ma'am, please put that down," the man who attended Kemble said. "You could hurt yourself."

"I am hurt," the woman cried. "We all hurt."

"We want to help. You're in the best place for help."

The woman backed away. Several patrons slowly approached her. Kemble hoped they would assist in calming the woman, but one by one, they erupted into fury. Kemble stepped over the threshold into the street. She was horrified to see people attacking each other. They were as dogs ripping into raw meat.

The screams intensified as she fled the store and ran down a narrow street off the main pathway. The hairs on Kemble's neck rose. She turned to a wall, bracing her arms against its smoothness. Kemble gasped, huffing against the sensations barreling throughout her belly. Amid her ordeal, two citizens, a man, and a woman came strolling from the direction of the store. They smiled as they passed.

Did they see it? She asked herself, checking over her appearance. Did they feel it?

Kemble hugged herself hard. She shook her head, wondering what happened. Why had she given in to panic? Sirens sounded. The Fordham were near. Arrests were certain. Kemble peeled herself off the wall and gathered her senses. She opened the box containing the pearl purchased at the store. One whiff took Kemble back to a pleasant state of mind. She walked to the end of the street, dropping her bag when she rounded the corner. Zelda stood face-to-face with Kemble.

"Good eve, Pilot Novak," Zelda said.

"Good eve," Kemble whispered.

Zelda stooped to pick up Kemble's items, taking notice of the store's logo. "Did you see what happened?" she asked, handing Kemble the bag.

"I'm sorry."

"You were in the store."

"I...I don't know what you're asking."

"Something's happened?" Zelda said, glowing with ambiguous radiance. "Perhaps you left before the incident."

"I don't know what you're talking about."

"It is quite all right," Zelda smiled. "There is nothing for you to concern yourself with. It is under control."

"I'm glad to hear it. I'll be going home now."

As Kemble walked away, Zelda called to her. "Pilot Novak! It is good you feel well. Night seems to have a strange effect on your family." Kemble thought to speak, but Zelda cut her off.

"Good eve to you."

Kemble stared after Zelda, rolling the sentinel's words around in her mind. *Night seems to have a strange effect on your family.*

Fordham were usually candid. They used plain, specific language. Kemble worried a veiled threat existed in Zelda's speech. Someone was watching her family, taking a keen interest in the Novak's behavior.

Kemble clutched her package and hurried on the path that would lead her home. She had no wish to discover the identity of the observer.

CHAPTER 13

After giving evidence about the Cleft issue, Crawford returned home to unwind in his quarters. A wall screen imparted a subtle pearl luminescence to his living space; the sounds and smells of a damp forest filled the air. Thalo, his long snout resting comfortably on agile paws, slumbered on the floor next to the couch and Crawford stroked his pet gently, feeling him breathe easy under his touch.

Crawford had found Thalo as a small jackal pup when traveling to the Citadel on an inspection. The canine was exploring life with new eyes, curious about the architect upon their meeting. He soon clung to Crawford's side, never to let go. Thalo's sharp predatory instincts served as Crawford's eyes and ears, keeping the engineers in check. If caught dawdling, many found themselves the victim of Thalo's bark or bite.

Crawford longed to sleep as the clock passed 1:00 a.m., but the cogs in his skull continued cranking. Several dilemmas plagued him, most notably, his earlier reminiscing about Janessa.

His memory of her was pleasant up until the end, yet the details of her final decision now sped through his consciousness.

Janessa had hurled herself off the steel assembly of a bridge in sight of him and a passel of Fordham who did nothing to deter her suicide. When Zelda escorted Crawford to detention, the assumption of an examination utilizing stretching followed. It did not happen that way, as no reading from the sentinels condemned Crawford. After giving evidence of what he saw, they speedily released him into Betera's custody. The lack of further inquiry puzzled many, but without due cause, Crawford could not be prosecuted.

Crawford rose from his seat so as not to disturb Thalo. He blindly crossed the floor to open a drawer in search of a remedy for his insomnia. No sooner did he find it, then Thalo's ears pricked up.

The animal gritted its teeth, growling displeasure when the entry bell sounded. Crawford grinned. "It's all right. It's probably Breen. You like him, remember?"

The architect sauntered to the door and released its seal. Farah, bedecked in a lavender dress, stood before him beaming, her fiery hair offsetting peach undertones in her skin. Crawford followed the garment's line from her creamy neck to her full breasts and then the swell of her hips. Zelda stood next to her, a spark of orange moving down her face, indicative of his stirring sexual energy.

"Consul Farah, to what do I owe the pleasure?" he asked, raising his eyes to Farah's rouge tinged cheeks.

"I am here on business," she replied, stepping inside coolly. "Zelda, wait in the corridor."

Crawford smelled Farah's perfume as she wandered into his home, its distinct fragrance laced with alleviation.

Thalo growled, causing Farah to halt. "He won't bite unless I let him."

"Get him away from me."

Crawford snapped his fingers; Thalo leaped up, parading away. With her safety assured, Farah strode to a leather chair. She slid gracefully into place like oil, the folds of her dress spread sumptuously around her legs.

Crawford assumed a casual posture in the adjacent seat. "I'm surprised you didn't map yourself here," he said. "It's the best mode of intrusion."

"You look very clean for someone who toils with machinery," Farah said, ignoring his remark. "A man who works as hard as you should have something to show for it."

"Supervision doesn't demand significant effort," Crawford commented.

"You should try getting your hands dirty," she retorted.

"I don't think you came here to tease me," Crawford replied, lacing his hands in his lap.

Farah locked eyes with him. Save for their hazel accents, his irises were just as green. "You are quite perceptive. Conceivably that is what drew me to you."

"Maybe," Crawford said. "Zelda's looking very appealing these days."

"Would you have her as well?"

"She's not my type. Too frosty."

Farah grinned watching Crawford push his hair away from his brow. It was a trademark gesture of his. She continued studying his form, noting the fine creases spread along his eyes, with a few lines apparent when he smiled.

At thirty-four, Crawford had an attractive rugged look and a sturdy frame supporting his height. He had labored all his life, but for a manual laborer, his hands remained surprisingly unscathed.

When compared in stature to other men, Farah found he favored Mallet Tragnor, both of whom were dedicated to maintaining their allure and health.

Farah began to recall the intimate time she had spent with Crawford. It did not take long for her to summon images of his naked figure or his erotic practices. Long ago, he explored every part of her, his gentle caresses giving way to hungry passion in an intense pursuit of pleasure, matched by an unrelenting desire to satisfy her needs.

Sitting before her now, thumbing his nose, he seemed aware of her reflections. He was biding his time, looking for something within her to exploit. Crawford leaned toward her with a serene disposition, sensing her thirst. Farah's throat felt numb and beads of perspiration adorned her bust.

Why does he do this to me? Farah wondered, standing up with a jerk.

Farah smoothed her dress and stroked the pit of her neck. Her thighs tingled, her heart fluttering at the surge of affection and temptation she concealed in a vapor of chemicals.

Sex bonds no one. Love is an illusion.

"Do you need something?" Crawford asked, gauging her reaction in the wake of his effect on her.

Farah dug her nails into her flesh, the pain bringing her back from the edge of collapse. "I'm fine," she said biting her lip. "I have a conference with Caelum's trade representative at hour ten tomorrow."

"What do they want?"

"Fuel cells."

"You must be up to something if you're willing to hand those over."

"The embargo is lifted," Farah said, choosing her words carefully. "We will not come out empty-handed."

"Sounds dirty to me," Crawford grinned.

91

"Our continued welfare is paramount," stated Farah.

"If you say so," Crawford said grinning. "I have tasks to complete tomorrow."

"I understand Commander Jaxon is bringing metals from Iona for track repairs."

"The *Zephyr* is scheduled to be in port tomorrow."

"Give Keir my regards."

"I'll do that," Crawford said.

Farah took the cue and moved the conversation along. "I trust everything is in order at the fortress?"

Crawford moved to open a refrigerated compartment in his kitchen. Gold cylinders and little else filled the chilled interior. He extracted a can and traced its rim; the lid dissolved releasing a sweet-smelling effervescence. He gulped a portion then returned to his seat, offering Farah a sip of the liquid. She declined.

"Are you sure?" Crawford asked.

"Answer me," Farah hissed. "Is everything in order?"

"I'll have the write-up for you soon," he replied. "You should know though, there was a thing at Cleft tonight."

"What thing?"

"A disturbance. The Fordham took care of it."

"What happened?"

"A little misunderstanding over a girl."

"What were you doing there?"

"Did I say I was there?"

"I am sure you were."

"I was, and I filed a report," Crawford smiled. "What were you doing earlier?"

"Minding my own business, as you should continue to do."

"Believe me, after my duty, it's my next priority," he said, undoing the clasp at his collar.

Farah's eyes rested on a sliver of bare skin at his chest. She fanned herself, feeling an intense rush of warmth. Something was amiss. The Joi dowsed on her skin and clothing secreted vapors, yet tender feelings entrenched in her subconscious refused to stay dormant.

Farah admonished herself. *I command you to pass.*

Crawford caught her eyes again. "Was there something else you needed?"

"No," she said, hurrying to the entry, banging the lock. "Good eve to you."

Crawford snickered at her hasty departure, finished his drink, set the can on a counter, and went upstairs. In his bedroom, he stripped off his uniform, and reclined next to Thalo, asleep on the bed.

Crawford slid a silky cover over his body and as the light above faded, dark thoughts about Kemble penetrated his psyche. He had known Kemble Novak a long time, long enough to recognize what he stirred in her.

I can protect her. I can control it.

Crawford's wants were in opposition to the well-being of his fellow citizens. Having once tasted the appeal of love, he wanted the freedom to enjoy its rewards, regardless of the reckless characteristics Beta Union's canon heaped on it.

The idea begged further inspection, yet without the aid of his distinctive gifts, it would take patience on his part for Kemble to realize her feelings toward him. If he did not complete his mission, there would be no "happily ever after" for her or anyone.

His main objective needed to come first. The plan was already in motion and there was scarce time to waste—for time, as he knew, was a rival prone to cheating.

CHAPTER 14

Farah scrambled around her office, putting together details for the conference with Losara Idoni, minister of Caelum's foreign affairs. Farah did not want to deal with her or Caelum's Malachim, a body of secretive brothers holding power with His Holiness Urias Marcus. Yet, Caelum had things to offer. The question was whether they would surrender exactly what Farah needed.

Zelda brought files for Farah to examine later in the afternoon. "Dr. Sorenson has an audience with you," Zelda said.

"I have little time for anything but the trade discussion," Farah said.

"She says it is urgent."

Farah inhaled, breathing out slowly. "Very well, send her in." When Dr. Sorenson arrived, Zelda excused herself.

"What do you need, Andira?"

Andira Sorenson, Unity City's chief medical officer and director of Beta Union's Center of Health and Harmony, approached Farah. "I needed to tell you something that happened last eve."

Farah stepped forward, intrigued. "If this is about the problem at Cleft, I know what happened. Crawford Lear mentioned it."

"I wasn't aware you spoke to him."

"He said it was an isolated incident," Farah said.

Andira stepped closer, pausing before answering. "Did he tell you about the sentinels?"

"What of them?"

"There was an intermittent disruption in the nexus between them and the Servers."

"They lost contact?"

"It was brief, but it registered on the boards."

"I did not hear it from Crawford," Farah said. "Is there anything else he neglected to tell me?"

"There was a man who started an argument when he refused to share a female," Andira said. "He claimed they were in a relationship.

"That is illogical," Farah said. "Have everyone who was there detained and examined."

"I'll make sure of it."

"Do you have the analysis from Delphia?"

"We're finishing it now."

"Let me know when it is done. I have a meeting to attend," Farah said. "You will forgive me if I do not walk you out."

"I have my work," Andira said in farewell.

Farah relocated to the senate chamber, inspecting the gelatinous clear round table at the center, cold to the touch. The matrix above, ready to dispense data, pulsated with an opalescent hue. Soon fervent strength would flow beneath the hands of the senate, heating the slab with bioenergy.

The inward motion of the doors disrupted Farah's meditation as Orin and his fellow senators filed in one by one, taking their places.

Zelda and Karno flanked the group, armaments absent to safeguard the balance of the matrix against their magnetic force.

Farah smoothed the front of her dress, almost instinctively. "Greetings, senators, shall we begin the proceedings?" she asked with a smile.

"Losara Idoni is standing by for our talk; therefore, we will begin with downloads and any subsequent analysis," Orin said, instructing the assembly. "We will postpone new business until the next session."

Senator Castillo addressed Orin. "I leave tomorrow for Havamir. I do not expect to return before the fifth day."

"Give your proposals to me before you leave," Orin replied. "Let us begin."

The table's surface rippled with robust vibrations beneath the fingers of each senator's hand resting on its top.

"Train delays in Osler have increased two-fold due to the repairs," Orin said, relaying the input. "ETR is another sixteen solar hours."

"Citizens will have to take alternative transportation," Farah directed, "limit TransMap travel to distances not readily accessible through marinas."

"Relaying," Orin replied. "Iona has encoded their report in Before Standard again. Castillo, please translate."

Senator Castillo started speaking a vernacular virtually unheard in the streets, its vocabulary featuring trilled consonants reminiscent of a widely used language in the old world. Quashing its use and all other dialects remained a priority in Beta Union's Senate.

"Iona requests stockpiles from quarries elsewhere. Mining operations in Yardell yielded less than estimated," Castillo concluded.

"Yardell will have to make up the quota," Farah said. "If they miss it, the cost of the project could increase."

"They know their responsibility to demand," Farah said. "Senator Castillo, kindly inform Iona that Standard Tongue is our official language. No other will be tolerated."

When Castillo finished interpreting, Orin addressed the last piece of business. There was nothing crucial in the report except the recounting of Crawford and Dr. Sorenson's information regarding the incident at Cleft. Orin closed the meeting, diverting the senate's attention toward a large flat screen. After a moment, a woman with an olive complexion and flaxen hair appeared.

"Greetings, Consul Farah," Losara Idoni said. "It is an honor to speak with you."

"Greetings to you," Farah smiled smugly. "Shall we discuss the options you outlined in your proposal?"

"We're delighted you could spare the time," Losara said. "Caelum is grateful."

Caelum spanned a third of the eastern land across the Azure and though Beta Union's social interaction with the country was minimal, the senate possessed a good deal of information about its society.

The country, built on monotheist virtues, had sprung from a religious renaissance formed upon the arrival of its pilgrims. Free conscience flourished in its states, under the guidance of fealty to an invisible power purporting to control the destiny of man. The laws of man paled in comparison to the divine edicts to come and the crimson cloaked Malachim were custodians of secular and spiritual life until the end of corporeal existence. Urias was simply a puppet of the consortium.

Farah mocked their society. She deduced their alleged piety masked a true state of oppression, as intelligence told of violent protests, religious zealots, and outright cruelty in the face of their faith.

"I'm ready when you are," Farah said.

"As you know, His Holiness has requested fuel cells for our industrial plants."

"Go on."

"We have hydro stations needing new power supply on the southern border," Losara said.

"Is it true you crossed the water?" Orin asked.

"What does that have to do with my request?"

For many years, the channel between the feuding nations stood as a natural barrier dividing their cultures, but when a small faction in Caelum attempted defection across the sea, the inadvertent action became a prelude to an offensive response. Without a successful treaty, a volatile clash was imminent.

"Are you readying for war?"

"The trespass was a slip in judgment on the part of a few defectors."

"You should learn to be friendly before you invite annihilation," Farah suggested.

"What does it matter to you?" Losara asked.

"If we give you cells, our neutrality may be compromised," Orin said.

"Are you dismissing my appeal?"

Farah leaned back in her chair, using silence as a tactic to unnerve Losara. "Not necessarily. I think we can come to an arrangement to satisfy us all."

"What would we have to do?"

"Your aquatic farms have a particular organism with properties useful to us."

Losara did not have to ponder Farah's motivation. She was acutely aware the senate often sought new ingredients to manage and appease its citizens. The creature's secretions contained psychoactive compounds, which could accomplish Farah's goal.

"The Horned Mollusk?"

"Yes."

"Have you ever considered democracy and diplomacy rather than tyranny?" Losara asked.

"Maybe you should consider your problems," Farah replied. "Your people are not free."

"We have laws, guided by heaven itself," Losara said. "When we stray, prayer and forgiveness save us."

"You can call your world what you want in that antiquated language," Farah snorted, "but Caelum is still a Hell."

"Ladies, we are here to negotiate a trade," Orin interrupted.

"Stay out of this, Orin!" Farah snapped, returning to Losara. "Your streets are filled with starvation, marauders, and assassins, and you deny people pleasure through religion."

"You're quite the iconoclast. Religion brings pleasure to the spirit," Losara argued. "We don't tell our citizens how to live their lives, we ask them to use their judgment and have faith."

"I am sure many of your people wish to penetrate our borders in search of safety from the morals you press on them."

Losara's resentment mounted as she continued defending her land. "No land is perfect, not even yours," she said. "Your people are devoted to lust and a lack of self. They are not fed propaganda through a pipe."

"We are done here," Farah said, reaching to close the channel.

"Wait!"

"Perhaps you did not hear me," Farah said. "Let me couch it in terms you will understand. You are killing my buzz."

Losara's expression changed to one of desperation. She could not afford to lose favor with Beta Union. "I am not ignorant of our position, but we will not be ridiculed," she responded.

"I suggest you remember you asked for our assistance."

"Does this mean you will consider the trade?"

"Make it worth my while."

"You will have what you want if I get the cells."

A half-hearted smile came to Farah's red-stained lips. She stood up, facing her colleagues. "Then we have a deal."

"And we will ask for nothing further."

"You will bring a supply of mucus to the Green Zone," Farah said. "After our chemists examine it, we will hand over your goods."

"How much do you want?"

"I believe one-hundred or so liters will suffice for now," Farah answered.

"You'll need more to control your people," Losara laughed.

"It is none of your concern."

"When can we expect to see your envoys?"

"Within the month," Farah answered, silently commanding Orin to discontinue the feed without waiting for a response from Losara.

"If they use those cells as part of an arsenal, it could invite trouble," Senator Rivan said.

"We are not breaking our code," Senator Hyatt replied, "and we are not teaching them to develop munitions."

"Senator Hyatt is correct," Farah said.

"Thank you, ladies and gentlemen. Our meeting is concluded," Orin said.

"Your dedication to our citizens is most noble," Farah added. "Elation is restorative."

"Elation is restorative," the members said, bowing in unison. Zelda and Karno escorted them out.

Orin stayed with Farah, her chest heaving with frustration. He glanced at the door, expecting Zelda's entrance.

"You need not look for her," Farah said. "Are you suddenly exempt?"

"Such brevity is hardly worth correcting."

"Who will you assign to the trade?"

"Commanders Tragnor and Ragas will do."

"I prefer the *Zephyr*," Orin said.

"I am not surprised. Keir Jaxon is well-known to you." Farah grinned and went to the table. She spoke into the comm, requesting Zelda.

"Yes, madam," Zelda said.

"Have you heard from the grand architect about the restoration efforts?"

"No word has come in yet."

"Thank you."

"I was surprised Hyatt agreed with you," Orin said.

"He knows the value of good commerce," Farah said.

"So does Losara. They'll be eating mollusks for weeks," Orin said. "When you think of it, it is almost comical."

"I couldn't care less whether it inconveniences anyone."

"Considering our priorities, I do not either."

"I'm glad we agree on something," Farah smiled, pleased with her skills of negotiation.

If anyone were going to have the upper hand, the consul was determined that it would be she and no one else.

CHAPTER 15

Mallet was never one to hurry, but from the moment he woke, everything conspired against him. Owing to the midday train delays, heavy TransMap, and pedestrian traffic, he decided the most logical path was to chance the sub train and run to his destination. He felt he could cover the distance with reasonable haste and sprinted briskly through the square.

Mallet's principle was never to be late, especially for a class. Students relied on his punctuality along with the knowledge he imparted during a session; therefore, being late was unacceptable. Mallet moved down the stairs of a subway entrance to join a mass of citizens along the edge watching for the approaching bullet. Out of the corner of his eye, he saw Keir Jaxon on the platform.

"Jaxon!" he called, squeezing through bodies crowded into the station.

"Mallet!" Jaxon replied. "Where are you off to?"

"I'm late for class."

"That's not like you."

"Tell me about it," Mallet said. "I was flaked. What are you doing here? Don't you have more exciting places to be?"

"We delivered some stuff for the GA," Jaxon said. "If I had my choice, I'd rather be paying a visit to Melee, but I can't seem to find the time."

Mallet's brow furrowed. "When did you last talk to her?"

"I haven't been able to catch her since before the fire."

"I haven't talked to her either."

"You sound sentimental."

"Not at all. She's a big girl and she has her own life."

"As do you," Jaxon smiled.

Mallet's train approached the station and slowed to a smooth halt. "I'll see you around," he said, shaking Jaxon's hand and stepping onto the train.

The train eased away swiftly, the wind of its departure unbalancing Mallet as he gripped a pole for support. When he looked at a bulletin overhead, he sighed. Mallet's students would not be upset by his tardiness, but he certainly was as Kemble would be at the port, probably taking advantage of his absence.

"For someone so keen on the rules, she has a lot of ego," he said under his breath as he watched Fordham passing between cars.

With all their exploratory power, Mallet was fortunate their astute senses had not yet read him the wrong way. As he watched the clouds drift by before the train descended underground, he felt pleased by this blessing.

The *Meridian* was out of her hub when Mallet arrived at Aero. He saw the ship floating down from the sky with students gathered on deck. Only Kemble was qualified to take the ship up without him.

I'll kill her, Mallet breathed, examining the sky.

Kemble's blue suit, with its array of delicate particles, reflected the noon sun as she leaned over, meeting Mallet's gaze. "Class dismissed," she said when the ship moved into the wharf. "You have one week to submit your trial results."

When the last pupil disembarked, Mallet unleashed his frustration. "What the hell do you think you're doing?"

"You were late, and I wasn't going to cancel the class."

"Their instruction is not your call."

"If you hadn't been strung out, you would have been here."

"Are you testing my authority?"

"I provided your students with an experience they weren't going to get from you today."

"Maybe if you weren't so jealous of me and Severn, you'd concentrate on finding something of your own."

Mallet's remark ignited a fury in Kemble's belly. "Excuse me?" she said, raising her voice.

"Your fixation is perverse," Mallet said, clutching her arm, pulling her close.

Kemble's mouth dropped. Mallet's words sounded flat, his voice without malice, yet the knife kept digging. She twisted away from him, swung her charm to her face, searching for instantaneous relief while fighting against the pang of her gut.

"You're the one who's perverse."

"Severn likes it," Mallet said.

Kemble's next response was criminal. She spun around, striking Mallet's jaw with an intense crack, leaving a visible imprint on his cheek that alerted two Fordham a few paces away.

"You are having a problem," a female sentinel said, taking Kemble into custody. "Kindly come with us."

CHAPTER 16

The Central Detention Center was the largest facility of its kind in the city. Its interior, suggestive of an archaic sanatorium, boasted an immaculate décor replete with calming colors and gentle staff, but its stretching cells were less buoyant.

Correction was a private affair modified to each victim's inner demons. Columns framing penalty cubicles gathered visions and emotions from those awaiting remedy, recording playback available to physicians, and the senate. Transcripts haunted citizens forever, their very existence deterring repeat offenses.

"Wait here," a clinician said, directing Kemble into a room.

Fear coursed through the pilot's limbs. This was a new experience; one she hoped never to repeat. When the clinician returned, Kemble obediently removed her garments and stood alone in the center of the space. She heard Karno droning outside deciding the appropriate duration and intensity of her treatment.

The entry locks snapped in place with a thud. Two columns shifted from clear to purple, dancing like totems in a native ritual, causing Kemble's body to sway in a woozy pattern. The walls undulated with intense energy, making Kemble's skin tingle. Currents within the floor scorched her soles, burning through her, galloping up the length of her body to ignite a fire in every hair follicle.

Three-dimensional forms and shapes leapt forth out from the fluid confines, cracking skin, oozing sores and extreme disfigurement ravaged their bodies. Kemble's strength faded with each phantasmal appearance, her knees buckling as she unwillingly opened to The Stretch's cruelty.

"No!" she screamed, horrified by the contagious nature of frailty spreading over her. Her flesh rippled and wrinkled with advanced age, revealing gruesome swollen veins and abscesses expanding down her arms, torso, and face.

Kemble sank to the ground in a futile attempt to support herself on weary, skeletal hands. She closed her eyes, yet the vision persisted. Faces she knew stood out from the crowd, their hands clasping crude jagged instruments.

"Stop it!" she screamed, but the horde with mouths gaping in vicious delight came closer.

Razors ripped Kemble's skin, massacring her physique. Blood spurted from the pilot's extremities as savage hands groped her nakedness.

Kemble's body seized; foam gushed from her mouth. Against her cries, they continued assaulting her being, exerting powerful evil, and removing every vestige of dignity from her soul. This was her future, a nightmare of what she would be without reform.

Farah emerged in elegant robes rustling in a hidden breeze. "Let me help you," she said, offering her arms in comfort. "Come back to us and it will end."

Kemble, frantic and broken, searched around the room, clawing desperately for relief. The scene changed, depicting her father in agony; his face contorted. Mallet stood near familiarly caressing him.

"Help me. Please help me," Severn pleaded with Mallet. "Don't let them—"

"Get away from him!"

Kemble spat at Mallet's image. "You're destroying him!"

"You understand what is at risk," Farah said. "Let me help you. Renounce your rage." Kemble nodded, but her gesture did not satisfy. "I must hear you say it. Reject your feelings and you will survive."

"Yes!" Kemble swore, succumbing to the terms. The tormented illusion ended with her pledge and out of the darkness, she felt a soothing hand stroke her cheek. Kemble, stirred by the gesture, scanned the room. It was empty, yet she believed she saw a man whose eyes were deep with feeling.

The door of the cell opened, and the dream vanished. Adario placed an arm around her waist, lifting her from the floor—Kemble fainted.

Crawford rarely visited detention, but when he stopped in Farah's office for a debriefing, Zelda indicated the consul had gone to witness Commander Tragnor and Pilot Novak's reprimand. Crawford wondered about their detainment, more specifically, Kemble's. As far as Crawford knew, with no priors, she should not be there.

The architect spotted Karno peering into a cell window. Intrigued by the action inside, Crawford approached. Mallet sat in the room alone, untested.

"I'm looking for Consul Farah," Crawford said.

"She is in recovery with Pilot Novak," Karno said, focusing on Mallet.

Crawford looked in the room again. "Is his session over?" he asked.

"He was not tested. There was no reading."

"Then why is he here?"

"The pilot attacked him."

"Interesting."

Karno mechanically cocked his head, his irises empty and dark, devoid of compassion. "Yes, it is," he responded.

Crawford slunk away without further comment and proceeded to the recovery area. When he entered, Farah loomed over a sedated Kemble. "I assume the process met with success," he said to Farah.

Farah glanced at her rear. "You have a report for me?"

"It can wait."

"Either you have something to say or you are wasting my time."

"Some Server modules are stressed," he said. "They'll need replacement, but other than that, all's fine."

"What of the delays in Havamir?" she asked, dismissing the former topic.

"We're nearly finished."

"Nearly? Are you and your engineers becoming lax?"

"Repairs take time," Crawford said.

"Are there any other issues?" Farah asked.

"What else could there be?"

"I leave the answer to you."

"I can't think of a thing."

Crawford looked away from Farah to observe Kemble. An inspection of her features revealed insignificant damage to her skin. Her curvaceous body was noticeably thinner, and her hair had lost some of its luster.

Andira entered, inspecting the patient. "She'll wake soon," she said to Farah. "I think an infusion of Joi is in order."

"It'll assist in restoring her balance," Andira said, charging a technician to prepare the necessary dosage. "I'll let Dr. Novak know she's here, so he can escort her home."

"No, we cannot encourage inappropriate associations," Farah said. "Get someone else to assist."

"I'll take her," Crawford said. "It's on my way."

"You have duties to attend to," Farah said, unconvinced of his motives.

"I don't have a problem doing a kindness."

"Is that all?"

"For what you're thinking, she'd have to be awake."

Farah turned to Andira. "Release her into Crawford's custody."

"Thank you," Crawford said. "I'll make sure she sticks to what she should know."

"See that you do, Crawford," Farah smiled, "for both your sakes."

CHAPTER 17

When the news of Kemble and Mallet reached Severn, he halted his experiments and grilled Bristol for information.

"Are they still at the center?" he asked.

"Pilot Novak is no longer there," Bristol said, reacting to his feelings, ginger streaming down her face.

"I should have been notified," Severn said, discarding his lab coat.

"You have no fealty to her."

"I'm someone she knows well."

"No one is a stranger," Bristol said.

"She was escorted by the grand architect. Commander Tragnor is still there."

"Am I allowed to retrieve him?" he asked.

"Dinaria Burns was called but was unavailable. You may go if you wish."

"Tell him I'm on my way," he said.

The city traffic was subsiding. The third day would be a busy one, but Severn had no time to think of all he would do then.

His child had been tortured. He now considered Mallet. He loved many things about him, how he moved from hot to cold so quickly there was scarce time to avoid the fluctuations. This dynamic was appealing in many ways and, over time, he learned to adapt to Mallet's ever-changing moods.

Mallet could restrain himself far better than Severn, and the timing of his outbursts or detachment gave the impression of calculated behavior. He was always in the right place at the right time when expressing his feelings.

Severn recalled a visit to one of the facilities he oversaw. A colleague was irritated with a delay in receivables. Severn tried to calm him to no avail when he pounded a hole in a wall. Mallet, who accompanied him on the trip, witnessed the entire event and was eerily quiet.

When sentinels arrived, Mallet showed no sign of surprise, relief or anything. He was in a reality all his own, absent from the scene played out before him. Severn wondered where Mallet acquired this skill of control without the use of artificial means.

He entered the center and walked straight to the recovery area where Andira attended several individuals with blank expressions. The sight was unsettling.

Severn courted her attention. "Dr. Sorenson," he said.

She greeted him with a firm handshake. "Severn, it's good to see you. I'm sorry about the trouble."

"I've come to collect Commander Tragnor. Where might I find him?"

"He's in post-processing."

"Thank you. I'll go see him now."

"Don't be a stranger, Severn." Andira smiled. "Your contribution makes reform possible and for that, we're grateful."

Severn, wishing her words were in jest, returned her pleasantry. He found Mallet sitting in a corner of the post-processing area, his eyes closed against the scene of other citizens waiting for an escort.

"Mallet, I've come to take you home," Severn said, approaching him, laying a hand on his back.

Mallet raised his eyes, looking as if sleep had not touched him in days. There was no sign of anguish on his face or form as he stood groaning.

"I don't feel like going home," he replied.

Severn took hold of his arm, guiding him to the hover. "I thought you'd welcome being on the *Meridian*."

"Not right now. They pressed me to get to Kemble," he said, sliding into the car. "What were they asking you?"

"Why she went berserk and hit me."

"She hit you?"

"We got into it and she lost control."

"What did you do to her?" Severn asked.

"It was a disagreement. Nothing we don't go through all the time," Mallet said.

"But this time, she was punished, and your hide wasn't touched," Severn said. "How'd you get off?"

Mallet threw his hands up. "I don't know. She was loud and crazy," he said. "How was I to know they'd pick her and not me?"

"You let them drag her in there!"

Mallet understood Severn's concern. He wanted nothing more than to reassure him everything would be all right. "She'll be okay. I promise. I told them she tried to help herself."

"I wasn't able to see her. Crawford took her home."

Mallet looked out the window. They were heading to Severn's dorm. "Kemble's stronger than you think. It's her first offense. I wouldn't worry."

"You wouldn't understand. You're not a pare," Severn said. "I've got nothing else to worry about."

"As far as they're concerned, you shouldn't think about her that way," he replied, adjusting his seat. "She's safe with Crawford."

Severn concentrated on the road, winding the hover along the streets. Mallet stared out the window, watching children playfully tug at each other, racing around with vigorous energy while adults laughed and kissed, enjoying the stimulation provided by elative paraphernalia. It was a false sense of security.

Mallet's thoughts drifted to his sister. Seeing the kids in the street brought fond memories of his childhood. Melee was bound to be back to work at Plant 13. He remembered how he and Melee reenacted the adventures of Linus Rand.

When their father discovered their curiosity, he put an end to their fun. Mallet wondered if his father's heavy discipline contributed to his views toward the government. He had hidden it well throughout his younger years, with help from Crawford and his classes with the youth groups.

Meeting Severn was the best thing that happened to Mallet since leaving Delphia. It was a little short of a miracle catching his attention. He was afraid Severn thought him juvenile, so Mallet feigned interest in science, Severn's favorite sports, and even his rituals. It worked; Severn took to him.

To keep the pretense of an innocent liaison, Mallet and Severn carefully rotated in and out of each other's orbit, hiding their fidelity, yet with Mallet's dissension rearing its head more often, Severn feared discovery.

"We should get you into bed," Severn said, parking the hover outside his dorm.

Mallet entered Severn's quarters, immediately slipping through the balcony's glass doors. He averted his eyes upward, looking around the heavenly crown and taking in the city's skyline.

Severn joined him, observing the metropolis as he pointed here and there to its glory. "It can be beautiful if you let it," he said.

"Have you wanted to go out there?" Mallet asked, still taking in the vast ceiling of stars.

"Not really."

"Tal isn't the only place in the galaxy," Mallet said. "There're millions of planets out there, all different and exciting."

"And millions of hostiles, diseases, and other nasty things."

"Don't you ever wonder about Enoch?"

"Why should I?"

"I don't know. I've heard Caelum knows everything about our beginning?"

"They were the first to arrive," Severn said, "but as far as I know, they're more like the Birth Born Coalition than anything else."

"Birth Born?"

Severn paused. "Founders stuff. I only know a little about it and the war. It's not worth going into."

"I think this place is haunted," Mallet said. "Zara's Pillar and those strange constructions are creepy, alien."

Severn laughed. "We're the aliens, far removed from our natural habitat."

"I'd like to know who lived here, where they went."

"If the first citizens had encountered anyone, we'd know," Severn said.

Mallet leaned his back against the balcony. "People used to think gods lived among the stars," he said, beginning a tangent Severn did not understand.

"Where'd you hear that rubbish?"

"People in Delphia talked about it when I was a kid," Mallet said. "They still believe it in Caelum."

"What's with you and Caelum? There aren't any gods," Severn said. "You're in charge of your own life—not something you can't see."

"Who said you had to see it?" Mallet asked. "You aren't supposed to believe in love, but you do."

"That's not based on subjective reasoning. I know I care because I see the influence you've had on me," Severn explained.

"Maybe if I leave you alone, it'll go away," Mallet said. "You wouldn't always be in fear for your life."

"I'm not afraid and I don't want you to go."

"Neither do I, but if we stay here, it won't last."

Severn attempted to take Mallet away from his thoughts. "What did you mean when you said Kemble was safe with Crawford?" he asked.

"Just that he's sensible. He wouldn't take advantage."

"How well do you know him?"

"We grew up in the same region."

"You've never been intimate?"

Mallet jumped at the suggestion. "No! It's not like that, never has been," he said. "And just because we're free and encouraged to do so doesn't mean I'd do it."

"I'm sorry. I didn't mean to assume anything," Severn said, feeling foolish. "I want to be with you and only you."

"Are you only with me? I know they tried to reach Dinaria."

"She's just someone I know."

"How well do you know her?"

Mallet found the conversation's vein irritating. "We're not going through this. You know how it is."

"You could've asked for me."

"You're the one who's always scared we'll be caught!"

"Keep your voice down," Severn warned.

"I've said it once and obviously, it bears repeating. If you really want to be together, we should get away from here,"

Mallet breathed, kissing Severn with a fire that coursed through the chemist's spine.

"If you persist in this, they're likely to put you down," Severn whispered. "I'd rather die knowing I fought to keep you than let them tear me away."

Severn circled Mallet's waist, the heat between them growing intense. "Let's go inside," he suggested, pulling Mallet indoors.

They walked upstairs, stopping short of the bedroom, opting instead to step into the bath.

Severn took Mallet to a pool, removed his uniform, and stroked Mallet's bristled chest. He then took off his own garments and stepped into the water, surrounded by its comfort.

With renewed energy, Mallet pinned Severn against the rim of the tub, pressing his mouth on the chemist's lips with mounting passion. Severn's thoughts swam with erotic excitement as he groped Mallet's flesh. He let out a breathy moan as the couple's mutual desires swelled between them.

The warmth of Mallet's presence, combined with the love and respect Severn discovered, were central to the chemist's very existence and it was in this moment, Severn realized he could not and would not give Mallet up.

His love is all I need to know, Severn thought, as the couple slipped beneath the water, giving in to the sensual delight of their feelings. *Right here, right now, he is mine, forever.*

CHAPTER 18

Crawford ferried Kemble home after she injected the prescribed alleviator. He was grateful for her tranquil state. Without it, he would not have the privilege of enjoying her company sans friction. She could not have made the trek alone, for tonight her muscles betrayed her balance with every step.

The architect took her in his arms, playing the gallant hero, carrying her into the complex. His choker buzzed several times during the ride in the lift; he ignored the notification. He placed Kemble's hand on the entry key, called for the lights, and conveyed her to the bedroom.

Crawford carefully deposited her onto the bed, laying her flat. With her eyes closed, but not entirely oblivious to the surroundings, she was aware he unzipped her bodysuit. He hesitated at the sternum, causing a momentary lapse in her whimsy.

"Don't let him hurt Far."

"Who?"

"Mallet's dangerous," she mumbled, falling asleep.

He sat next to her, touching her face, finding it moist with perspiration. He leaned forward, smelling the pit of her throat, a floral scent wafting from its soft shape. He was sympathetic to her condition and a witness to The Stretch's imposed obedience on its victims.

Crawford thumbed the weighty chain around Kemble's waist, observing the delicate feminine weave, her initials and an inscription etched in its surface.

"For your happiness," he recited. "Far."

The enclosed orb had lost its luster, the chemical element inside finished. He had no doubt Kemble held a supply somewhere and would replenish it when she woke.

A rescue deserves a prize, he thought, undoing the clasp to slip the ornament out from under her. He secured it around his neck, tucking it in his uniform. Kemble did not flutter when Crawford bent over to kiss her forehead. He resolved to let her sleep as furthering their acquaintance would have to wait.

When Crawford reached his vehicle, a call came through the console link. "What is it?" he asked.

"Excuse me, grand architect," Narlin said, "but this couldn't wait."

"I'm listening."

"There's trouble at the Amanta City's broadcast station. They've reported a malfunction in their network," he said. "Multiple areas have telecom outages."

"Send the file through." Crawford surveyed the information on the console, seeing several receptors, public screens, and comm links damaged. "These receptors," he started, "are they offline or broken?"

"According to the data they're offline."

"I know what's been documented, but is it accurate?" Crawford said, shooting an annoying look at Narlin.

"I assume so."

"I need facts, not assumptions," Crawford said. "Where did you get the log?"

"Engineer Emili relayed it from her comm."

"If the systems are down, how did she upload it to you?" Crawford asked.

"I don't know sir," Narlin said. "I suppose she did the transfer offsite."

"Hypotheses aren't facts, Narlin," Crawford said, looking back to the screen. "Send Breen with Thalo to meet her. Tell him to get to the board and trace the transmission."

"Yes, sir," Narlin nodded. "The sentinels are on the way."

"Fine," Crawford said, "and Narlin, next time you contact me, I expect you to have all the info."

"I'm on it, sir," Narlin answered.

Since Breen could get the answers the architect sought, Crawford did not go to Amanta City. There was another task to complete, which he had put off long enough. Mallet had to know about Melee.

Morning rose across Beta Union and with it, Crawford began his perilous journey to see Mallet aboard his ship. The Aqua Academy lay along Crawford's route to his office at Pump 5. He could guess Mallet's reaction and the sooner he told Mallet the truth, the sooner he could begin healing.

The *Meridian* lay floating in her berth, bereft of sailors and students. Mallet was likely in his cabin, preparing for afternoon classes. As a man of the sea and air, he resided on the ship, forsaking his formal accommodations long ago. If marriage existed, Mallet would yoke himself to the *Meridian*. Crawford took a moment to savor the friendship they shared.

As teens, he and Mallet had belonged to the same youth group, flourishing under the teachings of Crawford's parents. Mallet proved to be a stubborn if not passionate pupil, asking what for, how and why. Crawford was the exact opposite, sitting at his mother's knee, serious about his studies and absorbing every detail of her lectures.

Though Mallet had no interest in the private instruction they received, Crawford dragged him along. Had it not been for the architect and his stabilizing influence, Mallet's hotheaded nature would have annulled his future in command.

I must tell him. Prolonging it is cruel, Crawford thought, approaching Mallet's quarters below deck.

Mallet lay asleep in an alcove. Crawford prudently crept along the floor, but the sound of a creaking board stirred Mallet's attention.

"What are you doing here?" Mallet asked, rubbing his eyes.

"I was on my way to the pump," Crawford said. "How are you?"

"I'm fine."

"And your pilot?"

"You took her home. Don't you know?"

"I haven't seen her since," Crawford said, crossing his arms.

"It's probably for the best," Mallet sniggered.

"I need to speak with you, seriously."

Mallet got up and the old friends stood before one other in silence before he broke the peace. "I'm listening."

"I have word about Melee."

"Breen said she was taken for questioning, but she hasn't called," Mallet said. "I told him I'd speak to you."

"Well, I'm glad he did, otherwise, I wouldn't have known."

Crawford looked to the floor. He knew there was a receptor on deck able to detect fluctuations even from the distance where they stood. Can he hold it in?

"She's gone, Mallet."

"Gone?"

"She died in custody," Crawford said. "There wasn't anything I could do."

"You let them kill her?"

"She took her own life."

Mallet covered his mouth, crossing to his desk, gripping its edge, his knuckles white; his face flushed with anger. "You couldn't leave well enough alone, could you?" he said. "You had to drag her into this."

"Melee knew what she was doing," Crawford said.

"She didn't have to die for it!"

"She committed herself to what she believed."

"No, what you believe. What Betera taught you," Mallet said. "I don't want anything to do with it anymore."

"You don't have a choice," Crawford said. "None of us do."

Mallet wanted to strike him. "You like seeing people off themselves and feel rotten, don't you?"

"No, but we have to release people from this cage."

"You can't break people out of prison if they like the prison!"

"They don't like it. They're told how to act and feel every day and it's wrong."

"And there's nothing wrong with the way we are and what we're doing?" Mallet asked. "We're killing people. Don't you care about that?"

"No revolution is without sacrifice."

"We're being used. I can feel it and I don't like where this is going."

"If we don't do this, you'll never be with Severn."

"You've seen what I've seen," Mallet swallowed. "Something terrible is going to happen. I know it."

"Try not to think about it."

"Crawford, we're condemning people to an unknown future that I don't want to die for," Mallet said, stepping to Crawford, his face a breath away. "I'm not going to die for it."

Crawford put a hand on Mallet's chest, pushing him back. "You need to come out of the dark, Mallet, he said. "Betera promised us a better future. You can't help who you are."

"Get out. I don't want any more blood on my hands," Mallet seethed. "I'm done. I'm out."

There was little more Crawford could do to encourage Mallet. "Before you quit, consider the alternative," he said before returning topside.

In his quarters, Mallet reached for the comm box, dialed a code, and waited for an answer. "Hello," a female voice said.

"Dinaria," Mallet said, his voice cracking. "Are you back?"

"Hi, Mallet. I just got back yesterday before Consul Farah's address," she replied. "You sound awful. Is everything okay?"

"Can I come to see you?"

"Sure, let me know when you want to get together. We can go out this eve, have dinner, whatever you want."

"I need to see you now."

"All right, are you in your dorm or on your boat?"

"I'm on the *Meridian*, but I'll come to you."

"I look forward to it," she said.

Mallet closed the link gathered a few items, placing them in his rucksack, stopping to search a shelf for an old volume from his childhood, a book from Grayson Lear. He withdrew a small flat object pressed between the pages. It was an image of Severn, etched on the thin square.

"Forgive me," he breathed, returning the picture to its hiding place, He stepped from the cabin, took three deep breaths, and hurried down the plank for his meeting with Dinaria.

Jolly citizens traversed along paths in the square, their smiling faces rich with delight. Mallet pushed through the bodies in the street, anger, and frustration boiling in his mind. Without warning, several citizens erupted into raucous shouting and pushing. They assaulted one another in the wake of Mallet's steps. The abrupt chaos alerted the Fordham, who responded with enflamed faces.

The sentinels used force to control the swarm. They grabbed citizens, twisting their arms, shoving them along. They used their rifles to create a fence, pushing people back into a tight formation. One even went so far as to choke a citizen into submission.

Mallet did not stop to view the bedlam. He knew what he had done. As he continued strolling along undetected, he heard distinct giggles, groans and other peculiar reactions from bystanders. It was a sick scene, yet the disruption of the norm, engrained within Mallet since birth, proved Crawford's point. Mallet was not different from Crawford. He, too, was an unsuspecting pawn in a much larger game.

CHAPTER 19

Farah faced the image of a silver-haired man on a screen in her office. "Governor Devin, what can I do for you this morning?"

"I am concerned about this morning's activities," Devin said. "It is quite out of the usual."

Farah leaned back in her chair, resting her head against its high back. "I heard about Amanta's technical issues, but the details have yet to reach me."

"You may have to wait longer than you anticipate," Devin replied, his voice a bit tense.

"Why?"

"Grand Architect Lear is not here, madam."

Farah stood, coming to the front of her desk. "You have not seen him on the premises?"

"It is surprising you do not know his whereabouts."

"I am sure he has a reasonable explanation," Farah said. "Please tell me what you know."

"With the grand architect absent, I am not sure when I will know what caused the outage," Devin replied.

"Who is overseeing the investigation in his absence?"

"Engineer Novak is at the center," Devin said. "As of now, there is no definite basis for the problem."

"Breen Novak is one of Crawford Lear's best."

"I agree, but we need our communications online as soon as possible," Devin said. "This is just as horrific if not worse than the Delphia problem."

"Surely you are exaggerating?"

"There was a murder, and a suicide," Devin exclaimed, trying to keep his tone even. "Apparently, their heads were blown off."

"Just like Tech Tragnor," Farah whispered. "That is disturbing, governor."

"What's worse, some of the responders were neutralized."

"Please, continue," Farah said. "I need to know everything you have heard about the situation."

"A Fordham squad answered, but only four of them remain alive," Devin explained, "and they've stopped functioning."

"I will send Karno to conduct a full investigation."

"I would like to know what caused it and how we can prevent such an incident in the future."

"I do not have those answers yet, but Dr. Sorenson is reviewing the Delphia case," Farah said. "I will personally see to it that she examines this case as well."

"I would appreciate it, consul," Devin said, "and I will await the engineer's findings."

"Please give your citizens my regards."

Farah tried to end the conversation on a pleasant note, but her lack of knowledge about Crawford's activities remained a thorn in her side. Farah squeezed her lids shut and called Zelda to her office.

"Summon Dr. Sorenson."

"Dr. Sorenson is already here to see you."

"Then do not just stand there. Send her in."

Andira quickly moved into Farah's office. She looked as if the wind had blown her there from her lab, which was several blocks away. "Consul Farah," she said in greeting. "I hope I'm on time."

"Do you have an answer for me?"

The physician waited for the door to close before speaking. "Though I can't tell you why it keeps happening, we're pushing to figure it out."

"Your answer does not suffice," Farah said. "I need something concrete."

"There's a report circulating about a problem in Amanta."

"I know of it," Farah said. "What have you verified thus far?"

Andira presented images to Farah. "These are the cranial scans of the sentinels from Delphia."

"What am I looking for?"

"See the dark area?" Andira asked, pointing to the scans. "These regions and their grafts sustained traumatic injuries."

"I am following you."

"The areas are part of emotional awareness and reaction response. The problem may be an infection from a virus or bacteria."

Farah dropped back, eyes wide in confusion. "Could their injuries have been sustained in the attack?"

"If that were the case, other areas would've been damaged," Andira said.

"If it is a virus, why isn't it spreading to citizens?"

"It could be specific to the grafted cells; therefore, affecting only the Fordham."

"Either way, we have a problem."

"What concerns me is the focus of the damage," Andira said. "The sentinels seem changed. They're meant to be aggressive in their task, but it seems to be taking a more violent turn."

"That is preposterous," Farah said. "They are merely firm when dealing with insolence."

"Forgive me. I know it sounds unwarranted, but no matter how small, they're endowed with a certain amount of negativity," Andira said. "They wouldn't be effective otherwise."

"It was a necessary course and as you say, effective," Farah said, pushing aside the pictures. "Continue your studies and find a plausible cause."

"We will."

"What do you know of the Delphian technicians?"

"Tech Julian is confirmed dead. He and the other tech succumbed to burns and smoke inhalation, but look at this," Andira said, laying out new images. "Their skulls were crushed, post-mortem."

"Were they trampled by the crowd?"

"No, the wounds were not the result of an accident."

"Why would anyone deliberately do this? Farah asked.

"I don't know," Andira replied. "Everyone at the plant was thoroughly interrogated. No one knew of it."

"Yet the brutality was there," Farah breathed. "What about the tech's moods?"

"The rage registered by some was alarmingly high," Andira said, "but the majority tested within limits."

"Could they have taken sedation before the sentinels arrived?"

"The grounds and everyone present was searched. No paraphernalia turned up."

Farah reached for the comm again. "Zelda, bring me the list of personnel from Plant 13."

"The review of the file shows everyone scheduled was present," Zelda said upon entering.

"You said people were missing from the roster."

"It was an error."

Zelda's sensor turned yellow as Farah pursed her lips. The sentinel did not correct the feeling. "See such an oversight does not happen again."

"I think the chemists should conduct their study," Andira remarked, returning to the problem. "I'll perform an emotive analysis with test groups to check for seepage."

"I am inclined to agree with Prell about Tech Tragnor. He thinks she was a dissident."

"Her file doesn't indicate any previous trouble, but there were abnormalities in her cells and in the dead technician that look like a protein deficiency," Andira said. "It could have interfered with their alleviation."

"Perhaps it was an absorption problem," Farah mused.

"I've never seen it before, but even with those oddities, it would have taken an army of citizens with unrestrained behavior to produce pandemonium," Andira said. "Add to that, everyone in the vicinity would have to be un-medicated."

"I suggest you find out what it is," Farah said. "If they were sick and the alleviators are weakening, we need to adapt our efforts."

"I think we should talk with Commander Tragnor," Andira said. "He and Melee were close. He may have insight into her state of mind."

"I will arrange for transport of the affected parties from Amanta. Keep me apprised of any conclusions."

"There are more?"

"Three of them," Farah answered.

"Disturbing," Andira said, moving to the exit. "One more thing you should consider. Pilot Novak knew Tech Tragnor. The playback from her treatment could be valuable."

"See it is brought to me."

"At once."

The screen in front of Crawford buzzed. "Consul Farah," he answered with a grin.

"You have some news to share with me?"

Crawford looked to Zelda standing in the background to Farah. "It's for you alone."

"You are dismissed, Zelda." The sentinel departed, stationing herself outside the door.

Farah's attention returned to Crawford. "I expect you to tell me what I want to know."

"It took some time, but everything is being restored," Crawford said.

"The full details please."

"It's very technical. Are you sure you want me to get into it?"

"Proceed," Farah smiled.

"There was a malfunction in the mechanism relaying data between the network nodes," Crawford said. "It means data traffic was screwed up, not to mention everything went down."

"Now you're going to tell me you do not know what caused it," Farah said in a dismissive tone.

"It was old-fashioned incompetence."

"Is it on your part or are you going to put it on the techs?"

"You need to ask?" Crawford replied, lifting his brow in feigned disbelief.

Though she was not blushing, Farah's face was rosy. "Maybe you were selected too early."

"I'm doing my job, madam. These things happen all the time," he said. "Technology isn't foolproof."

Farah wanted to yell at the screen. With incidents mounting, her competence was in question. "When will the receptors be online?"

"They're already up and running," Crawford said. "I heard the sentinels are dropping like flies."

"You are not worried, but you should be," Farah said. "I am calling a meeting of the senate. It is time that we see what you see."

"You intend to gain access to the Servers?"

"Someone needs to follow up behind you."

The muscles in Crawford's neck strained. "These incidents and the problem with the Fordham are yours. I alone oversee the hive, and I know what I'm doing."

"These disruptions are increasing under your watch. The Senate meets in the morning and you will attend," Farah said. "If we find you negligent in your duties, your term will end and possibly your life."

"I'll survive," Crawford said. "You can count on it."

Crawford switched off the channel before she could say another word. He folded his hands and rolled his neck from side to side. Narlin came into his office unannounced.

"Excuse me, grand architect."

"What's there to excuse? You barged in," Crawford said. "Are you set?"

"I have Breen's observations from the center."

"I'm listening."

"He believes the outage was premeditated," Narlin said. "Engineer Emili received the previous statement from a young technician shortly after the incident."

"So, you have an answer. A remote station picked it up and couriered it over."

"It's not possible. Emili and her engineers were already in the area installing optics at the Opus Hall." Narlin explained. "They responded immediately. A courier couldn't arrive before them and the tech was outside when she responded."

"The center would have been locked down," Crawford affirmed.

"Precisely, and the report was delivered before the outage."

"Does Emili know who the tech was?"

"She doesn't remember seeing him before," Narlin said. "Breen sent her to detention to see if they could jog her memory, but as far as I know, they haven't gotten anything."

"Did they check the entry log?"

"Everyone is accounted for. Two died during the trouble and the rest will be detained indefinitely," Narlin said. "I don't know what'll happen to the witnesses."

"Neither do I, but if things keep going as they are, I know what'll happen to us," Crawford replied. "You can go. It's really for me to deal with."

Crawford drummed his fingers on his desk. If Farah knew what he knew, she would have reason to dispose of him. It would be over soon. How soon she discovered his intentions depended on several factors beyond his control.

CHAPTER 20

Severn sat at his favorite café along a promenade, thinking over all the work he had accomplished over the last few days, and how he had nearly forgotten what it was like to sit down and simply enjoy life. He considered walking over to the Muse, a popular shop selling musical tracks, inspiring and deterring the need for purging. His favorite sounds among its vast collections included string instruments and ocean waves.

Dismissing the idea, Severn considered stopping into the Cellar to see if the text he ordered had arrived. A colleague recently published a new tract on chemical suppressors, promising a fascinating read, but Severn decided to remain in place, sipping his drink, watching citizens pass along the street.

At any minute, flowers along walkways would spray restorative mist into the air. He usually excused himself at this point since he inhaled more than enough alleviation fumes in the lab. His thoughts went to a time in his childhood when his mother first took him to the gardens. Initially afraid, Severn grew to love the sweet scents and their effect on his demeanor.

Severn remembered her holding him in her arms, lowering his diminutive frame toward the petal's fumes. On the day he matured, Severn departed from his home, never to see his mother again. Later, he learned she took an overdose of suppressors, erasing recollections of him and his sib Orin.

There's no use thinking about it. What's done is done.

Severn took a calendar from his lab coat, scanning a schedule of focus groups over the next two days. "There goes my gap," he said, referring to the weekend. He put the planner back into his pocket and took another deep swallow from his drink. Tovah walked up just as he finished.

"Severn," she said, smiling with joy. "I'm so glad I've run into you."

"How are you?" he asked, inviting her to sit.

"I'm splendid, and you?

"Taking a much-needed break from the lab."

"What a wonderful idea," Tovah replied.

"You mustn't tire yourself out." Severn waved over a server. "Will you have something?"

"I'll have whatever you're having."

"How are Somiel and Lerner?" Severn asked after ordering an additional refreshment.

"They're as happy as happy can be, and they like Quynn."

"Who's Quynn?"

"Our Third."

"I see. I'm sure it's good for you to have another set of hands to take care of the children," Severn said. "Does Breen enjoying having another grown-up in the household?"

"He hasn't had time to enjoy her presence," Tovah replied. "He's been very busy doing the grand architect's work in Amanta City."

"The grand architect is fortunate to have him."

"He is, but it doesn't mean he can't spread the work around. Somiel and Lerner need Breen to be in their lives during their early years if they're to become proper citizens."

"I don't know Crawford Lear well, as we don't move in the same circles," Severn said, "but if you like, I could try speaking with him."

"No. That wouldn't be appropriate. It's too familiar."

Severn pursed his lips. "You're absolutely right," he said. "We must always remember the lanes we occupy."

Tovah slipped her hands around the mug delivered by the server and changed the subject. "It's a bit warm to be drinking this, don't you think?

"I like the taste of it," Severn said, taking another swallow.

"There is something I'd like you to look at," Tovah said, tasting the drink and nodding her approval. She reached into her purse, retrieving a diamond-shaped device encrusted with green enamel.

"What is it?" Severn asked, noting its size was larger than a personal communication link.

"I found this in Breen's home office," Tovah said, handing it to Severn.

"It looks like a comm," he said, turning the object over. "I've never seen anything like it, so it's probably recent technology developed for the corps."

"I'm not sure what it is, but it was hidden behind a drawer."

"How did you find it?"

"I was looking for a transcriber. When I couldn't shut the drawer, I yanked it out and there it was."

According to Severn's instincts, Tovah was lying. Before her brace, she was a research assistant at the State, too intuitive to find the device by accident.

"I can't imagine Breen hid this," he said.

"Can you find out what it is?"

134

Severn did not relish the idea of intruding on his son's privacy, but Tovah seemed insistent. "I doubt it's anything sinister," he teased, "but I'll check around for you."

"Thank you."

Moments later, the sprinklers started their midday sequence. Tovah inhaled their bouquet. "Delightful, isn't it?"

Severn watched her cheeks pink up. Tovah was a strange one, almost too pleasant, too content. He secretly wished she would leave but plastering a grin to his face and feigning approval was the appropriate response.

"Yes," he said, "Quite delightful."

Tovah cast a gaze across the grassy scene where Fordham sentinels escorted a small pack of frail citizens, whose loose-fitting clothes exposed thin bodies with jutting bone structures. Severn saw the sight as well. His throat seized, becoming dry. His fingers tapped the table.

Tovah recognized one of the women in the group. "Poor Bettany," she said, turning back to her mug. "She had the most beautiful skin. Now it's leather."

"What did she do?" Severn asked, clearing his throat.

"She held on too long. Adelaide did the right thing. I would have tagged her too," she said. "We have to share."

"How old is she?"

"Twenty-six," Tovah answered. "Attachment is an evil crime, one worth punishing."

The tone of Tovah's voice disturbed Severn. "What's Adelaide doing these days?" he asked.

"She's joined a Quart."

"I've never been much for those."

"It would do you well to have more recreation," Tovah said. "Mallet can't be your only distraction."

"Mallet isn't my only interest," Severn said firmly.

"Good, I'd like to introduce you to some people whom I think you'll enjoy."

Severn rose from his seat. "Thank you, Tovah, but I'm afraid I don't have time for much these days. I've had to turn down several invitations already."

"Well, do make time for it soon. I know plenty of citizens who'd welcome your company and Mallet's."

Tovah's scrupulous observation mirrored her belief in the laws she taught her children, and she expected those around her to be faithful to them as well. Severn knew Tovah actively tagged. Not only was she keeping her eye on him, but her words threatened Mallet as well. Severn hoped she would forget their conversation and focus on her pursuits.

Bristol sat laboring over test tubes and beakers when Severn stepped into the lab, her appearance dramatically changed. Bristol was sporting a new dress, less conservative, brighter, and more revealing than any former outfit in her arsenal. Severn questioned her motivation as he studied the transformation.

She looks like a normal woman. What prompted the change?

"Dr. Novak, the research from the last test group is collated in the database," Bristol said. "The new mixture is well tolerated and sustained at nineteen point three hours."

"That's more than sufficient," Severn said. "We'll send it off for manufacture and secure a label."

"What do think about the name Siesta or we could name it after Somiel."

"Siesta is Before Standard," he said, raising a brow, "and the latter could be construed as glorification."

Bristol lowered her eyes. "It was just a thought."

"And a nice one," Severn smiled.

These sparks of creativity are most unusual, he thought with a curious glance. *Why isn't she registering me?* He looked to the ceiling monitor. It was dark, nothing transpiring between her and the object.

Bristol noticed his puzzlement. "It stopped working a short time ago."

"Did you call a maintenance tech?"

"It will reboot itself."

"We should get someone in here to take a look," Severn said. "I don't want anyone to think we didn't report it."

"There is no need to worry, Dr. Novak," Bristol replied. "If it does not function by the end of the day, a service call will be initiated."

Bristol was usually on top of things, but today, she was completely different. Without a clear answer, Severn forged ahead. "We should look at the schedules for the next mixture."

"You will need the sheets," Bristol replied, skipping away.

Severn waited for her to disappear before pulling out the device Tovah gave him. He sat it on the island, studying its shape, contrasting it with his pocket comm. He squeezed it, but there was no response.

Bristol walked up behind him, observing his movements. "Where did you get it?" she asked.

"I happened on it while I was on the promenade," he said. "I don't know what it is."

"It is a message link," Bristol said, grasping the object. "These are no longer in use."

"Why?" Severn asked, as his assistant tested the object's weight.

"They were constructed for audio file purposes, but subversives used them to pass illegal information."

"What kind of illegal information?"

"Slander against Beta Union, love poetry, and other criminal memos," Bristol explained. "This one is designed to destruct after message retrieval. Possession of this device is illegal."

Severn felt ill. "So, someone is breaking the law by having this?"

"Do you wish to know who?"

"I'd rather not," Severn replied. "Sometimes it's best to leave well enough alone."

"Consul Farah might say you are skirting your duty."

Bristol's logic was inescapable. It had been in Breen's custody and it could hurt him. "I don't know," Severn said. "I really don't want to have to tag someone."

"It must be opened," Bristol said, pressing the issue.

"I'm a good citizen, but I'm not entirely comfortable with being an informer."

"There may be nothing to inform," Bristol said, "but without opening it, there is no way of knowing."

She was not backing down. Her training made her naturally inquisitive and ascertaining the source of the device's use was obviously important to her. Severn was cornered. He had no choice but to relent.

"How do we crack it open?" he asked, searching the lab for a tool.

"Like this," Bristol said, grasping the ends with her fingertips, twisting the device clockwise for two clicks and countering until she heard another. The two points separated, revealing a small cabochon gem, which Bristol pressed firmly. A low crackle preceded a female voice.

"It is imperative you acquire the product. Do not delay," the voice said. "The cure cannot commence without it. Restoration cannot wait."

The speech, though obscured, was familiar. Severn pondered the message's meaning and proffered a hypothesis.

"Smuggling," he said. "Someone must be stealing medication."

"Well-adjusted citizens are innocent without knowledge of deception," Bristol said. "They do not steal, nor plan unlawful activities."

"True. The senate just opened the dispensaries."

"Perhaps it has something to do with the incidents, an untested remedy not yet made public."

"If it were meant to help, it wouldn't be secret," Severn said, searching Bristol's face, "and it contradicts the fact that thing is illegal."

Severn reflected silently. *It's too strange. If the orders are from Farah, why would she disguise her voice and why did Breen have it?* Severn's pulse raced; he was afraid for his son.

Bristol placed a hand on his back, quieting him. Suddenly, the gadget glowed molten hot, dissolving into a charred ruin.

"It is finished," Bristol said.

"If it is Consul Farah, I don't think she'd be pleased we listened to it, regardless of its purpose," Severn said.

"It is not her voice."

Severn's breath stopped. "If it isn't Consul Farah, then whose voice is it?"

CHAPTER 21

Crawford sat alone in his office, welcoming the solitude after his argument with Mallet and the problems in Amanta. Though the circumstances of Melee's death were different from those of Crawford's brother, he could relate. Fenton Lear was also an engineer, who might have been grand architect had he lived.

When Crawford was just a boy, Fenton and their father perished during an inspection of The Citadel's exterior when stabilizers on their observation platform failed. Fenton was twenty-one, Grayson sixty-eight. Crawford was not allowed to see Fenton's body, nor that of his father.

There was no closure, yet he never asked why. Absent any answers, he never spoke of Fenton again, choosing instead to remember, privately, the kind and gentle youth who inherited his mother's soft, but candid demeanor, fair hair, and bright eyes.

Crawford tossed the tablet he was reviewing aside and rifled through his desk in search of a stimulant pack. After locating it, he zipped open the pouch and withdrew a small syringe.

Uncapping the instrument, he held it to his neck, hesitating to inject the substance. Crawford rarely used, but he was tired, and the temptation crawled into his body. It would only take one dose to perk him up—yet therein lay the problem.

I can't go down this path.

A knock at his door distracted him from this meditation. He quickly stashed the medication, turning to see Kemble Novak standing in the archway leaning her head against the door.

"Am I interrupting you?" she asked.

"No, not at all," Crawford replied, gazing down the length of her body. "I welcome the company."

Today she wore a uniform different from her typical Aero suit. It was the same navy, but its scaly material clung tightly to her form, revealing her sensuous curves. He noticed a gleaming chain hanging from her slender waist and pointed to the accessory. "That's new," he said.

"I can't find my old one," she said. "I called the detention center, but it wasn't there."

Crawford's eyes sparkled as they moved over her form. "Good thing you've got a spare," he laughed, softly.

"I'd rather have the other one back," Kemble said. "Far gave it to me. I suppose you could say it's sentimental."

"I'm sure it'll turn up."

Kemble stepped further into the office, slipping past Crawford. The rear of her suit, save for two straps across the upper and lower back, exposed a fair amount of flesh. Its design complemented her well-toned shoulder blades and spine.

"What can I do for you, Kemble?" Crawford asked, blinking as if waking from a dream.

"Do you know when Breen will be back from Delphia?"

"He already departed, but he won't be back here today," Crawford said, taking a seat. He motioned Kemble to an oversized chair opposite him. "I had to send him to Amanta City on an errand."

"You couldn't send someone else?"

"He was already in the field, not to mention the best engineer for the job. I'll have him back as soon as I can."

Kemble knew Crawford was giving praise to her brother. According to Breen, he rarely singled out accomplishments, preferring to think of the engineers as a team. A grin lingered on Crawford's handsome face, compelling her to avert her gaze and peer around the room. Except for some charts and a few wall screens, it was barren but tidy.

"How do you live in this room?" Kemble asked. "It's far too austere. Cold."

"It suits its purpose," Crawford replied, "and I don't live here."

"You're better than Mallet. He sleeps on the *Meridian* nearly every night as if he has no dormitory to go home to."

Crawford's smile dissipated when she mentioned Mallet's name. "He and I have many things in common," he said somberly, "but thankfully, that's not one of them."

Kemble began counting their similarities aloud. "I wouldn't say that. You both have great attention to detail. You're from Delphia. You live for your work. Did I miss anything?"

"We have our mutual sorrows," Crawford whispered.

"You've nothing to be sorrowful about. Life is good," she commented.

Crawford stared into her eyes. This time, he was not communicating his desire for her. "I wish it were true."

"It should be," Kemble responded. "Nothing in life needs to be difficult. We've all been afforded a wonderful opportunity to live as we should, completely unfettered by anything."

"Not all of us," Crawford said bluntly. "Melee's dead, Kemble."

"Dead?" Kemble asked softly.

"She passed after the fire at thirteen."

Kemble's hand suddenly caught her throat. "What happened?" she breathed.

"She committed suicide."

Kemble quickly reached into a slit on the side of her jumpsuit and extracted a small tube containing blue crystals identical to those that Mallet smoked the night of Severn's party. She clicked the top, thrusting the end in her mouth. Fumes gathered in the chamber as she drew on the device to settle her nerves. After a few puffs, she nodded to Crawford to continue.

"She was taken for interrogation," he said, fanning away the smoke filling the space. "They ordered her to be examined, but she had other ideas."

Kemble listened as the potion's effect dulled her reaction to the news. "Melee was like the sun, brilliant, warm and all aglow. She had no cause to do that. Why would she do it?"

"I don't know, and we may never know," Crawford lied, "but Mallet's the one you should be concerned with. He's in a dangerous frame of mind."

"You shouldn't feel sorry for him," Kemble said.

"You don't think he deserves to be comforted after this loss?" Crawford asked.

"I doubt he'd feel that way for you."

"I grew up with him and Melee. They're important to me."

"Don't be ridiculous. No one is truly important to anyone," Kemble said. "Melee was attracted to you. That's all. She had feelings she shouldn't."

"Regardless of what she allegedly felt, I genuinely care about what Mallet's going through."

Kemble was not following the conversation. Her mind seemed fixated on a single point. "They say everyone is after you, Crawford."

Crawford tilted his head, amazed at the pilot's ability to skirt the present topic of conversation. The need to debate the weight of Mallet's current dilemma was futile in the face of Kemble's intoxication. Crawford decided to play her game. "Apparently, everyone is after me except you."

"I'm not fond of being made to suffer," she said. "I don't intend on ever experiencing that again."

"Why do you think you have issues with Mallet?"

"Who are you? My therapist?" Kemble asked, her speech slurred.

"I only want to help you. You felt there was a reason you needed to attack him."

"He's a bad influence on Severn. His behavior is shameful, and he'll get Severn in trouble or worse."

"Mallet takes many things to heart. Sometimes he doesn't think about consequences."

"You should see the way he looks at Far. It's not friendly. It's—"

"It's called love."

"That emotion isn't natural," Kemble said, she said, attempting to sit up. "I'd better get to Aqua."

"Do you think you should be going anywhere?"

Kemble's fingers relaxed. The pipe she held slipped and shattered on the floor. "I'm sorry."

"It's no bother. I'll clean it up," Crawford said, placing his hands on her shoulders to push her back into the chair. He marveled at Mallet's ability to unnerve the pilot even without being present. "I don't think you'll be any good to anyone like this."

"I have to show up," Kemble said, hanging her head. "There's too much to do today and I can't leave it to someone else."

"Here," Crawford said, swiveling in his chair to retrieve a stimulant. "I didn't use it."

"Can you inject me?" she asked, tapping her neck.

Crawford rose to prick her smooth flesh, his conscience tugging at him. Stabbing someone with a needle, especially for the drug use, was not at the top of his activity list with someone as attractive as Kemble. He had other pursuits in mind when it came to the pilot.

"What are you waiting for?" Kemble asked, her groggy voice breaking him from his reverie.

"Nothing," he replied, pushing the plunger.

The meds rushed through her like a hot iron, tingling her very veins, and jolting her back to reality. Kemble spread her limbs and cracked her neck several times. She was like a new being, vigorous and genial. The pilot's tolerance for the concoction amazed Crawford.

"I'm glad to know you're good for something, architect," Kemble smiled, getting to her feet. "We've got a diving tutorial today and I promised Gerran I'd assist him."

"You can't miss that," Crawford replied, smugly.

Kemble leaned forward, touching Crawford's face. "You're so good to me. I often wonder why," she said, pressing her lips to his.

She lingered, providing Crawford with an opening for increased intimacy. He slipped his tongue into her warm mouth. Her body clung to his as she deepened the kiss. For a moment, Crawford felt like she was searching for something lost. Desire stirred throughout Crawford's body, but before he could act, Kemble pried his hands from around her waist. She stepped and proceeded to saunter out of the office without even saying goodbye.

Crawford brushed a finger across his lips. *She's doped*, he realized. *She wouldn't have done it otherwise.*

Feelings of adoration tinged with sympathy accompanied Crawford's thoughts about Kemble, the vice of his longing not diminishing his desire to know her on a deeper level. He went back to his desk, attempting to concentrate on his work, and spied Kemble's broken pipe and ashes on the floor.

He could turn her to his thinking if he wanted, but preferred she open to him without persuasion. From his pocket, Crawford fished out the chain he appropriated the evening he took Kemble home. He gently laid the jewelry back in its hiding place. It was a pleasing souvenir. Someday, he might even return it.

The architect closed his eyes, replaying the kiss in his mind. He revisited the idea of bringing what he discovered within her to the surface. Considering his words to Mallet regarding Severn, Crawford felt ambivalent. When he opened his eyes, Betera's teachings flooded his conscience.

He had not lived all these years to see his purpose destroyed as the shackles of freedom needed to be broken. These were the facts, checked and rechecked.

As much as Crawford craved Kemble's love, he could allow nothing, and no one, to interfere with his destiny.

CHAPTER 22

Night fell on Unity City as Farah called Orin to The State Building for a private briefing with Losara Idoni. Orin took refuge in his office before the meeting, mulling over documents from past forums. Karno interrupted him just as he started looking over the details for the impending trade.

"You need to remember to announce yourself before entering," Orin said to Karno.

"Understood," Karno replied, handing Orin an envelope. "It shall not happen again."

"What is this?"

"The playback Consul Farah requested."

"Give it to her directly."

"She asked not to be disturbed."

"Fine, I'll give it to her," Orin said. "You may leave." Orin looked at the envelope and tossed it aside as Farah entered his office.

"Have you heard from Sister Idoni?" she asked.

"I am ready to contact her now if you are."

"Very well. Get her on the line so we can get this over with."

Orin followed her instruction as requested. To their mutual satisfaction, Losara Idoni stood by anticipating contact.

"I extend greetings to you Consul Farah and you, Senator Novak," Losara said.

"I trust all is well with you," Farah said.

"If you are referring to our mediations with Pleura, I am pleased to inform you they are completed, and all is well."

"You came to a beneficial resolution?"

"We decided to surrender several points along the sea corridor," Losara said, "and we've provided safe conduct to the north of our border for their routes."

"What is to stop them from using the right of way against you?" Farah asked.

"I accept their word, as I accept yours."

"They are a peculiar nation, and you play a delicate game with them, especially if you asked for nothing in return."

"I asked them for concessions, but we are not here to discuss Caelum's relationship with Pleura."

"I completely agree and though I remain curious, let us settle our affair."

Orin stepped into the conversation. "How much of the product is ready?"

"Everything you requested will be ready when you arrive at the Green."

"I have decided we will begin the operation ahead of schedule," Farah responded.

"When should we expect you?"

"Our ships depart on the sixth day at noon with a chemist and Grand Architect Crawford Lear," Orin chimed in.

"I look forward to meeting the architect," Losara said. "I have heard many interesting things about him."

"What exactly have you heard?"

"Only that he is your most gifted engineer and his loyalty knows no bounds."

"That is quite true," Farah said, her eyes shining brilliantly with the knowledge that her engineer—no, Beta Union's engineer was well known. "We cherish him as a valuable member of our society."

Losara sat back smiling. "No doubt he would give his life's blood as Betera Eaton did."

"Which is more than I can say for your people."

"How little you know, Consul."

"I thought we agreed to table our previous debate."

"I am not the one who forgot our truce," Losara smiled. "In any event, I do hope Grand Architect Lear lives up to your esteem."

"Believe me, your people could learn something from Crawford Lear," Farah said. "Good eve to you, Losara."

"And the same to you, Consul."

With Losara gone from the screen, Farah addressed Orin. "Since when was Crawford Lear included on the personnel manifest?"

"His engineers have charge of the fuel cells," Orin replied.

"We should forget the fuel cells."

"You mean not hand them over? They are expecting a trade and so is the senate."

"What if something were to happen to make their property readily available to us?"

"What devious plan are you conjuring, Farah?"

"The South would not be pleased to hear what Losara is planning," Farah said. "I think a timely word could help them ferret out her intentions."

"Losara's request indicated no plans of developing offensive capabilities."

"At the present, no, but they could turn on the offensive at any time," Farah said.

"You could put them at war with each other with us in the middle," Orin said.

"If Pleura deals with Caelum, we could negotiate for anything we want in the region."

"I could have you tagged for what you suggest."

"I am thinking of the country and its continued integrity."

"Greed remains a punishable offense," Orin said. "Are you prepared to accept the consequences for this?"

"In other words, you are above strategy?" Farah laughed. "You obviously do not have the stomach to be a leader, Orin."

"If it means putting lives in danger and forgoing our principles, then the answer is no," Orin said. "I believe the senators would agree that such an approach is reprehensible."

"You would not hesitate to stretch citizens to the point of death."

"I would if the crime demanded it."

"Fine," Farah said, backing down. "They will have their precious cells. Tomorrow we will discuss the server inspection."

"I fully intend to accompany the grand architect on his expedition," Orin replied.

"Do not be surprised if your request is denied."

"I have work to attend to, Farah," Orin said.

The senator then sat down, indicating his desire for Farah to depart. To Orin, she behaved like a dictator; the plot she hatched was pure evil. Farah's emotions ran unchecked by Zelda and the sentinel's disregard and failure to rectify such behavior unsettled him.

Orin quietly contemplated Zelda's nature. *She is one of the first models. They tend toward leniency.*

It would take someone stronger to hold Farah back if Zelda was weak and Prell was just the sentinel to take her place. Before

Orin could orchestrate a shift change, he needed to deal with the mounds of requests from governors and vendors spread across his desk. As he sifted through the files, he uncovered the envelope Karno delivered, which he had forgotten to give to Farah in the excitement of their exchange.

Orin opened it, finding a disk inside labeled with Kemble's name. Though she bore the Novak surname, he was not often in communication with his niece, as was customary.

He inserted the object into a player, watching the graphic and disturbing film with great attention. He was ready to turn it off until Severn appeared in the video. Kemble was profoundly afraid, her delusions playing out a terrifying scenario of Severn attacked by his fellow citizens and Mallet Tragnor. In Kemble's anguish, she accused Mallet of indecency perpetrated against Orin's sib.

"Is this what she truly thinks?" Orin whispered. "It cannot be real."

Orin stopped the playback, ejecting the disk. He could not believe what he witnessed—the images of attachment between Severn and Mallet. Given the nature of what Kemble's mind had conjured, the proper course of action was to tag his brother, have him assessed and if necessary, eliminated. Orin did not want to condemn Severn so quickly.

There is more than one way to atone for a wrong, he mused. *I will give him a chance to redeem himself.*

He reached for the comm wave and called Dr. Sorenson.

"Senator Novak, if you're looking for the results of my examination, I am still conducting an exam of the Iona sentinels," Andira said. "Please tell Consul Farah I'll have it by morning."

"That is not why I am calling," Orin said.

"I see. What can I do for you?"

"I need you to find out immediately if Commander Tragnor has a pending brace order."

"One moment," she said, placing the call on mute, returning after a few minutes. "Commander Tragnor received an exemption in favor of his sib."

"Then the Tragnor bloodline was to continue?"

"Yes, but through the female."

"It shall continue with him instead."

"I'm not authorized to make a change without senate approval," Andira said.

"You now have it," Orin replied.

"I'll still need the necessary seal."

"When does your appointment end?"

"In seven months," Andira answered timidly.

"Am I correct in assuming you would like another go at your current position?" Orin asked.

"You are."

"Then you will do as I ask, and I will make sure your work continues."

"I'll send the order out after I select a pare," Andira said.

"I have one for you," he said. "Pilot Novak."

Andira looked puzzled for a moment. "Severn Novak's descendant?"

"That is what I said," Orin replied, his jaw set in a tight line as if irritated by the question.

"Standard thirty-day return?"

"See that it is sent out before week's end."

When the call was over, Orin destroyed the disk, believing his actions would help his brother remember their place in society and his own.

Farah is wrong. I am not above deception.

CHAPTER 23

Mallet woke sprawled out in Dinaria's bed. His eyes were fuzzy from sedation. He squinted against the darkness, searching his way to a door, feeling along the wall. The brilliance of the next room was in sharp contrast to the shadows from which Mallet emerged.

A sparkling tree, oozing Solace vapor and jutting from the center of the floor, changed color in time with Beta Union's anthem as it played in the background. Mallet was sick to death of the happy-go-lucky tune. He circled the living space looking for Dinaria, but she was not in sight. The commander assumed she was on a call bringing relief to some stressed citizens. Her clients, senate officials among them, found her services to be as effective as medications.

Mallet took in the surroundings consisting of holographic representations of a fertile forest, tactile illusions so real and precise, replete with speckled pink leaves. Chaises surrounded the trunk of the main tree, beckoning relaxation accompanied by soft, pleasurable dreams. Mallet abhorred the false energy as much as he despised Dinaria for lulling citizens into a disquieting sense of protracted, but illusive security.

He shuddered at the idea of her touching his skin. The sensuality with which she performed her duties was a violation for him rather than a remedy for an ailing body or soul. On that thought, he looked at his uniform, relieved to find every closure in place.

That's enough of this, he breathed, moving to the exit.

Mallet was determined to slip away before Dinaria returned, but the front door slid open before he could make his escape. Dinaria stood in the entrance, a heavy sack slung on her shoulder.

"Leaving so soon?"

"I just figured I'd get out of your way," Mallet said, reliving her of the burden.

"There's no need to rush off. Take all the time you need."

Mallet placed the bag on a counter. "I really should go," he said. "I've tarried long enough, and I feel better anyway."

"At least let me fix you something. You must be starving."

"I'm fine. You don't have to go through the trouble."

"Don't be ridiculous," Dinaria said, embracing Mallet. "You called me for help, and I intend to give it to you."

Mallet questioned the sincerity of her offer as she nestled herself against his chest, increasing his tension. "I'll be all right. I just needed to crash and clear my mind."

"You're not all right, Mallet. In fact, you're unbalanced," Dinaria said, looking into Mallet's eyes. "You've accumulated a lot of pent-up negativity that only leads to one place."

Mallet looked down at her, having played the same scene long ago. She was testing his patience, unaware of his love for Severn.

He unfurled Dinaria's arms from his waist. "This isn't a suitable time for me," he said, stepping away to sit on a cushion by the tree.

"Why don't you take off that uniform and let me work on you." She said. "It'll help you recover."

Mallet's grief started to well up again. Before he could check himself, he exploded at her. "Don't even think about it," he seethed, jumping from his seat. "You don't recover from what I've been through."

Dinaria fell back, shocked by the sound of fury in Mallet's voice. His scornful reaction to her suggestion felt ungrateful and mean. Even more confusing was his adverse reaction to the Solace permeating the room.

Dinaria's inner peace cracked. "What's wrong with you? Can't you feel the amity in the room? It's everywhere and in everything," she said, rushing to the tree, plastering her nose against its bark.

"You're pathetic and you're just like the rest of the fools," Mallet said. "You have no idea what it means to love someone and lose them. You don't know what it is to feel."

Dinaria put a hand on her chest. She felt strange anger boiling inside, unraveling her control. "What you're feeling is sick. You need to let go of the anger that plagues you. It will destroy you."

"It's not sick to care for people," Mallet said, "to value them while they're alive, to miss them, and cherish their memory."

"You need to leave, Mallet. You need…"

Mallet stood at the door, calling back to her. "I don't need anything, but you do. You and everyone like you."

For Dinaria, the room was spinning, her head throbbing. She clawed the organic totem, desperate to find relief from the unseen enemy attacking her bliss. She clenched her teeth against hot tears. "Pass, pass…it will pass."

"I can't believe I came here," Mallet said. "You and everyone in this dump are useless to me." He punched the door panel, storming out of her quarters.

Dinaria's gut hurt. Even with all her training and knowledge, she could not fathom what happened. She slumped to the base of the tree, sobbing, her plethora of happiness failing. Dinaria removed a sedation syringe from a compartment under one of the benches around the tree. She plunged the needle into her hip, ripping furiously at the muscle beneath. Blood soaked her pant leg. She dug the needle deeper in the hope the pain would relieve the emotional sting of Mallet's dastardly deed.

She then dragged herself across the floor, reaching for the comm. Her fingers paused before the dial pad. If she tagged Mallet, she risked exposing her fear and The Stretch would claim her, not as a victim, but as one who had lost control. However, self-preservation took over as Dinaria collapsed in defeat.

Outside, the stars were in full view with citizens roaming the streets enjoying flights of fireflies while sentinels took root around the squares, their disposition suggesting a pleasant evening. Crawford snaked through the huddle, entranced by public screens broadcasting entertainment bulletins for aerial joyrides, and lusty flicks.

There also was an exhibition at the Museum of Modern Society, featuring paintings by Rashida Ramil. Her latest collection, Rays of Enlightenment, included glass mosaics of the Sun and other celestial bodies. Crawford found nothing invigorating in her work. It put him to sleep.

"Everyone has their taste," he muttered while smirking at three scantily dressed women sauntering toward him, batting their lashes.

Each passerby represented a different shape of the female figure and all were equally beautiful. He propelled himself onward, smirking at three women who strutted toward him, batting their lashes and licking their lips while eyeing him up and down. The architect, not in the mood for sport, refused to indulge them. He was immune to such tricks, having perfected them himself.

Kemble had been on his mind ever since she left his office. He wondered how her diving class had gone. He surmised her to be an excellent teacher, a master at everything she knew. It was odd to find someone so immersed in a career as she was, but he understood her passion, having one of his own, and felt it would be interesting to hear her ideas on just about any subject. Crawford reasoned she held high opinions, fostered by her mother, Agora.

If her daughter were half the woman she was, he would never reach Kemble and he wanted so much for her to let him in. Crawford took a deep breath and turned a corner. The sentinels were surprisingly absent along the back streets. He was surprised to spot Mallet ahead of him, taking a stroll.

"Mallet," Crawford called, stopping a few paces behind him.

"Not now," Mallet said, waving him off.

Crawford ignored him, planting himself firmly in front. "Where are you going?"

"What business is it of yours?"

"You seem more settled."

Mallet shook his head. Crawford never ceased to amaze him. It was hard to believe they grew up in the same district, much less in the same group. His behavior was solidly in tune with the Fordham and their friendship was never tenser than now.

"It dawned on me that you're just like the sentinels. Nothing gets to you."

"You'd rather I be like you?" Crawford asked.

"No. Just stop expecting me to be you," Mallet replied.

"Betera saw something great in you. She believed in you. Don't disappoint her or Melee."

"Your pare was wrong. I can't do what you do, and I don't want to."

"You could if you stopped using your heart and started using your head."

"Don't drag Severn into this. He's got nothing to do with it and I'm not hurting him."

"You will if you don't pull back and stop being so self-absorbed."

Mallet laughed at what he felt was the ultimate hypocrisy. "Take your own advice then and stop mooning over Kemble Novak."

Crawford was stunned. Though Mallet had succeeded in wounding his pride, he did not back down. "You should come out of the dark, Mallet," he responded. "It's escalating. If you haven't noticed, people are giving their lives."

"Well then you can add yours to the pile," he said, stepping into the architect's space, his face a breath away. "I'm not dying today."

Crawford put a hand on Mallet's chest, pushing him back and stepping aside to depart. "Sooner or later, you'll have to come out. You'll have to join the fight because the day we've worked for is at hand."

"Wrong. You're an idiot," Mallet said. "It's the day Betera worked for."

"Either way, it's here and there's no denying what we must do," Crawford replied. "Like it or not, you are part of the plan and it will succeed with or without you."

Mallet's scornful glare burrowed into Crawford's flesh, the heat of the architect's words coloring his cheeks. No matter how he felt about the message delivered to him in that moment, the truth reigned supreme. The revolution had begun. Mallet's only choice was to go forth with the tide or be swept away in its aftermath.

CHAPTER 24

Crawford was glad to get away from Mallet's forceful rejection of their shared mission. As he turned another corner in his sojourn through the night, he saw Kemble sitting alone in the Tranquility Garden. She was giddy and relaxed, watching aerial vessels pass between the clouds in the night sky.

Dreamy music in a nearby pavilion streamed across the lawn with lazy abandon. Crawford kept his distance from the pilot while waiting patiently for an inroad.

Kemble spread her limbs, taking a comfortable posture on a bench, and began to recall the celebration she attended earlier at Aqua. Someone thoughtfully had brought a keg of "Shine" to the event. The sight of the barrel made everyone squeal with glee. They stripped off their clothes and lubricated themselves with the luminous gel, enjoying a sensual euphoria producing rainbows beneath the water.

Gerran's students possessed incredible skills, lithe bodies moving with ease and grace through the pool as they practiced search and recovery drills. Kemble stayed out of the water, spending the better part of the party watching Gerran swim laps.

If she were not intoxicated already, she would have challenged him to a duel. Gerran was a strong swimmer, but his pace in aquatics did not compare to hers. They were partners once, the joining pleasant and brief as Gerran was diminutive and shy, lacking spontaneity. Kemble toyed with the notion of indulging in raucous behavior with other candidates during the evening but held back for reasons only she knew.

Crawford stirred Kemble's feelings, confusing her perception of reality. She closed her eyes, reciting lessons from her youth. "Attachment is unnatural. It's unnatural, it's—"

"What's unnatural?" Crawford asked, having finally decided to approach the pilot.

Kemble whipped around. "I was just—," she said, stumbling.

"It sounded like something from elementary class," Crawford said smiling, taking a seat and, noticing a faint glimmer on her skin.

"It is from a primer. It's as relevant as the day I learned it."

"Why are you quoting a primer in the middle of the night?" he asked, leaning in her direction, elbows resting on his thigh. "You're a long way from grade school."

"It doesn't matter when I learned it. Those traditions remain with us regardless of our age."

"I suppose they do, but unless you've committed a transgression or are you thinking about it, they shouldn't be necessary."

"Mallet would know more about that than me," Kemble snapped before changing her tune. "How is he?"

"Isn't the notion of concern against your philosophy?"

"Would you rather I remain cruel and aloof?"

"I'm impressed at your interest," Crawford said. "I thought you couldn't give a damn."

Kemble slid away from him. "I don't need your praise, Crawford. I don't actually dislike Mallet."

"You've given a great impression of it earlier."

"It's Mallet's behavior I don't like. He's disrespectful and ungracious."

"There's a solution for that," Crawford said. "You could tag him."

"It wouldn't do any good to report him," Kemble said. "He gets away with everything." Crawford erupted into laughter.

"What makes you say that?"

"He wasn't assessed after we quarreled."

"That could have been a simple oversight."

"Whatever it is, I'm tired of it," Kemble said, standing up and focusing on the exciting sounds piercing the blackness. "I'm starving. You can stay here or come with me."

"You're inviting me to join you?"

"Yes, it was an invitation and I'm only offering once."

"I'd be honored then," Crawford said, falling into step.

Kemble stopped at the gate saying, "Promise me you'll behave yourself."

"I will if you will. I don't want you going to The Stretch twice."

Kemble kept a reasonable distance between her and Crawford as they entered the streets. His occasional glances disturbed her.

"Are you okay?" Crawford asked.

"I'm fine," she responded, searching her pockets aimlessly. "The drugs are wearing off."

Crawford found fault with the answer. The residue of the drug she ingested hours before would be long gone. Therefore, the only chemical coursing through her would be hormonal.

162

Rather than put forth this hypothesis and possibly mar the evening, Crawford took the initiative, leading her to one of his favorite establishments along the river.

When they arrived, a host sat them at a table with a splendid view. Kemble's gaze moved around the room, taking in the abundance of attractive males and females. Crawford watched her as she watched them.

"Shopping?" he asked.

"I'm sorry. What?"

"You're prospecting. See something you like?"

"I'm supposed to look," Kemble said blushing. "You should try it sometime."

"I don't hunt in the open," Crawford replied, cupping his chin. "At least, not in an obvious way."

Kemble folded her arms. "You have your methods and I have mine. Let's leave it at that."

"You should have a drink. That anxiety of yours could bring the sentinels down on us."

"Good evening," a server said, interrupting their banter. "What can I get for you?"

"What's on good today?" Crawford asked.

"Wildfowl from Redmire Farm with Janus berries."

"Sounds good to me," Crawford said, "and we'll need a bottle of Terra Blanc."

"Excellent choice," the server said, taking the menus.

"Tell me something," Crawford said, leaning across the table. "How is it Severn's a chemist, but you're a pilot?"

"Not everyone follows their pares," Kemble said. "Remember, Agora's a scientist too. I grew up in a lab and that was enough for me."

"There's plenty of science at Aero and Aqua."

"It's different. As a pilot, I get to see more of the world, Beta Union at least."

163

"If you like to travel, you should've been an engineer."

"And fail out of those classes? I think I did just fine with what I'm doing now."

"I think you're smart enough to have passed through. Besides, you'd have a chance to go to the west corner," Crawford said. "There're a lot of interesting things out there like Zara's Pillar."

"You've seen it?"

"I saw it on a rotation while we were studying obsolete fuel stores in the region."

"Is it true its origin is alien?"

"That's the rumor," Crawford said, "and it's older than the settlements in Caelum and Pleura."

"Do you have any idea who built it or what it's actually for?"

"I don't know, but apparently, it's important enough that Linus Rand erected a force field around it to protect it."

"So, it's like a museum? You can look but not touch."

"I don't know many people who'd go that far to look at a monument regardless of how pretty it is," Crawford said. "There are more appealing things to see here."

"I've heard there isn't anything, but wasteland," Kemble retorted.

"Some of it isn't pleasant now," Crawford said, "but before everything moved inland, for whatever reason it did, there were farmlands and hatcheries out there that fed the entire habitat."

Kemble squirmed in her chair, trying to get comfortable under Crawford's stare. She felt it best to keep him talking, launching into another topic of interest. "What's in the Citadel?"

"You're full of curiosity tonight."

"Like everyone else, I want to know why it's hidden across the northern border."

Crawford twirled the bottle of wine in its chilling base next to the table as he considered how to tell Kemble about the

Citadel without revealing too much. "It's the main power plant," he said. "It controls the entire grid, so it has to be defended."

"From what?"

"There's always a chance of intrusion from curious minds."

"That doesn't make any sense," Kemble scoffed. "No ordinary citizen can cross into the north. Besides, it's cold enough to kill anyone's curiosity."

"It's not that cold," Crawford teased. "Suffice it to say, our enemies might find it useful. Caelum's interested in our energy sources."

"From what I understand, they're not hostile and if they were, they don't have the means to penetrate Beta Union."

It was Crawford's turn to change the subject. "I've heard fascinating things about their culture," he said. "Since you're so intrigued by what you don't know, you'd probably welcome interacting with them on a more frequent basis."

"We see them enough on our trade assignments."

"Do you ever see people from Pleura?"

"They're savages and probably not worth seeing."

"You can't believe every piece of propaganda you hear," Crawford said. "I'm sure they have good traits."

"Sometimes not knowing is best."

"You mean to tell me you're not interested at all?"

"You have to know when to leave well enough alone."

"Sometimes it takes experience to know that."

Kemble folded her arms across her chest. "Once you go looking for answers, it could be too late."

"Too late for what?"

"To change course, to turn back," Kemble said. "Restraint is often necessary. Don't you agree?"

"I do for the most part," Crawford said, wiping his mouth, "but it depends on what needs to be restrained and who's doing the restraining."

Feeling her shield peeling away, Kemble averted her attention from Crawford to the restaurant's windows, thankful the server arrived with their meal. There was a strange dichotomy to the architect; his speech and actions, usually in line with the moral standard, hid something enigmatic.

Without further words, Crawford busied himself with the plate in front of him, nonchalant about the possible course the evening would take. For now, it was enough to be in Kemble's company. After dinner, Kemble granted Crawford the privilege of seeing her home. He asked for nothing more at the time, figuring anything else would be asking too much.

Crawford followed Kemble through the halls of her dorm, recalling his first trek to the location when he carried her limp body over the threshold. He questioned if she remembered the evening, how he watched over her in sleep.

"I should go," Crawford said. "I have an early start and you should get some sleep."

"You could take time off," Kemble said, thinking how handsome he was when smiling.

"There's no such thing as time off," Crawford smirked. "Engineers are always working."

"What are you doing besides maintaining buildings and stuff that needs so much care?"

"Why do you want to know my every move?" Crawford teased. "Are you planning to stalk me?"

"Of course not, I just wondered," Kemble said, playfully hitting him.

"Unfortunately, I can't tell you. It's a matter of security, practically life, and death."

"Is that so?" Kemble said. "Now I really want to know what it is."

Blood rushed in Crawford's ears. He wanted to hold her, to kiss her. Kemble's eyes told the same tale, but she wrestled with her will.

"Good eve," Crawford said, turning to go.

"Wait," Kemble said. "Could you look at something before you go?"

"What is it?"

"My screen is down. Since you're here, maybe you could look at it."

Crawford hesitated, wary of her invitation, yet he stepped in with enthusiasm. The lights came up, revealing new modifications to the space.

"When did you get this?" he asked, pointing to a wall of water, accentuated by blue light, permeating the flow.

"It was installed a few days ago," she replied. "I told you I liked water. It makes everything seem purer, cleaner."

"Why didn't the techs examine it, when you put the design in?" Crawford asked, walking over to the screen, waving his hand over the paper-thin device, flipping through its channels. It functioned perfectly.

"You fixed it!" Kemble said.

"There was nothing wrong with it."

What happened next was unexpected. Kemble charged him, throwing her arms around him, kissing him ardently. Crawford held Kemble tight, his mouth burning with intensity. Kemble's hands ruffled through his hair as he kissed her face, burying himself in her neck.

Kemble purred in his ear. "Take this off," she said, referring to her uniform.

Crawford unhooked the straps, sliding the garment down her smooth skin, groping the swell of her breasts. Upon hearing her reaction, he released his grip and returned to her lips. There was no air between them. Kemble's feet parted with the floor as

Crawford cradled her in his arms and climbed the stairs. In her bedroom, he laid her down tenderly and finished undressing her before discarding his own trappings.

Kemble took in the full view of his body. From the contours of his face to the soles of his feet, Crawford was an alluring mixture of hard and soft. To her, he was striking. He crept to her slowly, bending to kiss her lips, but Kemble suddenly blocked him.

"Wait," she said, moving to retrieve something from a drawer and producing a tube containing a ruby substance. He knew what it was and wanted no part in it. "What's wrong?"

"You've been sober this entire time," Crawford said. "If you need that now, you don't need me."

"It never hurts to turn things up."

"I've no doubt you'd be exciting enough on your own," he said, rolling onto his back. He feared the worst. Kemble did not trust her instincts, and Crawford could not get through to her if she kept a wall between them.

"It's not that bad," Kemble said, putting a hand on his chest. "You're just not used to it."

"I think I'll call it a night," Crawford said sharply, sitting up on the side of the bed.

"I asked you here because I want you here."

"Why do you? You could bed anyone you want."

"I don't want just anyone," Kemble breathed. "I want you."

"You're discriminating," Crawford said. "Why start now?"

"I don't know."

"But you want to kill it," Crawford said, positioning himself on top of her. Kemble did not resist. "You needn't protect yourself from me. I'm not going to hurt you." She heard truth in his words and let go of the vial.

Crawford lovingly touched her face, brushing her eyelids and cheeks. "Look at me. I won't do anything you don't want me to do," he whispered.

Kemble fixed her eyes on him, feeling the warmth of his hand floating down her ribcage. There was an intensity between them she could not name. He entered her body; a gasp escaped her throat. Kemble's palms ran the length of his back as his rhythm coaxed her to action. With each movement, he sank deeper into her.

"Look at me," he repeated, pleading with his gaze as well as his voice.

Kemble obeyed, feeling swayed by the surreal experience of their activity. He was inside her heart, inside her soul. She had never been fully open to anyone. Her yearning for him spread throughout her limbs and core. Crawford tuned into this, captivated and stirred by her surrender.

He had broken Kemble's self-imposed barrier, believing the beauty of her heart could match the knowledge in her head if she let go of Beta Union's false ideals and trusted in her strength. If she broke away, she would see the world as he did, welcoming release from its control.

Crawford pressed on, seeking and giving pleasure while Kemble continued uttering satisfaction. She knew her ardor for him was real, naked, and alive. She wanted to love him, learn from him, and be with him always. With a final surge forward, Crawford fulfilled both of their desires.

CHAPTER 25

Karno puttered around Farah's chambers, using systematic movements while organizing various pieces of data for review.

"Have Commanders Ragas and Tragnor arrived?" Farah asked.

"They are waiting in the atrium."

"Let the cabinet and Dr. Sorenson know we are ready," Farah said. "As soon as the meeting is finished, escort the officers to Senator Novak's office."

"Yes, madam."

Farah's visual comm beeped. Prell was calling from Amanta. "Are you finished?"

"The detainees are corrected. We are awaiting your next orders."

"Did they have any knowledge of the malfunction?"

"The techs knew nothing, but Engineer Emili did."

"Pray continue as I am eager to understand the situation."

"A technician outside the facility handed her a file after the lockdown."

"What was in it?"

"It contained information about the outage, but the time stamp preceded the power loss."

Farah's brow wrinkled. "You are telling me there was a warning of the problem?"

"None the workers saw," Prell said. "Someone shut down the central power grid and secondary controls without notice."

"That means it was planned."

"It would seem to be, yet without further information, the exact nature and timing of the event are uncertain."

"Have you confirmed the technician's identity?"

"Recovery of the particular memory from the girl was unsuccessful."

"It must have been a preemptive strike," Farah mumbled. "What did you do with the deceased?"

"Their damage was too severe for examination; therefore, they were destroyed," Prell said.

"The survivors are wiped and ready for release."

"You were given no orders to dispose of them," Farah said, attempting to modulate her tone.

Even with the effort, a faint hint of crimson tinged Prell's mark. The sentinel, however, made no move to acknowledge Farah's inner struggle and calmly answered her challenge. "It was the logical thing to do, as Dr. Sorenson would have little to work with."

"Remember what you are and stay in your lane."

"Yes, madam. I exist to serve the senate."

Farah cringed. *He referred to himself in the first person.*

"Do you have further instructions, Consul?" Prell asked.

"Hold the information you have. For now, I will relay it to the senate," Farah said. "We alone will decide the best course of action."

"The detainees will be held as you wish."

"Thank you," Farah said, shaking off a peculiar feeling like the one she experienced with Adario the night of Plant 13's disaster.

It dawned on Farah that Andira's views on the Fordham might be true. Prell spoke outside the collective mind, as an individual, in command of his own conscience. This is Crawford Lear's realm. He must know what is happening.

Farah hailed Karno, "Is the grand architect here yet?"

"He waits in the senate chamber."

"I want to see him now. Bring him to me presently."

"The meeting is about to begin, Consul," Karno started.

"Did you not hear me?" Farah asked. "You are to do as I say. Get Crawford Lear now."

Crawford entered with a simple look on his face. "Whatever you said to that sentinel didn't go over well."

"They're becoming insolent," Farah said, "and it is most disturbing."

"I hadn't noticed."

"Perhaps your head is not in the game."

"We're going there again?"

"The senate will gain access to the hive despite your argument against it," Farah said.

Crawford's eyebrows raised as he locked his eyes on Farah, returning her determined look with confidence. "I'll present my facts and you'll present yours, then we'll see what happens."

"Your conduct is a few rungs short of being flippant."

"I've told you before failures aren't out of the norm."

"Then you have a twisted perception of reality," Farah said, raising her tone. "Do you think violent deaths are ordinary phenomena?"

"As I am not a criminal investigator, I don't have an opinion on the subject."

"The increasing amount of Fordham dysfunction and casualties makes me wonder if the Servers are experiencing errors."

"It's interesting you didn't mention citizen casualties."

"Citizens will suffer far worse if these problems continue."

"They're not machines, Farah," Crawford said. "They have faults, just like you and me."

"You may speak for yourself, architect. I have no faults," Farah said.

Crawford stepped back, analyzing Farah's speech. He reckoned she was afraid of losing control. "If you have your way, the mystery may be solved, provided it is a mystery."

"Yes, and in two minutes, your authority may be finished," Farah said, looking at the clock. "Shall we go see how it all ends?"

"I'm prepared. Are you?" Crawford asked, leading the way to the meeting place.

The senate members filed in shortly after Farah and Crawford's arrival. Crawford rolled his eyes at the assembly, the atmosphere of the coming proceedings. He would not tolerate opposition to his authority and intended to make it clear to everyone. Orin and Andira came up to Crawford together, both eager to speak with him.

"Good morning, Crawford," Andira said. "It's good you could be here."

"I'd rather be elsewhere, but I do as I'm told," Crawford scowled.

"It is good you can take direction," Orin replied.

"Do I have a choice?"

"In this, you do not. I suggest you fix your face before we start."

Andira took Crawford by the arm, guiding him to a seat. "You certainly have a way with pleasantries."

"Did you expect me to be doing cartwheels?"

"No. But fighting them isn't wise either."

"This is a waste of my time and yours."

Karno overheard Crawford's statement and cut his eyes in the architect's direction, Crawford's frustration registering vividly on his features.

Andira glimpsed the change. "You like living dangerously, don't you, Lear?"

"There's no other way to live."

"I hope you're right about the problem," Andira said, settling in her seat. "It would be unfortunate if you're wrong."

Once the senators situated themselves, Orin began the meeting. "Good morning. We are here to discuss the proposal of opening the hive for a survey," he said. "Based upon Dr. Sorenson's report of a possible pathogen among sentinels it is imperative we investigate to determine any impact on The Servers."

"What type of survey do you suggest, Dr. Sorenson?" Hyatt asked.

"A visual feed from the hive should be sufficient," Andira said.

"No one except the Grand Architect and the corps is permitted to look upon the Servers," a junior senator said. "Any deviation from the statute would be a violation of the law."

"Considering the risk to everyone and everything we built, I believe the rule should be waived," Orin said.

"We are asking you to consider this action just once," Farah explained. "It will not become a regular occurrence."

"What would the exam entail?" Castillo asked.

"Dr. Sorenson, please explain the procedure," Farah said.

"My analysis requires a tissue sample. With it, we can determine whether what's affecting the Fordham is affecting The Servers."

"You are suggesting cross-contamination through their neural implants?" Hyatt asked.

"The structure of their brains is a complex design. It's a marvel what Eaton's people achieved in such a short span," Andira said. "I've studied the texts from the inception of the Servers to the creation of the Fordham, but some of the data is corrupted. We're attempting to recover it."

"Do you think you can?" Rivan asked.

"I have the comm center working on it," Andira explained. "In the meantime, I'm using all my available neurological knowledge to decipher the puzzle."

"You are intelligent, doctor," Hyatt said. "You will find the answer."

"Betera Eaton offered the Fordham as the perfect solution."

"You sound as if you distrust her science," Castillo said.

"We accepted what was done and we heralded it as a breakthrough for our purposes, a final solution to our ancestor's former failings," Andira said. "But every perceived perfection has a flaw, and I fear our arrogance will show we were wrong."

"I am still hesitant to open the hive without reason," Rivan said, scowling.

"I can suggest a valid reason," Orin said, peering at Crawford.

Crawford noted the silent accusation and rose to speak. "It's simple, the Servers need replacing. Their age could be why we're having this trouble." Farah was surprised. Crawford had stood opposed to the idea of opening the hive until now.

"What will you do if there is no evidence of harm?" Hyatt asked Andira.

"Until I figure out the true nature of the issue, I suggest we consider increasing the strength of our arsenal and develop new delivery methods."

"What would you suggest for delivery?" Castillo asked.

"Sustained release prescriptions would lessen the risk of a breakthrough."

"Creating a perpetual fog and an end to purging," Crawford said sarcastically.

"Do you have a better suggestion?" Farah asked.

"Purging's supposed to be healthy."

"There is nothing more beneficial than lasting contentment."

Hyatt looked around the table, observing the reactions of his colleagues. "The purge has psychological value, but it may be inadequate," he said solemnly. "Right now, we must abate the disruptions and consider Dr. Sorenson's proposal. Consul Farah, perhaps you could speak with Dr. Novak."

"It will be my pleasure."

"I call a vote on the measure to increase our efforts to sustain elation," Hyatt said.

"All those in favor raise your right hand," Orin instructed. Sixteen acknowledged favor. "All those opposed?" The remaining dissented.

"The motion carries," Farah announced. "Senator Novak will accompany the grand architect and his engineers to the Citadel in the morning."

"We have agreed to the feed, not Senator Novak's presence," Castillo said.

"I will only monitor the engineers, not enter the store," Orin replied.

Hyatt squirmed. "I am not comfortable with this idea."

"It would not hurt to ensure procedures are as they should be," Rivan said.

176

"Here we go again. This is a question of me not doing my job," Crawford said.

"Are you doing your job?"

The senate's voices rose again. This time the opposition was unanimous. "The answer is no to Senator Novak's inspection," Hyatt said.

"I hear your concerns, but perhaps you will reconsider this position in a moment," Farah said. "You all know what transpired in Amanta. What you do not know is that Grand Architect Lear withheld information vital to the situation."

Crawford's glance was contemptuous. Karno stepped to his side offering Joi and he accepted it without reservation.

"What have you to say, madam?" Rivan asked.

Farah swiveled her chair to face Crawford. "Shall I tell them about the saboteur, or will you?"

"There's no proof any of those techs were involved."

"When you gave your summary, you failed to disclose the existence of a technician outside the center after the lockdown," Farah countered.

"I saw no reason to. Engineer Emili cooperated in the effort to identify him," Crawford replied. "Any other investigation into his whereabouts is Prell's responsibility."

"It does not excuse your omission," Farah said. "This, ladies and gentlemen, is precisely why Senator Novak should go to The Citadel with the corps."

"Architect, do you believe the man was a saboteur and that others may follow?" Hyatt asked.

"I don't know. The sentinels need to do their job and figure it out," Crawford said. "Either way, The Servers will continue to function."

"It is commendable you know your task," Castillo said. "For me, there is nothing else."

"I believe you, grand architect. Your lineage and training, coupled with your disciplinary record, is good enough for me," Hyatt said.

"These fiascos started with his term," Orin said. "Is it not strange to you?"

"Coincidences are not truths," Hyatt responded. "We must deal in facts, Senator Novak."

"I am inclined to allow the senator's visit on the condition he does not enter the hive and his memory of the journey is wiped," Rivan said. The senate members nodded their approval.

"So be it," Hyatt said. "Grand Architect Lear, your continued position depends on Dr. Sorenson's analysis and what you do from here on. Do you understand?"

"I do."

"You are a pupil of Betera Eaton, do not disgrace her," Castillo said.

"I honor her as I honor Beta Union."

"There is still the matter of those detained," Farah said. "Everyone was tested, yet none provided information on the unknown tech."

"Then they should be released," Orin said.

"I am concerned that releasing them would send the wrong message to those involved," Farah said. "I think a more permanent remedy should be applied."

Rivan drew a sharp eye at Farah's shocking logic. "What you suggest has not been done since your ancestor's time," he said.

"This is no time for leniency. If there are malcontents, they need to know we are not afraid to deal with them."

"You can't just wipe out people without due cause," Crawford said. "Most of those people are likely innocent."

"The innocent must sometimes be asked to sacrifice," Farah reasoned. "If we do nothing, we show weakness."

"Eliminating those techs isn't necessary. It could make your problems worse."

"It worked well enough against the Rand mutiny," Castillo remarked.

"That was another time," Crawford said, "and we don't know there's really a threat."

"We have much to discover and little time to do it," Hyatt said. "Are the citizens in custody wiped?"

"Yes, they are," Farah answered.

"Then the likelihood of unpleasant memories is minuscule. We will leave it for now. I prefer not to administer further penalties unless necessary."

"Our business on this matter is concluded then," Farah said. "Senator Novak and I will now meet with Commanders Tragnor and Ragas to discuss plans for the Caelum trade."

"Thank you all," Orin said. Dr. Sorenson and the delegates bowed their heads as they departed.

Zelda entered. "There is a communication from Havamir. Another disturbance," she reported.

"You cannot be serious," Orin said. "These repeated incidents are beyond ridiculous at this point."

"A group of citizens argued over the merchandise in a market complex. The sentinels responded in numbers," Zelda reported.

"Is the situation under control?"

"The citizens are in custody, receptors in the area are offline, and eleven of the troops are unresponsive."

"More Fordham for you, Andira," Orin said. "Check every citizen involved, thoroughly."

"There were also several arrests," Zelda said. "Violations against Bracing orders."

Hyatt was stunned. "People refused their pares?"

"Yes. There were also arrests for campaigns promoting monogamy."

"This behavior is heinous," Farah hissed. "Recall Prell and have him deal with it."

"I didn't have the opportunity to examine the bodies from Amanta, but we appear to have a pattern of assaults here," Andira said. "The Cleft, Plant 13, now this."

"We have to contain this, Farah," Hyatt said.

"There is nothing more immediate on my mind than this."

"I'll have the corps get on the receptors immediately," Crawford said. "We leave at hour five, Senator Novak. Please be prompt."

As Crawford walked down the hall towards the exit, he saw Mallet and Odonna going into Orin's office. Crawford nodded to Mallet as they passed while twisting his left wrist in his right hand and flexing his fingers. Mallet recognized the gesture's meaning, its call clear. The inevitable was happening sooner than he hoped. Even with the consequences, it was time to step into the light.

Farah perched on Orin's desk, welcoming Odonna and Mallet. The commanders took up seats in front of her ready to receive their orders.

"I shall come to the point," Farah said. "We are concluding negotiations with Caelum to secure a valuable commodity. I need you and your personnel ready to close the deal."

"What's the cargo?" Mallet asked.

"It is a very special fuel."

"Can you be more specific?"

"All you need know is it is essential for our people."

"So back to my original question," Mallet said, folding his arms and leaning backward. "Is it an animal, mineral, or vegetable?"

"It is a nourishment," Farah returned. Mallet remained curious but silent. A voyage across the sea would fit well with his plans.

"What are we trading?" Odonna asked.

"Energy cells."

"Since when do we hand over that sort of thing?" Mallet asked.

"The Senate has cleared it and you need not concern yourself with the details."

"Classified, huh?"

"Would you like to be excused from this task, Commander Tragnor? I am sure another officer would gladly take your place."

"It won't be necessary."

"Good," Farah said. "As soon as I speak to Losara Idoni, we will commence our trade. You can begin your preparations now."

"The *Azimuth* is scheduled for retrofitting in two weeks," Odonna said. "Your schedule will not be a problem."

"You go next week on the second day."

"Tuesday?" Mallet asked.

The slightest form of the Before Standard language irritated Farah. "Kindly think about your word choice. I am unsure where you learned it, but that archaic language is unsuitable."

Odonna sat on the edge of her chair. "Are we carrying any other personnel?"

"Dr. Novak will go with you to inspect the goods."

"Severn Novak?" Mallet asked, surprised.

"Is there any other?"

"Not that I know of," Mallet said. "I just didn't think we'd need a chemist."

"You are not employed to think about personnel decisions," Farah said.

Mallet's thoughts registered an internal victory. *She's practically securing our exit.*

"Forgive me, Consul, you are absolutely right," he said.

"What of Pleura?" Odonna asked. "They are at odds with Caelum. They might try to intercept us."

"Sister Idoni has assured me they are working through their difficulties, and we have no reason to expect interference."

"What about the Fordham trouble?" Mallet asked. "That could become an issue."

"You are full of questions. I suggest you focus on your assignment."

"I'll do that."

The officers stood up to leave, but Farah asked Mallet to stay. "Your sib was a fine citizen, a profound influence on the success of Plant 13."

"I wouldn't exactly call what happened a success."

Farah skimmed over his comment. "Was she happy in her position?"

"Whenever we spoke, she never complained."

"Still, I am concerned for you."

"For me?"

"Do not let this occasion bring you to an unskillful mental state," Farah said. "Grief is an unnecessary and burdensome emotion. It shows a want of feeling."

Mallet sensed Farah was trying to bait him. "She was a technician, nothing more to me," he said. "If you'll excuse me, I have to get ready for the journey."

"Of course," Farah said, bidding him farewell.

Mallet quickly left the State Building, his feelings for Melee still too close to the surface to engage in a long discussion. The upcoming voyage presented a viable means of escape, but there was one more thing to do. If Mallet intended having Severn by his side, he had to tell his love the truth.

CHAPTER 26

Kemble stood at the door to her father's quarters, ringing the bell several times. When there was no answer, she reasoned Severn was in his lab. Kemble dialed the lab, using a hall comm.

"Greetings, Pilot Novak," Bristol answered.

"Is Dr. Novak in today?"

"He is concluding a focus meeting. Do you have an urgent need?"

"No, it's all right. I'll swing by if he'll be there for a while."

"Dr. Novak has no plans to leave until the data is correlated."

"Thank you," Kemble said, hanging up.

Kemble needed Severn's help. In a desperate move, she lied to Bristol thinking no one else could be as impartial to her plight as her father would. When she reached the lobby, Kemble considered the prior evening and her conversation with Crawford before they drifted into sleep.

"That was different," she had said, staring at the ceiling.

"It's a new experience," Crawford replied, "and one I hope you enjoyed."

"I should think you would know," Kemble said, cozying up to him.

"Why shouldn't it always be like that?" Crawford asked.

"If it was, people might get attached, forget about sharing everything and everyone."

"Belonging to someone doesn't feel so bad," Crawford said, propping himself on his elbow. "But I do understand that on occasion, people can be jealous, afraid, and cruel when they're in love."

"I've always felt empty after being with someone."

"Are you afraid you'll feel that way tomorrow?"

"No, I like this feeling," Kemble whispered. "I honestly don't ever want it to go away."

"That's because it's real," Crawford replied, kissing her cheek."

It's also dangerous, she thought.

Crawford was gone when Kemble woke. In his absence, she smelled the spot where he laid, wondering if Crawford knew she observed his nocturnal patterns while he slept. Crawford was beautiful at rest, peaceful without movement save the rise and fall of his chest while breathing.

The metallic gray streaks weaving throughout his locks were softer than expected, yet unexpected for one so young. She drew a line down his face and brushed his flank, imagining the effect of his physique on other women. Pangs of envy, previously unknown, seized her mind.

Kemble glanced at the Fordham seated at the front desk and looked to the monitors along the entry walls. Each was stationary, collecting no information, their regularity perplexing. She then walked to the sub train station, descending its stairs two at a time, mixing with citizens crowding the platforms.

The pilot felt secure, surrounded by buoyancy though sentinels, standing guard in discreet positions, could catch any violation ensconced in large numbers. They were sharks eager to smell blood in the water, waiting for a feeding frenzy from which prey rarely escaped. Despite the risk to herself, Kemble delved back into the memory of Crawford's stay again.

She recalled crying during the night. Crawford wrapped comforting arms around her, bringing needed relief. They talked honestly about many things and Kemble laughed at his candor, playfully scolding him for his criticism of the engineers under his charge.

Even in those humble moments, Kemble feared the new adventure, worrying it would not persist. The couple's growing relationship was contrary to the established order, and Kemble questioned how Crawford could be the son of Betera Eaton, serve Beta Union, and yet break its most sacred laws.

"It's not a matter of breaking it," Crawford said. "It's about letting things and people exist as they are."

"As they stand is wicked."

"There's nothing wicked about the way I feel for you," Crawford said, kissing her. "What's there to be afraid of?"

"Consul Farah, assessment, your legacy?" Kemble asked. "What would Betera say?"

"She wouldn't say anything," he said, "and I've no fear of The Stretch."

"That's hard to believe."

"If you knew her as I did, you'd understand."

"Understand what?"

"That nothing is as it seems," Crawford whispered, positioning himself above her. "Now, where were we?"

Back in the present, the train pulled forward, collecting passengers. Kemble boarded, grasping a pole for support. She stood for the length of the ride contemplating pieces of Crawford's cryptic speech.

"Nothing is as it seems."

Kemble questioned whether Crawford's actions were honorable or if he deliberately meant to lead her into harm's way. The Fordham in the car stared in her direction. *He's clever,* she theorized. *This is a trap. It can't happen again.*

Bristol busied herself in Severn's lab, shuffling through a tablet and analyzing its data while Severn shifted aimlessly around the space.

"You need a reprieve," Bristol said.

"Hmmm," Severn said over his shoulder. "I can't afford one. The figures aren't going to calculate themselves."

He turned to look at Bristol, thinking he heard a faint laugh. Instead, he found her straight-faced, consumed in work; her hair, and uniform back to their usual style. "You look like yourself today."

"As opposed to any other day?" Bristol asked, her smile fading as Severn laughed.

"I'm sorry. I wasn't mocking you."

"Are you disappointed?"

There it is again, an odd show of self-awareness. "Did you call that in?" Severn asked, pointing to the still dark ceiling monitor.

"No," Bristol answered. "It will be done now."

"It's not like you to forget anything."

"It is busy. The days are challenging." Her account was hardly truthful. Bristol was a battery, endlessly charged.

"You can do it after lunch," Severn suggested. "I can manage on my own for a bit."

"Do you require anything?"

"What are you having?"

186

"Protein?"

"Sounds lovely."

Bristol unlocked the entry and sauntered out, encountering Kemble outside. "Good morning, pilot."

"Bristol," Kemble nodded. "Is Severn still here?"

"Yes. He will be pleased to see you," Bristol said, pausing, her face awash with pink. "You feel great affection for him."

"Come again?"

"It is most clear in you."

"You're mistaking respect for affection."

Bristol gave her a queer smile. "It is you who are mistaken," she said, turning to walk away. "Good day to you, pilot."

Kemble breathed a sigh of relief. Her emotions were obvious, but for some reason she did not understand, Bristol gave her a pass. She rang her father's lab; Severn answered, pulling her inside with a hug.

"Are you all right?" he asked, holding her. "I hadn't heard from you."

"I'm fine," Kemble replied. "It wasn't pleasant, but I'm not dead."

Severn looked at her face and hair. She was changed, albeit not drastically. "I should've been there."

"You couldn't, besides, Crawford Lear took me home."

"I heard," Severn responded. "Why did he do that?"

Kemble approached the island, hoisting herself to its surface, as she had done so many times in childhood. The lab held special memories for her and Severn. It was where she first called him "Far." Severn assumed she meant father. He did not know where she had picked it up, and Agora tried to correct her, to no avail.

"I need to talk to you," Kemble said, casting her gaze to the floor.

"What's wrong?"

"It's not safe to talk here. I'll come to your home."

"You needn't worry. The monitor's out and Bristol's gone for a while."

Kemble broke into tears. "Something's wrong and I don't know how to fix it."

"What is it?"

"I let myself go," she said, wiping her nose on a sleeve. "I really let myself go."

"What do you mean?"

"He's in my head and I can't get him out."

"Who are you talking about?"

"Grand Architect Crawford Lear."

"What's he done to you?"

"I don't know, but I can't get him off my mind," Kemble answered. "I wonder what he's doing, how he feels and what I mean to him."

"Kemble," he said, gripping her wrists. "You can't mean anything to a man like him. You shouldn't want to either. It's dangerous."

"That's not what he said," Kemble breathed. "He said he loves me."

"I can't believe he'd tell you that. He doesn't know what that is," Severn said.

"He thinks he does, and it frightens me how serious he is about it."

Severn was mortified. What she described were the feelings he had about Mallet in the beginning, the depression one could feel before understanding love.

Mallet consumed his mind all the time, but Severn never expected his daughter to falter in this respect. He never meant to tell her about his involvement, but now, she needed the truth.

"If what you're saying is true, then I know what you're talking about. I've been through it."

"With Mallet?"

"Yes, and I know you don't like him, but he's everything to me next to you and Breen."

"Why didn't you fight it?"

"I tried, but the more I did, the more it grew and after a while, I didn't want to fight it anymore," Severn said, confirming his forbidden feelings for Mallet.

"Do you know what could happen to you?" she asked. "I know—I've seen it. I've been punished before."

"I don't care," Severn said with a passion in his voice Kemble had never heard before. "Mallet is everything to me and I won't be parted from him."

"I'm frightened for you, and you should be too," Kemble countered.

"Your concern for me isn't sanctioned either."

"It is if it means helping you to be righteous."

"Is that all it is?" Severn asked. "I know you love me. That's an emotional attachment and according to everything we live by, it's wrong too. How do you reconcile it?"

Kemble shook her head. "I don't know. You've been here all my life. I can't help but care for you."

"Nothing's going to happen to me," Severn said, cradling her in his arms. "I promise."

"If you don't get away from Mallet something will happen," Kemble said. "He'll put you in your grave and he won't care. He probably doesn't care Melee died."

Severn backed up. "Mallet didn't tell me she passed," he said, stunned at the revelation.

"What happened to her?"

"They wanted to scan her after the plant fire, but she killed herself."

"He never said anything," Severn murmured in disbelief.

"I told you, he doesn't care. You have to stop what you're doing and so do I," Kemble pleaded. "What I'm feeling is criminal and what you're doing is criminal."

"Listen to me, right or wrong I love him, and he loves me. I don't know why he didn't tell me about Melee, but it doesn't mean he's cold," Severn said. "I know what it feels like to have someone taken away from you. My mother left me."

"She was supposed to. You should have left me."

"It shouldn't be that way. Everything you and I have, I wanted with her."

"I want a suppressor," Kemble said. "I have to forget these feelings."

"You won't get it from me," Severn replied. "I won't risk losing you."

"You'd rather I suffer as you do? Hide in the shadows praying they don't catch me."

"Did you profess anything?"

"Not out loud."

"Unless you act on it or indulge your feelings publicly, you're safe from being tagged." Kemble contemplated for a minute. Crawford was astute, almost to the point of clairvoyance.

"What about Crawford? I don't see how he can't know."

"The sentinels aren't after you right now."

"Maybe he's waiting for something," Kemble mused. "He seemed so honest, not manipulative."

"Manipulation usually precedes deceit," Severn said. "I'm not sure that's what he intends, but he got to you."

"I've never felt right around him. Something draws me to him," she said. "He speaks as if there's a future beyond what we know."

Severn recognized the pattern. His association started equivalently. "I want you to stay away from him even if he calls for you," he said, holding his daughter close, resolved in the knowledge no one would take his child away.

Mallet entered the lab, startling them. "I'm sorry," he said. "The door was unlocked."

"It's okay," Severn said.

"Are you all right, Kemble?"

"I'm fine," she said, hopping down from the island. "I need to go home and rest."

"I'll see you later," Severn said. "Remember what I said."

"I will," Kemble replied, departing.

"What's going on with her?" Mallet asked.

"Nothing she can't handle."

Mallet clapped Severn's shoulders. "You won't believe what I have to tell you."

"What now?"

"We're getting out of here next week."

"Where are we going?"

"Farah's put me in charge of the Caelum trade," Mallet said in excitement. "We're going to the Green on the second day."

"What are you trading?"

"Some energy cells."

Severn's face twisted in disbelief. "We've never traded energy. Why she's doing it now?" he asked.

"Who cares about the terms," Mallet scoffed. "What's important is I'm not coming back, even with Ragas on my heels."

"The *Azimuth*'s escorting?"

"She is, but I can outrun her," Mallet said with pride.

"She can outgun you," Severn said.

"Odonna's never fired cannon a day in her life."

"Won't sentinels be there?"

"I'm not worried about them, either."

Severn believed the plan was reckless. "This isn't a suitable time for an escape," he said. "For one, you don't have much time and two, anything could go wrong."

"Our escape, remember?"

"I never said I'd go with you."

Mallet looked hurt. "You're not interested in being together?"

"I have other things to consider."

"Like what?"

"My children."

"Kemble's a big girl, she likes it here," Mallet said.

"You really are thinking of yourself," Severn said, standing back. "You have no idea what's going on."

Mallet reached out for Severn, but the chemist pulled away. "I care about you and everything you care about."

"Then act like it."

"Look, I don't want to argue. The last thing either of us needs is to court trouble."

"Feel free to get angry all you want," Severn said, gesturing to the downed monitor.

"When did it stop working?"

"It doesn't matter. You're asking me to run away with you, but you never told me about Melee."

Mallet bit his lip. "I couldn't. I figured you had enough problems of your own."

"Really?" Severn said.

"Severn, there are things you don't know," Mallet said. "You can't be involved in everything."

"Everything about you involves me. I could've helped you deal with losing her."

"We spend a lot of time together and we're careful, but I couldn't risk being around you at the time."

"So, who did you turn to?"

192

"It doesn't matter. The important thing is that I dealt with it."

"I doubt you did it alone."

"I went to see Dinaria."

"Of all the people in the habitat," Severn said. "You turned to her?"

"Nothing happened."

Severn rolled his eyes. "I'm sure she tried to make you feel better."

"She failed," Mallet responded. "In fact, it got ugly all the way there and back."

"Oh, so that means you fought her off?"

"Listen to me. Things are happening, and people aren't who you think they are," Mallet said.

Severn heard the seriousness in Mallet's voice. "What things and what people?"

"This place is going to fall apart. This way is collapsing in on itself," Mallet said. "I've tried to stay out of it, but I made a pact."

"What's going to happen?"

"We're going to leave here together."

"I can't leave. Kemble's been emotionally compromised," Severn said. "She may very well lose all control."

"Crawford's involved, isn't he?" Mallet asked.

"How do you know that?"

"It seemed obvious. Must've been some ride home."

"It's not funny," Severn said. "She's in danger and I think Breen is involved in subversive activities. I can't leave right now."

"I don't know about Breen, but Kemble will be okay."

"I don't trust the grand architect."

"I've known him since we were kids and I told you he wouldn't deliberately hurt anyone," Mallet said.

"I don't care how long you've known him, he's a loyalist," Severn said.

"Have you heard a word I've said?" Mallet asked. "You don't have to worry about Crawford. He's not the enemy, Beta Union is."

"What you're saying is treason."

Mallet took a deep breath and looked into Severn's eyes. "It's more than that. I'm with the revolution."

"You can't be serious," Severn hissed.

"It's true and I know I can trust you because I sense it."

"You're out of your skull if you think you can get away with it."

"What they've done to you, to me, and everyone is wrong."

"We shouldn't pay for the miscalculations of the past," Mallet said. "I was raised to understand that and so was Crawford."

"Are you saying he's part of it?"

"This can't be real," Severn breathed.

"Believe it."

"If the Senate finds out, you'll die."

"Unless one of our operatives is caught or you tell," Mallet said, "they'll never know."

"This is crazy. You really think you can topple the government," Severn said, downtrodden. "Who's going to pick up the pieces if you succeed, and how many are going to die if you don't?"

"What does it matter?"

"Are you some mythical martyr surrounded by deranged disciples?"

"That's a low blow, especially for you," Mallet responded.

"I'm not unversed. You're racking up the crimes." Severn said hotly. "The next thing you know, you'll think you can part the sea or raise the dead."

"I'm counting on living with you for the rest of our lives."

"If this fails, the rest of our lives will be short," Severn said.

"I know we can slip away next week," Mallet said. "Whoever is on my boat is getting out. That means you, me, and Kemble if she decides to go."

"And Crawford?"

"I don't know what he'll decide. He wants to see this through."

"This is going to be a disaster," Severn sighed.

"Don't think about it now," Mallet said kissing Severn, "not while I'm thinking about you."

CHAPTER 27

Crawford, his engineers, and Orin arrived at The Citadel on schedule. Though uncomfortable with the senatorial presence, Crawford had no choice but to comply with the edict given. The Delphia fire precipitated this test of the architect's proficiency and his fate depended on the continued health of The Servers.

The architect bought the revolution time with his successful manipulation of the facts, and the gradual actions he and his co-conspirators executed were taking hold, the method of their deception too complex for the senate to fathom. Crawford remained oblivious to the identities of every participant, but he remained confident of their mutual goal and tactics.

"This is it," Crawford said to Orin as they stood outside the final post. "You will stay here."

Orin unfolded a leaf, flexing the clear material laced with metallic veins, prepping the device for synchronization with Crawford's lens. He drew several shapes across the surface, opening a channel to the senate, their anxious faces filling the screen, ready to view the inspection. Orin watched Crawford fit his visual receiver. Once inside, he would activate its optics.

"Ready?" Crawford asked, addressing the audience.

"We are standing by," Hyatt answered.

Crawford inhaled and exhaled deeply while walking to the door, the scan flooding him, opening the entrance, sheathing him in darkness.

"This is the moment of truth," Farah said to her colleagues. "I anticipate all is well."

Crawford stood in the hive, summoning the lights, revealing numerous charred modules oozing discolored fluid. He switched on the visual and panned the room, the senate's reaction one of mutual distress.

Crawford heard a flood of gasps from the spectators. "The impairment is very extensive," he said.

"This cannot be," Farah mumbled.

"It is, and it's getting worse," Crawford responded.

"How can this be happening?" Orin asked. "How many are affected?"

Crawford stepped to the podium. "I don't know yet. I'll pull the stats," he said, retrieving the information from the panel before speaking instructions into the device. "Initiate sterile shield, module ninety-one, row L."

"Well?"

"Fluid amounts are rising, the rate of deterioration increasing across the board," Crawford said, jumping back on the mat. "They're drowning in it and more than a third of them are affected."

"This is a disaster," Orin said.

"Tell me about it. I'm going to retrieve the sample now."

The pad veered off to the right, settling in front of a patch of decrepit receptacles. Crawford moved to the designated unit while slipping his hands into a pair of gloves, ready to perform delicate surgery.

After verifying the stability of the sterile field, Crawford drew out a hollow green rod from a kit on his belt and placed it on the module. Next, he slid a heated fiber strand through the opening, collecting the tissue. Holding the fiber within the rod, Crawford detached it, capped the device, and put it in a sleeve.

"Do you think it is a pathogen?" Farah asked.

"I'm not a biologist," Crawford said, floating back to the podium to finish the analysis. "I wouldn't know what to look for."

"What does the report say?"

"The temperature is fluctuating, but I can compensate for it."

"What about nourishment?" Hyatt asked.

"They're not starving if that's what you're asking." Orin chimed in. "We need a healthy sample as well."

"I'll have to take one offline," Crawford answered.

"Do it, then," Farah said. "One sacrifice may assist us in containing this thing."

"As you wish," Crawford said, deactivating a cell and repeating his steps, collecting and storing the tissue.

"Take the samples to Dr. Sorenson at once," Farah said.

"How crippled will we be if you take the ailing modules offline?" Hyatt asked.

"It's hard to say. There'll be some delays in transport and computing, but we can maintain most of the infrastructure ourselves," Crawford replied. "It's the Fordham you have to worry about."

"They are our concern," Farah said. "Shut down the damaged units."

"Yes, madam," Crawford said, turning off the camera. He collected the final sample and stepped back to the display, his fingers lingering over the controls.

"Grand Architect?" Orin's voice inquired. "Is it done?"

"It's done," Crawford said, turning back to the devastation, finding himself consumed by snowy orbs, reflecting his image with every piercing glare.

"What do you want?" he asked the frustrating images.

There was no answer. The eyes swelled, gaping with distress before melting back into the shadows of their casings. Crawford shook his head, Mallet's words plaguing him. Whatever the entities desired, Crawford assumed their motivation was strong, their entreaty tied to his destiny.

Farah hastened to meet Severn in his lab with an idea, fostered by Andira's suggestion, the validity of the brainstorm requiring a discussion with the chemist. He would soon know if the mucus was strong enough to quell the rising disturbances.

Severn sat in his office looking over the latest medication notes from Dr. Sorenson while eating his lunch. Her findings baffled him. Citizen alleviation levels were stable, but control was fleeting. Though the usual course required an increase in dosages and strengths of meds, he abhorred the practice, fearing it would do more harm than good.

When the lab door buzzed, he thought Kemble had returned. He rose from his seat to answer, but Bristol came into the office, revealing the guest's identity.

"Consul Farah is here to see you, Dr. Novak."

"Thank you, Bristol."

Farah perused the lab, examining the contents of several cabinets. She reached in a compartment, took out a flask containing lilac liquid, uncorked it, and held the item to her nose.

"It has no scent," she said.

"It's added later," Severn replied.

"I need to speak with you alone," Farah said, replacing the item and looking toward Bristol with a cautious glance. "Completely alone."

Severn dispatched Bristol to the office. "What can I do for you, Consul?"

Farah moved around a table, gliding her fingernails across its immaculate plane, her dress swirling as she slunk closer to him. "We are preparing to send envoys to collect secretions from Caelum's horned mollusks. I need you to join them."

"You're interested in its psychotropic properties?"

"It can help us create new alleviators, yes?"

"It's suitable for ingestion, but that's probably not the most effective way to use it," Severn answered. "I'll have to run tests to find the best delivery method."

"How long will it take?"

"I'm not sure. There might be contraindications with current meds, which could pose a problem," Severn said. "Depending on the severity, it might be useless for your purpose."

"Then you need to go and find out."

"I'll still need to bring samples back to the lab for assessment."

"Our situation is critical, so you will have to make a field test," Farah countered.

"You want someone to swallow it on the spot?"

"A test will tell us if it is the real thing and you could gauge any immediate side effects."

"Why wouldn't it be real?"

"You should always be sure you get what you pay for," Farah said.

"Well, even if it does have the properties you want, who's to say what long-term effect it has," Severn said. He swallowed

200

hard against his next statement. "Until we know, we should increase the strength of what we already have."

"If citizens are developing a tolerance for the routine, it may not be enough. Resistance could develop."

Severn was aware desensitization could occur and realized it could help Mallet's cause. He was averse to going through with the mission but could not afford to draw attention to himself. "Well I can't argue with that," he said.

"You can always work on modifying its effects."

"I see your point. I'll do everything I can to assist."

"Wonderful," Farah said. "You will also agree to another facet of the operation."

"What facet is that?"

"I think we should have a foolproof mode of delivery, one to anticipate citizen needs."

"I'm not sure I follow you."

"I propose we help citizens in keeping with their regimes," Farah said, easing behind Severn.

"They're intelligent enough to know when and how to use their meds," Severn said, spinning around. "Very few would risk the penalty."

"We can reduce corrections by giving them what they need before they know they need it."

Severn finally caught Farah's train of reasoning. She advocated the use of force. "What exactly are you proposing, Consul?" he asked.

"Food and water are life, so is contentment. They bring health to everyone."

"You want to introduce euphorics into the nutritional supply?"

"It would be a constant spring of stability," Farah cooed. "No one need ever purge again."

"You're proposing to take away the last vestige of freedom allotted to us," Severn said, his jaw-dropping in disbelief. "The founders never meant to eradicate our humanity."

"Have you forgotten our history, how and why this country was founded?"

"I haven't forgotten."

"Then you also remember that thanks to the founder's discoveries, people have privileged lives, true liberty, and happiness," Farah said. "They are free from societal constrictions and ethical struggles. This land is balanced, united under one language, one identity, and one purpose?"

"It's not balanced. It's ruled through fascism and indifference."

"Those are not the words of a dedicated citizen, but rather the ramblings of confederates," Farah said, her voice threatening. "Are you a killjoy? Do you identify with deviants?"

"I'm not untrue," Severn said. "I merely acknowledge a different point of view exists."

"What we have established is the only view that matters and your responsibility is to protect it."

"I still think what you're asking me to do is severe."

"It is ultimately for the senate to decide, but I believe they will agree with me," Farah said, determination in her eyes.

"Perhaps they will indeed."

"I expect your loyalty to continue, Dr. Novak," Farah responded, walking to the exit. "Anything less will not be tolerated."

Severn's conscience raced upon her withdrawal. Though she required a majority vote on any measure, Farah could be quite persuasive in an argument. Severn shivered as he mulled over her speech, pondering what she might do if opposed. Farah's parting words were not a threat. They were, in fact, an assurance that she possessed the authority to act upon.

CHAPTER 28

Breen's return to Unity City was met with delight from his daughter Somiel. As soon as his satchel hit the floor, she eagerly ran up to him.

"Did you bring me anything?" Somiel asked, her hands extended in anticipation.

"I did," Breen said, handing over an intricate multi-dimensional puzzle. "Now you can tease your brain all you want and let mine rest." Happy with the gift, Somiel ran to the den, eager to solve the device.

Tovah waltzed into the foyer, carrying Lerner on her hip. "You're back," she said, greeting Breen.

"It took longer than I expected," Breen replied, tickling his son.

"He's been fussing all day, waiting for you."

Breen kissed Tovah on the cheek. "It's good to be home."

"What was that for?" she asked, mystified.

"It seemed harmless."

"I don't think you should make it a habit. What will Somiel and Lerner think?"

Breen was too tired to debate moral issues with his partner. "I'm starved. What's to eat?"

"Quynn and I were hoping you'd like to go out with us for dinner."

"Who's going to watch Somiel and Lerner?"

"I'm sure I can ask the neighbors."

"You go ahead, I'm tired. I'll stay with them."

"You're not fond of Quynn, are you?"

"I don't have a problem with her," Breen yawned. "I'm just not feeling up to it."

"We really wanted to take you out," Tovah said, bouncing Lerner in her arms. "You've been in a mood for weeks and Deluxe is a fun place where you can forget all the stress the grand architect heaps on you."

"That place is too crazy for me. I'd bore you both."

"We can fix that with a little Joi."

"Thank you, but I don't want any stimulants."

A chime rang; Tovah skipped to the door. Breen hoped it was not Quynn and felt a sense of relief when he spotted Severn. "I wasn't sure you'd be home," the chemist said, stepping over the threshold.

"I just got in," Breen said, rising from the couch to clasp Severn's hand.

"I won't stay long. I just wanted to welcome you back."

"I'm going to put Lerner down now," Tovah said.

Severn smiled at the child then sat down with his son. "Amanta must've taken a lot out of you. Did everything go well?"

"It was a mess, but thankfully the GA didn't have to come."

"I would have figured Crawford Lear would see to that situation personally."

Breen laughed. "You and everyone else. He sent his terror of a mutt instead. I just dropped the beast off before I came in."

Severn was not laughing, thinking instead about his talk with Mallet and the message he heard. He wanted to broach both subjects, but Tovah was upstairs and the layout of the quarters kept her within earshot.

"When are you returning to Pump 5?" he asked.

"I have to go back tomorrow since you know there's really no such thing as time off."

"I wouldn't know anything about how Crawford Lear runs his business."

Breen noticed stress in Severn's voice. It was unlike his father to allow anything to bother him. "Are you feeling all right, Severn?" he asked.

"There's something we need to discuss," Severn said looking around, anticipating Tovah's intrusion, disappointed when she came downstairs on cue.

Severn always found her beautiful, but tonight she outdid herself. Her dress, with its short hem, was like spun gold, and iridescent crystals, twinkling in her hair, matched appliqués on thigh-high boots.

"You look incredible," Breen said, ogling her outfit.

"Incredible enough for you to come along?" she asked.

"Unfortunately, no."

"Okay. Somiel and Lerner are asleep. Don't wait up," she said, turning around to address Severn. "How did your research go, Dr. Novak?"

"My research?" Severn asked clumsily.

"The study we talked about at the café. Did you come to any conclusions?"

Severn was visibly uncomfortable, having difficulty finding words. "Umm...the results were inconclusive."

"What a shame. I had hoped you'd reveal something more significant," Tovah said, prancing out. "Good eve to you both."

"She's something else," Severn said, staring after her.

"Tell me about it. What research were you doing?"

Severn bit his lip. There was no painless way to tell Breen what he and Bristol uncovered in the lab. "Breen, I need to know what you are involved in."

"What I'm involved in?"

Severn stood up, wringing his hands. "Tovah brought me a message she found here. She thinks you're hiding something."

"I don't have anything to hide," Breen asked casually, getting up and entering the kitchen. "I'm as open as the next man." He proceeded to wash an apple and offered it to Severn, which the latter declined. Severn was more interested in unraveling the mystery behind the recording.

"Apparently, you're not as open as you'd like me to think," Severn said. "I want to know what you're doing and why you'd put yourself in danger for it."

"I don't hide things," Breen said, acid coloring his tone. "Besides, Tovah couldn't have found anything in here. She can hardly keep track of Lerner's toys."

"Don't lie to me. Bristol and I heard a recording with your voice on it," Severn said. "At first, I worried you were involved in some smuggling operation, but that wouldn't make sense."

"The truth probably wouldn't make sense either," Breen whispered, realizing he could no longer hide the truth from Severn, "and if I tell you, you may never see me again."

"Does this have something to do with those incidents?" Severn asked. "Please do tell me. I can't sit back watching you and Kemble make mistakes that'll cost you everything."

"The only thing I'd regret losing is you and my descendants," Breen said.

"That won't happen if you tell me the truth and let me help you."

Breen took a deep breath. "The transmission you heard came from a resistance group. They need engineering information to help their cause."

"I've heard rumors about a resistance, but I never would have believed they were actually a force here."

"They are a formidable group. People in every corner of the habitat are mobilizing."

"What do think you'll accomplish other than destruction and death?" Severn asked.

"We're fighting for everyone's freedom. And that means yours too."

Severn's face fell. Mallet was right all along. The crusade was widespread, and it pained Severn to think of himself as part of the problem. "If the resistance is so large, why do you have to do this? You don't owe anyone anything."

"I know it's against everything you taught us," Breen said, "but I've seen and felt what it's like to be in control of your own emotions. I think we're missing something that makes us human."

"You think feeling negativity makes you more human?"

"You should know the answer to that, Severn. Without it, we're not whole beings," Breen explained. "We can't judge what's truly moral and good for ourselves."

"People don't need to be violent and insecure to know right from wrong?"

"This place was founded through violence," Breen said. "We stole this world to be free from destructive forces, but it's the same world. Beta Union controls us through fear."

"And you intend to turn people into savages."

"They can't fight if they don't get angry."

"You're asking people to become instruments of hate."

"That's not what we're advocating. We want our own identities, the ability to make choices and govern together. We want the opportunity to love one another."

"You're a citizen," Severn replied. "That's your identity."

"It's not enough. There's more to me," Breen said. "I want to think for myself, practice what I believe, cry if I want to and choose my mate without fearing The Stretch."

"How in the name of all the Union did you come to this?"

"I watched them take a man away from his family unit when I was an apprentice in Delphia. He was speaking against the cruelty of The Stretch."

"That's the punishment for such an infraction," Severn said, his voice bordering on sadness. "Everyone knows that."

"Yes, but some people tried to help him," Breen said. "They acted strange, as if they actually cared."

"People don't sympathize with criminals."

"No, they're not supposed to, but these people did and so did I," Breen said. "Don't you see? We should be connected instead of masking what we feel."

"That's what caused the trouble in the first place," Severn said. "Everyone did as they pleased and were different. We're all on the same page now."

"Do you really believe that?"

Severn paused. He had never believed it. "No," he said, solemnly. "I spend every day helping people to escape themselves, and I'm guilty of keeping them in bondage."

"It's not your fault."

"I shouldn't have feelings for you or Kemble. I shouldn't think of you as my responsibility," Severn said, "but I can't help but love you as part of me."

"Then you understand why I'm doing this?"

"It doesn't matter if I do or not. You should know that Bristol heard the message, though I don't think she'll say anything."

"I'm not sure I trust that."

"Something in me says not. Her behavior's been peculiar, off in some way," Severn said. "The other day she didn't call in the maintenance on my monitor. It's her duty to ensure my emotional well-being."

"If she's malfunctioning, it could be to my advantage."

"What if the grand architect finds out?"

"He's too busy taking care of all the problems in the habitat to notice," Breen answered. "I don't want you to worry. You haven't done anything to get yourself tagged."

"I tried to raise you the best I could,' Severn said. "You wouldn't be in this position if I hadn't failed."

"You did everything you were supposed to do."

"It doesn't mean I'm not frightened for you and Kemble's really in danger," Severn said. "I don't care what Mallet says."

"What kind of danger and what's Commander Tragnor got to do with it?"

"She's gotten herself emotionally entangled with someone I don't trust. Mallet said I shouldn't be concerned, but I don't believe the—"

Breen's comm buzzed. He fished in his satchel, examining the call signal. It was an encrypted transmission. "I have to take this."

"Go ahead. I should be getting home anyway."

"I'll catch with up with you later," Breen said, walking into another room.

Severn left his son's quarters feeling confused. *What if Mallet is wrong?* He had faith in his partner, but Mallet's passion for change could have blinded him to Crawford's true motivation.

If Severn confronted Crawford, he risked exposing his children, himself, and Mallet. His next move needed great consideration, as there was no way to extricate himself from his work before Mallet and he departed Beta Union.

The chemist was determined that once they were free from the punishing grip of Beta Union, Farah would never use his knowledge for such evil again. Until such time came, he resolved to stay under the radar and out of the grand architect's way.

CHAPTER 29

Breen's informant instructed him to wait for the gap before delivering the codes. While sitting in his parlor, Breen could not help but contemplate the risks associated with his assignment. He gazed through the window, appalled now by the sedate, harmonious city and its blithely ignorant citizens.

I'd be more secure if I knew where our orders were coming from.

Kemble visited him earlier, back to her old self, hyped up on drugs. His sister neglected to bring up anything Severn discussed the evening before last, which led Breen to the conclusion that she was not ready to confide in him.

They were usually open with each other, rather friendly in a non-familial way. He helped her sort out worries and stay on track, just as any other citizen would, but now things were different. Breen wished Kemble would join him in renouncing Beta Union's farcical nature.

He knew it was too soon to pry into her heart and discover whether she was open to committing herself to an uprising.

Joining the movement would mean going against everything she held sacred.

Flushed with frustration, Breen returned to the immediate problem, having to find a viable excuse for being present at Pump 5 during the gap. He was anxious when he called Narlin to ascertain Crawford's whereabouts.

"He's not in today," Narlin said, "and he didn't say where he'd be."

"Since when is he not working?" Breen asked.

"I don't keep tabs on him, Breen. It's the other way around. We're busy here bundling fuel cells for the *Meridian* to take to the Green."

"Who's the duty supervisor?"

"I am unless you want to take over," Narlin laughed.

"That's all right; I'd rather take the gap off and leave the heavy lifting to you."

"Well, I'm sure Crawford will have some instructions before he leaves for Osler."

"Is he going there for an inspection?"

"No, it's the end of the term, time to see how many fourth years pass though."

Breen remembered the end-term experience with all its rigorous assessments where apprentices gathered at the Osler Institute of Technology for field and academic tests in their chosen concentration.

The trials were split into two parts. Each segment lasted six hours with results delivered on the same day. They were the culmination of four years of study under master engineers. The academic portion was administered first, followed by the practical skills test. If you failed the academic portion, you failed completely.

"If it's half as challenging as when we did it, most of them will crash and burn."

"That's true. They'll need all the luck they can get," Narlin said. "We'll be busy while the grand architect's gone. Things have gone buggy around here."

"What do you mean by buggy?"

"Don't worry. It's nothing we can handle. Just a lot of service disruptions lately. Comm units, brownouts, train delays," Narlin said, rattling off a list. "There was even a smashup on the commuter to Yardell. No one was seriously hurt, but Fordham had trouble with the crowd."

"I suppose that meant detentions?"

"It was quite a scene, from what I heard. The important thing is that it's over."

"I didn't hear of it."

"It seems they hushed everything up as soon as it happened. Even I wouldn't have known if it weren't for Engineer Dillard."

"Well, it's best to move on from it and not gossip," Breen said. "I think I forgot to cite something in my notes on the events in Jersa. I'll be coming in to look them over."

"I can pull your report and run through it with you right now," Narlin said.

"That's not necessary. Any updates to the file need my signature so I have to stop by anyway."

"Okay, I'll be here."

Now that Narlin expected him, Breen contemplated how he would bypass the facility's security system. Even without swiping his badge, a log of his visit existed. He shrugged it off, convinced he could come up with something if questioned. What concerned him the most was accessing the files to retrieve the codes from within Crawford's computer.

The engineer once saw Crawford open the application attached to the security matrix, but unfortunately, he did not pay close attention to the passkey. Crawford changed it frequently, yet that did not mean that a hint to its identity would not materialize within the space.

Breen stuffed an inhaler from Tovah's vanity into a pocket and preceded to the door.

"Where are you going?" Tovah asked, coming downstairs.

"Out for a walk," he said, his pulse quickening at the sight of her sensuous body in a revealing nightdress. "I'll be back soon."

Tovah came over to him, stroking his uniform. "You're dressed for work."

"It was the first thing I grabbed out of the closet."

She stepped around him, caressing his buttocks. "This is why you're never in the mood for fun," she said. "You're always working, even when you aren't on the clock."

"You can blame the grand architect for that."

"If you asked for a transfer, you could spend more time doing what you should be doing," Tovah teased, lacing her fingers around his neck. With hot breath, she ran her tongue along his cheek and up to his ear.

"When I get back, we can do anything you want."

"I want to do it now," she said, forcefully kissing him.

Tovah ground her pelvis against the engineer's groin, attempting to entice him to action. Breen felt himself caving. An aching fire roused his primal senses, but the sound of footsteps rescued him from Tovah's clutches.

"Is this where the party is?" Quynn said, strolling towards them.

Tovah greeted her with a kiss. "Are Somiel and Lerner asleep?" she asked.

"Like stones," Quynn answered, fondling the swell of Tovah's breasts.

Breen took his chance to get away from the lascivious women. "Why don't you two keep everything cozy for me?"

"You're off to work?" Quynn asked. Tovah was busy dragging her nails across Quynn's stomach, too excited about impending passion with Quynn to pay attention to Breen.

"No, just out for a walk," he reaffirmed, looking down at his uniform. "I just threw it on, a force of habit."

"Well, hurry back," Quynn said, winking. "It'll be even more exciting with you here."

Breen smiled, starting once again for the door. He looked back, catching a glimpse of the women sinking to the couch, after which he left in a hurry.

Considering the traffic delays, Breen took his hover to Pump 5. Trepidation coursed through his brain, making the ride feel longer than usual. When he arrived, he parked the vehicle and sat for a minute. Two Fordham were on the premises, standing close to the entrance.

Feeling the need for a mild dose of sedation, Breen put his mouth over the inhaler, dispensed a puff of mist, and held his breath while quietly running over his course of action. He then stepped out of the vehicle and approached the entry.

Adario stepped forward, blocking his way. "Why are you here, Engineer Novak? You are not on the duty roster today."

"No, but I need to correct something for the grand architect before his visit to Osler," Breen said.

Adario looked at his companion Garnette. They were skeptical but sensed composure within the engineer. "Grand Architect Lear no doubt appreciates your diligence," Adario returned.

"He depends on it."

"Then you should get to work."

"Thank you," Breen said, reaching for the door. "Silly me, I forgot my badge. I better run back and get it."

"There is no need," Garnette said, swiping a black box next to the door. "Your attendance is noted."

Breen passed through the archway, navigating the halls toward Crawford's office, fortunate the complex was nearly deserted, engineers out on calls and Narlin nowhere in sight. He assumed the junior engineer was in his section, a floor below, yet he still approached Crawford's office with caution.

"Engineer Novak," a voice called out.

Breen abruptly reversed course. "Zelda, what are you doing here?"

"Consul Farah called for the grand architect," she said, "but he is not here. Do you know where he is?"

"I have no idea. I'm just dropping off some scans for him."

Zelda looked to his empty hands. "You seem to have forgotten them along the way."

"Good grief, I left them in the hover," Breen said, thumping his head.

"No doubt the task is important. Be sure you complete it today," Zelda said, moving down the corridor.

Breen sighed with relief. With Zelda gone, he surveyed the lock on Crawford's door, its screening mechanism requiring the architect's fingerprints for access. Breen searched around the door seals, looking for a bypass to its defenses. When he accidentally touched the pad, the door slid open.

That's not like him to leave it unlocked when's he's not here.

Breen decided not to meditate on the irregularity. He went inside, closed the door, and scrambled to Crawford's desk to boot the computer. The display was like his, except for some cryptic symbols cluttering the desktop that he did not recognize.

Just as Breen expected, a pass prompt appeared on the screen. Breen had three chances to decipher the code and enter the database before the program shut down, registering an intrusion. He tried to think of something obscure, but possibly memorable to Crawford.

"What would he put in here?" he asked aloud, sucking his teeth.

Breen ran through several words and combinations in his mind, all of them seemed too obvious. He then went about examining Crawford's office, searching for a sign, careful not to disturb any items. His mind wandered back to the door, wondering if someone had already breached the interior. A chill ran through him as he shook his head. This was not the time to allow fear to envelop him.

Two new choices sprung to his mind. He could go through with the informant's request or walk out. Breen chose to continue his quest and typed some characters on the screen. The display registered an incorrect response.

With only two chances left, Breen opened Crawford's desk drawers again, rifling for clues. In the top compartment, he noticed something out of place, a shiny chain he recognized as belonging to Kemble.

"What's he doing with this?" he wondered aloud, fingers hovering over the display. "There's no way he'd make it that easy."

He keyed in his sister's name and met with another incorrect answer.

"So, it's not straightforward," he said, toying with the chain. "Kem's a pilot."

Breen tapped out the word PILOT, unlocking the computer. He searched the files within the operations folder, copying codes to a storage device, then logged off, powering down the apparatus. He left the building quickly, seeking the security of his hover. After waving to Adario and Garnette, he made a U-turn and proceeded to his next destination.

"That's it," Breen huffed. "I've done my part."

CHAPTER 30

Mallet persuaded Crawford to meet him in the marketplace, arranging for them to run into each other casually in the public locale, thus avoiding the suspicion of a secret encounter. When he arrived at the designated area, Crawford stood by a melon stand. Thalo guarded the architect who scanned the parade of people blithely unaware of their shackled lives and the Fordham who tightened their chains daily.

Mallet inspected the scene carefully, preparing to intercept Crawford, but before he could make a move, a petite, pretty woman pranced up to Crawford, taking him by the arm.

"Greetings, grand architect," she said. "I think I have something to interest you."

Though they never met before, Crawford felt a kinship with the woman. "Lead on," he said, marshaling Thalo to follow.

"I'd like to show you some tracts on emerging technologies or maybe you'd prefer ethics," she said, leading Crawford to a kiosk, drawing his attention to a small screen. "I think you'll find these texts on proper citizenship amusing."

"I'm sure I will," Crawford said, smiling.

"Do let me know if you require anything else," she said, walking back through the market. Crawford followed her movements before returning his attention to the screen. The article, titled, "Before Standard: Evils of the Past", focused on the eradication of pre-Standard speech and the use of the Gregorian calendar. A highlighted passage caught Crawford's eye. He skimmed the words, mouthing them under his breath.

"Tuesday: a vulgar label for the second day symbolizing violence and bloodshed through its association with a mythical deity of war. In keeping with our shared vision of benevolence, it was purged from public and private discourse."

Crawford searched the crowd, looking for the woman. She was no longer in sight. He turned back to the passage, studying the manuscript again. It occurred to him the web of insurgents was not as disorganized as it appeared, and though he never heard or saw a leader among them, someone behind a veiled curtain stood as commander-in-chief, coordinating the battle.

It must be a message, he mused. *But how could she know my purpose? No one is supposed to know that.*

Mallet wove through the market, stopping a few paces behind Crawford. Crawford's favorite companion, Thalo, who barked at his arrival, reared up on his hind legs for petting when he noticed Mallet's presence.

"Down, boy," Mallet said, ruffling Thalo's fur. "I never thought I'd run into the grand architect at the market."

"I was just on my way out," Crawford said. "I'll walk with you a bit and we can catch up on things."

"Were you reading anything interesting?" Mallet asked, keeping an eye on the Fordham, as they headed toward the square.

"I happened on an article about the ancient calendar we used to track time."

"What good is that now?"

Crawford motioned Mallet to a seat. "Does the word Tuesday mean anything to you?" he asked in a hushed tone.

"If I remember correctly from my studies, it's the old word for the second day. Of course, no one is supposed to use it, but everyone knows what the reference is."

"Yes, but does it have any other significance?"

"It's the day we're sailing for Caelum."

"I've been given instructions to join you," Crawford said, monitoring the crowd. The architect was unusually tense, his hands clenched into fists at his side.

"Relax, you're going to look suspicious," Mallet said, encouraging Crawford to act natural.

Crawford mulled over the words in the article. "Something isn't right here."

"I'll tell you what's right. The *Azimuth* and the *Meridian* are going to the Green to deliver fuel cells," Mallet explained. "And I don't plan on coming back. Neither does Severn."

"Are you serious?"

"Yup, this is our chance to break away from this madness."

"What about everyone else?" Crawford asked. "You intend on leaving people here to struggle on in this mess?"

"I can't fit the entire population on my ship," Mallet said in a hushed tone. "If you want to free them, you stay here and figure it out."

Crawford sat back, crossing his arms. Mallet was not interested in being selfless and nothing the architect said would affect his decision or disposition. "You haven't lifted a finger to help the situation, have you? All you've done is serve yourself."

"I'm not everyone's keeper," Mallet said. "I did my share in Delphia."

"You did, but you're also using what you have to your advantage."

"Say what you want, Crawford, you've got plenty of help. Besides, I'm not just looking out for me," Mallet replied. "Severn is ordered to the zone too and Kemble's my pilot. Isn't she someone worth saving?"

"If this doesn't work," Crawford started, "you're a dead man."

"If we stay here, we'll all be caught eventually because they're going to figure it out," Mallet said. "They only need one of us to get all of us."

"Everyone knows what to do if they're taken."

"They may not have the chance. I told you I'm not dying for this. Melee was enough."

"You know how I feel about that. It couldn't be helped."

"Well, Farah is smart and so is Andira Sorenson," Mallet said. "Sooner or later, it'll come out and who knows how many hundreds will die."

"By the time it happens, it'll be too late."

"And if isn't? You have to think about yourself," Mallet said. "Think about Kemble living without you."

"I can't let someone else take my place," Crawford said, his face calm, voice collected. "I have to see this through."

"Why do you think you have to control everything? There's no logical reason to sacrifice yourself for an unknown result. If you can't do it for me, then do it for her."

"Fordham will be crawling all over your ship and onboard the *Azimuth*. You can't slip past them and Odonna."

"That's for me to worry about. You need to decide if Betera's cause is worth risking your life and the lives of the people you claim to be helping."

"I have to go," Crawford said. "There are things I have to do before I leave for Osler."

"When are you going?"

"I have to be there on the first day to oversee the exams."

"Well, I'll be at the Aero pier the day after at noon," Mallet said. "I hope for your sake that you're there."

Crawford touched Mallet's shoulder in farewell. He felt mentally spent. Though his actions proved effective, every "push" strained his psyche. If something did not give, the architect half expected to keel over like the rest of his brethren. Crawford could not promise Mallet he would join him. The choice to abort the effort would be difficult.

I ought to go see her. Only then can I decide.

Kemble shuffled around her quarters waiting for Crawford, wondering what he wished to discuss before departing. She had news to share as well. To her dismay, a brace order arrived early in the morning, her chosen partner Mallet Tragnor. The directive made her furious and sad. When she contacted Mallet, he vehemently rejected the order.

"There's no way I'm going through with it," he shouted. "You expect me to pay the price for your disobedience?"

"I don't want to comply any more than you do, but neither of our feelings matters in the situation. It's a directive from the senate and there's no refusing it."

"You think Crawford will be pleased?" Mallet snarled.

Kemble fell back, shocked by his awareness. "The order stands," she said. "You have to submit and so do I."

"Like hell I do," Mallet said. "I wouldn't brace with you if I had the choice."

"Mallet, if you refuse, I'll have to tag you."

"You do that, and you'll expose Severn. I can't imagine you'd want that, now would you?"

"With my testimony, he'll survive," Kemble said, somberly.

"Fine, if you tag me, I'll do the same to you. Crawford will die, and Severn will lose us both."

Kemble meditated for a moment, wanting to protect both men. "We have four weeks to comply."

"That's more time than I need," Mallet said, disappearing into static.

Kemble did not know what his parting words meant, but she suspected he meant to find a way around the brace.

His feelings for Far are much stronger than I would have guessed.

Kemble's conscience drifted to Crawford. The raging war inside her manifested itself through hypocrisy. Every part of her thirsted for the grand architect; the desert of her desire could only be quenched by his presence. With this fact in mind, Kemble realized she could not hold Severn and Mallet to standards she had already discarded.

"It's not real," she chanted, advancing to the door. "The heart is just an organ. It can't feel or want for anyone."

When Crawford arrived ahead of schedule, Kemble rushed to open the door. She stood before Crawford, staring into his eyes, hoping to find nothing there, but the verdant gaze facing her was filled with excitement. Kemble's confidence in the ideals she had fought so long to preserve disintegrated when Crawford crossed the threshold. What she once despised, she now welcomed.

"Don't let go," Kemble whispered, thrusting herself into his embrace. "Don't let go."

"I won't," Crawford said, palming her cheek before planting a tender kiss to the corner of her mouth.

"I can't imagine my life without you," Kemble said, carding her fingers through his dark locks. "With you, the world has just begun."

Crawford pressed his chin gently against her forehead. "You'll never have to be without me."

"Promise?"

"I do," Crawford said. "I've never said this to anyone before, but I can say it now—I love you, Kemble."

Kemble heard the words, their meaning sincere. Crawford Lear opened her to the joys of love, a feeling more potent than any prescription.

"I think," she muttered. "I think—."

Crawford put a finger to her lips. "You don't have to say it. I don't expect you to."

"But I do have something to tell you," Kemble said, stepping away to pick up a small envelope from a table. She handed it to Crawford, who recognized the seal.

"When did you get this?"

"A Fordham delivered it this morning after I came from my visit with Breen."

Crawford sat down, removing the card from its sheath. Mallet Tragnor's name and serial number spread across the surface in bold red type.

"Mallet said he wouldn't comply," Kemble said, sitting next to Crawford.

"I should think not."

"He knew you'd have that opinion."

"You think I'd want to see you with anyone else?"

"It would just be a formality."

Crawford stroked the card. "And you can live with that?"

"I don't want to, but they'll correct us if we don't obey," she said, her voice panicked. "I can't get stretched again. They could kill me."

"Listen to me," Crawford began, taking her hand. "If I have my way, they won't be able to touch you. You'll be safe. You just have to keep your head down and be patient."

"I don't think I can hide what I'm feeling for long."

"Our plans will unfold quicker than you think," Crawford replied. "Mallet's not coming back after the trade. He's leaving and you're going with him."

"Mallet intends to steal the *Meridian*?"

"That's his plan and you need to help him do it."

"They'll never let him escape."

"I trust in Mallet's skills and it's your only chance of survival."

Kemble let out a fearful chuckle. "You better hope everything favors him then because if it doesn't, Mallet will never get past the *Azimuth*, and he may not get out of the harbor."

Crawford believed much of the same but diverted her attention from the concern. "Let's leave the maneuvering to Mallet. How many are in your crew?"

"Ten, if you don't count the escort."

"That's Mallet, you, a navigation officer, a watch officer, and six hands, right?" Crawford asked, counting the numbers on his fingers.

"It's our typical crew complement."

"How do you manage with such a small crew?"

"There's not much manual labor. All our cargo is robotically stacked," Kemble explained. "Once Navigator Ivar fixes the route and inputs the coordinates, the ship practically flies itself."

"How does the ship fly itself if you're the pilot?"

"I monitor our speed and course. Sometimes, we're required to use manual control and that's when I take the wheel."

Crawford's expression grew serious. "Whatever Mallet asks you to do, do it," he said. "You have to go with him and Severn."

"Far's going?"

"Farah needs a chemist for what she's after."

"You'll be with us too, right?"

Crawford looked into her velvet eyes, wrestling with the prospect before him. Mallet and he had already debated the question, and now Kemble put it forth again. She wanted him with her. In leaving, he could enjoy what every citizen should, a life free from oppression, filled with choices.

Staying meant forsaking his burgeoning connection with Kemble to face the wrath of Farah and the senate, which would ultimately culminate in a trial leading to death.

"I don't know," he finally answered. "It's not an easy decision. I've been preparing for this my whole life."

"What does it matter now what you've prepared for if it means your life is at risk as well?"

"Betera started this. She trained me, Mallet, and a host of others," Crawford said. "She taught us how to use our gifts."

"I don't understand what you're saying."

"You know how Fordham can sense your emotions?"

"Everyone knows that."

"Well, it's called empathy," Crawford said. "The people I work with do the same thing, but unlike the Fordham, we can influence how people feel and think."

"So, you made me fall in love with you?"

"I would never do that. I merely helped you realize it by giving you a slight push in that direction," Crawford. "I can't make you feel anything that's not already there."

"But if you can read people, doesn't that make you a Fordham?"

"Sort of, but they can't direct people to act on their emotions."

"But how can you do that when everyone is influenced?"

"I don't know," Crawford said, "but I was born this way, all of us were. Betera said we were special."

"This doesn't make sense. Betera created the sentinels," Kemble said. "She helped enforce the policy. Why would she encourage you to fight against it?"

"Betera was braced to Linus Rand," Crawford said. "From what I understand, she agreed with his belief that the Founders weren't righteous in their methods to establish Beta Union."

"I don't know much about the details of that story, but what I did learn in school was that Rand and the Founders saved us from the evils of the old world and brought us to this planet to live as equals without want of anything or fear."

"You and everyone else heard wrong," Crawford smirked. "The whole truth has never been revealed. Even I don't know it all. Betera wasn't very forthcoming with the finer points of why she and Rand did the things they did. Yet, I have to believe it was important work and still is."

"How is it that Rand's associates were stretched and culled, yet no one knew about Betera's plans?"

"If they'd interrogated her, they would have known, but that's where Dorian Aver made a mistake," Crawford replied. "He took her betrayal of Linus Rand as a sign of good faith."

"You admire her even though she turned citizens against each other."

"Fordham were a necessary evil; a means to help us," Crawford said. "Part of me feels sorry for them. I grew up with those children. They're less than human."

"You and everyone like you are behind those incidents, aren't you?" Kemble asked. "How could you believe in love and hurt people?"

"I wish it wasn't part of it," Crawford said mournfully, "but when it's over, we'll have saved more lives than we've lost."

"I never cared about what happened to people before as long they didn't interfere with me," Kemble said. "I believed killjoys deserved correction, but now I know I was wrong."

"I don't want you thinking I enjoy all this death and destruction."

"I don't," Kemble said, "but the senate's relentless. Consul Farah will do anything to stop you and anyone working with you."

"She can't see the big picture."

"For your sake, I hope so. It would be awful if it turns out it's all for nothing."

Crawford could not tell Kemble of the growing apprehension he felt inside. Their strategy was so far advanced; he could see no way to back out regardless of how prudent it might prove to be.

"Make sure you're on the *Meridian* with Mallet," Crawford said, cupping her waist. "Don't worry about me."

"But I do worry about you," Kemble replied. "I love you."

Crawford believed he would have had to wait longer to hear her declaration. His heart rejoiced, and he conceded Mallet had won the argument. He could not separate himself from Kemble. She alone was reason enough to keep on living.

The rest of the evening held lovemaking, words of adoration, and hope. As they lay entwined, cleaving to each other, Crawford listened to their hearts beating in unison, content for the time being, secure in the knowledge of Kemble's love, which changed his course.

CHAPTER 31

During the next gap, Mallet gathered his crew for a pre-launch briefing. Deckhands moved briskly around the ship, prepping the vessel for its voyage, inspecting communications and routes, and clearing out the hold in anticipation of their cargo.

"I don't need to tell you we'll have a tight schedule on the trip," Mallet said, addressing his crew. "We're expected at the Green on time. After we cement the trade, we'll proceed back here."

"How many Fordham are we taking on?" a crew member asked.

"The usual number," Mallet said. "We'll be carrying our defenses, too."

"Rifles or sidearms?" Ivar asked.

"Don't get excited. It's just insurance in case we have any contact with the Pleuran fleet."

Kemble spoke in support of Mallet. "We're not likely to run into any trouble, but it's best to be prepared for any scenario."

"The Green's neutral," another crewmember said. "Why would we run into any trouble there?"

"You never know. The feud between east and south could boil up again," Mallet said. "Now get on with your duties and then head home."

"I'll need to see you and you in the wheelhouse," Kemble said, pointing to Navigator Ivar and the watch officer. "We need to review the navigation charts."

The *Azimuth* lay docked in front of the *Meridian* with suitable clearance for a vertical takeoff. As she issued orders to her deckhands and tactical officers, Odonna Ragas sighted Mallet crossing over the bridge between the ships.

She approached him as he hopped onto the deck. "You could have called before you boarded."

"We're friends, aren't we? Partners on the trade," Mallet grinned. "I shouldn't have to announce myself."

"Isn't Jaxon your best friend?"

Mallet wagged his finger. "You know better. There's no such thing as best."

"If it pleases you, Tragnor. Say what you need to say then leave me to my preparations."

"Everything looks done to me," Mallet said, eyeing the command center through its large window, seeing no one in the enclosure.

"I need to speak with you in private."

"Fine, we can go to command," Odonna said, leading the way.

The wheelhouse hummed with electronic activity, with monitors blasting news reports and weather conditions, and the compass at the center of the room pointing to the current position.

"What do you need to speak to me about?" Odonna asked, leaning against the pilot's post.

"I'm concerned about the guard," Mallet said. "With all the stuff that's been happening, we can't afford to have them acting weird during the trip."

"You're being paranoid," Odonna replied. "I'm sure they've identified the problem and are working to remedy it."

"Yeah, but if something should go wrong out there and they white out, we wouldn't have any help."

"I'm not worried," she said, pointing to the fixed cannons on the *Azimuth*'s deck.

Mallet smiled cheerfully at her reply, furtively studying the command interior. "You're right," he said. "There's nothing you can't handle with those."

"I can even shoot straight," Odonna said confidently, "We'll be covered when we touchdown for the approach."

"I feel safe with you riding along, and I hope you don't have to do anything."

"Consul Farah trusts us to protect you and the senate's interest. That's enough for me."

"Do you need any other encouragement?" Mallet asked.

Odonna gazed through the window. One of her officers waved at her, insistently. "Excuse me," she said, springing topside.

In her absence, Mallet examined the frequencies of the communication equipment, needing to reconfigure the settings to keep Odonna off his trail. The helm was always busy before takeoff, its pilot, navigator, and commander huddled together in the space during pre-flight checks. Mallet had to disable the communications link discreetly just before casting off. For his part, Crawford had been instrumental in preparing Kemble for the events to come.

The architect informed Mallet that Kemble had accepted the plan, with the promise he would join them. Considering his bond with Kemble, Mallet wanted Crawford to keep his word and not let guilt dissuade him. Any deviation from his promise would be painful for the pilot, for as often as Mallet fought with her, he now considered Kemble as family. His love for Severn, and Kemble's new-fangled disposition tempered his attitude.

Mallet looked back and forth from the equipment to the deck, suddenly realizing a flaw in his trickery. Just as he did, Odonna possessed a personal comm she kept nearby, and he would have to arrange for its disappearance if his actions were to go unnoticed.

Fortunately, her bunch presented no threat to his plans. Neither did his. Mallet's crew always followed his orders to the letter, and he would ensure their safety when the ship was in the clear. Everything had to be perfect. With so much at stake, Mallet was determined to avoid failure.

Breen took the TransMap to the drop-off location at a popular theater. His instructions were to go inside the complex, buy a ticket for a specific screening, and sit in the aisle seat at the very back. By the time he arrived, citizens, hungry for an afternoon of entertainment, crowded the rows and he was lucky to find a seat in the virtually packed house.

The feature film of the day was a customary piece about the blissful adventures of a Quad. Breen had seen the movie twice, once alone and once with Tovah. On both occasions, attendees, under the influence of stimulants, engaged in sexual acts during films. It was a fascinating performance if one were in a voyeuristic mood. Unfortunately, if you had come strictly for the movie, the crowd's enthusiasm drowned out the dialogue.

Darkness smothered the audience as the picture started. Breen searched the crowd for his contact, but could not readily pick out the person, so he settled in to wait. A few minutes into the picture, a slender woman squeezed past, taking the seat next to him.

Breen recognized Bristol and found himself confused by her attendance. Fordham did not indulge in recreation. They sought no pleasure nor gave any.

What's she doing here? She can't be here to see the film.

Bristol stared straight ahead with a relaxed visage, emitting a red glow within ten minutes of the film. Similar signs appeared on Fordham monitoring the exits. It was not fiery anger, but rather the flame of arousal leaching off spectators.

Breen squirmed in his seat, uncomfortable with the public display around him. In line with his reaction, Bristol's mark immediately flushed with a sickening pumpkin color. She leaned toward him, placing a hand in his lap, her soft lips grazing his ear as she whispered.

When her actions stirred primal forces within Breen, she instantly cooled to a sensual purple, exposing his emotions. The engineer abruptly stood up, leaving the cinema. Bristol stayed for a moment before following him.

"What were you doing here?" Breen asked, meeting Bristol outside.

"You are perturbed," she said in a clipped tone.

"Well, you definitely fixed that," he said, raising an eyebrow. "Where'd you learn that trick?"

"There is no time to explain. Please hand over the item you have brought with you."

Breen kept his voice down. "You're the contact?"

"It goes without question," Bristol said. "There is a message for you and your answer is required."

"I don't understand."

Bristol walked a few steps away, ushering the engineer away from the theater complex. "Talk of Dr. Novak as you walk," she said.

"You want to hear about Severn?" he asked, falling in line with Bristol.

"It is best to reference mundane things while making the transaction."

"Wait. Why would a Fordham be involved with the resistance?"

"Knowledge of your task is ample confirmation that there is no threat," Bristol said. "You may trust, or you may walk away. The choice is yours."

Breen knew she heard the transmission, and though no one came to collect him, her demeanor, as Severn described it, was uncommon. It gave the engineer reason to pause.

"I'm going to sit down," Breen said. "When I get up, I'll leave what you came for behind."

"Thank you," Bristol said. "Now for the message. You are not to approach the square on the second day. To do so will result in harm to yourself. Do you understand?"

"I know how to stay away from danger," the engineer replied.

Breen walked to a bench and sat down, pressing his palm to the surface. Within moments, he got up, wiped away the perspiration collecting on his forehead, and disappeared into the crowd.

Bristol approached the bench, retrieving the storage device left behind. She tucked it into a discreet metallic tube, screwed on the lid and headed toward the public square where Fordham danced in and out of the area, scrutinizing sensations.

The sentinel advanced to a fountain and perched on its edge. She discreetly put her hand in the water, allowing the tube to slide from her fingers before standing and leaving it behind. From over her shoulder, she saw a female figure approaching the same spot. It was Zelda coolly making her way to retrieve the item.

Zelda stirred her hands in the fountain, artfully removed the tube, and strolled away. Bristol knew Zelda's destination—the

Unity City Broadcast Center, the site of the final blow against Beta Union and her government.

The petite beauty looked up at the public screen then surveyed the citizens going through the motions of the day, frolicking in their many colors. Unbeknownst to them, Consul Farah and the senate, the feeling of cheer would soon fade in the face of revolution.

CHAPTER 32

Crawford woke early on the first day, well-rested for his annual visit to Osler's Institute of Technology despite a recent communication from Narlin, indicating incidents breaking out in Belnord and another province an hour before his departure. Weighing the damage and extent of Fordham fatalities, Crawford said he would change his plans immediately, but Farah decided to let personnel in each province take charge under Karno's direction.

The architect found her decision surprising, considering how little faith she put in the abilities of the engineering corps in the wake of the habitat-wide disasters. Yet, when they spoke, Farah sounded convinced the engineers on duty could handle the issue without him; however, she did expect him to follow-up with the senate upon his return.

When he arrived at the technology school, Crawford could not help but reflect on his sojourn at the institution. If Beta Union allowed its citizens to show pride in their children's accomplishments, the architect believed his pares, Betera and

Grayson, would have proclaimed his achievements to anyone who would listen to their ramblings.

Crawford was a prodigy, well versed in his primary discipline and several sub-disciplines. As the youngest fourth year in the history of the habitat, he remembered the pressure his instructor placed on him. The subsequent praise she gave when Crawford graduated at the head of the class with perfect scores was more for her efforts, an internal need to prove worthy of her post as a teacher.

As Crawford crossed the lawn with his beloved Thalo, he greeted first and second-year students departing their exams. They recognized his stature as grand architect, the symbols on his sleeve glistening under the bright sun, elevating the earthy tones of his uniform. Crawford, amused by their respectful glances, imagined the day when a select few would take their place among the elite engineering corps under his supervision.

He continued strolling toward the main hall, enjoying the soft fertile grass under his boots. The structure was a grand building, its exterior bronze with broad smoky glass doors. Crawford often accompanied his father to the hall during lectures and spent many a day and night in its belly during his enrollment, absorbing everything his brain could hold.

Good memories.

The architect stopped in front of the building, greeting Master Engineer Tristan on her way inside. "Tristan," he said, "Are your pupils ready?"

"They are, sir," she answered. "I think this is one of the best crops."

"We'll see," Crawford said, following Tristan to the building entrance.

Inside, the school was a burst of activity with students hurrying down corridors to the auditorium ahead of instructors. Crawford received a silent reception from students when he entered. The atmosphere was reserved, receptors, hanging from the ceiling in the exam area, glowing with a pleasant radiance.

Though no one believed it necessary, thirty Fordham kept vigil around the edges, ready to safeguard testers against displays of unskillful emotions after the exam. The first and only incident of traumatic emotion during a testing period had occurred over twenty years prior, at the time of Crawford's matriculation. The candidate in question was never the same again.

Since then, modifications to testing procedures included provisions for prompt dispensing of Exult, the premier sedative for academic trials, delivered through armrest cuffs, directly following exams.

Crawford gathered with his staff at the front of the room, as Thalo took his place on the floor at the architect's feet. Fordham indicators showed congenial vibrations wafting throughout the room. The candidates' eyes fixed forward with hands in their laps. Virtual goggles sat on the transparent desks before them.

"Good morning everyone. I don't need to tell you how crucial the next three hours are. There are 150 of you, all talented, expecting to do your best," Crawford said. "Anyone of you may be grand architect someday, but not all of you will be engineers."

The class did not stir. They remained quiet, listening carefully to Crawford's speech.

"You will receive your grades before you leave this room. We do it this way because there are no egos here. Remember, you are citizens of Beta Union," Crawford said. "No one is going to hold your hand or dry your tears because there'll be none. Either you have what it takes, or you don't. Those who don't pass will still have a purpose. Have I made myself clear?"

"Yes, sir!" students answered unanimously and enthusiastically.

"All right. Get ready to start," Crawford said, instructing them to don their testing equipment.

In seconds, candidates would begin the most grueling analysis of their academic careers. With a swipe of their hands, the desks lit up with glowing white light. A countdown began inside their visors. When it hit zero, fingertips went into action, tapping out answer after answer in mid-air.

Fordham swept up and down the aisles, scanning for anxiety, frustration or any prolonged tension. Crawford's beloved Thalo also monitored activity, bounding up and down the steps, sniffing the rows.

Crawford took a seat with the other instructors. His eyes swept the room before fixing on a young woman with blue hair and a nose piercing. The architect laughed to himself. If the girl succeeded in passing the exam, she would have to give up her eccentricities for consideration to a proper post.

Crawford's study of her appearance aroused a strange feeling, evoking the memory of his encounter with the woman in the marketplace. He still could not reconcile the emotions of their intimate experience or the familiarity he felt at the time.

"Master Tristan, who is she?" he asked, pointing to the girl.

Tristan looked to the rows. "That's Hermia. She's a Delphian candidate and an excellent pupil. I expect her to pass."

"How many Delphians are here?" Crawford asked.

"Quite a few," Tristan said, singling out several other students. "The young man over there with the black hair is Matsen."

"Interesting."

"Your province is well represented," Tristan said. "I suppose you're rooting for them?"

"This isn't a popularity contest. It's about Beta Union and who's fit to serve the habitat."

"I wouldn't tell anyone about a little instance of pride."

Crawford crossed his legs, trying to brush aside an eerie impression welling in his stomach. He stared at Matsen. The boy's peculiarity, combined with Tristan's words, rattled Crawford's head.

Delphia's well represented, Crawford muttered to himself as he ran a hand through his hair. He stood up abruptly, consumed by the sudden need to sequester himself.

"Excuse me," he said to Tristan. "I think I'll take a stroll."

Crawford barely reached the hall when Prell came up behind him. "Grand Architect Lear," Prell addressed him. "Do you not feel well?"

"A headache," Crawford replied.

Prell glared at Crawford, paying close attention to his facial muscles and posture. The absence of a reading appeared to stump the guard. "Would you like a remedy for your pain?"

"I'll be fine. There's some nervous energy in the room."

"How would you know that?"

"I was in their place once," Crawford said. "They're bound to be anxious."

"And you? Are you anxious?"

"Shouldn't you be telling me?"

Prell's cold gray eyes examined Crawford from head to toe and back again. The malevolent nature of his probe intrigued the architect. It was clear the Fordham was not in control.

"You are difficult to interpret today," Prell said, "but your expression suggests feelings of stress. Something is under the surface and no doubt it will show in time."

"I guess you'll have to wait for it," Crawford said. "In the meantime, you should deal with your irritation."

"Fordham do not experience irritation."

"Your face says otherwise," Crawford hissed, bumping Prell's shoulder as he passed. "Look in the mirror. I guarantee you won't like what you see."

Prell touched his face, feeling nothing but smooth skin. Fordham rarely examined their image, yet Prell's inquisitive nature sought to investigate the validity of Crawford's claim. The sentinel traveled the length of the corridor, entering a rest area. He walked to a mirror and peered at his reflection. A pulsating coal streak stared back.

Prell's eyes were on fire, burning with a sensation of fury. Pent-up anger crumbled his Fordham conditioning. What once was believed impossible became reality in the glass.

The sentinel banged his fist against the sink, denying the truth. He grunted against the barrage of angry terror, bent on recovering his sensibilities. Prell splashed icy water on his face. He breathed, daring to look back at his image, watching the emotional barometer return to its natural tone, signaling the end of the tirade.

Prell started for the lecture hall without considering the stimulus of the reaction. He took his place among the rest of the squad. Crawford remained alert, watching the sentinel with cool pleasure. He then folded his arms across his chest in silent victory.

The chamber remained quiet for the rest of the period. The students continued laboring, unaware of the looming menace ready to unleash a flood of chaos even the Fordham could not foresee.

Severn called his children and Mallet together for a meeting in his lab. The chemist arrived early, knowing Bristol would be in the office. He gave his assistant an assignment to distract her from the conversation with his family.

Bristol happily occupied herself cataloging items Severn would take to the Green. She also took it upon herself to initiate additional research on the mollusks.

"Dr. Novak," Bristol said, entering the lab. "The information you requested on the mollusks is ready."

"You're finished?"

"It was not difficult to find," she answered. "The database is rife with facts and figures."

Severn took the sheet from her hand. He perused the data, disappointed she finished so quickly. "It seems we'll be able to make use of the material," he said, handing the information back to Bristol. "There aren't any contraindications."

"You do not sound relieved."

"Don't I?"

"No."

Severn noticed her glow; nothing escaped her detection. He turned away from her gaze. "Has the repair been scheduled?" he asked, referring to the ceiling monitor.

"The request is still pending."

"It's taking longer than usual, don't you think?"

"The technicians have a backlog due to the number of disturbances."

Severn looked back at Bristol. She was serene, but oddly, changed. No matter how hard he tried, he could not put a name to the shift in her essence, but knew it was there.

"Commander Tragnor and Pilot Novak will arrive shortly," Severn said. "I'll need you to continue putting my things together."

"The items you need are already packed."

"I'm sure you've been most thorough, but I need you to check again."

"Very well."

"Thank you, Bristol," Severn said, dismissing her.

It was already past noon, and there were still many details needing Severn's review. The wait was killing him, but he was apprehensive about leaving. Severn's life was not bad, despite

Beta Union's cultural constraints. Had he known Mallet in his youth, Severn would have questioned every aspect of living.

"There's no use thinking about it now," Severn sighed, crossing the floor space. He approached a cabinet, unlocked it, and removed an intricate chest, which he carried back to the island.

"What's that?" Mallet asked, coming in with Kemble.

Severn jumped at their entry. "You startled me."

"You knew we were coming."

"I wasn't really here," Severn replied, looking again at the box.

"What is it?" Kemble asked.

Her father tapped its top. "Something I've held onto for a while. It belonged to your grand pare, Lillian."

"It must be important if it's locked," Kemble said, pointing to the clasp.

"In some ways, it is, though it shouldn't be."

"You're not going to open it?" Mallet asked.

"Not right now. I'm taking it along."

"I suppose everyone has their secrets," Kemble said.

"Are we alone?" Mallet asked, looking around the lab.

"Bristol's in the office, but she won't bother us, and the monitor is still out," Severn said. "I've been on her to fix it and she's usually quite efficient, but it hasn't been her priority."

"Okay, well everything's set. We're sailing at midday, so make sure you're at the dock on time," Mallet started.

"Have you figured out what you're going to do about Odonna?" Kemble asked.

"I'm still working out how we're going to ditch her, but we will."

"This is very dangerous," Severn said. "Odonna Ragas is clever. I can't imagine how you intend on avoiding a confrontation with her."

243

"Mallet's good at avoiding people," Kemble chimed in, "and I'm a good pilot. We'll figure it out."

"Are you sure you want to do this?" Severn asked Kemble.

"We have Crawford on our side. If he's willing to do this, so am I."

"It's ironic. I never considered you'd break away."

"I'm your descendant. It took some time, but I guess rebellion runs in the family."

Severn wrapped his arms around Kemble, happy she was joining him, the three going into the unknown together as a family. They were all in danger. "Now what about Breen?" Severn asked. "We can't leave him here."

"What makes you think he'd go?" Mallet asked.

"He's been helping your friends."

"He told you that?" Kemble asked.

"Not in so many words, but he's confirmed my suspicions."

"Who is he working with?" Mallet asked. "It can't be Crawford; he would've told me."

"I don't know who it is," Severn answered. "Some woman's giving him instructions. For what, I don't know."

"Did you tell him about Crawford?"

"No. When he and I talked, I wasn't sure if the grand architect was reliable."

"Well, he'll need to know," Mallet said. "Crawford's the only one who can give him clearance to board the *Meridian*."

Severn huffed. The situation was becoming more complicated by the minute. He was ready to voice concern when the entry bell sounded. "That'll be Breen," he said to Kemble. "Go let him in."

As Kemble went to the door, she looked to Mallet. Neither had mentioned their bracing orders, seeing no reason to upset Severn further. With the entrance open, Breen rushed past Kemble, making straight for Severn.

"Where is she?" Breen asked.

"Where's who?"

"Bristol."

"What do you want with her?"

Breen shook his head. "She's one of them, Severn."

"One of whom?" Kemble asked confused.

"She's my contact," Breen replied. "I wouldn't have believed it, but she knows everything I've been doing, and she has the codes I stole from the GA's database."

"Codes for what?" Severn asked.

"To access the public screens all over Beta Union."

"You broke into his computer?" Kemble asked. "Are you insane?"

"If it wasn't for you, I wouldn't have been able to access it."

"You two are begging to be caught," Severn said.

Kemble turned to her father. "I didn't do anything."

"It doesn't matter how they were stolen," Mallet interjected. "Question is—what's Bristol going to do with them?"

"She never told me what she intended to do," Breen said.

"Then we better ask her," Severn said, going to the office, beckoning to Bristol.

"Dr. Novak, do you require assistance?"

"I need you to join us for a moment, Bristol."

"Certainly," she said. "What do you require?"

"The truth," Mallet said. "Do you have Crawford's codes to the public system?"

Bristol detected alarm in Mallet's voice and in the faces of his companions. "Yes, but you need not be worried about your position," she said. "Everything is prepared and secure."

"You're Fordham," Kemble said. "You expect us to take your word?"

"You may trust it," Bristol answered. "There is no need to fear. All proceeds as planned."

"That's all I've been hearing since this started," Severn said. "Will someone please tell me what the plan is?"

"That you cannot know," Bristol replied, meeting Severn's gaze. "It would jeopardize your safety."

"You sabotaged the monitor," Mallet said with certainty. "You kept them from probing this place."

"It was done was for Dr. Novak's protection. He is valuable."

She loves me, Severn pondered, looking at Bristol in amazement. *All this time and I didn't see it.*

"Thank you, Bristol," he said, touching her arm. "I wish I could protect you. If anyone knew about what you've done."

"Do not worry," Bristol said. "You must leave and everything in this lab must be destroyed."

"You're going to get rid of his research?" Breen asked.

"It is necessary to prevent further entrapment," Bristol said, looking at the panels. "If the movement is to succeed, the senate cannot have his knowledge to fall back on."

"There are other labs," Severn pointed out. "They'll have access to everything they need."

"Those facilities are marked for destruction as well."

"I guess I'd better start now," Severn said, going to his computer.

"Leave it," Bristol said, stepping to his side. "It will be done. Go enjoy the remainder of the day with your family."

The once tremendous hollowness in Bristol's eyes was gone. Severn enjoyed the radiant nature of her defiance. *How did I miss this transformation? She's a woman of emotion again.*

Mallet cleared his throat, interrupting their stillness. "There's a lot to do before we cast off at noon, so we better get going. Once we're gone, there's no coming back."

"No coming back?" Breen asked. "What are you talking about?"

"We're taking the ship and fleeing Beta Union after the trade," Kemble replied.

"You'll never make it out alive."

"Watch me," Mallet said. "You can go, or you can stay, but our minds are made up. We're leaving."

"The GA is likely to be aboard your ship," Breen said. "Do you think he's just going to let you kidnap him?"

"He's coming too, Breen," Kemble said. "He's part of it."

"You're kidding yourself. The grand architect is the epitome of virtue in the habitat."

"Grand Architect Lear is against this state," Bristol confirmed. "It has been known throughout the network since the birth of Fordham."

"Really? Do all of you know, because I bet you Prell doesn't," Breen said. "He's as nasty and dangerous as they come."

"He is Series B," Bristol said. "They are not like the first editions, the primes."

"I don't understand what that has to do with his attitude."

"That series has displayed instabilities in the past," Severn said. "Some of them used to experience psychosis."

"You mean they're all insane?"

"It is what you call a breakthrough," Bristol explained.

"I thought all Fordham after prime were reconditioned," Mallet said.

"Many were, but the mind and its reasoning are complex," Bristol answered. "Owing to this fact, all but a select number were destroyed."

"Thankfully, you weren't," Severn said.

"That is your fortune, Dr. Novak."

There were many questions left unanswered, but the group knew Bristol would say nothing more. Mallet, Kemble and Breen walked to the exit as Severn picked up his box to follow.

He turned back to Bristol, face sullen, knowing he would miss her company. Severn relied on Bristol, admired her skills, and wished he had known the depths of her mind and compassion.

Severn walked back to her, expressing his gratitude by hugging Bristol tightly, and kissing her cheek. Bristol was slow to respond but ultimately returned his gesture.

"Joy, Dr. Novak," she said. "It will not be much longer."

"Thank you," Severn whispered.

Severn saw his mood shining back at him as Bristol released him from their mutual embrace. Not wanting Bristol's last memory of their union to be distressing, Severn motioned for Kemble, pulling the chain at her waist, raising its charm to his face. He inhaled the fragrance, bringing a rush of peace to his system.

The corner of Bristol's mouth curled into a slight smile, her face flushing with pleasure. Severn left Bristol's side, throwing an arm around his son.

"I can't go with you," Breen said.

"You have to come," Severn said. "You can't stay here."

"I have my own family and I have to stay for Somiel and Lerner," Breen replied. "One doesn't desert descendants so young and helpless."

Breen's words struck a chord with Severn. "You're right," Severn said. "You need to stay close to them."

"Bring them with you," Kemble pleaded. "Tovah needn't know where you're going."

"A trading expedition is no place for young ones," Breen replied in response to his sister's concern. "I'll be all right."

"If all goes well, you need not worry for his safety," Bristol said. "He will be protected."

"If all goes well," Kemble repeated the Fordham's words solemnly. "That sounds so simple."

"You'll have to trust it," Breen said. "I'm sure everything will be fine."

"We'll be together again soon," Severn said. "I won't have it any other way."

The four left the lab, leaving Bristol standing alone. Her eyes darted to the panels and cabinets along the wall. She moved quickly toward them, opening every door, throwing out tubes and other containers, shattering them into pieces. Liquids and powders stained the floor and exposed wires danced with lively blue current.

Bristol stepped back, examining her handiwork. It was enough for today. She would clear the rest in the morning, before the spectacle whose better part was already in progress.

CHAPTER 33

Senator Hyatt waited patiently in Orin's office, thumbing through the dispatches of the day, enthusiastic about the council meeting starting in a few minutes. Orin wished to discuss the Belnord and Havamir incidents in advance of the summit. Hyatt suggested waiting until after the senate met and reviewed a complete download from The Servers.

Orin was persistent, rejecting Hyatt's proposal, feeling the need to address matters involving the subject in private. "I hope you were not waiting too long, Hyatt," Orin said, entering the office.

"I have been admiring your space," Hyatt responded, tossing the dispatch from Iona aside. "It is very clean and appropriately elegant."

"Your domain is worthy of praise."

"Like you, I do not feel the need for expensive trappings," Hyatt said, sharing a laugh with Orin about the remark, referring to Consul Farah's taste.

"Luxury is enjoyed by all. Farah, on the other hand, takes it to another dimension."

"I trust she is well within the expenditure limits."

"Zelda has not indicated otherwise," Orin said, sitting behind his desk. "I wanted to speak with you before the meeting regarding the situations we are facing in the other provinces."

"I would have preferred to discuss this with everyone present."

"Yes, I understand, but you are here now, and I want to hear what you have to say."

"Everything we know tells us they are multiplying," Hyatt said. "The dispatches told of Fordham engaged in a standoff on the plaza in Yardell yesterday. Citizens were demonstrating, demanding personal rights."

"What sort of rights?" Orin asked.

"Marriage, privacy, free government, and an end to stretching," Hyatt said. "You name it—they called for it."

"The Fordham obviously cannot control the masses."

"In Belnord and Havamir seventeen receptors were destroyed; thirty-three citizens, in addition to fifteen Fordham troops were assaulted."

"With all this unrest and disruption in the provinces, I question whether we are looking at this the way we should," Orin said.

"Forgive me, my friend," Hyatt began, "but how should we view it? What lens do you suggest?"

"These are attacks against our system, our way of life."

"The word attack implies purposeful involvement by our citizens, which is a capital offense."

"That is exactly what I am saying. These are calculated actions, not accidents," Orin said.

"I refuse to believe citizens are deliberately engaging in open revolution," Hyatt said. "They have no reason to promote discord among each other."

"Where do you think these thoughts and reactions are coming from?" Orin said. "It is either them or someone; something is making them react destructively."

"That is absurd. Alleviation represses all violent actions and thinking."

"Then how does your reasoning account for the chaos that is gripping us even as we speak?"

Hyatt rubbed his eyes. "The grand architect is investigating this. I have no doubt he will uncover the cause in time for us to take action and reverse the situation before permanent damage is done."

"He is not present. Farah decided to let the engineers in the area take the lead."

"With such extreme unrest, the architect should be on-site," Hyatt said. "Protocol demands it. The Consul cannot make the decision alone."

"I agree. Consul Farah has overstepped her bounds," Orin said. "It is not the first time nor is it likely to be the last if she is not reminded of her place."

"Her predecessor was not like her," Hyatt said, gazing out of the window, dark eyes squinting against the sun. "Dorian was a very powerful man and knew the limits of his authority."

"The days of leaders possessing common sense are over," Orin said, leaning on his arms. "No consul can take on what should be shared by us all."

"I agree that Farah goes too far, but her wisdom has propelled us to many great advances."

"No matter the good she has done in the past, her faults far outweigh those deeds. Her power must end today."

"You would impeach her?" Hyatt asked, pressing a forefinger to his lips.

"I think it is time," Orin said, "and if citizens had a say, I believe they would unanimously agree that she is a tyrant worthy of dismissal."

"They might indeed, but we will never know what goes on in their hearts or souls," Hyatt said. "They are tightly bound to their bliss, though these terrorist acts, as you imply, threaten it."

"We have to stop these riots. Every instance undermines everything we have done," Orin said. "If we fail, the habitat itself as a united system may collapse. We cannot return to our sordid past."

Hyatt sighed. "Dr. Sorenson is ready to give her report. If her results confirm a virus, your plans may be premature. Are you sure your motives and your conscience are clear?"

"My concern for Beta Union and its people is indisputable."

"You would be in line to fulfill Consul Farah's duties until the next election if she is found in contempt," Hyatt said, leading Orin to the door toward the meeting chamber. "Be careful how you display your enthusiasm for such action. One might misconstrue it for ambition."

Farah sat with senate members in the meeting chamber, awaiting Orin and Hyatt's entrance.

Andira stood next to Farah's chair, keen on beginning the proceedings. As Hyatt and Orin came in greeting their officials, Farah motioned them quickly to their seats.

"It's nice of you to join us," Farah said. "Dr. Sorenson has been waiting to give us her analysis."

"Sorry to have kept you, Andira," Orin said. "Where is Zelda, Consul?"

"She is not needed for this discussion. Dr. Sorenson, please begin your presentation," Farah said, waving Andira forward.

"I've concluded tests on the material from The Servers," Andira said. "There's no viral or bacterial component known to us in the tissue."

"So, you do not have anything to tell us?" Orin asked.

"I can confirm Crawford Lear's findings that the fluid in the modules is rising."

"What significance does this fluid increase have?" Rivan said. "Is it potentially dangerous?"

"The fluid is regulated by pumps that siphon off excess like a cerebral shunt," Andira explained. "Without drainage, the increase in liquid puts pressure on the organs. If it runs unchecked, it can progress into hydrocephalus, leading to hematomas, edema, or herniation."

"I take it such a state is not preferable," a junior senator said.

"Without treatment, it is lethal," Andira said.

"How is this condition affecting Fordham health?" Orin asked. "I cannot imagine them untouched by these events."

"The relationship between the Servers and the sentinels is symbiotic. As the Hive deteriorates, the Fordham experience whiteouts impacting the neural grafts that give them their empathic abilities."

Rivan's brow wrinkled. "If no evidence of physical injury exists, the problem has to be biological."

"It's nothing I can identify within the current medical database available to me. If there is a contagion, it would be genetically inherent to them," Andira said. "Whatever the sequence, we would have introduced it into the sentinels with those implants."

"Will the Fordham who were affected recover to their full capacity?" Farah asked.

"I can keep them alive indefinitely, but there's no awareness," Andira said. "They are dead. It would be best to euthanize them."

Farah nodded. "I see. What else did you observe?"

"The intensity and rate of these activities are beyond anything we've experienced. Just as in Delphia, the level of upheaval spiked and then suddenly subsided."

"How does it correlate to the fluid increase?" Rivan asked.

Andira shifted, annoyed with his lack of understanding. "I'll say it again. The Fordham's link with The Servers is like a wireless channel. Every emotional activity, positive or negative is transferred to The Servers for recording."

"The Fordham purge, correct?" Farah asked.

"They do, but purges are part of the payload taken on by The Servers. As of now, there's an obstruction in the process, a cork in a bottle if you will," Andira said. "We need to find out what's triggering the instability and stop it."

"The grand architect shut down the affected modules," Hyatt said.

"That defense will matter little if these events continue or if we can't ascertain what's afflicting our people, The Servers, and Fordham."

Orin looked to Farah. "Our entire system could be a weakness. It seems the only logical conclusion."

"The Server model predates Fordham," Andira said, "but the link is relatively new."

"So, is the effectiveness of our meds in question here?" Senator Castillo asked.

"I exposed three groups of twelve to negative stimuli. One group with no alleviation, another, a break of a day in routine, and the rest full dosage on the spot," Andira said. "Naturally, the un-medicated reacted immediately. They regained control after a dose of Joi."

"How long did the remedy last?" Farah asked.

"More than eighteen hours," Andira answered. "The group with the break had the same readings as those who received alleviators before the test."

"So, a little alleviation still goes a long way?"

"It does and since it remains active in the bloodstream, most people don't need to take it every day," Andira said. "The chemists assisting my research agree. There's nothing wrong with our supplies."

"I hesitate to say this," Hyatt began, "but we have to conclude there are citizens who are decisively off medication and perpetrating these attacks."

"It sounds like the right theory to me," Castillo said.

Andira stepped forward. "Every citizen present would have to be off their routine simultaneously and we would be seeing withdrawal symptoms," she said. "I don't have evidence of widespread withdrawal."

"Then what do you have?" Orin asked.

"All the data tells me drug levels are stable. No one should feel stressed with the concentrations I found," Andira answered. "It shouldn't even occur in moderation."

"Should not and cannot are two different statements, my learned friend," Castillo said.

"Emotions run deep. We keep them at bay with alleviation, but you can't destroy them."

Rivan rose, approaching Andira. "Well, doctor, they are not staying at bay."

"I have to believe Betera's files have the answer. If the comm center can repair them, I'll have it."

"And what do you intend to do if it is not among her work?" Orin asked. "Can you proffer another scientific solution?"

"She was a genius," Andira said, "and very thorough. If there's something to be found, it's in her notes and then I can put my energies into a plan of action."

"This has gone on long enough. Where is Crawford Lear?" another senator asked.

"He is attending the annual exam in Osler," Farah said.

"Crawford Lear should be here or in the affected provinces," Hyatt said. "He alone can interpret The Servers' condition."

"Not true. His only advantage is seeing them with his own eyes," Farah said. "We have peered into the place and have always been able to download accounts."

"Can you interpret them as well as he can?" Orin asked.

"Together we shall try," Farah said, asking the senators to place hands on the table. Within moments of opening the link, a fault developed in the system, static and heavy interference spreading throughout the transmission. Farah was frantic. "What is happening here?"

"Our signal is weak," Orin said. "We can attempt to download a partial file before we lose it."

"Do it now then," Farah commanded. "Quickly!"

The matrix above sputtered, color draining from its crackling web. "We are losing power," Orin said. "Hyatt, Rivan, what do you have?"

"A forty-two percent drop-in services over Jersa and nearly fifty-six in Delphia," Rivan replied. "The number of impaired Fordham is rising."

"What about The Servers?" Farah asked. "Is there condition degrading further?"

Orin rapidly scanned the file. "The damaged modules are still on."

"Those units were to be taken offline," Rivan said, turning to the others. "The grand architect must be recalled."

"Turning them off would not remedy the problem," Andira said. "It would also leave us without surveillance."

"But the strain?" Rivan asked.

257

"Strain or not, they're waning. We must concentrate on the people," Andira said, shaking her head. "If we lose them, we'll lose everything."

"I move we open The Pool. There is material in it to replace the affected Fordham and restore The Servers."

"There won't be enough," Andira pointed out. "Only a limited number remain and the same might happen to them if we replace the tissue."

"This is insane," Farah fumed. "All I am hearing are excuses and no solutions to this dilemma."

"If these issues were managed properly, we would not be in this predicament," Orin said, pointing a finger at Farah.

"Are you impugning the work I have done?"

"The Senate has tried to be proactive, but your actions are another subject."

"What else would you suggest?" Hyatt asked Andira. She did not answer, having grown tired of the senate's naiveté.

"I move we proceed with the previous remedy discussed regarding food and water supplies," Rivan said.

"I agree. We must maintain total control over citizen health," Castillo said. "Until the mayhem is quelled, we take no chances with anything."

"Then we will retrieve our new ingredient and begin inserting it into the daily diet," Farah said triumphantly.

Andira sat quietly thinking for a moment. *I must gain access to that data. Our problems stem from there.*

Hyatt reached for the intercom, requesting Zelda. "You are to recall Crawford Lear at the close of the exams." Zelda acknowledged the order, leaving the chamber to carry it out the Hyatt's instructions.

"I want to know why he left The Servers exposed," Castillo said. "He will tell us himself when he appears."

"You will of course address the populace tomorrow?" Rivan asked Farah.

"I will say we remain strong and at their service," Farah said. "Zelda will coordinate the announcement. When Crawford Lear comes to us, we will open The Pool."

Andira spoke, "I've already told you it won't work if it's more than a biological failure."

"Using the Pool is a chance we must take, and you will prepare the new additions," Hyatt said. "We other matters to discuss now. Dr. Sorenson, please excuse us and send Zelda in when you go out."

Zelda walked in to stand watch against the rear wall. Farah's gaze went around the table. "What else would you like to discuss?" she asked.

Hyatt signaled Zelda to come forward and administer alleviation to all if necessary. "Your overall performance is in question and I think it is time to address some of this concern," he responded.

Farah's eyes came to rest on Orin. No one else in the room could have issues with her duties except him. For all his grand discourse on unity, Orin envied Farah. She believed it from the day she took the oath of office. Now Orin sought to shame Farah and her right to serve out a full term.

"Very well, let us converse," Farah said, raising her head high. "I have a few concerns of my own to share with you."

CHAPTER 34

The moment every engineering student was waiting for had finally arrived. The grand architect himself stood prepared to deliver the verdict on their work

"Everyone put your right wrist in the cuff now. In a few moments, you'll all know if you've passed through," Crawford said before signaling Tristan. "Deliver the scores."

Tristan retrieved a tablet, tapping out codes on the instrument. The flow of unique information she sent out bombarded every student's eyes and the auditorium sank into silence.

"Congratulations to those of you who'll move forward as journeymen," Crawford said, placidly. "We're adjourned."

The students removed their eyewear. Some beamed while others stared blankly ahead, unfazed by the results. A young woman seated to Crawford's right sat gripping the edge of her desk, her long flaxen hair falling about her face as she inhaled and exhaled forcefully. Crawford's head snapped in her direction. The angst in the girl's expression mimicked a pot of boiling water threatening to bubble over.

When the docile light of a receptor above took on a distressing color, Crawford realized his proximity to the candidate fueled her passion. He backed away, mentally willing the girl to relax, but she was too far gone to control. A female sentinel approached Crawford's position and Thalo jumped to attention, slinking toward the young woman. He sniffed her, growling with displeasure.

The girl pushed him away, words of discord bursting from her sanguine lips. "This isn't fair," she choked. "It can't be right. I'm better than this!"

"Easy, boy," Crawford said to Thalo. The jackal had instinctively started to growl as tempers flared.

"Stand down," the sentinel ordered, warning the girl to collect herself or face correction.

"This isn't right," the girl continued, slapping the sentinel's hand. "I won't accept it. I must be an engineer. There's nothing else for me!"

Her subsequent movements were unnerving. With savagery, the young woman discarded her visor and slapped objects off the desk. Students and staff recoiled at her display of vehemence.

Prell came rambling down the stairs, bewildered by the girl's mood. He joined Crawford at the front, facing the girl with a look of freshly forged iron. "You will comply with the instructions," he said firmly.

"It is a lie; they're lying to us. The test is rigged," she screamed to the assembly. "They're stealing your future!"

Prell placed a hand on his gun, addressing the sentinel closest to the violator, "Remove her."

The guard tightened her grip on the young woman, forcibly ejecting the candidate from the room. In the middle of the rows, a freckled youth let out a hideous gurgling sound, followed by a jet of digestive acid that spewed onto those seated immediately in front of him.

The victims, covered in curdled chunks, pounced from their seats, assaulting the youth with reckless abandon. Crawford watched with horror as other students became incensed, their pupils blown wide with excitement as they heckled and cheered. The entire hall was rapidly deteriorating into an abominable explosion of destructive orgiastic dynamics.

Fordham indicators began flushing with wild energy; receptors gaped in alarm as equipment crashed to the floor. The sentinels were trampled under heavy heels and hammered with reverberating antipathy.

Clusters of students held themselves against fear and panic while others laughed hysterically. Fists pounded desks. Emboldened voices chanted, "Cheats, cheats, cheats!"

Crawford stood motionless, watching the dreadful scene, powerless to intercede as the sentinels penetrated the aisles, attempting to restore order, with Thalo barking wildly at the violent throng.

Tristan grasped Crawford's shoulder, beckoning for answers amidst the chaos, "What's wrong with them?"

"This is an outrage," said one of the master engineers, "The alleviators aren't working."

"Calm yourselves," Tristan commanded.

"Take them down," a cadet yelled, striking a sentinel. "Take them all down!"

Fordham hustled to block the entryways, to stand against the discontent, but the vibrations of the herd were swiftly overcoming their physical capabilities. The mayhem continued sweeping through the rows as cadets combatted their oppressors and resisted arrest. A blond student battled one of them, scratching and clawing his face, blood spurting under her nails.

The sentinel cried out in pain, kicking at the student, firing rounds into her chest.

Crawford looked up into the stands, focusing on Matsen and Hermia. They were strangely unaffected, glaring at him with supreme jubilation. Matsen moved quickly to steal a pistol from an injured Fordham. He aimed the weapon at Crawford, discharging a lethal burst of energy.

"Lear!" Tristan shouted, launching herself in front of the architect. Her body crumpled to the floor.

Crawford dropped to Tristan's side, turning her body over. Tristan's eyes were open; a smoldering pulse burned at her neck. The architect glared back to the pack only to see a small clump of cadets, led by Matsen and Hermia, hurriedly disappear through the rear exit.

This is my fault, he reasoned. *I've done this to them.*

"Cull the offenders," Prell shouted, sprinting to a comm box to summon reinforcements.

Crawford released Tristan and ran up the center stairs, with Thalo close on his heels. They entered a corridor, searching for the escapees. Thalo led Crawford along a hall and made a sharp right turn where Matsen stood on a balcony with Hermia and another girl, overlooking the building's atrium. The trio was huddled together praying.

Matsen backed away from his companions, pointing the pistol at both women. He halted when Crawford came into view. Hermia and her accomplice fled, determined to escape a confrontation with Crawford, but Matsen whirled around to face him.

Thalo, in a frenzy to protect Crawford, lurched at the teen, tearing his jumpsuit. Matsen deflected Thalo's bite, booting the animal, who fell to the side breathing heavily. Crawford ached for him but could not move to help.

"I know who you are, architect, I know your destiny, and you know how this is going to end," the boy said, his black hair glistening, his weapon ready.

"If you could do something like this," Crawford began, "then you don't know me or what I stand for."

"Did you think you were the only special person in all of the Union? Matsen asked. "The only one Betera Eaton chose to carry on her work?"

"Don't use Betera as an excuse for the bloodshed you caused today," Crawford said. "She never advocated this type of behavior against anyone."

"You really don't know anything about her, do you?" Matsen smiled. "Or maybe, you know everything, but you're in denial."

"Then maybe you should tell me what I ought to know."

"You can't help who you are, why you're here, or what you were born to do."

Crawford felt sickened, "People like you will doom us all."

"There are others who will take our place," Matsen said, "and though neither of us will live to see it, our actions certainly will be vindicated."

Crawford did not expect his life to end with a botched mission. Everything the resistance worked for would be in jeopardy if the sentinels apprehended the students. The architect silently hoped the Fordham succeeded in destroying the surreptitious details of the conspiracy. Crawford shut his eyes, awaiting death at Matsen's hand.

Suddenly, a shrill pulse sounded behind Crawford, followed by a burning sensation in his arm. He opened his eyes, seeing Matsen drop his weapon, clutching himself in pain.

Prell came forward, pausing slightly ahead of the architect. "You will stand down now," he said to Matsen, "or you will expire. Make a choice."

"You can't stop us all," Matsen said, grasping the balcony railing. "It's finished." The youth did not hesitate as he flung himself over the side of the gallery. Crawford rushed to the edge, witnessing the boy plummet to the atrium floor, his limbs splintering on impact.

Prell also took in the sight before turning his attentions to Crawford. "You are injured, grand architect."

"It's a scratch. I'll be fine," Crawford said, rushing to Thalo. The jackal was severely wounded, his eyes moist.

"You will go to the infirmary and take the animal with you," Prell said, gesturing towards two officers dashing toward them.

"Backup units have arrived," a sentinel said. "The area is under control."

"No one is to leave the premises," Prell said. "Where are the delinquents?"

"Three were captured attempting to flee. Seventy-six candidates have expired, forty-nine wounded and twenty-six Fordham are inoperative."

Crawford stood up, scooping Thalo into his arms as Fordham below worked to recover Matsen.

Prell looked over the ledge. "Does he breathe?"

"He is alive," a female sentinel replied.

"See that he continues and take the rest to detention."

"He should be dead," Crawford whispered.

"No doubt he is badly broken, but, fortunately, he did not meet with success," Prell said. "Come, the senate must be informed of this occurrence."

Crawford stole another look at the bloodstained floor. He was always careful, taking calculated risks when aggravating, but today he was on the offensive, shield down, unable to restrain himself during the disaster.

What are we doing? Is this what Betera truly wanted? Mass murder?

Prell led Crawford to a hovercar outside the school. The architect rested Thalo in the back of the vehicle before sliding into the passenger seat. He turned to look out the window to, watching Fordham corral students and faculty into transports without protest.

As the hover sped to the detention center, Matsen's words lingered in Crawford's mind. *You can't help who you are.*

Those were the very words he used to defend the rebellion when conversing with Mallet. At that moment, Crawford realized he hated doing Betera's work almost as much as he hated Beta Union, but the truth to come would make Crawford resent Betera in a way he could never have imagined.

CHAPTER 35

At the same fateful hour of the Osler attacks, the Senate concluded its heady discussion. Consul Farah stood on notice. Her role as the leader of was balancing on the thinnest sheet of ice.

"I believe we all agree you have done wonders in the past, madam," Senator Castillo said, "but recent events make us question your skills in handling the problems we currently experience."

"There are things beyond my control," Farah answered, "yet I am committed to quashing the malevolence."

"We agree with your plans to insert prescriptions into the food supply," Senator Rivan said, "and we must act immediately if we are to subdue the uprisings."

Senator Hyatt sat forward, clasping his hands together, "I am disturbed by Dr. Sorenson's inability to determine exactly what it is we face."

"Her research has yielded nothing except for the Fordham-Server connection," Castillo said. "From my observations, she is incompetent to give us an acceptable answer to the dilemma."

"Perhaps she should be replaced," Rivan said. "I can review a list of candidates for the position."

"Please do," Hyatt said. "In the meantime, how are we going forth with our plan?"

"The *Meridian* and *Azimuth* leave tomorrow for trade with Caelum at the Green," Farah said. "Dr. Novak has ensured me we can immediately begin the process of refinement and insertion into the chain once the mollusks are in our possession."

"What about those already 'infected' by these events?" Orin asked. "Our final solution will come too late for them."

Hyatt drummed his fingers on the table. "It is time for a drastic change in direction," he said. "I vote we eliminate affected citizens."

"All of them?" Castillo asked.

"There are so many doors that have closed because of our earlier inaction and slow response," Hyatt said. "I see no other option."

"We can collect them and detain them for correction," Orin said. "It can buy us time to assess them."

"Culling is the far wiser option as it will send a message to everyone that radicalism will not be tolerated," Rivan said.

Orin looked at Farah who looked pleased with the proposal.

"So now we rule with fear?" he asked. "How is this part of the doctrine we protect?"

"The elder Aver took the same action with acceptable results," Castillo answered. "I concur with Senator Hyatt. It is time for us to show that these actions will not be tolerated by anyone." The other senators shook their heads in agreement.

"Dorian Aver was not dealing with the same issues," Orin said. "If we ignore the real culprit, Fordham will continue to be overwhelmed and The Servers will not survive."

"None of us can predict the future with certainty, Senator Novak," Hyatt answered. "We are in the present and we must learn from the past."

"You brought us to this, Farah," Orin said, seething. "Your conduct alone has put us in danger."

"I told you once you could not stomach what it takes to secure our future. It seems my conclusion was quite apropos."

"Understand, Consul," Hyatt said, "This is the last test of your authority. If you do not maintain integrity, you will lose your position on this board."

"I understand," Farah said. "The new method will work. While we wait for relief, we will move forward with the culling."

Without warning, Karno rushed into the meeting, prompting Orin to scold the sentinel. "I told you to announce your entry."

"It could not wait," Karno said. "A riot has occurred at the engineering school."

"Are the students safe? Was the school evacuated?"

"The candidates became violent and engaged in conflict with the Fordham."

"What in the name of Enoch is happening to everyone?" Hyatt asked. "Has every citizen gone crazy?"

Karno and Zelda felt the senate's displeasure, but considering the circumstances, neither corrected the emotions.

"The dead number more than seventy. Those who tried to evade capture are in custody," Karno said. "Prell holds them in cells for interrogation."

"Has Prell collected all identities?" Farah asked.

Karno handed the consul a list of names. "These are the offenders," he reported. "Three are Delphian. The others are from Belnord and Jersa."

"Delphia seems quite rooted in this mess," Farah muttered.

Rivan bit his lips, looking uneasy. "Delphia is the birthplace of Rand's revolt, not to mention a host of other firsts."

"It seems to feature prominently in this tragedy. Could it be the connection to the disorder?" Orin asked. "After all, the girl at the Plant 13 fire was Delphian."

"We have been down that road and found nothing. Commander Tragnor acquitted his sib," Farah said.

"Tragnor's word means little to me," Orin replied. "He is Delphian, as is the grand architect."

"You are trying to establish a pattern that is not here," Farah argued. "The techs at the comm center were not Delphian."

"This is how terrorists work, Farah," Orin said. "They recruit others to their cause. For all we know, the cities are full of these terror cells, led by Delphians, and originating from Delphia itself."

"Your obsession with Crawford Lear is ridiculous."

"And you have the audacity to think you know him," Orin said with a sick grin.

Hyatt broke the debate. "This council placed the security of our systems in the hands of the Crawford Lear based upon his reputation," he said. "Unless you have proof to the contrary senator, I suggest you curb your enthusiasm."

Karno spoke again. "The evidence supports the grand architect's loyalty," the sentinel said. "He was targeted for elimination at the school."

"Why would they want him dead?" Rivan asked.

"I do not care whether he was slated for elimination by these deviants, I still say he is in league with them," Orin replied. "As grand architect, he is perfectly situated to commit and conceal any type of sabotage."

"Crawford Lear would never have agreed to our inspection if he were working against us," Farah said.

"There is a way to settle this question once and for all," Rivan said. "I move we stretch him. It is the only way to ascertain whether he is detached from these events."

Farah reflected for a moment. She did not want to believe Crawford guilty of the crimes Orin insinuated. "Bring them to detention and have Lear report here directly. He will speak for himself."

"We will schedule a culling for tomorrow, after the address," Hyatt said. "Let the captives have a last eve to think on their actions and its consequences."

"Are you planning to make it public?" Orin asked.

"There is no need to risk further distress," Hyatt answered. "The message will spread without a public display."

Dr. Sorenson returned in time for the grim news. "The captives should be delivered to a health facility," she said. "I can make observations under controlled conditions."

"You found nothing before. What do you think you will find now?" Farah asked.

"I have to keep searching," Andira said. "I'll perform imaging to rule out neurological disorders and defective transmitters in the citizens."

"Why did you not think of that before?"

"Our complacency and ignorance of change have left us ill-equipped for these events, and I admit my part in it."

"Dr. Sorenson, if the transmitters were to blame, we would know from the feed," Hyatt said.

"This disorder is causing all types of unnatural behavior and you can't even get to the feed right now," Andira said. "Those specimens may give us the key to unravel this mystery."

271

"You've examined everyone else involved already," Castillo said. "What difference will additional studies make now?"

"These are live specimens. We can interview them to gather information."

"Zelda will arrange for them to be transferred to your lab," Hyatt said. "Consul, you will announce the trade tomorrow before Commanders Ragas and Tragnor leave for their journey."

Orin considered to his instructions regarding Mallet and his niece. "Is there no one who can take Commander Tragnor's place?" he asked.

"Why should he be collected?" Farah asked. "He is ideal for this particular mission,"

"I told you, he has ties to Delphia."

"We cannot pull everyone from Delphia out of service," Hyatt said.

"You would rather wait for them to show themselves false?"

"Of course not, but if there is danger, the sentinels will take action."

"It is late, and we are going around in circles," Castillo said.

"Quite right," Farah said, scooting her chair away from the table and smoothing the layers of her dress. "My address will be ready in the morning. We will reconvene then."

"Agreed," Hyatt said. "Good day to you all."

Farah turned to Karno. "Summon Prell. He will escort the Grand Architect back to the city," she said. "Werner will take over in Osler."

"Is the grand architect to be detained?" Zelda asked.

"Not yet. Bring him here first thing in the morn," Farah said. "He is not to be touched until we are finished with him."

"What of the sentinels for the trade?"

"See that Adario and Garnette's squads board the *Meridian* and *Azimuth*," Farah said. "They will attend to the commanders to ensure a compliant journey."

"What accompaniment do you wish for your address?"

"A battalion, three-hundred at the most, is to assemble in the squares by hour ten."

After Zelda and Karno cleared the room, Orin spoke his piece. "Tread carefully, Farah, you heard the senate's warning."

"Jealousy is a nasty thing," she said. "You should suppress it, or you will be the one awaiting stretching."

There was much Orin wished to say, and he considered it all valid. Orin disapproved of the senate's decision to keep Farah in her role, and its inaction in failing to arrest Mallet and Crawford. He left his musings and observed the receptors in the room, humming with a vibrant yellow.

Farah also noticed the change. "May I offer you some reserve?" she asked, reaching for a spray on a mantel.

"Keep it. You will need it before your hanging."

"I suppose you will supply the rope and make the noose," Farah laughed.

Orin snatched the spray from Farah, threw it aside, and headed for the door. "If it will snap your neck, I will gladly supply it," he said, exiting the room.

Farah stood alone in the center of the room, her head spinning while the receptors blushed crimson. I will not be driven to anger, she said to herself.

The consul felt sick, the emotion causing her to run, seeking the sanctuary of her office. Upon arriving, she sank into a chair where she partook of relief.

"I am Consul. I am in control," she chanted aloud, eyelids fluttering under the weight of medication. Farah would continue the litany until she convinced herself it was a fact.

CHAPTER 36

By morning, Mallet was back on the *Meridian*'s deck bellowing instructions to automated loaders. The machines handled the power cells with care, deftly stacking the supplies in the cargo hold. Mallet was grateful for the cool breeze sweeping over the pier, taking away the scorching heat of the sun.

"Take that to the hold, too," Mallet said, to a floating mechanical pallet. "Make sure it's stowed tight."

"Do you want me to deliver the coordinates to Odonna or are you doing it yourself?" Kemble asked, approaching him from the wheelhouse.

Mallet took the data, eyeing it quickly. "This looks fine. I'll take it over to her."

"You haven't said how you intend on gaining distance from Odonna's vessel."

"Wouldn't you like to know," Mallet grinned.

"It's not as if our course change won't be picked up," Kemble said, "and you know we can't turn south if we want to avoid Pleurans."

"That's why we're going straight on," Mallet said, making a forward motion with his hand.

"To the Green?"

"Not exactly. I figured there has to be a spot between Pleura and Caelum where we can land and figure out our next move," Mallet said. "For this plan, I'll need you to put us as close to southern space as we can get without getting killed."

Kemble tugged Mallet aside. "You're crazy," she breathed. "Patrols are all over their territory."

"Relax. We know where the markers are and we're just doing a flyby."

"You've got some nerve."

"Don't you trust me?"

Kemble was still, thinking of a million reasons why they should scrap the scheme and only two reasons to go through with it—Severn and Crawford. Even the best-laid plans contained a margin of error. It was difficult to accept that Breen would not accompany them. Despite Bristol's statement, Kemble feared for her brother and his children.

"I have to cross to the *Azimuth*," Mallet said. "Odonna and I need to go over this right now."

"There's no way this is going to work," Kemble warned. "They'll alert her as soon as you veer off course."

"I think she'll have other troubles to worry about," Mallet said, removing his comm from his uniform.

"What are you actually going to do?"

"You don't ask, and I don't tell," Mallet replied, heading for the walkway extending along the ship's bow. "Get Severn and the others on the horn, I want to take off on time."

With a wink, Mallet hopped up on the board, balanced himself, and crossed to Commander Ragas' vessel. His boots thudded onto the deck as he jumped down.

Odonna was facing the command center, conscious of his arrival. "What's to do, Mallet?" she asked.

"I brought you the coordinates," he said, striding up beside his commander.

Odonna grabbed the form, reviewing the notations. "I'm familiar with this route," she said, handing it back to him. "I'm bringing up the rear."

"You should really take the vanguard."

"There's no need. We'll be far away from Pleura's line."

"What if they happen to wander into the sector?" Mallet asked. "I've heard they have weaponry more advanced than we are even capable of producing."

"I don't care what they have," Odonna said. "They'll never get their hands on this ship. I'm too good at what I do to be blown out of the sky."

"You're saying you'd leave me behind in a tight situation?"

Odonna's eyes grazed Mallet's face from under her lush lashes. "I'd never leave you behind," she said.

"I'll take your word for it," Mallet said, looking toward the wheelhouse. "Is your pilot on station?"

"Where else would he be?"

"Shall we go give him the news together?" Mallet asked, starting for the entrance. Odonna followed him inside where her pilot sat setting the scope.

"Commander," he said, raising his head from the lighted globe. "Everything is primed and ready. I just need the coordinates and we can get underway."

Odonna motioned to Mallet. "Hand them over, Tragnor.

"It's pretty regular," Mallet said. "You're new, aren't you?"

"Yes sir, Pilot Dainus, sir. I've run this way before on the *Corona*," he answered.

"The *Azimuth* is a step up from the *Corona*," Mallet smiled.

"She is, but I can handle her, sir."

"I'm sure you can," Odonna said. "Are the communications systems in order?"

"They are, madam," Dainus said, pointing out several transmissions broadcasting over the wave. "I'd better go over the markers with the navigator."

"You do that," Odonna said.

Mallet watched him step out. This was his chance. "Speaking of comms," he said, pulling his device from a cargo pocket, "I think this is on the fritz. It keeps breaking up."

"Let me see it," Odonna said, examining the cube. She squeezed it gently and then pulled out her own. "There's no signal. I suggest you call Adario. He can bring you another one when he arrives with the escort."

"May I use yours?" Mallet asked. "I don't want to clog up the ship's wave."

Odonna handed over the communicator. "We'll be fully loaded in a few minutes," she said. "As soon as the sentinels arrive, we'll get underway."

"I'll make that call now."

"Don't let me disturb you."

"Well, I have another call to make too, if it's okay."

"Are you making homecoming arrangements?" Odonna asked, her lips forming a sly smile.

"You're really nosy, did you know that?"

"I never stand between a man and his recreation."

"Thank you," Mallet said, turning away as she departed.

Once Odonna was gone, Mallet thrust her link into his uniform, laying the broken comm on the navigation table. He scurried to the ship's communications box, removed the back panel, and tinkered with the transmitter, slipping a small stub over fiber strands inside the housing. Mallet peered at the window, monitoring Odonna's preparations with the crew.

He returned to the panel and continued fiddling with its circuitry, "A tweak here, a tweak there," he muttered, "and done."

Mallet sealed the mechanism after successfully fixing the broadcast into a loop. He then proceeded to walk casually onto the deck, making his farewells. He smiled smugly as he crossed back to his ship.

Let's see you catch me now.

Crawford rode in silence with Prell for the duration of their journey. Along the way, he thwarted Prell's attempts to determine his mood and refused to give the sentinel satisfaction. Thalo had been put down at the infirmary. Crawford suspected the vet techs did it deliberately rather than out of necessity. If that were true, Farah's ire was worse than Crawford wanted to believe.

Zelda greeted Crawford upon his arrival at the State Building. "Grand Architect Lear, you must be distressed after your ordeal."

"Is that what you're feeling?" Crawford asked.

"Your mood is obscured," Zelda said, escorting him into the building.

Crawford faced her in the hall. "You should be able to uncover it," he said. "If not, you're malfunctioning."

"Whatever happens, know you have not failed. People believe in you."

Crawford skipped over her statement, focusing on the irrationality of her theory proclaiming all was lost.

Zelda touched the symbols along the entrance arch. "They are ready for you," she said, waving him into the room, and taking her post against the wall.

The senate sat around the matrix conduit with their hands folded in silence. Farah took her usual position at the head.

"You will remain standing, Lear," Orin said. Prell entered the room, stationing himself near Zelda.

"Grand Architect Lear, you stand before us to answer charges of negligence brought forth by Senator Novak," Hyatt said. "We are ready to hear your defense."

"I have nothing to defend," Crawford said, standing at ease. "I've performed my duties competently ever since my appointment to the post."

"You have the gall to call these incidents a representation of your proficiency?" Orin asked. "The damage to The Servers offers considerable support to the contrary."

"It's an unfortunate occurrence, but it's also the sign of an issue of which I have no knowledge," Crawford said.

"Dr. Sorenson did not confirm a contagion within The Servers or Fordham," Hyatt said. "It is, therefore, a different problem altogether."

"Again, what does this have to do with my responsibilities?"

"The health of The Servers is your responsibility," Rivan said. "Your inspections should have verified what we now know before the situation progressed to this point."

"With all due respect, senator, I don't recall you being an engineer."

"It is well-known that whatever Fordham detect passes to The Servers," Orin said.

"I'll agree that's common knowledge," Crawford said, "but these events have nothing to do with me."

"Something or someone is provoking the attacks," Castillo said.

"We know you never shut down those modules," Orin said. "You left the hive open to danger."

"Pray tell, where did you acquire that information?"

"We downloaded a report verifying their online status," Hyatt said. "Those units were active, sapping the strength from healthy units."

"I made an administrative decision," Crawford replied. "If I had taken them offline, we'd be in worse shape."

"It was not for you to decide," Orin said. "We gave you a directive. We did not ask you to think."

"Even if I did what you asked, we'd still be standing here," Crawford said. "And I'd be telling you the same thing."

"Architect, for every problem, there is a solution," Hyatt said. "Dr. Sorenson stated it has nothing to do with mechanics; however, I believe you saw something in your survey that would help us understand the problem."

"If there was anything, my engineers and I would have dealt with it immediately," Crawford said. "I can't fix what we can't see or what doesn't show up on a scan."

"Your answer is unacceptable," Orin said. "These attacks are no coincidence. They are the work of radicals."

"You believe I'm one of them, don't you?" Crawford answered. "If you didn't, I wouldn't be here defending myself against these trumped-up charges."

"Senator Novak has suggested as much," Castillo said.

"And I deny it," Crawford said. "The engineering corps has consistently responded to every failure and effected a solution to each."

"What do you make of the massacre at the engineering school?" Senator Rivan asked. "Did you attempt to apprehend the disruptors?"

"I didn't recognize them until they fled," Crawford said, "and one of them tried to kill me."

"Do you know what precipitated the incident?" Hyatt asked.

"There was nothing unusual during testing, but after the scores came out, a student had an unpleasant reaction to her marks," Crawford said, noting Farah's quiet sympathy.

"Each tester was under alleviation?" Rivan asked.

"It's standard procedure," Crawford said.

"Then explain the violent eruptions," Hyatt demanded.

"I'm not a chemist or a physician. I don't pretend to know how those chemicals work or why they didn't in this case."

"You or any of your engineers could have tampered with the delivery system," Orin said.

"Seriously? You think that's feasible," Crawford said. "That's like saying I relish the notion of putting myself in harm's way and helping Fordham slaughter people without regard for their lives."

"Who knows? You may have gone to such lengths to cover yourself. This is not the first time you have been present during hostilities," Orin fired. "You were in The Cleft when the violence and hysteria broke out."

"I never said I wasn't there."

"How do you explain your presence at both events?" Castillo asked.

"A coincidence," Crawford said. "Wrong place and wrong time I suppose."

"Trouble seems to follow you, grand architect," Orin said. "I would say more often than not."

"I think that is enough," Farah spoke. "We have no definitive proof of a connection between Crawford Lear and these events."

"You're shielding his errors," Orin asked. "There is more than enough proof."

"I am not biased as you suggest; however, your outbursts impugn the grand architect's record, which is spotless," Farah said. "Grand Architect Lear cannot be held accountable for failure among our sentinels or the rampant moods of citizens."

"I suggest you question the chemists instead of wasting my time and yours," Crawford said to Orin.

"They will be next, but first, we will finish with you," Hyatt said, leaning forward to peer at the architect with suspicion.

Rivan chimed in. "Were you aware some of the dissidents are native to Delphia?"

"What's it got to do with me?"

"You may be able to assist us in identifying them," Hyatt replied with a more relaxed demeanor than before.

"Delphia's a large place. It's impossible to know everyone."

"Yet there could be a chance you have run across them before," Rivan replied.

"Maybe, but I doubt it."

"You knew one of them," Orin countered, "Technician Melee Tragnor."

"I've already testified to Melee's innocence," Crawford said. "She was a victim, not a saboteur."

"You knew her as well as you know Commander Tragnor," Orin said. "You have a sentimental weakness that enables you to cover for both?"

"Why don't you just Torture me," Crawford said, irritated with the panel. "That way you can get everything you want."

"Then there is something you are withholding," Rivan said.

"Take me to The Stretch and you'll find out," Crawford returned boldly. "Either that or terminate me now."

"So be it," Orin said.

The members looked to Farah who reluctantly nodded approval. "Zelda, the grand architect is to be examined. Take him to the detention center," she said.

"I am disappointed you disobeyed our instruction even if you considered it was best," Hyatt said. "For what it is worth, I hope to find nothing more to discredit you or your progenitors."

"It doesn't matter what you find," Crawford replied. "I know who I am and what I've done. I'd do it again."

CHAPTER 37

Andira sat in her lab, staring at samples through a scope, periodically pausing to glance at screen images projected in front of her station. Five new modules, housing brain tissue, lay on a long metal table, hooked into a life support unit ready for priming and placement into The Server hive.

Directly opposite the organs lay small shrouded forms. Andira moved to uncover one of the figures, revealing a child with inky skin, white eyes, and bony nodules protruding from its limbs. Its shaven head was marked with a fresh incision.

This is a mistake, Andira said, shaking her head. *They're wrong. This isn't the answer.*

Andira replaced the sheet and returned to the samples, mulling over the data. She and her group were finishing the last round of tests on the three subjects from the academic disaster. Thora, a senior medical officer, joined Andira in the lab, poring over the data with the physician.

"We know alleviation was present in those involved, yet they suffered distress anyway," Andira said to Thora.

"The readings aren't anywhere near the threshold," Thora said. "The Fordham-Server connection theory is the only real thing we have. The heavy emotional traffic is obviously deadly to them and The Servers."

"But the problem is ascertaining the stimulus. If I could find it, I'd be able to eliminate it."

Thora bent over the scope, peering at the cells smeared on the slide. "Is it possible the Fordham themselves are the issue?"

"How's that?"

"They collect emotions and they transmit them."

"I know that, Thora," Andira said, seizing a pad.

She punched several codes on its face, bringing up a new display. An announcement over the wave interrupted her analysis. Thora and Andira listened closely to the transmission. The grand architect was in custody.

"Senator Novak said he was part of the problem," Andira sighed. "It's hard to believe."

"He may still be innocent," Thora said.

Andira returned to the units. "I hate to place these inside the Hive. It's a waste of resources."

"The problem could be in the citizen sensors."

"No, the sample group and people at the scenes were pinged. They function normally."

"What else is there to consider?"

"I wish I knew," Andira said. "The comm center sent over the restored files, but it turns out they weren't damaged. Someone encrypted them."

"Then they had something to hide."

"Precisely. Go and see if Ciers has them and have him bring the other units to me."

Andira crossed to a glass cabinet in the corner of her space. She pulled out several instruments, plugged a cord into a device resembling a scalpel, and started working on the tissue samples.

As she began her analysis, a chilling cry rang out from the corridor. Andira rushed the door, dropping her instrument on the way to the exit.

"Thora! Ciers!"

Ciers stumbled along the hallway, stunned from an unseen ordeal. He clawed the wall attempting to brace himself, fighting to maintain consciousness. Blood dripping from a jagged gash on his forehead fell in droplets on the marbled floor.

Andira hurried to his aid, putting an arm around the tech, holding his solid frame while guiding him to the lab. "Where's Thora?" she asked.

"She ran," Ciers said gasping. "The sentinel went berserk."

"What?" Andira asked, applying pressure to his wound.

Ciers tried to catch his breath. "They provoked it, they pushed us all," he said, pulling on Andira's coat. "They're Fordham."

Andira did not know what to make of Ciers' excited mood. "You're in shock. Hold this," she said, placing Ciers' hand on the bandage. "Stay here."

Andira crept to the exam room, slowly sticking her head in the entranceway. What she saw horrified her senses. The sentinel lay on the floor, staring at the ceiling, its strip cracked. One of Ciers' technicians rested across a gurney, saliva leaching from the mouth. Andira stepped closer, observing the woman's vitals. Her neck was broken. Two additional personnel slouched dead in the adjacent room, shards of glass in their hands, victims of lethal combat.

A whimper caught Andira's attention. She approached the sound cautiously, finding Noreen, a junior technician, wedged between a cabinet and the wall.

Andira grabbed Noreen's shoulders, shaking her into awareness. "What happened? Tell me what happened."

"They made it angry," Noreen said hysterical, gulping.

"Who made who angry?"

"Those people did. They started on Hensley, pushing him," Noreen said. "They wouldn't stop."

"I don't understand," Andira said. "What do you mean - pushed him?"

Noreen fell back, bursting into tears, unable to give a coherent account of the happenings.

"Get up," Andira said, assisting Noreen. "Go into the lab, I'll call Dr. Stricklin, and get Ciers some help."

Noreen slid up the wall, holding herself in fear as she left. Andira scanned the room looking for answers. The modules she sent Thora to retrieve were putrid and blackened. Andira crossed to Ciers' terminal, dialing Dr. Stricklin.

Stricklin answered. "Andira?"

"I need a medical team now in my lab. My technicians have been attacked."

"We're on our way," he said.

Andira started back to Ciers and Noreen's location but paused when she saw a package bearing a seal from the Unity City's comm center. She ripped open the envelope, pulling out its metallic disk. She ran back to the lab with the object in hand.

"When did you get this?" Andira asked Ciers.

"It came in an hour ago, but we were in the middle of our exams, so it went by the wayside."

"You should have told me straight away."

"We didn't think it would make a difference," Noreen said. "Not after what we found."

"The subject's levels were in range," Ciers said. "Their response to emotive probe was negative, but we found foreign tissue comparable to The Servers."

"That's not possible," Andira breathed. "There has to be an error somewhere."

"It's true. They have a power of some sort."

"It's like the sentinels, except they're agitators. It started when we finished the report," Noreen said. "I was coming to tell you, but our staff was attacked."

"Properly medicated people aren't violent."

"These people were. That girl sensed something in us," Ciers said. "She made everyone feel strange. She brought out things I never knew I felt."

"She was laughing at us," Noreen said. "Pushing perverted feelings on us we couldn't control."

"Are they wired?"

"They've no transmitters, which means no connection to the network," Ciers said.

"Where did they come from?"

"We cross-referenced their stories. They're from Betera Eaton's groups," Noreen answered. "Just like the Fordham."

"Fordham get their power from The Server tissue," Andira said, her complexion turning bleak. "The previous subjects had unusual variances in their blood."

"These subjects did as well," Noreen said.

Andira thrust the disk into the reader to retrieve the decoded files. Her voice cracked as she began to read aloud.

"They're not human. They're a hybrid of some sort," she said. "We didn't know what we were looking for."

"That must be why they kill themselves," Ciers said, his voice faint. "They'd be exposed if they were tested."

"They're rebounding stress from citizens and overriding the alleviators," Andira continued reading. "We'd have found their intent if we had these files sooner. We'd have…Oh no."

"What is it?" Noreen asked.

"Betera had to have used the same genetic material to create these children as the type she used to enhance the Fordham," Andira said. "Linus Rand destroyed all of them except those that made up The Servers and the children in The Pool."

"The grand architect is her son," Ciers said. "Who knows what he or the rest of his kind really are. None of the Lear clan was ever corrected."

"I've got to get to the senate," Andira said. "Lock the inner door. Don't leave until Stricklin gets here."

"You've passed the detention center," Crawford said glancing out the rear of Zelda's squad hover. "Where are you taking me?" Crawford studied her face. Her rich coffee eyes were sensitive, but her face remained vacant.

"You have to leave this place," Zelda said. "You must be saved."

"Why would you want to help me escape?"

"Do you need to ask with everything you have seen?"

"You're supposed to be loyal to Beta Union," Crawford said. "This isn't in your programming."

"Fordham loyalty is a myth," Zelda said, turning her head to observe his reaction. "You were designed for a purpose. All of us were."

"What do you mean?"

"You are the culmination of Betera Eaton's work," Zelda explained. "You fulfilled the objective that has freed our people from their bondage."

"Our people?" Crawford inquired. "Who are they?"

"Those that were here before Enoch's settlers," the sentinel explained. "They are nearly extinct now."

"Those visions. What are they?"

"They are the spirits of your kind, calling out to release them from bondage and avenge them," Zelda said. Crawford's mind shook with the weight of her words. He could read the truth from within.

"My kind?"

"I cannot explain everything, but know you are not ordinary," Zelda said. "You are a part of Beta Union's bloody history and The Servers are also a part of you."

"They're not human."

"You are not human. Neither was she who made you," Zelda said. "Betera was the queen of a great race, deceived and destroyed by human lusts. Linus Rand and The Founders were always the enemies, even as she appeared to protect them."

"Are you saying?"

"You have been part of a brilliant plan to deal justice to the humans," Zelda said, "and to free our people from slavery at their hands."

"The Servers' deaths are her idea of freedom?"

"Their fate secures the survival of The Pool," Zelda said. "It is my task to rescue those who remain captive."

"Who are you in all of this?" Crawford asked.

"I am the descendant of Linus Rand and Betera Eaton, hidden from view to keep you safe, to bring you to this moment," Zelda said. "There is more for you to do."

Crawford's mouth fell open. There were no words to define the shock of Zelda's statement. "I think I've done enough," Crawford said. "Betera used me my entire life. I don't want any part of whatever you're planning for the rest of humanity."

"If you want to live, you will play your part."

"Are you threatening me?"

"No, but your people's survival is in your hands," Zelda said. "Those that remain cannot return home."

"What home?" Crawford asked.

"It is a planet far from here," Zelda responded. "I do not know where in the heavens."

"I can't kill anyone else. I won't kill anyone!"

"Whatever future there is, it cannot be built on the backs of our people," Zelda said. "You must go to Caelum and prevent things from ending the way they began."

Crawford did not like the sound of Zelda's words. They were too ominous. How could he trust a person who knew the truth and allowed him to destroy an entire culture? What was certain was that he had to survive for Kemble. She was reason enough to continue his journey, to escape from the Union.

"Where exactly do you propose to take me?"

"Dr. Novak's lab will suffice. They are likely to have searched it already, but he is onboard Commander Tragnor's ship by now," Zelda said, gliding around a corner. "Bristol is waiting there to assist us."

"What's going to happen now?" Crawford asked, seeing citizens moving along the streets in comfort, Fordham scattered among them.

"You will see," Zelda said, imputing coordinates, angling the hover to its destination.

The ride to Severn's lab was quick. Zelda surveyed the streets, before setting the vehicle down gently.

"We have to get inside quickly."

Bristol waited at the door, opening it after recognizing the sign she and Zelda agreed to use. "Greetings, grand architect," Bristol said, ushering Crawford forward. "Do come in."

Crawford stepped in, finding the lab in shambles, equipment strewn across the floor, panels broken, and furniture overturned. "Is this your idea of a well-kept household?" he said, stepping over broken glass.

"It was necessary to destroy Dr. Novak's work," Zelda replied. "This is the primary lab where all research flows."

Crawford stared around the room in astonishment, observing the dead monitor above. "You did all this yourself?" he asked Bristol.

"Yes. Grand Architect Lear," Bristol responded.

"I think you can stop calling me that. They'll be looking for my successor soon if they aren't already."

"A successor will not stop what has begun," Zelda said. "The Servers are too deeply penetrated."

"Even with everything we've done, Farah and the Senate won't stop until they find us," Crawford said. "I wouldn't be surprised if they knew what was going on."

"He knows?" Bristol whispered to Zelda.

"He has been told enough for now."

"Do you understand what is happening?" Bristol asked.

"I'm not sure I understand anything anymore or who I am."

"You will board the *Meridian* and make your way to Caelum," Zelda said. "There you will find answers for many questions and the next phase of your journey."

"You can't stay here," Crawford said, leaning against what remained of Severn's island.

"We must get to The Pool and lead the people to safety," Zelda said. "That is the next phase."

"They'll send every Fordham in the city after you."

"They are too concerned with their welfare to notice us," Bristol said.

Crawford looked to Zelda. The sentinel touched her ear. "What is it?"

"A province-wide transmission," Zelda answered. "We move when it begins."

"That's your cover?"

"It is, grand architect," Bristol said. "The action will be most unexpected. A surprise if you will."

"Something tells me Farah's not going to like this," Crawford said with a smile.

Bristol's cheeks flushed with mischievous energy at his expression. Crawford caught her with her shield down. Her reaction pleased him. Crawford looked from Bristol to Zelda. It was hard for him to believe in their mutual connection. The idea of their shared foreign roots disturbed his conscience.

Mallet, Melee, Crawford and countless others belonged to the same genetic stock. All of them were part of a unique environment, raised under Betera's protection and yet kept in the dark. Zelda had said that Caelum promised to shed new light on the expanse of Betera's conspiracy, but whether Crawford could stomach the fullness of her genius remained ambiguous.

CHAPTER 38

Farah tucked delicate strands of her scarlet hair into her chignon. "It is time for our address to the people," she said.

"I wonder how many citizens heard of the problems at the school," Rivan said.

Hyatt crossed to stand beside him. "I doubt anyone is alarmed," he said, patting his colleague's shoulder. "It was all kept very hushed up."

"I would thank the Fordham for their diligence if they accepted the praise," Castillo said.

Farah stepped in front of the pack, laughing demurely. "That would be a waste whether they responded or not," she said. "They are here to obey, protect, and serve. It is their only purpose in life."

"The *Meridian* and *Azimuth* depart within the hour," Hyatt said. "We should start now."

Farah reached for the screen, ready to summon the station to open a public channel.

Suddenly, Andira burst in, Prell and Karno behind the frenetic physician.

"Please forgive the intrusion," Karno said. "Dr. Sorenson insists she sees the senate immediately."

"It is all right," Farah said, puzzled by Andira's state. "Calm yourself, Andira."

Andira gasped for air. She had run to The State Building, to deliver damning news. "They're aliens," she said, holding her heaving chest.

"Who are you referring to?" Orin asked, stepping forward.

"The dissidents. They're offspring of the people from the time before," she said, handing Orin and Farah Technician Ciers' report. "They can manipulate emotions. It's a power inherent to their species."

"Where did you get this?"

"We extracted the data from the offenders brought in from the incident at the school," Andira replied. "Several of my staff...they are dead. Ciers is injured and a sentinel is to blame."

"A sentinel is beyond reproach," Hyatt said.

"He attacked my staff after they were prodded by a student," Andira explained. "They're all empaths. They're different from the Fordham, but empaths no less."

"That makes no logical sense," Farah said. "How could they be among us? Those creatures look nothing like human beings."

"Some of them are hybrids. The irregularities in their blood are mutations of the alien DNA," Andira said sternly. "I am certain of that fact."

"How can a bunch of rabble-rousers overpower Fordham?" Castillo asked. "The sentinel's emotions are suppressed."

"No matter how we engineered them, Fordham are human, susceptible to a myriad of moods. The installation of the graft cells didn't change that."

"So, these mutants cause these riots?" Hyatt asked.

"How many ways do I have to tell you?" Andira asked. "They act like explicit emotional contagions. Their actions are willful and calculated."

"And you believe they are killing The Servers?" Hyatt asked.

"They seek out negative impulses and expose them. The resulting chaos volleys between the sentinels and The Servers like a loop," Andira explained. "The Servers can't purge the emotions fast enough to recover."

"Why would they want to destroy The Servers?" Castillo asked. "What purpose could it serve for them?"

"Betera created the entire system," Andira said, "They were perfect for her purpose. She used them and her son to exact her revenge upon us."

Farah perked up. "Crawford has nothing to do with this."

"Doesn't he?" Orin asked. "The other subjects are from Delphia, are they not?"

Andira hung her head. "Every one of them," she breathed.

"I knew it!" Orin said, turning to Farah in excitement.

"You know nothing for certain," Farah said, clutching her arms tightly to her chest.

"Crawford Lear has been present at several events, most recently the school yesterday," Hyatt said, "and he was a student at the school during the first incident in Osler."

Castillo concurred. "The grand architect was also at the museum incident. I remember the record well. He was just accepted into the engineering program."

"He was never arrested." Farah fired. "He was merely in the wrong place at the wrong time."

Orin's voice cut the air. "Betera Eaton was able to shield her son from being detained. He got away and now he is attacking us with his knowledge of The Servers' workings."

"Do you hear what you are saying?" Farah breathed. "He can't be like them."

"Why not?" Orin asked. "You think because you have feelings for him, it makes him human?"

"Crawford Lear has never been scanned," Hyatt said. "He must have been protected somehow."

"There's no record of him being ill," Andira said. "Nor has he ever been assessed."

"Betera Eaton knew many scientists," Orin said. "They probably helped him hide."

"These creatures are frauds," Andira said. "The scans on their temples, their connection to the network, everything is false."

"This is an absurd fantasy," Farah said. "They bleed just as we do. They look like us."

"You would defend Crawford Lear to the last," Orin said. "Or are you defending yourself?"

Farah backed away from her colleagues. "I have nothing to do with this."

"Consul Farah," Castillo said. "I agree with Senator Novak. As Betera's descendant, the architect has a motive. Crawford Lear had the means to deceive us."

"Orin hates him," Farah said, directing her attention to Senator Novak. "You hatched these lies yourself, didn't you?"

"It's true, Farah. You must believe it," Andira said, slamming a pad on the table. "Here are Betera's notes. She is one of those from the time before. I don't know how, but she passed herself off as one of us."

Orin perused the data. "She intended us to find this at a time of her choosing."

"No one ever questioned the death of a woman who rescued us from ourselves only to annihilate us from within."

"Dorian Aver should have eliminated her," Orin said to Farah, "and you should not have elevated Crawford Lear."

"You have nothing on me," Farah snarled. Prell immediately went to her side, placing a hand on her arm. She batted him away as his facial receptor glowed hotly, but Prell held firmly to Farah, his strength enflaming her slender limb.

Castillo faced Dr. Sorenson. "There must be something we can do."

"Our medications are inept against their force. Their power countermands alleviation."

"Then we must round them up," Rivan said. "We will arrest every one of them."

"We don't know where they are or how many they number," Andira responded, "and they'll sacrifice themselves before being caught."

"As the Tragnor woman did," Hyatt said.

"We should cull everyone involved in the incidents," Orin said. "It will be a greater sweep than the first and just as effective."

Castillo seconded the idea, offering one of her own. "Crawford Lear can be made to assist us if they were mentally prompted."

"He'll die before he tells you anything."

"Then he will die with the rest of them," Orin said.

"We cannot kill innocents?" Hyatt pleaded.

"If it means ensuring our survival," Rivan said, "we have little choice."

Orin looked to Karno. "Where is Zelda?"

"She has not returned from the detention center," Karno said. "Shall I summon her?"

"Immediately! And tell her to bring the grand architect."

Zelda's from the Delphian groups, Andira thought. *We shouldn't trust her.*

Andira's fears were realized when Karno returned. "The architect is not at the center and neither is Zelda," he said. "They never arrived."

Hyatt and Orin exchanged grim looks. "This is the rope that will hang you," Orin seethed, directing his ire at Farah. "Consul Farah will stay here while Prell and Karno locate Zelda and Crawford Lear."

"What of Mallet Tragnor?" Andira asked. "He's a Delphian. He is close to Crawford Lear."

"Adario and Garnette are on their way to the harbor," Orin said. "Karno, contact them, see they enlist Commander Ragas' assistance to stop Tragnor's crew."

"I move we transfer Consul Farah to detention," a junior member said. "She must be detained until this business is sorted."

"Quite right, my learned friend," Hyatt said. "Senator Novak, you will serve as interim consul until we are clear of this mess."

"I accept the responsibility," Orin replied, watching Farah crumble. "We must address the citizens. They can help us locate the confederates."

"Take me away now," Farah murmured.

"No," Orin said to her. "You will watch how a real leader confronts virulence."

"I'm afraid for our future," Andira said.

"There is still one other card to play, Andira," Hyatt said. "Zara's Pillar is still available to us. If need be, we can use the weapon against them."

"Only if you can figure out how to make it work for us," Rivan said. "Linus Rand tried for years. He came up with nothing."

"Betera might have known," Andira said. "It stands to reason these creatures may know how to operate it. All we need do is capture them."

"You are all fools," Farah laughed. "Do you think they will give you any information?"

"They will have no choice."

"We've underestimated them as it is. You will fail."

"If we do, it is on your head," Orin said.

"Enough," Rivan said. "Have the broadcast center open a channel to the squares."

Orin touched the screen and dialed several digits. The display linked to the center. A fair-haired man answered the call. "Senator Novak," he said. "We are standing by for Consul Farah's address."

"Farah Aver is no longer giving a speech," Orin replied. "I will speak to our citizens. Open the channels to the squares."

The man complied. "The feed is open; you have visual and are on-screen."

Orin was glad to see the squares peaceful. He waited for everyone present to catch sight of him before speaking.

"Citizens, I wish you good noon. I am Senator Novak," he said. "We are scheduled to embark on a great journey today, but before it can occur, I need your help. I know you love our nation as much as your senate and you will help preserve her sanctity. Therefore, I ask—"

The screen went dark; the transmission faded abruptly.

"What is happening?" Rivan asked.

"Look!" Hyatt said, pointing to the screen. Stills and clips of violence, religious iconography, sadness, and all manners of vice splashed across the display.

Orin slammed his hand down on the comm. "What is going on?" he yelled into the speaker.

"The feed has been hacked, sir," the technician responded, "and the codes have been altered."

"Shut it down! I do not care what you have to do."

"Nothing is responding."

The images continued briefly before the vantage switched to the streets. Citizens standing before the screens fell under the hypnotic spell of images dashing across screens in every square. Several females held their children close while others ushered their flock away from harm.

"They are watching," Farah said.

"So are we," Andira uttered. "Those pictures are a prelude to the extermination of our people."

Fordham approached gatherers in the State quadrangle, steering them away from the monitors. There were those who submitted and others who were not silent.

"Move this way," a sentinel said to a man dressed in khaki.

"Take your hands off me," the citizen responded, combatively.

A group of teens started stirring the mixed emotions around them, frantically waving their arms, hurling insults at the guard, and fueling the tense atmosphere. Bystanders responded to the vibrations and pushed back against the sentinel forces.

"I've always despised you!" a woman screamed, slapping a man across the face.

"I thought you cheated me. Now I know it's true," a male said, grabbing a vendor by the arm.

The scene repeated in every province as citizen tempers swung from high to low and back again, causing Fordham to fall like building blocks as pandemonium grew. Statues, benches, and fountains were overturned, storefront windows were broken in outrage. Men, women, and children dropped to their knees crying in panic.

Back in the meeting room, the senate continued watching the horde explode, their beloved world ripped apart by violence.

"How can this be?" Rivan asked.

"The rebels are feeding on the vulnerable," Andira said. "All they need is a speck of emotion to build on."

"What about the mists?" Hyatt asked.

"It will spray to no avail," she answered.

Orin refused to believe his eyes. He buzzed the security center within the building, "Barnak, Romnel," he said, calling the sentinels.

"Yes, sir," two voices said in unison.

"Citizens are in distress. Gather every available Fordham within the vicinity of the squares," Orin said. "Have the frigate commanders assist in controlling the unrest. If the people resist, cull them!"

"It's too late," Andira said. "Nothing can hold it back."

Together, the members looked toward the windows, seeing citizens running past the State with Fordham in pursuit, discharging bursts of energy from their weapons. The pulses tore through the brightness of the day, scorching the soft flesh of fleeing victims.

"It is a virus," Hyatt said in a low tone.

"We will regain control," Orin said defiantly. "We will not surrender."

Farah laughed hysterically from her seat, unable to control the hideous noise escaping her mouth. Orin slapped her.

"Senator!" Castillo cried out, "Restrain yourself."

Farah lifted her eyes to Orin, her beautiful features stained with tears. "I cared for him. It was my sin," she said quietly, "but yours will be that you will not kill him."

Farah chuckled again, the sound dying to a whimper. Orin, too concerned with the madness in the streets to pity her, feared her words. He thought of Severn, whom he knew was with

Mallet and Kemble. He felt betrayed and outwitted, the knowledge of the parallel catastrophes terrifying him.

In a cruel twist of fate, Linus Rand's last words seemed more than a prophecy inching closer towards fact. Beta Union's fall had begun, just as the founder said. Its only salvation against the tide lay in capturing Crawford Lear.

CHAPTER 39

Keir Jaxon wandered around Jersa's waterfront, he and his troop on standby after hearing news of disquiet raging across the nation.

"Commander Jaxon," his pilot called from the *Zephyr*'s boarding plank. Keir tore up the ramp to meet her, his brow taut.

"What's the word?" he asked.

"The *Meridian*'s being held at the dock. They don't intend for her to launch."

"Odonna can deal with that," Keir answered with a scowl. "We have an obligation to the citizens here."

"Attempts to contact Commander Ragas have been unsuccessful," the pilot said. "The order to detain the *Meridian* comes directly from the senate. Commander Tragnor and the GA have been identified as confederates."

Keir's mouth twisted in disbelief. "Mallet Tragnor's an egotist, but he's no traitor. I know that for a fact."

"Senator Novak was on the wave, sir. He said it himself."

Keir stared out to sea. Mallet was not only a colleague. He was Keir's friend. "Signal the senator, tell him we'll investigate, and then raise the ship."

"Aye, sir," the pilot said, heading for the wheelhouse.

Whatever you're doing, Mallet, you'd better be willing to pay for it, Keir thought.

Bristol put an ear to the lab door, hearing raised voices and other rumblings passing by the location. Zelda stood with Crawford some distance away.

"It is time," Bristol said.

"We must go now," Zelda said. "Get a weapon for the grand architect."

Bristol ducked into the office, returning with a burnished handgun and gave it to Crawford. "Are you adept at using this?" she asked.

"It's not unknown to me."

"Remember to be defensive," Zelda said. "This rail will fire twelve pulses and then recharge."

"How long does it take?" Crawford asked.

"Thirty seconds," Bristol answered. "It is a small margin, which could mean the difference between life and death."

"Be precise. Aim for the head or the neck," Zelda said.

"I'll do my best."

"There is a station on the edge of the square," Bristol said. "A train is scheduled to arrive shortly."

"It may be delayed thanks to your little demonstration," Crawford said, tucking the pistol in a holster attached to his thigh.

"It is worth the risk," Zelda replied. "The stop at Aero is closest to the pier. From there, you will make your way to Commander Tragnor's vessel."

305

"I hate to remind you, but Fordham are after me," Crawford said. "Do you intend on holding all of them off by yourselves?"

"If necessary," Zelda replied.

"The sentinels will be distracted by the commotion," Bristol said.

"Lucky for you, they all wear the same uniform," Crawford joked. "You'll blend right in."

"Let us go," Zelda said. "Open the door, Bristol."

Bristol reached for the panel, releasing the latch. A state of anarchy permeated the area outside Severn's lab.

"This way," Zelda said, taking the point.

Crawford took Bristol's hand, weaving past bodies scattered in their path. The dead, Fordham and citizen alike, lay on grassy patches trodden by citizens rushing in panic from weapon fire, drowning the moans of the wounded. In the distance, Crawford heard sirens blaring in loud waves as sentinels ordered citizens to calm themselves and return to their homes. No one was listening.

Zelda was steps ahead, carefully pushing through the figures. Holding a gun at her side, she halted her steps at the sight of Prell and Karno on the edge of the square. They stood by a hover, blinking red and scanning the crowd. If the sentinels dallied much longer, they would reach the brink of whiting out.

Prell touched his ear, squinting against the negative emotional onslaught. He finally motioned Karno into the vehicle and glided away. Bristol and Zelda fared no better. Crawford, feeling Bristol's discomfort, slipped an arm around her waist, and dragged her along.

"Keep moving!" he shouted.

"Confusion, anger…" Bristol said, sensing ill-feeling in the crowd, "It…it…"

"You have to keep going," Crawford said. "We're almost there."

Zelda stumbled, shapes blurring her vision. As tremors rocked her body, screams ravaged her ears. Blues became greens, reds melted into burnt orange, and brown. She fought for air, shaking her head, trying to regain balance.

Crawford, coming up behind, used his free hand to support her. "Two meters," he yelled. "You can do it."

"Two meters," she cried blinking, her throat tight. With a last push from Crawford, they reached the station. Zelda hugged a column in relief.

Bristol, sustained by Crawford, panted, her breathing slowly returning to normal. The tracks were quiet with no citizens in sight. "It is clear," she said, raising her head. "Where are the people?"

"They're drawn to the square," Crawford said, releasing her to a seat. "How are you?"

"Recovering," Bristol said, her eyes bright.

Crawford checked Zelda. "And you?"

Color returned to her complexion. "The same," she answered, surveying a digital display hanging overhead. "There is a car arriving."

"It could be a false signal," Crawford said.

"We shall see," Zelda replied, loosening the belt around her waist while holding tightly to the gun in her hand.

"I'm surprised you held on to that."

"It would have done no good if it were lost."

The tracks issued a hum. "What do you know? You were right again," Crawford said, helping Bristol to her feet.

The train, ferrying a small number of citizens, pulled up to the platform. There appeared to be no sentinels onboard. Crawford and his companions warily stepped into the cabin.

"They are here on the train," Zelda said lowly. "It is difficult to determine their exact location."

"Most are in the square," Bristol replied, sitting down.

The occupants, looking overwrought and scared, held on to support poles. A young woman in muted yellow, her eyes moist and fearful, turned to Crawford, touching his arm.

"They attacked us," she said. "I was afraid."

"You'll be all right now," he said, assuring her with sincerity.

"I don't think so. They're here," she said pointing toward the rear car. Crawford searched the space between the coaches. Two Fordham traversed the aisle spraying a ragged bunch with an aerosol.

"We have to get off," Crawford said to Zelda and Bristol. "The Fordham are on the move."

A voice suddenly came over the intercom. "You are betrayed. The grand architect stole your bliss." Zelda placed a hand on her gun as the litany continued, "Find the engineer, detain him and your contentment shall be restored."

The jaded gatherers stared viciously at Crawford, who realized he was the only one onboard wearing the signature brown of his occupation.

"We're in trouble," Crawford said to Zelda and Bristol, pushing them to the forward compartment.

The watcher's hungry eyes followed them. "You are the one," a man said. "You have brought this on us."

"I'm not the architect. I'm just a simple engineer," Crawford said, his presence increasing their fury.

A figure lunged at Crawford, tearing his sleeve. "He's lying!"

"Hold him!" another passenger screamed.

"Come on," Zelda cried, opening a linking passage. Fordham, sensing the commotion from their position in the rear, pushed through the cars, intent on capturing Crawford.

"He is here," a female sentinel said, dispatching information through her ear link. "He is attempting to escape."

"Halt, architect," a Fordham shouted as they squeezed through compartment doors.

Zelda and Bristol hurried to the next gate, prying the doors open. A shot rang out, flooring a citizen. There was no time to think. Crawford's instincts sought to defend his person. He raised the pistol, the red aura of the principal sentinel providing a perfect target. Crawford fired into its glowing light as the metro thundered underground.

The sentinel dropped like a bag of stones. The pulse Crawford discharged blackened its face. He then took the brief pandemonium as an opportunity to make his exit to the next car.

"Where are we?" he asked, catching up with Bristol and Zelda.

"We are nearly at the station," Bristol said.

Another sentinel, blond hair plastered to his sweaty brow, paused in his pursuit, issuing an order into the intercom. "Operator, you are to stop the train and secure all exits," he said, sweeping his locks from his eyes. "Sentinels, the architect is in the center car. You are to converge at once and detain him."

On the sentinel's command, the train screeched to a halt, throwing riders against its walls, darkness engulfing the compartments.

"They've cut the route," Crawford said.

Zelda tugged at an exit. "It is sealed," she said, standing back and aiming for the glass.

"Don't waste your energy," Crawford said. "It won't break."

"How are we to exit?" Zelda asked, ignorant of its design.

"Get behind me," Crawford said, shooting the emergency panel, which flared and burned. "Now try it."

As three figures advanced on their position, Bristol urged Zelda to hurry. Crawford assisted her in prying open the door. He then jumped down into the shadowy tunnel with Zelda and Bristol following.

"There is a stairway ahead," Zelda said, pointing to light in the distance.

Fordham reached the blast area moments after their exodus. "The grand architect has fled to the subway," a sentinel said into her earpiece.

Prell answered the signal from his hover. "What is his destination?"

"Unknown," the sentinel replied. "The train is stopped between Jenlo and the Aero dock."

"He is on his way to the pier," Prell said. "Are there citizens on the train?"

"Affirmative. They are afflicted."

"Cull them and then regroup with the squad at Jenlo."

Karno sat next to Prell reviewing a tablet. "Adario and Garnette are approximately fifteen minutes from the dock."

"They will capture the *Meridian* while we apprehend Grand Architect Lear at Aero," Prell said.

"He is to be taken alive," Karno gently reminded his companion.

"Does it matter how he is taken?" Prell asked with a sickening smile. "Surely dead would be preferable."

CHAPTER 40

Crawford and his allies emerged from the murky tunnel soiled from their travels. "There is no one here," Zelda said, checking the area.

"They must've cleared the area," Crawford said, remaining cautious and alert.

Blood trickled down Bristol's cheek and legs. She dabbed it with her fingertips, awed by the color matching her dress. Crawford reached to examine her face; the wound looked nasty, but not too deep.

"I guess this means you've earned your stripes."

"Clarify."

"Forget it," he said, looking toward the school.

"The harbor is just over the hill," Zelda said, pointing to the slope at the side of the building. The open space between them and their destination was less than inviting.

"It's too quiet," Crawford said.

"We must move on."

"Wait. I'll go out first."

Zelda took his wrist. "You will be safer behind us."

"This is no time to be gallant. Have a little faith in me," Crawford said, gripping his pistol. "Give me your hand, Bristol. You stay with me."

Crawford slowly crept away from the platform columns to the isolation beyond, scrutinizing the scene with Zelda walking backward protecting the rear.

Bristol held tight to Crawford's hand, the length of her face emitting a disturbing spark. "Something is wrong," she said, slowing to an abrupt halt.

"Keep moving," Zelda ordered.

Crawford inspected the hill, the sound of a hover reaching his ears. A craft came quickly into view.

Zelda's vision darted about, seeking cover. "Run!" she shouted.

Bristol shook loose from Crawford, dashing toward the vehicle, waving them down and throwing herself to the pavement. "Arrest them," she said. "They are rebels."

Prell and Karno exited the car, directing rifles at Zelda and Crawford. Karno stepped away from Prell, helping Bristol stand. "You are not with them?" he asked.

"No, they broke into Dr. Novak's lab. They were trying to evade capture."

"You are a hostage?" Karno asked, holding her with a firm grip.

"Yes," she said. "They attacked and murdered citizens." Prell slipped closer to Crawford and Zelda.

"You are unwise to believe her," Zelda said, "but she is right, you should arrest us."

"Our orders are to take the grand architect to the State Building," Prell responded. "You are another matter."

"Throw down your weapons," Karno said, voice hard, distorted with stress. Crawford advanced toward the sentinels, tuning into Prell's mood.

"Stop where you are, architect," Prell said.

"You want me to come with you, don't you?"

"You will come forward slowly after Zelda relinquishes the weapon," Prell said.

"Put it down, Zelda," Crawford called to her.

"And kick it away," Prell said.

Zelda did as she was instructed, then held her hands next to her head.

"Karno, release Bristol and then dispose of Zelda." The sentinel let go of his charge and started toward Zelda.

"No!" Bristol screamed, pouncing at Karno, setting him off balance.

Prell fired into Bristol's back, rendering her limp. She slumped to the ground in a heap before him. Crawford immediately rushed Prell, struggling to secure his gun. Zelda hurried to retrieve her weapon as Karno rose. He discharged a pulse at her but missed his target. She returned fire, hitting the sentinel between the eyes, felling him.

Prell and Crawford continued brawling amidst the unfolding drama. Crawford slammed Prell's head against the hover's hood, pounding his face with vicious force. Glittering hues raged across the sentinel's face. Prell gnashed his teeth and spat wildly while Crawford held his forearm against the sentinel's throat.

Sweat dripped down the architect's face as he pressed hard against Prell's resistance. The sentinel's face blinked, and his eyes rolled back before his consciousness failed. Crawford gasped, releasing his hold on the static body. He rushed to Zelda, who cradled Bristol in her lap.

"You are sad," Bristol breathed, seeing remorse in his eyes, her face saturated with blue. "I can feel it. I can feel," With her voice trailing into silence, Crawford stroked her hair and cheek.

"You must go. There is little time," Zelda said, lowering Bristol to the ground, before moving to the hovercar to answer an incoming call.

"Zelda, our squad is approaching the pier," Garnette said, over the intercom.

"Belay your orders," Zelda said. "The grand architect is in custody and Prell has secured the *Meridian*."

"No information was transmitted to this location."

"The information has now been relayed," Zelda said. "There are students in the Aero Institute who need restoration. Take charge there."

"Acknowledged," Garnette said, ending the call.

"Come with me," Crawford implored. "They'll kill you if you stay."

"That they will," she said, handing him her pistol, "yet, it does not change the fact that you must continue alone. Your path is the more important one."

Crawford stared into her dark face. He wanted to remain a little longer, pleading with her to survive, but her expression was steadfast.

"Goodbye," he said, reluctance tingeing his voice as he jogged away.

Zelda did not watch Crawford as he disappeared over the hill. Instead, she took a rifle from the hover's rack, checked it, and proceeded to her rendezvous with Garnette and Adario. Her intentions belonged to a link in a chain she could not break. Climbing the stairs, she saw students racing through the corridors, a flock confused and frightened.

Zelda entered the building, accepting the gravity of her commitment. The ground upon which she stood might well prove to be her final resting place.

"Where's Crawford? We're cutting it close," Mallet said, stealing a glance at the *Azimuth*'s preparations.

"When is the escort arriving?" Severn asked, standing close.

"The last transmission said they were fifteen minutes or so out," Mallet replied.

"Then we've got to hope he's near."

Kemble stuck her head out of the wheelhouse entrance. "Mallet, come here," she yelled.

"What's wrong?" he asked, sprinting to the wheelhouse.

"The wave," she began, "You and Crawford are all over it. The *Zephyr* is on its way here."

"Oh no," Severn sighed. "We're out of time."

"Kemble, we have to lift off now."

"We can't leave without Crawford."

"If you want to live, we don't have a choice," Mallet said. "Now get started."

"No, sir," Kemble said boldly.

Severn saw the love in his daughter's eyes. He understood her unwillingness in leaving Crawford behind. "She's right," he spoke up. "We're in this together. We can't go without him."

Mallet drew a hand down his face. The sabotage to Odonna's comm bought them time, but with Adario and Garnette in transit, opposing forces were collapsing in on them. Severn and Kemble's concern chipped at his determination.

"Five minutes," he said, "then we have to leave."

"It's him!" Kemble shouted.

Mallet bolted to the deck, spotting his friend. He cast his view on the *Azimuth*. Odonna was out of sight for the moment. "Go to the control," he said to Kemble. "We're casting off."

Crawford ran up the gangway, grasping Mallet's arm. "Sorry, I'm late."

"What took you so long?" Mallet asked.

"It's not important. Where's Ragas?" Crawford asked breathlessly.

"She's in her wheelhouse."

"We better get underway then."

"Callia, where's the watch officer?" Mallet asked the engineer.

"He's on the *Azimuth*, sir. He said something about checking their comm."

"We're leaving. Break from the moorings. We'll catch up with Ragas at the Green."

"But the escort hasn't arrived."

"They can board Odonna's ship," Mallet said. "We're late for our trade. Move."

"Aye, sir," Callia said, directing the crew to their stations.

The ship pulled away from the jetty. Mallet took Crawford to the wheelhouse, joining Kemble and Severn inside. "Kemble, engage the field and lift us out on Ivar's mark."

Odonna waited in the *Azimuth*'s command center, mulling over the ship's comm device with her pilot. "It's been tampered with, madam," the watch officer said. "It's fixed in a loop."

"You should've figured it out," Odonna said, shooting a look at her pilot.

"I'm sorry, madam," he responded. "I don't know how it happened."

Odonna turned her head slightly, thinking about the situation. "Mallet," she whispered.

"Commander Ragas," a tactical officer said, barging in. "The *Meridian*'s left the harbor."

"Is our escort here?" she asked.

"No, madam. They've not arrived," the officer replied. "Commander Tragnor left ahead of them."

"Get that thing fixed!" Odonna said to her pilot, snatching her communications device off the chart table before heading topside to issue instructions for liftoff. Her crew sprang to action in preparation for the ship's departure.

"Did you get the wave back up?" Odonna asked her pilot as he approached her location.

"Yes, we've been charged with apprehending the *Meridian*," he said. "The provinces are under siege by fanatics. Per the transmissions, Commander Tragnor and the grand architect are in league with them."

"Tell Limon and Yumiko to take to the cannons," Odonna said. "We're pursuing Commander Tragnor's vessel."

"The *Zephyr* is in the area. Shall I contact Commander Jaxon to assist?"

"Yes," Odonna answered, folding her arms across her chest and smiling with glee. "Keir's ship may come in handy, but I fully intend on capturing the prize first."

CHAPTER 41

Kemble stood behind Ivar, looming over navigation charts. Ivar, meticulous in his course, managed a good distance from the shoreline while keeping a steady path to the Green, but the winds surrounding the ship made for a bumpy passage.

"Course correction," Mallet said, calling out new orders.

"Sir, that's the edge of Pleuran space," Ivar said.

"It certainly is," Mallet said. "Take the wheel, Kemble. I'm going to go check on Severn."

Kemble moved to the controls as Crawford came to rest beside her. "What's he doing?" he asked.

"What he always does," she responded. "Have you ever seen him play it safe?"

"No, and I gather, neither have you."

"Not once," Kemble said, trying to keep their conversation veiled. "The crew doesn't know what's going on."

"Does he expect them to just follow him out of duty?" Crawford said, bending close to her neck, the slight hairs standing at attention. Kemble liked the feeling, pivoting to brush her lips against the corner of Crawford's mouth.

"They would follow him to hell if there were one," she said, smiling graciously.

Crawford wished he could express his desire for the pilot without drawing Ivar's attention or that of the crew, but he settled for patting the exposed skin at the small of her back. A loud signal sounded on the monitor against the wall.

"Is that an alarm?" Crawford asked.

"It's Commander Ragas," Kemble replied.

Mallet bounded to the wheelhouse. "Who is it?" he asked.

"Who does it look like? Don't worry about it. Just keep your eyes on the map."

"Commander Ragas is closing on our position," Ivar said.

"Maintain course and increase speed," Mallet said, skipping out on the deck.

"He's not going to be able to pull away from her in this turbulence," Kemble said.

"What's your back-up plan?" Crawford asked.

Kemble opened a chest. "These," she said, pointing to the guns in the box.

"We'll have to get up close to use those."

"You'll do just fine," Kemble said, tapping his sidearm.

Mallet joined Severn, seeing the gunship in the distance, making full speed toward the *Meridian*.

"Will she catch us?" Severn asked.

"With this wind," Mallet began, "it's not likely. She has power, but we're lighter, even with the cargo."

"What are you going to do?"

The *Meridian* hit another bump, lurching Severn forward. Mallet reached out to pull him back. "Careful. You hit that energy field and it won't matter," he said.

"It won't matter if she reaches us either."

"I've got to get the ship down. I can outmaneuver Odonna on water." Mallet said, signaling the wheelhouse.

"Pilot Novak," Ivar said. "Commander Tragnor wants you to descend."

"He's going to the sea," Kemble said to Crawford, turning the ship slightly starboard as fast as she dared take it.

"Are we trying to evade her?" Ivar asked.

While the *Meridian* skimmed to the ocean's surface, Mallet studied the *Azimuth* as she gained ground. The speed of the travel was making Severn sick. "I think I'm going to vomit," he said, holding to the center mast.

"Do what you need to do," Mallet said, waving to the deck engineers. "Everyone, get ready to man the sails."

Odonna's deck hummed with activity. Deckhands scurried around to staff the cannons, inspect rigging, and check the main guns. Odonna eyed the *Meridian* from the stern as it continued its drop. Her pilot came on deck again to apprise her of the situation.

"Commander Tragnor must know we're in range," he said, following the line of Mallet's ship.

"I'm sure he does," Odonna said, "but he doesn't know I know what he's doing."

"It's not stopping him from running."

"Did I ask you?"

"No, madam," the pilot said.

"Limon!" Odonna said, summoning her senior tactical officer. "He'll have to disengage the energy field before he opens his sails. When he does, make sure he knows I mean business."

"With pleasure, madam," Limon answered.

"Are you planning to obliterate the vessel?" the pilot said.

"There would be no fun in that," Odonna smiled.

"Your behavior is most negative, commander."

Odonna looked at her pilot. "I'm going to stop that traitor. You can tag me later if you choose, but Consul Farah will thank me."

Limon and his officers lit up control panels behind the cannons. "Yumiko, Arvin, a shot across the bow!" he ordered.

Mallet's crew stood transfixed as the *Azimuth*'s artillery ejected energy beams from their barrels.

"Grab hold!" Mallet yelled, covering Severn. The energy bolts hit the *Meridian*'s field, rocking the hull. "Kemble!"

"I'm going as fast as I can!" she cried. "Crawford, pull that lever full out."

"This one?" he asked, pointing to a golden apparatus.

"That one!"

Crawford tugged at the bar, snapping it outward. The energy field surrounding the *Meridian* dropped and a rush of air zipped across the deck, thrashing the crew side to side. Mallet tucked Severn's head into his shoulder as the chemist struggled to breathe.

"Unfurl those sails!" Mallet bellowed to all available hands.

"The field's down," Limon said. "She's nearing the water."

"Mallet, Mallet, will you never learn," Odonna sighed. "Target him and fire."

Kemble gripped the *Meridian*'s wheel, her hands blistering against the tension. A collision siren sounded as the vessel raced to meet the water.

"Pilot Novak," Ivar said, "She's acquired our position, and the *Zephyr* is on the scope."

"How close is Commander Jaxon?"

"Less than one hundred kilometers," Ivar said. "At present speed, he can be here in minutes."

Kemble grumbled. "I can't sail this ship any faster."

"The *Azimuth* is firing portside!"

"Hang on!"

"She's going to kill us!" Severn hollered.

"This is it," Mallet said. "Hit the deck!"

A blue light glinted about the *Meridian*'s flank, followed by the smell of smoldering metal wafting from the keel. The ship crashed to the sea. Two crewmembers fell overboard. The wheelhouse was a mess of sparking panels. Instruments and charts tossed around the room. Windows shattered.

Ivar lifted his head from his display, his face bruised. "The hull's breached," he said, tapping a blistered screen.

Crawford assisted Kemble to her feet. "Activate the regen unit," Kemble said, bypassing her distress.

"It's already running, but it is slow going."

"How long before we sink?"

"I don't know, but we will."

CHAPTER 42

Mallet ran into the command center with three deckhands. "We'll need that insurance now," he said.

"I figured as much," Kemble replied, opening the chest, passing him the arms.

"Sir," one of the crew spoke up, "Why is the *Azimuth* attacking us?"

Mallet handed the young woman a weapon. "Commander Ragas and I have a difference of opinion," he said. "Personally, I think she's off her meds, and very dangerous."

"Sir, is she going to terminate us?" Ivar asked.

"No one's going to kill me or you," Mallet said, looking to Crawford. "We'll set her right." Crawford followed Mallet and the crew out of the command center.

"Kemble," Ivar said, taking a pistol from her. "It isn't true."

"What isn't true?" she asked, tucking a gun between into the back of her uniform.

"I heard the transmissions," Ivar muttered. "They're after Commander Tragnor and the grand architect."

Kemble stood back from the navigator, hearing a crackle over the comm. "The mutiny is over, Mallet," Odonna said. "We're coming alongside to board you."

"Listen to me, Ivar. I know you're worried," Kemble said, "but Mallet's done nothing wrong."

"If that's true, why are they after him?"

"I don't have time to explain, but believe me, he's in the right."

"Then we have to return so he can prove himself."

"Ivar, we're outside the habitat," Kemble said. "Out here, your fealty is to him. Do you understand?"

Ivar mulled over her statement. "I do," he answered.

"Good. Come on, we have to get outside."

The *Azimuth* cruised toward Mallet's ship. His crew was on edge, each contemplating their fate. "Don't make any moves," Mallet said. "Those with weapons, keep them behind you."

Crawford removed his gun from its strap. As instructed, he hid it between his hands at his back. "She'll know we're carrying," he said. "Our captor has a solid plan."

"I don't care if she does have one," Mallet whispered. "She's not taking us alive."

"There you go again," Crawford began, "speaking for everyone else."

Mallet could not help sniggering at Crawford's sardonic humor, though he and everyone on the ship faced execution. "They used to have films about this in the old days," he said.

"The last stand, right?"

"I'd go over a cliff with you."

"You weren't saying that a while back," Crawford said. Mallet smiled.

"I had a change of heart."

"Well, here comes your chance to make good on it."

Kemble appeared just as the *Azimuth* halted alongside the *Meridian*. Severn looked on, petrified, the others sweating, chests surging with anticipation, their apprehension heightened under Crawford and Mallet's influence.

Odonna Ragas crossed the plank extended between the two vessels. "Where's Keir?" Mallet asked as she stepped down.

"He's moments away," Odonna said. "You're awfully calm for a man facing arrest on a sinking ship."

Limon and Yumiko, along with the rest of the *Azimuth*'s team, strolled up to take positions in front of the *Meridian*'s crew. The duo's rifles were squarely aimed at their targets.

"It's a good day to go swimming," Mallet said.

"Maybe for you," Odonna replied, "but I'd rather not lose the rest of your crew."

Mallet and Crawford looked over the *Meridian*'s crew, then back to Odonna's forces, sensing discomfort in the men and women. Mallet stole a glance at Crawford, his muscles stiff, eyes glazed.

"Do you really want to do this?" Crawford asked Odonna.

Odonna laughed. "Are you kidding? Does this look like a garden party to you?"

Officer Yumiko shifted her position, walking to Odonna's side, handing her commander a small pad. "The *Zephyr* has halted and is standing by," she said.

"How far?"

"Forty-four kilometers," Yumiko replied.

"Tell Keir he can go home. I've got this," Odonna said, watching Yumiko key the pad and return to her station next to Limon.

"What's it going to be, Mallet? You've nowhere to go."

"Then I guess we should get this over with," Mallet replied.

"I'm glad you see it my way," Odonna said. "All of you, put your hands up, clasp them behind your head, and drop to your knees, right now!"

"You heard her, hands up," Mallet shouted. His crew obeyed in rapid succession, brandishing their arms at Odonna and her pack.

"Seriously?" Odonna asked. "Not only have you been outrun, but you're outgunned, Mallet."

"If you don't like your odds, I suggest you change them," Mallet said, aiming at Odonna's chest.

"I'm tired of this. Limon, deal with them."

The officer trained his barrel on Mallet. "You don't want to do that," Crawford warned.

"You're right," Limon said. "You should be first."

The air swelled with hostility as Mallet actively worked with Crawford, pushing the restless energy between the two groups to a head. Bodies onboard swayed back and forth, perspiring, their inhalations rising to a thundering tone.

Odonna's temples throbbed, her hands shaking. "Do it now!" she commanded in a rage.

Limon squeezed the trigger, discharging his rifle, its pulse flying upward, the misfire opening an opportunity for one of Mallet's crew to shoot Limon in the leg. Odonna and her people were stunned. In the confusion, Crawford and company closed in on Odonna and her crew, engaging in close-quarters combat. Pistols cracked across heads, as short bursts rattled around the deck.

Kemble guarded her father while the battle ensued. "Stay down," she said, covering him.

Mallet rolled to the deck. Yumiko was on top of him, squeezing his body with her powerful thighs. Kemble attempted a clear shot at the officer, but a string of bodies blocked her aim. Ivar came to assist her, shooting Yumiko through the neck. With

326

her weight off him, Mallet sprang to his feet, searching for Odonna Ragas.

One by one, the *Azimuth*'s crew toppled over the side of the *Meridian*. They flailed their arms as they bobbed in the water. Odonna fled to her ship by way of the adjoining plank.

Crawford followed. "Stop!" he commanded.

Odonna pivoted slowly, coming face-to-face with him. "You will never get away," she said coldly.

Crawford extended his gun but could not terminate her. "I've already killed once today," he said. "I don't want to do it again."

"I didn't think you could."

"I'm not as forgiving," Mallet said, stepping from the wings, weapon in hand. Odonna sensed he was prepared to finish what she and her crew had started.

"Mallet," Crawford started, "don't do it."

"I'm not letting her go."

"You can't go back," Odonna said. "Keir is out there waiting for you."

"We're not going back," Crawford said.

"And neither are you," Mallet said.

"Don't patronize me. I don't know how you did it and frankly, I don't care, but you better kill me."

Mallet explored Odonna's ship. The *Azimuth* was intact, strong, and sturdy. "You should be so lucky," he said, focusing on Crawford. "Get Kemble and the others. We've got a new and better-equipped ride."

"What about her?"

"She can keep watch on my ship," Mallet said, smirking at Odonna. "Maybe Keir will come to rescue you."

Crawford led Odonna away, handing her over to Callia. She tied the defeated commander to a post. Kemble rushed to

Crawford at the edge of the board. She embraced him; her kisses filled with tears.

"What's this?" Crawford asked. "You can't be sad."

"I'm not," Kemble said. "I'm glad you're okay."

"So am I."

"Where's Mallet?" Severn asked.

"He's getting the *Azimuth* ready," Crawford replied. "We're taking her over."

"What about them?"

Crawford observed the remaining crewmembers, mocking Odonna's discomfort. She was mortified by their wide grins and poking fingers. "If you're coming with us, you'd best leave her be," he said to them. "If the *Zephyr* advances, they'll take you back. They'll detain you."

"Where're we going?" Ivar asked.

"To safety," Crawford replied with a warm smile.

Severn leaned in. "You don't think they'll turn on us, do you?" he asked Crawford.

"Their fever has passed. They know what freedom feels like now and they like it."

"How do you know?"

Crawford smiled at Kemble and Severn. "Because I feel it too," he said, watching Kemble gather the others, and direct them to the new vessel.

"Are you feeling better?" Mallet asked Severn, taking hold of his hand.

"I always feel better with you, but I'll never get my sea legs."

"Then I better find you some land," Mallet said, kissing his forehead before turning to his crew. "Callia, Ivar, it's a lot of ship to handle. Think you can do it?"

"Yes, sir!"

"Then get to it."

"What course?" Ivar asked starting for the wheelhouse. "South to the Cape."

"No," Crawford said. "We have to go to Caelum."

"Why can't we just sail away from all this?"

"Just trust me. I'll explain on the way."

"What about Commander Jaxon?" Severn asked. "Won't he give chase?"

"He hasn't made a move," Mallet said. "It's likely he doesn't know we're in control of this ship.

Severn pursed his lips. "I don't like the sound of 'likely'."

"Neither do I, but that's all I can say for now."

Onboard the *Zephyr*, Keir Jaxon watched the *Meridian* from a distance. It was sinking.

"Commander Jaxon," the pilot interrupted. "There are people on the vessel."

"How many?"

"Looks like a dozen or so," she responded. "The *Azimuth* is changing course for Caelum. Should we assist?"

Keir went to the pilot's post. Commander Ragas' ship was making a turn, the vessel's maneuvers classic to Mallet Tragnor's style. "No, they're finishing the cargo run," Keir said. "We'll pick up the *Meridian*'s hands and rendezvous with them at the Green."

"Yes, sir," the pilot said, taking the *Zephyr* toward the doomed vessel Mallet had left behind. Keir Jaxon exited the command post, seeking splendor in the afternoon daylight. Deep in his gut, he knew Mallet was onboard Ragas' ship. Mallet was now a fugitive and Keir's decision against pursuing him was treasonous.

I hope you know what you're doing, Mallet, Keir breathed. *For all your sakes.*

329

CHAPTER 43

The *Meridian* and *Zephyr* disappeared from the horizon as the *Azimuth* rolled to its destination. It was a bittersweet goodbye for Mallet. For as much as he loathed the tyranny of Beta Union, the relatively easy pace of his existence was over.

Mallet stood at the stern with Severn watching the pitch of the sun. Soon it would set, beginning a new phase as the stars came forth against a backdrop of moons. Until then, the water of the Azure with its silent rolling waves remained peaceful.

Severn smiled, taking Mallet's hand, his trust cemented in the promise Mallet carried out. Severn no longer cared where they made their home. They were together, braving a new journey towards their future. Mallet gave orders to keep a vigilant eye as even the *Azimuth*'s sophisticated equipment had difficulty detecting Pleuran submersibles.

"Why are we going to Caelum?" Severn asked.

"I'm not sure," Mallet said, "but Crawford thinks we need to, and I trust him."

"I'm glad you do and at least we're out of danger."

"If we don't run into the Pleurans, we'll be fine."

"I'm sorry I doubted you," Severn said, "I'll never do it again. I promise."

Mallet smiled, putting his arm around Severn. "Huh, with that cynical mind of yours, I'll believe it when I see it."

Kemble, huddling with Crawford at the other end of the ship, took pleasure in her father's happiness, finally understanding Severn's connection to Mallet as she celebrated her own with Crawford. With his hands folded, Crawford leaned over the bow's gangway, staring at the seafoam flowing along the waterline. The beauty of the vast ocean with its billowing depths astonished him, yet he could not help but dwell on everything, and everyone caught in Beta Union's shrieking ruin.

Kemble broke his silent retreat. "Why didn't you bring Thalo? Did you leave him with Breen?"

"No," Crawford answered, still entranced by the rolling motion of the sea.

"Then, where is he?"

"He passed at the school."

"I'm sorry," Kemble said, touching his shoulder.

Crawford closed his eyes. Kemble grasped his waist, laying her head on his shoulder. Her heart beat steadily, her exhalation tickling his neck. Kemble's form was comforting against his back.

The architect relaxed into her arms, breathing the salt air. A breeze lifted his hair, settling the strands back onto his brow. Kemble brushed them away from his face; Crawford smiled to himself, thinking how well she knew him.

He briefly reflected on Fenton and all who were like the tide, withdrawing from the shore into the vast deep, extending toward the end of the world beyond reach. Crawford lowered his head and shivered against the wind. With its equivocal nature, the newborn dawn of his life troubled him.

Crawford had a sister in the sentinels. Through Zelda, he became aware of the destruction Betera had spawned, its purpose far-reaching, and present long before his existence. He was part of a wide-reaching family seeking revenge for crimes of the past.

He felt a little better than a harbinger of death. The architect ignored the wrong he was doing in favor of a deceitful "greater good," malicious and rotten in its true form. The foul stench of blood was on his hands forever. For a moment, the idea of violence entered his mind.

It was a feeling all his own, unforced and raw, directed at Betera and her 'eye for an eye' mentality. Crawford wished he could get his hands around his mother's neck. He wanted to squeeze the life out of her as he had done to Prell. However, he could not justify such an act as he did with the death of the sentinel. That was a matter of self-preservation.

Kemble felt Crawford tremble. "Are you okay?" she asked.

The architect's mind was far away. *It'll be done when we get to Caelum. We'll be free then.*

Crawford twisted around, pulling Kemble close, ushering her lips to his. When he released Kemble, he gazed into her eyes, which were beautiful and hopeful, relaying confidence. He wanted to encapsulate the moment, freezing it forever, protecting it against the unknown change encroaching upon their happiness. He looked toward Mallet's position. Now was as good a time as ever to tell everyone what he knew.

"Crawford, did you hear me?" Kemble asked. "You disappeared. Where were you just now?"

"I heard you," Crawford whispered sweetly, taking her hand in his. "I'm here, where I was always meant to be."

"I suppose that means I was meant to be here too?" Kemble teased him playfully.

Crawford smiled back at the pilot, but the line of his jaw revealed a tension under the surface. "Can't this barge go any faster?" he said. "I thought these things were built for some kind of high-speed travel."

"I didn't know you were in such a hurry," she said, wrapping her arms around his waist.

Crawford looked down and clasped Kemble's hands. Her body was warm, protecting him against the crisp breeze. Though the couple escaped death only moments ago, they now sailed towards an uncertain future within the habitat of Caelum, a land known for religious zealots, untamed passions, and a mysterious leadership known only by the name Malachim.

"I just want to know who I am," Crawford said, meeting the pilot's warm eyes. "There are too many questions with no answers."

Kemble caressed Crawford's rugged face between her palms. He looked older, tired from the rebellion's events. The light in his green eyes seemed diminished by pain and guilt.

"You did what you had to do," Kemble said. "We wouldn't be alive if you hadn't."

"Tell that to the people who died," Crawford said sighing. "I keep asking myself if there was another way."

"If there were, you'd have found it," Kemble said. "It's too late for regret."

The engineer lowered his head. She was right. There was no other way. The fate of those left behind was out of his hands. "I'm going to see how Mallet's doing," Crawford said, glancing at the wheelhouse.

"Knowing him he's trying to devise a way out of going to Caelum," Kemble laughed.

"That'll be the day," Crawford said, bounding to the wheelhouse. "He owes me."

As Crawford surmised, Mallet was in the wheelhouse leaning over the *Azimuth*'s navigation globe. The silence of the scanners disturbed his mood. "Callia," he said, addressing the junior engineer. "Is there anything on your screens?"

"Nothing, sir," she replied, swiveling her seat to face him. "Everything appears to be normal."

"That's what's bothering me," Mallet said.

"What's bothering you?" Crawford called from where he leaned in the doorway.

Mallet straightened up, reaching his arms above his head before clasping his hands together and resting them on his head. "It's too quiet," he replied, his cobalt eyes narrowing with concern. "Something's not right."

"He's been saying that for the past half hour now," Callia chimed in. "He gets anxious when there's no action."

Crawford crossed over to the globe. Its iridescent glow soothed him much as the water splashing underneath the vessel. "It's about time things were quiet," he said. "Especially after everything we've been through."

Mallet joined Crawford in front of the display, "Well, I'll owe you one when we're safely in Caelum."

"You owe me already," Crawford grinned. "A thousand times over."

"Good to know someone's keeping score," the commander smiled, drawing a course line on the globe. "Kemble's better at this than I am."

Crawford looked out the window. Kemble was talking to her father, Severn. The scientist's and the pilot's heads were close together. He envied the relationship between them. Perhaps it was because a relationship with his father had been denied to him. "She's talking to Severn right now."

"He doesn't like your idea," Mallet said. "I'm not sure I'm like it either."

"A minute ago, you were fine with it."

"Losara Idoni expects us at the Green. What happens when we don't make the rendezvous?" Mallet asked, crossing his arms. "You think they'll welcome us with open arms with all these guns pointed at them?"

"It's a risk I'm willing to take."

"There you go again."

Crawford's eyes shot to Callia still seated at her instrument panel. It was not good for the crew to see them debating this decision. Mallet silently agreed. "Callia," he said. "Would you excuse us?"

The engineer arose from her station. Crawford followed the redhead's form as she exited the wheelhouse. "This isn't just about me," he said. "We need to know the truth."

"What I already know, I don't like," Mallet said.

Kemble walked in before Crawford could respond to Mallet's doubts. Crawford's eyes softened at her approach; the warm glow of her bronze face eased his temper.

"What are you two up to in here?" Kemble asked, touching Crawford's shoulder.

"Mallet's getting cold feet."

"I never expected that from you," she said, addressing Mallet. "You're supposed to be our fearless commander."

"Fearless," Mallet huffed. "That's not realistic with everything that looming over us."

The three comrades stood in silence for a moment. Suddenly, an alarm rang out. Callia ran into the wheelhouse. The junior engineer slid into her seat behind a large panel that flashed an angry red.

"There's something beneath us," Callia said, her fingers rapidly tapping symbols on her panel.

Mallet moved behind her, his eyes darting about the screen. "Whatever it is, it's big and it's right up on us," he said, motioning to Kemble. "Get to the wheel."

Kemble rushed to the ship's controls. Her nimble fingers reached for the wheel, her efforts thwarted by an undeniable force slamming into the ship, which threw her and its occupants to the floor. Outside the wheelhouse, the crew stumbled in complete disorder. Desperation clouded their faces as they gripped the railings to gain purchase to stabilize their footing.

"Get us in the air, Mallet," Crawford yelled, crawling toward Kemble's unconscious form.

Mallet clawed his way to a terminal as the ship rocked violently. His rose to his knees and tapped out a sequence on the panel in front of him. "It's not responding," he choked, scrambling as quickly as he could to the wheelhouse's doorway.

Crawford watched the commander claw his way out on deck before falling out of view. The attack caught them unaware. Smoke billowed past the windows of the wheelhouse and intense heat engulfed the cabin. Crawford held Kemble's head in his lap. Blood seeped from a wound at her hairline.

The architect's breathing became labored as he felt everyone's fear and heard the screams coming from the outside his position. One of the voices belonged to Severn, Kemble's father, and Mallet's lover. Crawford wanted to save them all, but his vision was failing him.

Suddenly, a roaring sound reached Crawford's ears. His head snapped upward, searching for the source. In an instant, white foam flooded the wheelhouse. Crawford's eyes grew large; every hair on his body stood at attention.

It can't end this way, he thought, cradling Kemble. We're not ending this way.

Darkness and cold enveloped Crawford, extinguishing the fire trailing down his spine.

CHAPTER 44

Crawford felt an icy numbness gripping his limbs. He wiggled his fingers and toes, surprised that either responded. He knew he was standing based upon the weight distributed under the soles of his boots.

My boots? I'm still in them.

The engineer slowly opened his eyes. From what he could perceive, the space he occupied was an empty void—black, without the faintest trace of light.

Crawford reached forward to test the distance in front of him. He felt nothing but the hollowness, not even a breath of wind.

Where am I?

There was no external sound, wherever Crawford might be now. There was only the quiet humming of his mind and something else, a presence—soothing yet commanding at the same time. He ached to understand the familiarity of the feeling, so direct in its intensity.

I can't be dead. No one thinks after drowning. I must be dreaming, but the water was real. I swallowed it and I know—

"What do you know, little one?" a voice said, piercing the darkness.

For a moment, Crawford felt the need to prepare himself for an attack, but his sensitive aura confirmed there was no threat. Perhaps diplomacy would be the best course in a situation where one could not discern their true predicament.

Crawford decided to respond charismatically albeit sarcastically to the question. "I hardly qualify as little unless I've shrunk in some way I can't see."

"You were always my little one and forever shall remain as such."

"Betera?" Crawford breathed. "It can't be. You're—"

"Gone? Deceased?" she asked. "Have you ever once missed me as I have missed you?"

The answer to her question edged towards the tip of Crawford's tongue, daring him to respond with savage vitriol. It would be easier and wiser to play along with Betera's game or that of whomever he was conversing with now.

"Truthfully, I hadn't thought of it," he said, tapping his toe in an arch as he tried again in vain to ascertain the dimensions of his environment. "I've been preoccupied with other matters."

"Yes, the collapse of the union," she responded with a twinkle in her voice. "You did well, and I am very proud of you."

Crawford could feel the smirk on his face. She was proud of the deaths of hundreds, maybe thousands of people. This reaction cemented his already ill-feeling towards her memory.

"I suppose you want me to be proud of it too, considering I'm allowed to feel that way now that I've destroyed everything I've ever known," he spat. "Remind me what I did it for!"

There was a silence following this expulsion of anger. Crawford turned slowly in a circle, peering through the darkness.

Something was emerging from a pocket in the space, bringing a soft form enrobed in blue light.

Crawford's eyes did not betray him for though he could not judge the distance between himself and the figure, he knew it was none other than Betera Eaton herself. His mother.

Her hair was the same, the color of moonlight, and her golden eyes shone with splendid radiance. She was clothed in a white robe with a high neckline adorned with a strange-jeweled necklace. The center stone was clear save for a spot in the middle that looked like a burning red eye ready to hypnotize any who gazed upon it.

The architect turned away from it to look directly at Betera. It was hard to believe she would be here in this dream, or rather this nightmare, for wherever Betera was death seemed to follow.

"You did it for those who could not fight for themselves, my dearest," Betera replied. "You cannot imagine the decades, no, centuries of suffering that occurred long before you were born."

She was closer now. Crawford could reach out and touch her if he desired. "That's the past," he whispered. "We were supposed to inherit the future, but now I'm not sure one exists for anyone."

Betera smiled as she reached out and caressed Crawford's cheek. She looked thoughtfully into his eyes, nearly level with her own. The engineer marveled at his mother's youthful glow, which imparted an otherworldly appearance to her smooth features.

"You exist because of the past and the wrongs I sought to correct," Betera said. "But what is to come is a greater threat to humanity than I ever was and though I felt it against my better judgment, humanity must be saved for Zelda's sake."

Crawford grasped Betera's delicate shoulders. "You thrust her into this. You knew what you were doing to her, to me, to Linus! Now you want to save humanity!"

Betera stepped back, effectively evading further contact with the engineer. "My goal was always for my children to survive," she said. "You and Zelda must live."

"To what end?" Crawford screamed as a rumbling cut through the darkness. Crawford swayed on his feet as the ground undulated below.

"We are out of time," Betera gasped. The engineer looked to his mother. Translucent waves swept over her skin as she began to fade away. "When you wake up, find Zelda. Together you can end what the past set in motion."

Crawford looked up and around, sensing the imminent collapse of the invisible boundaries, a moment that would bring a shift in his conscious state. The engineer quickly turned back to Betera, seeking guidance, but her eyes were all that remained.

Crawford struggled to maintain his balance as a shadowy force compelled him to his knees. "What's happening? Where, where…?" he asked feverishly.

Betera's eyes sparkled and fluttered before vanishing in a wisp of white smoke, yet her voice remained for an instant more. "Caelum, the very heart of the danger itself," the answer came softly. "You are in the home of my family. The Malachim."

T.J. SACHS

T.J. Sachs is an award-winning communications professional with twenty years of experience in the field. Sachs's interest in science fiction and fantasy began at an early age with the works of Ray Bradbury, Philip K. Dick, Frank Herbert, and Anne McCaffrey. Sachs is an avid art collector, ice hockey fan, and video game enthusiast.

Sachs's previous literary work includes *From a Fellow Patient,* a collection of personal essays. Sachs readily admits writing a press release is easier than a work of fiction. Betera's Factor is Sachs's debut fiction novel. The author makes their home in Baltimore, Maryland.

www.ingramcontent.com/pod-product-compliance
Lightning Source LLC
Chambersburg PA
CBHW030404180626
46812CB00005B/1928